GREGORY'S ANOMALY

Richard Sessions

Lucky Bat Books

A Lucky Bat Book

Gregory's Anomaly

Copyright © 2013 Richard Sessions

Cover Design by Brandon Swann

ISBN 978-1-939051-57-8

Published by
Lucky Bat Books
LuckyBatBooks.com
10 9 8 7 6 5 4 3 2 1

"Richard Sessions has written a highly perceptive and intriguing story grounded in today's world but deftly leading the reader to explore and accept a brand new reality in the realm of science. *Gregory's Anomaly* will hook you from the first page and not let you go."

~ Carol Dersham
A life-long reader and devotee of the well-spun, exotic tale.

"A gripping and tightly crafted piece of fiction using a decidedly ingenious twist on recent scientific findings."

~ Ian Tattersall, Ph.D.
Curator Emeritus for Anthropology,
American Museum of Natural History; author of
Masters of the Planet: The Search for Our Human Origins

"Richard Sessions has given us another page turner. *Gregory's Anomaly* shows off Sessions' mastery of the language while keeping us intrigued and unable to stop reading. His attention to detail makes us feel as though we are right there with the characters. I can't wait for Sessions' next book."

~ Chuck Riley
Former Oregon State Representative

"Imagine an intellectually advanced Neanderthal family whose strange powers spark challenging medical ethics debates, arouse fear and rage in certain fundamentalist groups, and will delight those who love a fast-paced story told through cliff-hanger scenes and well-grounded scientific information. This lively adventure, rooted in a genetic possibility, skillfully interweaves an emotionally engrossing tale with apt forays into ethnology, paleontology, anthropology, and what it is to be human. Enjoy!"

~ Muriel D. Lezak, Ph.D.
Professor Emerita, Department of Neurology
Oregon Health & Science University
Senior Author, *Neuropsychological Assessment* (5th Edition)

"A fascinating, scientifically up-to-date read with an unusual story line. It is well worth your time."

~ Dennis Borden, Ph.D.
Professory of Biochemistry
Assoc. Provost for Health Sciences (Retired)
Northwestern University

Arthur H. Parmelee, Jr., M.D., Emeritus Professor of Pediatrics, University of California, Los Angeles;

Richard H. Goodman, M.D., Ph.D., Director of the Vollum Institute for Advanced Biological Research, Oregon Health and Science University;

Roger D. Cone, Ph.D., Professor and Chair, Department of Molecular Physiology and Biophysics and Director, Vanderbilt Institute for Obesity and Metabolism, Vanderbilt University Medical Center;

the memory of Morton I. Grossman, M.D., Ph.D., former Professor of Medicine and Physiology, University of California, Los Angeles, and former Senior Medical Investigator, VA Wadsworth Hospital Center;

the memory of William C. Beatty, Ph.D., former Emeritus Professor of Anthropology, California State University, Fresno;

and to all the scientists participating in the Infant Studies Project (UCLA), the Center for Ulcer Research & Education (UCLA and VA Wadsworth), and the Vollum Institute for Advanced Biomedical Research (OHSU), while I served at these research programs. I thank all of these scientists for inspiring and encouraging me to develop a lifelong interest in anthropology, infant and child development, physiological science, molecular biology, and neuroscience. Such inspiration led me to write this book.

ACKNOWLEDGEMENTS

I would like to thank the following people at Lucky Bat Books: Judith Harlan, co-owner, was always there for me. Louisa Swann, supervisor and editor, did a superb job. Brandon Swann showed his fine talent on cover design.

Many people read early or late drafts and gave excellent suggestions and/or provided kind words to be used with publication. These included Dr. Ian Tattersall, Dr. Roger Cone, Dr. Muriel Lezak, Dr. Andrew Soll, Carol Dersham, Chuck and Dr. Katie Riley, Dr. Dennis and Judy Borden, James Dana, Ina May and Henning Nilsen, and Dr. Dwight Sangrey. I am also indebted to my wife, Julia Surtshin, who provided great support.

The mutated forms of genes . . . remain in the gene pool sometimes for thousands of years, being eliminated on a regular basis, unless they find the right environmental circumstances—at which point they become visibly expressed . . .
~ Paul Shepard

No individual path of evolution of any kind can be predicted, either at the beginning or even toward the end of its trajectory.
~ Edward O. Wilson

The greatest successes in evolution, the mutants who have, so to speak, made it, have done so by fitting in with . . . the rest of life.
~ Lewis Thomas

If, by some freak of nature, *Homo erectus* and *Homo habilis* still existed, *Homo sapiens* would appear to be far less special than we like to think of ourselves.
~ Richard Leakey & Roger Lewin

CHAPTER ONE

THE YOUNG MAN STARED at the pearl-sized drops of moisture sliding down the front window of Valley Insurance Associates. The fog had not thinned. He looked once again at the appointment card his wife had tucked into his coat pocket and decided he must leave for the dreaded meeting. Dreaded, because once there, he expected the doctor to tell them that their baby had epilepsy. *God,* he hated that word.

He buttoned his coat and stepped outside. Cold, wet air stung his sinuses. His temples tightened as he moved onto the asphalt parking lot. Where was his car? As shadowy bumpers and fenders loomed before him he sensed a buzzing in his head. The sound suddenly roared, like a power edger hitting concrete. Next to his car, he gripped his head and stumbled. A dark circle began closing off his vision. He clutched at the door handle, but then his body began to shake violently. He sank to the ground as the light snapped off completely.

OUTSIDE THE CEDAR AVENUE Medical Center the fog disgorged and swallowed cars while depositing droplets on the sweaters, hair, and eyebrows of people standing at a nearby bus stop. Looking down from three thousand feet, the San Joaquin Valley appeared as a giant tureen of cotton candy. The Coast Range mountains to the west formed one lip of the bowl. On the eastern side, the towering Sierras held the thick, winter cloud with mountains' teeth. At the bowl's bottom, inhabitants of Fresno, the valley's largest city, existed for weeks without seeing the sun— unless they escaped to the mountains, the coast, or to southern California. Some took those winter breaks, but most persevered in the drab underworld until spring blew away the overcast layer, providing a pleasant interlude before the summer oven ignited.

The doors of a bus opened and a young woman, dark green scarf covering most of her rust-colored hair, stepped onto the sidewalk and made her way into the medical building. In The Pediatrics Group reception room sat three women with several children. One of the women held a baby. A Celtic tune on hammered dulcimer softly emanated from speakers on the wall. The nurse behind the counter welcomed the new arrival by name and said that Dr. Kalakian would be able to see her soon. The young woman sat down, shook out the scarf, and glanced at her watch. She was late, but her husband was even later. She watched a runny-nosed boy draw a stick figure of an outsized dog under a large sun.

"Mrs. Shenko?"

She stepped up to the counter and explained that her husband was still expected. "I know I gave him the right time."

"The fog must have delayed him," the nurse said. "Unfortunately, the doctor will have to see other patients, unless you want to go in now."

"I'll go in."

She was shown into the office of Dr. Richard Kalakian, who stopped writing and rose from behind a small desk. He raised his black, wiry eyebrows, causing the skin on his bald head to ripple.

"Hello, Mrs. Shenko. Please sit down."

"Thank you."

"You didn't bring Gregory?"

"I left him with my mother. You said it wasn't necessary . . ."

"Right, right."

"I didn't want to expose him to other kids in the waiting room."

"That's smart."

Kalakian sat down, opened a file on his desk, and read for a few seconds. Then he looked into her worried eyes. "Mrs. Shenko, has there been any more eye-rolling? Any blanking out?"

"No."

"Anything else unusual? Any quivering or shaking?"

"No."

"That's good." He looked again at the file. "Well, the blood tests and the urinalysis were fine. So what we're left with is some minor symptoms of possible neurological involvement. But it's hard to say what is causing his symptoms. The optimistic view is that he'll simply outgrow it. The worst interpretation is that there could be an epileptic syndrome."

He heard a sniffle and looked up. Corinne Shenko's eyes welled and tears began sliding down her freckled cheeks. Kalakian's face softened. He pushed a box of tissues to the front of his desk and waited as she dabbed at her tears.

"Mrs. Shenko, I know this is upsetting, but I don't think we have to worry too much at this point. Not at two small episodes. Tell me, are you sure there is no history of epilepsy or seizures in your family or your husband's family?"

She shook her head. "My mom and dad said there wasn't any in their families. Nick said he knew of nothing like that."

"Uh huh." Kalakian cocked his head from side to side, as if trying to stretch his neck free of his tight collar. "Well, there are two ways we can go. One is to keep a close watch on Gregory and see if the eye-rolling or blanking out happens again. Chances are it may not. The other option is to have him seen by a specialist and have an electroencephalogram. This may or may not tell us something." He turned his palms up. "Which of these would you want to do? I'm comfortable either way."

Corinne frowned. "I guess I would like a specialist's opinion."

"That's fine. Would you be willing to go down to Southern State University in Los Angeles?"

"If it would help my baby . . . of course."

"Okay, then. I'm going to make an appointment for you to see a Dr. Jared Weymouth at SSU. He's one of the top infant development doctors in the country. If anyone knows what that eye-rolling might represent, he would."

The door opened suddenly.

"Mrs. Shenko," the nurse said, "come quick. Someone from your husband's work is on the phone. There's been an accident."

Chapter Two

Mark Sandler, in one coordinated motion, tossed the two medical records on the small desk, twisted off his lab coat, and swung the door shut with his foot. He noticed the plastic nameplate on the desk matching the new one outside the door: MARTIN L. SANDLER, MD, PhD, and below that, PEDIATRICS. They certainly weren't wasting time, he thought. *There is a new kid on the block, everybody. Never mind that he hasn't seen a patient since finishing his medical residency in 1995 and has forgotten how to use his stethoscope. But folks, he is Columbia-trained, has a PhD in molecular genetics, and owns two pages of hot research publications on the human genome. Shouldn't that count for something?*

Mark wiped off his glasses, smoothed his dark hair, and reset the wire-frames on his ample nose. Would his move to California turn out disastrous, as his father had predicted? *We will see.* Like the faulted land outside the window, in only eight months he had put his life into upheaval—if that fairly described giving up a Harvard tenure track position, breaking off an engagement, and causing a father to stop talking to his son.

There was a quick knock and the door handle turned. The white hair and ruddy face of Dr. Jared Weymouth, head of the Division of Child Development, jutted through the narrow gap as the door inched open.

"Oh, good, you're here, Mark. I wanted to be sure you got the two cases I assigned."

"I did, Dr. Weymouth. I was just about to read them."

Jared pushed all the way in and crept into a chair opposite the desk. "Please call me Jared. We're not formal around here. Even though you're doing a postdoc, I consider you a colleague."

"Thanks, Jared."

"We can talk about these cases when you're ready. One is a Down's syndrome baby that has been coming to the clinic for about a year. Our staff pediatrician left—this was her office, actually—so we're reassigning her patients. This case is straightforward. The mother is naturally accepting and attuned to the baby's needs. The other one, Shenko, is a new referral from a pediatrician in Fresno. It's kind of puzzling, so I'll be interested in your thoughts. We will do a history-taking and a Peds exam, and the baby needs an EEG while they're down here. Anyway, these two should get you started. My secretary, Lena, will schedule them. At clinic, I'll show you how to examine six month olds."

"Okay, good. I'm looking forward to it." Mark's smile underscored his enthusiasm.

Jared saluted with one finger and was out the door as speedily as he had entered.

As Mark left the Southern State University campus that evening and pointed his Saab west toward Santa Monica, he couldn't help mulling over what he'd read in the Shenko folder. Notes in the medical record written by Dr. Kalakian described two occasions where Mr. and Mrs. Shenko saw their baby's eyes roll up into his head, showing all white with no pupils. Upon examining Gregory, Dr. Kalakian could find nothing abnormal, but he was worried about brain damage or epilepsy and had decided there should be testing done by an infant specialist. Thus the referral to Dr. Weymouth. The strangest part of the doctor's record was his statement that Mr. Shenko had died from a possible seizure the same day as the family's second appointment with Kalakian. The young man had died from self-asphyxiation in a parking lot.

The setting sun painted an orange patina on the sides of the houses he passed. Mark pulled into a driveway, drove beyond a two-story English Tudor, and stopped next to the guest house he had rented a week earlier. It was a single-story cottage with a bedroom and kitchenette. Its roof and exterior walls were shingled and the windows were mullioned with multiple panes. Between the cottage and the main house was a groomed lawn, spacious enough for touch football, and a tiled swimming pool long enough for serious laps. A brick patio had two tables with awnings and a built-in barbecue.

Mark checked his mail and phone messages and then changed into swimming trunks. He grabbed a pale ale, his cellphone, and a bag of pretzels and set up at poolside. After stretching his wiry six-foot frame at the pool's edge, he bent into the twenty-lap routine he had set for himself each day. Afterward, he flopped into a deck chair and sat, eyes closed, for several minutes. The fearful thought came again: Maybe the change to Pediatrics had been a bad decision.

No, no, it just needs time. God knows, I can't afford any more mistakes.

~

JARED WEYMOUTH hung his lab coat on a hook in the division's administrative office and smiled at his long-time secretary, Lena Washington.

"Did we win?" she asked, her mischievous eyebrows in motion.

"Yes, but not easily. I wish you could have been there. Vice-Chancellor Reese was out for bear, but the dean out-maneuvered him. Thank god."

Lena raised her arms. "Yes!"

Jared laughed.

"I still don't understand why the vice-chancellor was against Mark getting the fellowship," she said. "The stipend belongs to the medical school."

"It wasn't about money. It was about appearances and institutional reputation."

"Huh? You mean that controversy in the journals?"

"Meaning that it looks bad that Southern State accepted a brilliant young scientist who has thumbed his nose at Harvard and the whole biomedical establishment. So sayeth our leader."

"Oh my. Pardon me. That's so silly. This boy has decided to care for babies instead of doing boring bench research. That's all." Lena wagged her head.

"Well, I wouldn't call the Human Genome Project boring bench research. But yes, it's silly."

IN HIS OFFICE, Jared pulled out a spiral tablet with Mark Sandler's name on it. He entered the date and noted that Mark had caught on to the basics of a six-month infant exam, but would need more experience to grasp the nuances of development. Also, Jared wrote, Mark was stiff in his interactions with mothers, but this would probably improve. He reread a copy of Dr. Kalakian's letter. Jared agreed that the eye rolling could have resulted from *petit mal* seizures, or possibly neurological damage. He had seen babies with similar symptoms before. Most infants that age had immature nervous systems and would turn out normal, but he remembered one that had not. But the father's death from a probable *grand mal*, tonic-clonic seizure raised a big red flag. It could be a genetic syndrome.

Jared wondered if it had been wise to have assigned the case to Mark. Mrs. Shenko was in her early twenties with her first child. Young, anxious mothers with problem babies could be difficult for even experienced pediatricians. This one would be doubly difficult because of the husband's recent death. Jared drummed his fingers. He decided to let Mark keep the lead on Shenko, but to work very closely with him.

Pulling up his email program, Jared sent a message to Lena, copy to Mark.

Please have Lionel check the Beckman polygraph machine.
When last used, one of the pens was intermittent.

Jared hoped that the pediatrics department bioengineer wasn't too booked up. Nothing was worse than malfunctioning equipment, especially when used on out-of-town patients who could not be easily rescheduled. The next message was to his former bridge partner, Kurt Fonkels, now dean of the medical school:

Thanks for your support on Mark Sandler. I owe you one.
Jared.

Chapter Three

TALL COASTAL PINES waved and sparkled against the pale concrete walls of the mammoth health sciences building as the breeze blew eastward from Santa Monica Bay. Magnolia leaves, like tiny Viking ships, sailed in short spurts along the tree-lined walkways. Inside the multistoried structure, patients, doctors, nurses, and myriad others navigated the labyrinth of hallways. Only a few made their way to the hospital's northernmost corridor where the offices and testing rooms of the Division of Child Development were housed.

One of those few was a young woman with a baby in her arms. It was early Wednesday afternoon when she walked into the division office. She wore a stylish, dark-blue dress and matching pumps. She stooped slightly as she cradled the infant, making her five-foot-six body seem smaller. Lena smiled and came out from behind her desk.

"Mrs. Shenko?

"Yes, Corinne Shenko."

"Welcome, I'm Lena Washington, Dr. Weymouth's assistant. And this must be Gregory. Hello there, little guy."

"I'm sorry to be late."

"No problem," Lena said, extending a mahogany-colored arm to take the tote bag from Corinne. "Please sit down, Mrs. Shenko, and I'll notify Drs. Weymouth and Sandler. They're expecting you."

MARK ARRIVED JUST after Jared and was introduced to Corinne. Together, the two doctors, mother, and baby went into Jared's office. Corinne was seated in a large, cushioned chair. Mark noticed that she had not once smiled, even when Jared made clicking noises to tempt Gregory with some plastic keys on a loop.

Jared made small talk: How difficult it was for newcomers to find the division office. How was the trip down? Had Gregory slept in the car? The weather was rather warm and babies tended to get cranky in warm weather. Corinne responded courteously, but gave minimal answers to the friendly initiatives. Mark finally cleared his throat. "Mrs. Shenko, we were so sorry to hear about your husband."

Her eyes shot directly to Mark. She moved the baby higher on her shoulder and looked down.

"Thank you. I know you were wondering . . . uh, if I would be teary and all. But you know, my husband Nick and I only knew each other for a little more than a year. I loved him and will miss him, but . . . it's just not so terrible . . . or rather, I mean I'm just not the crying type."

Mark winced inside, thinking he should not have brought up her husband. "That's understandable. We're very appreciative that you could bring Gregory down so soon after the funeral."

"Well, it was good for me to get away from my relatives if you know what I mean."

"Sure." Jared smiled.

"Did you get everything from Dr. Kalakian?" she asked.

Jared nodded. "Yes, I got the records in the mail and talked to him on the phone this morning. He was most helpful, and he agreed with our plan for testing. So why don't I tell you what we would like to do, Mrs. Shenko?"

"Fine."

Jared explained that while Gregory was still alert there would be a pediatric developmental exam in a nearby room. After this, she should feed Gregory and get him to nap so Jared could take the baby for an electro-encephalogram, which was best done while he was asleep. While Gregory was having the EEG, Mrs. Shenko would meet with Dr. Sandler for some history taking. Jared took a framed photograph from his desk and handed it to Corinne.

"That baby is having an EEG," he said calmly, pointing at the photo, "and his mother is smiling because it's perfectly safe. We will put a little bonnet like that one on Gregory's head. All those wires are pasted to his scalp and it doesn't hurt in the least. We then record the natural voltage of his brainwaves with a machine. It only takes about twenty minutes."

"It doesn't shock, does it?"

"Not at all. There is no electricity in the wires, other than the infinitesimal amount from the baby's head. The recording device is very sensitive."

"I don't think he'll go with you without waking and screaming," Corinne said.

"Lena and I are very experienced with small ones. And we'll give him a gentle sedative to make sure he sleeps."

Gregory suddenly shouted. It was less a cry of unhappiness than an announcement he was ready for attention. Jared and Mark chuckled as Corinne kissed Gregory on the cheek and cooed, "You're okay . . . you're okay, my baby. Don't worry. I won't be far."

Mark picked up the brightly colored keys and dangled them a few inches from Gregory who watched wide-eyed. He reached out a tiny hand, grasped a pink key, and pulled it to his mouth. In watching the infant glance around, Mark was struck by his unusually large, blue eyes.

"Don't worry, the keys are clean," Jared said.

As Gregory mouthed the key and made happy sounds, Corinne managed a smile.

"He's enjoying that," Mark said.

She frowned with pride. "He's kind of a ham."

IN THE INFANT examining room Mark felt nervous. He was surprised that Jared expected him to do the exam. At least his mentor would be there to catch any mistakes. Mark tried to focus on the basics of examining six-month-old infants: Engage them in play, because they don't test well if they're crying. Keep the mother in sight of the baby. Converse with the mother to keep her relaxed and to have her voice keep the baby calm. Observe the baby's behaviors carefully. Do whatever procedures the baby allows first. Check the startle pattern last.

Mark worked slowly. He tested Gregory's attention and peripheral vision with a colorful object and rang a bell behind his ears for auditory response. He watched the gross motor and fine motor movements, gently pulled on arms and legs for reflexes, and lifted the baby up to check for floppiness. He felt lucky that Gregory did not cry or protest. Finally, it was time for the startle test. He looked at Jared.

"One second, Mark." Jared moved to the baby, took a small plastic ruler from his pocket, and measured the width of Gregory's eyes twice. "Mrs. Shenko, Mark is going to clap loudly behind Gregory. He'll probably cry, and you will want to pick him up. This is just to check his startle pattern."

The reaction was similar to that of other babies: Gregory stopped what he was doing, tensed, looked spooked, then cried vigorously. Corinne took him in her arms immediately and made soothing sounds. Mark noticed both fear and reproach in her eyes as she looked up at Mark.

"Okay, we're done with this test," Jared said. "He passed with flying colors."

Corinne looked skeptically at both doctors. "My baby's okay?"

Jared smiled. "We just need to do the EEG and then we'll know for sure, Mrs. Shenko. So now you can feed him in a private room and see if he'll go to sleep. Let's go back to Lena. She'll give you a hand. Are you giving him natural milk or bottle feeding?"

"I'm breast feeding."

"Good, good."

Lena led Corinne into a private room while Jared instructed the student employee at Lena's desk to hold his calls. Then he waved Mark into his office.

"So what did you think?" Mark asked.

"I think your exams have improved one hundred percent."

"Thanks. I meant, what did you think about the baby?

"First you tell me what you thought."

Mark smiled. "Well, he seemed okay to me on perception, gross and fine motor, curiosity, verbalizing . . ."

"Go on."

"And neuromuscular tension and the startle, even jumping on the hearing test."

"Yes, that's unusual, suggesting high hearing sensitivity. Anything else unusual?" Jared twisted a wisp of his white hair.

"His eyes are large."

"Yes, good. Let's see about that." Jared pulled a volume from a bookshelf and flipped to a dog-eared page. He moved a finger down a column of metric numbers. "Three standard deviations. Those eyes are abnormally large."

"What does that mean?"

"Nothing, yet. So, anything else?"

Mark thought, then shrugged.

Jared chuckled. "Gregory wasn't afraid when you lifted him for the floppiness test. I've never seen a baby not get concerned and at least whimper. That's either one trusting kid or it's a signal that something's not quite right."

Mark nodded, picturing the baby on his back in the air resting on Mark's large hands.

Jared made some notes in the spiral notebook. "Hopefully the EEG will tell us something. I'm going to grab a quick roll and coffee. When you do the history, ask Mrs. Shenko if she's noticed anything besides the eye rolling, and how long those particular episodes lasted. See if you can find out any more about the father's condition and if there are any medical peculiarities in the extended family."

Mark scribbled on a three-by-five card. "Got it. Good luck with the EEG."

As Mark accompanied Corinne to his office, he noticed that despite her recent pregnancy, she was trim. Her tummy pooched slightly and her bosom was full from the milk, but her waist and hips were shapely, and there was a springiness in her step. He wondered if she'd worked out during her pregnancy. She sat opposite him and watched as he opened the Shenko folder on his desk. Her thin eyebrows firmed down over eyes that caught a reflection from the afternoon sun, revealing gold ore veins in the hazel matte of her irises.

"So, what would you like to know, Dr. Sandler?"

Mark turned on a smile and began gently asking for routine information— her full name, address, phone number, birth date, occupation. He learned that she was twenty-two and not employed, but was attending Cal State Fresno, needing only one more year for her B.A. in anthropology. Her mother took care of Gregory while she went to classes. Gregory's father, Nicholas, had been an insurance salesman. Mark was surprised that Nick was only twenty-two when he died from the seizure. He and Corinne had met at college ten months before Gregory's birth and had married only six months before the baby arrived. At this revelation Mark fought a smile.

"An insurance salesman and he didn't even carry life insurance." There was bite in her words.

Mark shook his head. "I'm sorry. He of all people should have known better."

"He said it was a waste of money for young people."

Mark grimaced. "Mrs. Shenko, how long did Gregory's eye-rolling episodes last?"

"About five to ten seconds. One of us would immediately pick him up and the eyes would return to normal and then he was fine."

"Uh huh. Have you ever noticed anything else about Gregory that didn't seem normal?"

"Not really. Sometimes he screams loud."

"What about Nick?"

Corinne folded her arms. "What about him?"

"Did he ever talk about previous seizures, have other health problems, or take medicine?"

"No, but like I said, I only knew him for just over a year."

"Never passed out?"

She exhaled noticeably. "Not with me, but I recently learned from Rose, his mother, that he passed out a couple of times when he was a little boy."

"That's interesting."

"Yeah, it is. He never told me about that."

Something in her inflection connected Mark to a memory of his ex-fiancée. They had been joking around on the day she received her PhD. She was wearing a gown and mortar board and they were by a fountain with a reflecting pool. *You wouldn't dare push me in,* he jeered. *Yeah, I would.* They had laughed. Neither knew for sure if she would.

"Dr. Sandler? Do you have any more questions?" Corinne asked.

Mark blinked. He'd lost his train of thought. "Uh . . . sorry . . . I guess not."

"Gregory might be back now."

"Right, let's go see. Thanks for talking with me."

"Sure." She offered him a slight smile, the most genuine he'd seen yet. Mark smiled back, then realized he should have obtained information about the rest of the family.

IN THE DIVISION office they found Gregory asleep in an infant carrier and Jared speaking loudly on the phone at Lena's desk. Lena came over to them, her face flushed.

"Mrs. Shenko, our EEG machine is broken. It was supposed to have been fixed, and Dr. Weymouth's giving the engineer the what-for right now. I'm so sorry."

"So you don't know anything?"

"No, we tried, but some of the recording pens didn't work right. Gregory was just fine throughout—he didn't even wake up."

Jared hung up. "We're sorry for this problem, Mrs. Shenko."

"It's all right."

"Lena tells me you were driving back to Fresno tonight?"

"Yes."

"Could you stay over until noon tomorrow? We can do the EEG on another machine in the morning. An EEG really should be done on Gregory."

"Well, I don't know."

"Lena has arranged a room for you tonight and we'll pay for your lodging and dinner, since this was our fault. It's a nice place, just two blocks from here."

"You really shouldn't try to start that four-hour drive now," Lena said. "You'll feel much better tomorrow."

Corinne looked at Gregory, then back at the expectant faces. "Okay."

EVEN TWENTY-FIVE laps that night could not erase Corinne Shenko from his mind. Mark kept picturing her face, seeing the hard-won smile. He finally decided to call a familiar number.

"I hope this isn't too late, Mom."

"It's a little late, but it's good to hear from you, Mark."

"Well, I have an office now and Weymouth has given me two cases of my own. I saw the first one today."

"That's good. So you're completely settled?"

"Yep."

"And making some friends?"

"The Pediatrics people are nice—lower key than the colleagues I'm used to, but it's a welcome change."

"Mark, you could meet people at Hillel."

"Like a nice Jewish girl to replace Rachel?"

"That's not what I'm saying. You know I don't care if she's Jewish."

"Right. Is Dad there?"

"No, he went to a pharmaceutical meeting in Geneva."

"Is he still pissed?"

"You know I don't like that term. He's still upset, yes."

"Can't he some day understand I did it out of conscience?"

"You didn't have to publish that letter in *Science* and embarrass him and everyone else who has sacrificed for you. You didn't have to move so far from Pittsburgh."

"It's a career change, Mom. And Weymouth is tops in the new field I've chosen. It's not like I sailed to Tahiti and took up painting. Look, I'm in my early thirties."

"Well . . ."

"I'm sorry. I don't mean to raise my voice."

There was a pause.

"Rachel said to say 'hello'."

"God. It's late. I'm going to say bye, Mom. I'll call you in a few days."

The air was balmy and Mark sat for a minute thinking about Rachel, feeling guilty as he had so many times in the past few months. There was no getting around it. He had hurt her badly. He had, in a sense, wasted three years of her life. So how could she still want to say *hello*? He saw her face looking at him with dark, questioning eyes. "I'm sorry, Rachel," he murmured. A cricket fired up close by with a rapid tsk tsking.

JARED ARRIVED AT his office early the next day and began thinking about Gregory Shenko. If only the machine had not malfunctioned, he would already have all the data necessary. But the polygraph recorder *had* malfunctioned and in an unusual way. The pens tracing Gregory's brainwaves from the occipital area had jammed against their upper stops, unlike the other brain areas which had showed the usual mountain-like pattern in the 50-100 microvolt range. It was rather strange. Oh well, he thought. He eased his big-boned frame into his chair, feeling every one of his fifty-seven years, and began reading one of the sloppiest papers he'd seen in a long while.

~

TWO HOURS LATER, Corinne bent and kissed her sleeping baby on the cheek, avoiding the bonnet that had turned his head into a Medusa of wires. She and Lena headed to the cafeteria to have brunch while Jared and Mark, who held the infant carrier, wended their way to the Brain and Neurology Institute on the opposite side of the medical center.

Jared was not particularly happy that they had to do the EEG in the laboratory of Dr. Louis Fazzi, a professor of neurophysiology the medical school had recently recruited at considerable expense. He didn't have anything against Fazzi, even though the man had the reputation of an academic star who published only in the most prestigious journals and didn't like to collaborate with colleagues. What bothered Jared was having to rely on Fazzi's good graces. Also, Jared had to admit he resented that Fazzi's machine was newer and more elaborate. But working with the man couldn't be helped. The interest of the patient came first.

When they arrived, introductions were made. Fazzi, a stout, fortyish man, graciously allowed Jared to direct the technician in the method for the wire hook-ups and machine settings. After the apparatus was ready, Fazzi inserted the high capacity disk Jared had brought and made some adjustments to the amplifier that was connected to the polygraph. Gregory's little chest moved rhythmically with each exhalation as he lay cherub-like in the almost-horizontal infant seat. The only noise in the room was his breathing and the hum of the equipment.

"I think we're ready, Jared," Fazzi said softly.

"Okay, go ahead."

Fazzi nodded and pushed buttons that started the oscilloscope-like patterns appearing on a screen. They all watched the multi-colored display. Jagged lines traced normally on all the channels except for the ten occipital zones. Those lines were maximized against the upper range, leaving a fuzzy horizontal line. Jared stood transfixed. His eyebrow began to twitch involuntarily. For a full minute they all stared.

"Damn. Would you look at that," Fazzi finally said, touching one of the occipital input wires. He stepped to the equipment rack and turned several knobs on the control panel. Slowly the occipital lines moved down, tracing in the middle of their range, the same as the others. He turned another knob and checked a digital readout.

"Christ, there's four hundred ninety microvolts coming off those occipital electrodes. That's more than five times what it should be." Fazzi looked at Jared, his eyes burrowing. "That's one incredible anomaly. Do you believe that?"

Jared shook his head slowly. "I don't want to believe it, but it's happened twice now—on two different machines—my old pen machine and your new fancy one of video displays."

Jared looked at Gregory. The baby's chin quivered for a brief second. The enormity of what they were seeing enveloped Jared, like going under water without air. He struggled, but there was no other conclusion: the baby's neurons in the back of his cortex were firing to such an extent that tremendous voltages were being produced on the cranial surface. That could only mean something was horribly messed up inside. And yet, the baby had tested all right on the pediatric exam. It was simply incredible. Again he looked at Gregory—so cute, eyes shut, tiny little hands.

Jared then realized he would have to go back and see Corinne Shenko who would want to know if her baby's brainwaves were normal. He touched his twitching eyebrow, wondering what he should say to a young woman apparently numb at the loss of one loved one and now very nervous about another.

CHAPTER FOUR

"HERE'S YOUR MAIL, Dr. Weymouth." Lena handed him two folders, one with mail needing his attention and the other with stuff that Lena couldn't decide whether or not to throw out.

"Thanks, Lena."

"Also, here's another box of Kleenex for your desk." She smiled. "Hopefully, the next patient won't need so much."

Jared nodded. "Did Mark get the information on Gregory's grandmother and that Fresno pathologist?"

"Yes, and I got him a map of Porterville and Fresno from the Web."

"Great."

He pursed his lips. Had he been unfair to Mrs. Shenko? He'd told her the results of the abnormal EEG as gently as he could, but tried to leave her some hope by saying that the pediatric exam, being normal, was more important. Her reaction was as if she had heard only the bad news and had let loose with such racking sobs that Lena had rushed in to hold her.

Crying patients always made Jared miserable. Giving bad news to parents was the one part of his job that he had never mastered. But there was no way around it. Providing an inaccurate appraisal was equally bad. You were damned if you did and damned if you didn't. He had felt bad until Mrs. Shenko had called him when she arrived home, sounding much better.

MARK WAS IN A good mood as he drove north on I-5. He liked the rugged geology of Tejon Pass with its sedimentary layers upended like gigantic broken quarry tiles. He imagined the momentous tectonic collisions pushing up the mountains as if a western Zeus had stood in the Pacific and placed his shoulder against the shore. Once down into the San Joaquin Valley the flatness was less interesting and his mind wandered. He wondered if it were just coincidence that Jared had assigned Mark two cases with genetic etiology.

Down's or trisomy was one of the most well-known genetic syndromes. The mongolism resulted from an extra piece of chromosome 21 in some or all cells. The abnormalities from this one single error were enormous: retarded physical and mental growth, flat face with short nose, protruding lower lip, small rounded ears, fissured tongue, laxness of joint ligaments, and other unusual features. Why would Jared assign him such a classic case? The answer was fairly obvious: Jared wanted him to learn that the care of such children and their parents was a lot different from knowing the nature of the genetic defect. The map was not the territory.

Then there was the Shenko case—much different. While a genetic component was suggested, the nature of the problem—the etiology and the prognosis— were completely unknown. Maybe the child was normal and maybe not. Why would Jared have assigned him this one? Mark wanted to believe Jared actually needed his expertise on the case.

The agricultural town of Porterville, boasting a population of approximately 50,000, sat nestled against the Sierra Nevada mountains in the southeast corner of the San Joaquin Valley. Mark first saw tracts of stucco houses mixed in with olive orchards still resisting progress. He followed Lena's directions to an area of older homes near the center of the city. The wood frame bungalow hunched back on the lot, almost hidden behind mature cottonwood trees. A scraggly lawn languished in the dry soil.

Rose Shenko wore a faded, floral print dress and a misshapen, gray cardigan. She gave him a friendly welcome and led him into a tiny living room with a worn couch and matching worn chair. A large TV sat on a table in the corner. Dog-eared movie magazines sprawled on a small table. She served coffee, but with considerable difficulty. He thought she might be in her forties even though she moved as if she were older.

"You'll have to 'scuse me but I don't get around right well. See, I have rheumatoid arthritis. This is a fairly good day for me."

"I'm sorry to hear that. It must be painful."

She looked at him and smiled. "I get along. Anyway, about those seizure things. I've been thinking back. There was a couple of times when Nick was little that he didn't have control of hisself. I took him to the doctor but the man didn't find nothin' wrong with the boy."

"How old was Nick at that time?"

"Let's see, he must'a been 'bout five. We was still living near Lawrence in Kansas. I remember it good, even to this day. The kids was outside playing in this field next to the house. I think I was in the kitchen doin' dishes. It was summer and Nick started kindygarden later that fall. Anyhow, Zenya—she's his sister— she came runnin' in yellin' for me, saying something was wrong with Nickie. So I ran out to where he was on the ground on his belly, real still like. I called him to get up, but he didn't move. Then I took hold of him and he was real tight. All his muscles were tight and kind'a throbbin'."

"What about his eyes? Were they up behind his eyelids?"

"Nope, I don't remember that."

Mrs. Shenko looked at Mark as if anticipating another question. She lifted her cup slowly and hooped the hot liquid, not taking her eyes from Mark. "Nope, I don't remember that."

"So what happened next?"

"Well, I picked him up and he was like a board. I got real worried and took him in the house. By the time we was inside he had woke up and was okay. He was tired but talked just fine. Asked me what the matter was. He didn't remember nothin' about what happened. He knew he was playin' in the field with Zenya, the next thing he remembers he's in my arms in the house. I was still scared for him so we all got in the pickup and drove to Dr. Williams in Lawrence. Doctor checked him over a lot but couldn't find nothin'. Just said to take Nickie home and watch him close and let the doctor know if it happened again. He didn't give us no pills or nothin'."

Mark pictured the scene and imagined Rose Shenko as a young woman. He could see that she might have been attractive. "Did it happen again?"

"Uh huh, 'bout a year later. We had moved to Salina by that time and I couldn't take him back to Dr. Williams. I didn't take him to nobody that time. And it never happened again after that, far as I know." Mrs. Shenko eased back in her chair.

"I see." It hadn't been what Mark expected, but then he hadn't known what to expect. Somehow he felt there should be more. "Did Nick cry a lot as a small baby?"

"Well, he cried, but not no more than Zenya did as a baby. I don't think it was more than other babies." She looked out the back window.

"Was there anything else that might have been unusual, about Nick's health or characteristics that was unusual?"

"No, least that I 'member. Nick was a strong boy. He played sports in school. He was smart too. Got good grades. I don't know how 'cause he never studied. He developed faster than most children. One time a principal said he was pre . . . pre . . ."

"Precocious?"

"Yeah, that's it. He had a temper though, just like his dad. Zenya got afraid to be around him. He wouldn't mind me too good, and after he got big, I couldn't do much with him, 'specially when he got mad. But he always seemed sorry later." Mrs. Shenko paused and looked out the window. "I need to water them flowers. No, he wasn't really a mean child. In fact, he could be real sweet at times. I guess he was just a normal boy."

Mark wrote some notes on a pad. "Did Zenya ever have any seizures?"

"No, she never had nothin' like that. Never got sick much. She was a good daughter. Helped me a lot when I was sick. Cooked dinners and cleaned up. Stayed close. I was lucky to have that child. By the way, help yourself to more coffee in the kitchen. It's hot."

Mark headed out to the kitchen and poured himself another cup of the strong coffee. He studied the kitchen's worn and stained linoleum and the peeling walls. Part of him wanted to write a check to Mrs. Shenko and leave it on the dinette table with a note: For a new floor and paint job.

He resettled in the chair and let the hot aroma fill his nostrils. "Mrs. Shenko, what was your husband like?"

"Sergi? He loved those kids. Too bad he wasn't able to see them grow up. He died when Nicki was two."

"Really? How did it happen?"

"He was drivin' a tractor, plowin' to get ready for plantin' wheat on McConnell's farm. What they told me happened was he fell off the tractor and it ran right over him with one of the big tires. Broke his neck. Then he was dragged by the plow for a piece. When I saw him he was a terrible mess." She shook her head slowly.

Mark winced. "My god, did anyone see it happen?"

"No. One of the hands saw the tractor driving by itself, plowin' the wrong way. When they backtracked they found him dead and mangled."

Mark felt uneasy at her matter of factness. "I'm sorry, that's . . . terrible."

Mrs. Shenko nodded.

"Did your husband ever have seizures?"

She looked at him thoughtfully. "No, why? Do you think he had a seizure on the tractor?"

"I don't know, but maybe it was the same as what happened to Nick."

She looked down, her forehead wrinkled. "What do ya know," she said slowly. "Maybe that's what happened. I never did understan' how he could get off and the tractor keep a'going. If you're going to get off, you take it outta gear first, even if you're gettin' off while it's still rollin'. But if he had a seizure, that could be why."

Mark sipped while she covered long forgotten ground.

"He never had a seizure while I knew him and he never talked 'bout such a thing to me, but I didn't know him before we was married and he never said much about his growing up. His parents came over from Russia when he was a baby. Lived in North Carolina. I never met none of his family. His father and mother died when he and Galina—that's his sister—when they was small. Galina got adopted but Sergi spent his life in foster homes. When he came west, he lost contact with Galina."

"How long did you go together before you were married?"

She laughed. "Four months. We had to get married 'cause I got with child. I'm from the Ozarks—it's why I talk hillbilly. We moved to North Carolina so my dad could get work. Then I met Sergi. Only my mother knew I got pregnant—we never told Dad. After the wedding we moved away so people wouldn't know we was havin' a baby. Boy, what a time. Strugglin' with no money. We were crazy kids."

"How old were you when you were married?"

"I was sixteen and Sergi said he was eighteen. But I found out later he was fourteen. Looked eighteen, tho." Her eyes went past him. "And after we was married I began gettin' those terrible headaches, 'specially when he'd yell at me. I think that was the beginning of all my ailments. Those headaches went away for a while after he died, and I thought maybe they must'a had somethin' to do with him. But then I started gettin' them again after Nick was becoming a cranky one." She stopped abruptly and looked at Mark again. "What else do you want to know?"

He asked about family pictures and she brought out an album and opened it on Mark's lap. The father and son did look alike. Mark was struck by their large eyes and heavy eyebrows—they were like Gregory's. Sergi, Nicholas, and Gregory, a definite genealogical line.

"This is Zenya?" He pointed at a girl in the picture.

"Yeah, when she was about fifteen."

"She looks a little like you."

"Some, but she has both Sergi and me in her."

"Does Zenya have any children?"

"No, she never married. I shouldn't say 'never.' She's only twenty-five. But she is tall and not real pretty. She don't attract men and I don't think she cares to. She's in the Navy, you know. Yeoman First Class at the base in Key West."

"How did she take Nick's death?"

"Well, real sad like. She and Nick didn't get along as kids, but I think she was proud of him going to college, at least 'til he had to get a job. She couldn't get out for the funeral but I talked to her on the phone. She was broken up. It's only me and her now."

Mark sketched a genealogy tree in his notebook, putting in names and ages. "Do you know the names of Sergi's parents?"

"Let's see, it's been a while. Maria and . . . some funny name. Oh, Peotr."

Mark jotted down the names. "Do you think it would be okay if I talked to Zenya?"

"Oh sure. I'll give you her phone number. She'll probably call me tonight. She does most every Tuesday. I'll tell her about you."

Mark asked a few more questions and found out that nothing unusual ran in Mrs. Shenko's side of the family besides the arthritis. After that he finished off his coffee and brought the visit to a close.

THE DRIVE TO FRESNO from Porterville was a seventy-mile dogleg over to Highway 99 and then north. Mark had hoped to visit the Fresno County Coroner's office before it closed, but he realized he could barely get there by five o'clock. He'd have to go in the morning. In Fresno he exited at Belmont and found a motel with a heated pool. He swam several laps, limbering his muscles from the cramping drive. Back in his room he plugged in his laptop and checked his personal and Southern State email.

There were two messages. The first was from his mother. She was letting him know she had mailed a check for $500 and he would not have to repay it. She also provided the email address for Rachel, in case he wanted to send congratulations on her new university position. He didn't. The second was a copy of a message from Dr. Fazzi to Jared with Jared's reply.

> Jared—
> I hope things are going well in the management of the Shenko case. I was glad to be able to help with the EEG and want you to know my equipment is available to you as is any other assistance my lab can provide. The baby's occipital voltages remain baffling to me. While higher voltages are seen in biological systems such as electric fish and eels, these species have evolved nerve end bundles to transmit brief jolts, not sustained activity. If you can bring the baby back in, I'd love to participate in trying to characterize the neurological substrate.
>
> All the best, Lou.

P.S. I enjoyed meeting Mark Sandler. Congratulations on attracting such a nationally accomplished postdoc.

Dear Lou,
Thank you again for use of your facility. Unfortunately the Shenkos live in Fresno, so it may be difficult to bring them in. We are very concerned about the baby's brain functioning and will be attempting to better define the problem. Thanks for your offer of assistance. I'll let you know if/when it is needed. Jared.

Mark composed a quick report and sent it off to Jared:

Jared, my interview with Rose Shenko yielded interesting stuff on the paternal lineage. I'll try to go to the Coroner's in the a.m. and get back to SSU tomorrow evening before you leave. I'll also give Mrs. Shenko a call to see how she's doing. Regards, Mark.

And the following to his mother:

Mom, I'm in Fresno gathering info on one of my cases. Will be back at SSU tomorrow. Thanks for the money—it'll come in handy.
Love, Mark.

Mark tried to call Corinne Shenko, but the line was busy. Fifteen minutes later the line was still busy and the idea came to him to drive over to her apartment. Why not, he had lots of time on his hands.

The apartment was an older, three-story building with a garish front. The only saving grace was that tall juniper bushes hid part of the building. Mark recognized it as a student neighborhood from the cars with collegiate stickers and bicycle and ski racks. As he got out of his car, a drinking party could be heard in its early stages. A car full of young people hot-rodded down the bumpy street, whooping and laughing as if they'd taken their last tests for weeks.

The building's entry door was cracked open and he did not have to buzz. Inside the courtyard was an oval swimming pool, empty except for a pink rubber ball and a half-submerged beer can. He climbed two flights of stairs and found

#312, Shenko, across the court from an apartment with rock music blaring. He heard Gregory crying behind the door and knocked loudly.

The door opened just a crack and then swung wide. "Dr. Sandler! What are you doing here?"

"Hello, Mrs. Shenko. I hope this is not an intrusion. I was in town and I thought I'd stop by and see how you and Gregory are getting along." He smiled cautiously.

"Of course, come in. Please sit down. What a nice surprise." She pointed to a living room area. "I have to finish changing Gregory. I'll be back in a minute."

Mark eased down on the sofa and looked around, pleased that she seemed genuinely glad to see him. The beige couch and its matching chair appeared fairly new. A natural wood bookcase was filled with undergraduate textbooks, most on business, humanities, and the social sciences, especially anthropology. There were also paperback novels. A folded playpen leaned against the bookcase.

The crying stopped. After a minute Corinne came in with Gregory and sat in the chair facing Mark. She had on blue jeans, a dark-blue terry cloth top and colorful Chinese slippers. Her red hair was back in an untidy bun.

"So here we are, all clean. Dr. Sandler, would it be okay if I nurse?"

"Sure. Please, don't mind me."

She discreetly slid up one side of her top and Gregory began suckling with vigor.

"First, let me ask you a question, Dr. Sandler, while I'm thinking of it. Gregory doesn't much like baby food. Is there something wrong or is that normal?"

Mark took a deep breath. "Well, to be honest, I don't know."

"Really?"

"I guess I should tell you that I'm not a pediatrician."

"You aren't?"

"No, I went through medical school but became a geneticist."

"Oh . . . then why do you work in pediatrics?"

"I'm changing my medical career, to go into pediatrics. I recently started a fellowship with Dr. Weymouth."

"Oh, okay. So, uh, where did you work before?"

"Well, it's a bit of a complicated story." He looked at her expectant smile and noticed the curve of the breast Gregory was working on. She looked down, re-positioned the baby, and cocked her head again, listening.

"I was a lead scientist on the Human Genome Project at the Whitehead Institute at MIT. When the first phase of the project ended, the sequencing of the genome, I decided to leave."

"I've heard of the Human Genome Project. We discussed it in my biology class. So they've really found all the genes in the human body?"

"That's right."

"You seem kind of young. I mean, I don't know how old you are, but how could you be a lead scientist?"

"Well, that kind of science is mostly a young man's—person's—game. I had an aptitude for developing the computer algorithms. There's lots of math, working with DNA, finding proteins, sequencing. That sort of stuff."

She looked at him admiringly. "Yeah, I'll bet. So why did you want to leave?"

He frowned slightly. "Well, uh, I became troubled by the ethics of the whole effort, where it was going."

"How so?" She was listening intently.

"Well, I came to realize that the result of determining the genome would be that scientists would ultimately end up trying to change the human germline, you know, genetically alter human characteristics permanently. And while this would help get rid of some bad diseases, it would also lead to social and political problems —problems much worse than those solved—many unforeseen. The science wouldn't be controllable. Does that make any sense?"

She gave him an amused smile. "For sure. I think people are worried that we'll change into a different species, all geniuses and beautiful and living two hundred years or something. Some people will anyway, and others will be stopped from having kids."

Mark appreciated the succinct summary. "I just felt uncomfortable helping to create the situation where some in society will play God. The only way to feel good about myself was to not stay a part of that. So I threw everything in my car and came out here to become a family doctor."

"All by yourself?"

"I'm not married, if that's what you mean."

She turned red. "I meant do you have any family out here."

"No, they're all back east. My parents are in Pittsburgh, and, well, I broke off an engagement from someone. All my attachments were left back there."

She pressed her lips together and nodded slowly, then shifted Gregory to the other side.

"Well, welcome to California!" She laughed. "A lot of people escaped some-thing to come out here. Some have done well, and others—just like the gold rushers—it wasn't what they hoped."

Mark laughed. He hadn't expected Corinne's cheerfulness. She was a completely different person from the depressed woman he'd seen at the Division of Child Development.

"So how are things going with Gregory?" he asked.

"Okay."

"Have there been any eye-rolling episodes or anything abnormal?"

"No eye rolling. Nothing unusual as far as I can tell."

"That's good."

"You know, I'm sorry I lost it in Dr. Weymouth's office. I just . . . I don't know, maybe it was having my worst fears realized. He was trying to help me and I was making him feel bad, the poor man. Since I've been home, I've said to myself, just take it one day at a time. You know, don't expect trouble until it comes."

"No apologies necessary. We know you've had a rough go. I'm amazed you've handled it so well, Mrs. Shenko."

She looked at him piercingly for a moment, then looked at Gregory who was slowing the milk intake. "Thank you. You're very nice."

Mark looked away, embarrassed.

"And why don't you call me Cory. I don't feel old enough to be a Mrs."

He laughed. "Okay, Cory." He thought of telling her to call him by his first name, but decided it was too informal for a doctor-patient relationship.

She asked why he had come to Fresno and he told her of his visit with her mother-in-law in Porterville. He recounted the conversation in as much detail as he could remember. Nick's childhood seizures didn't surprise her, but she was very interested in Rose's headaches.

"You know, I get bad headaches too, and I've wondered if mine had something to do with getting pregnant. That's when they started, and I worry that some hormones changed or something."

"You didn't tell me you had headaches."

"Yes, I get them every so often, less now than a while ago, though."

"Well, I've never heard of pregnancy as a specific cause of headaches, but I suppose it's possible. Headaches are common to many people . . . somewhere around forty percent of Americans get severe headaches at one time or another."

Corinne nodded. "And I guess I'm one of those lucky ones. Who knows, maybe it's psychological. Now that Nick's gone they don't seem so bad."

"Maybe they'll decrease as your situation becomes more stable."

She nodded, seemingly unconvinced. "Dr. Sandler, did you come up to Fresno from Porterville just to visit us?"

"Yes. And also to go to the Coroner's office to see what they can tell me about your late husband's autopsy."

"Really! They never told me he'd been autopsied. I'd like to know what you find out."

"I'd be happy to let you know what I learn, Mrs . . . Cory."

She laughed.

Gregory was asleep on Corinne's midriff and Mark brought the visit to a close so she could put the baby to bed. Driving back to the motel he wondered if it had been appropriate to call on her. It was not completely professional, he decided, but he was glad he'd done it.

MARK ARRIVED AT the Coroner's office shortly after nine the next morning. He asked for a Dr. Leonard Lesser, explaining that he was from Southern State University Medical Center and that the father of a patient of his reportedly had been autopsied by a pathologist of that name.

"What was the deceased's name?" asked the young man behind the counter.

"Nicholas Shenko."

The clerk brought up a file on a computer screen. "Yes, we have that autopsy. Dr. Lesser did it on February twenty-eighth."

Soon Mark was sitting in the pathologist's office down a back hallway reading the autopsy report. Lesser, a thin man in his mid thirties, sported a handlebar mustache and long sideburns, perhaps to draw attention away from his baldness. When Mark first met the pathologist, Lesser had been wearing a heavily stained white lab coat that reeked of formaldehyde. Mercifully, he'd hung it outside his door when they'd reached his office.

When Mark finished the report, Lesser looked up from his desk.

"It's funny that you ask about the Shenko case because that one is strange. I showed the slides to our chief and he had never seen anything like it, and he's been in the business twenty-five years. In fact, we plan to present the slides at the next section meeting of the American Pathology Association to see if anyone knows of that kind of lesion. So it's interesting to find out that the man had a child with problems. What kind of problems?"

"We don't know but we are thinking it could be some form of early epilepsy. The EEG on the baby is abnormal."

"Makes sense," Lesser said. "We think the father had a *grand mal* seizure which led to his death. The proximal cause of death was self-asphyxiation."

"That's what we heard. How big were those giant neuron cells cited in your report?"

"Let's see. About ten times normal size for that area."

"Ten?" Mark said, incredulously.

"At least. I know it's hard to believe, but we have them on the slides."

"Did you save the brain?"

"No. We dispose of all brains."

"How big an area was it where those neurons and heavy mitochondria were?"

"We didn't do a lot of cuts, but from what we did, I'd say the size of a fist in the thalamic and limbic area, reducing to a narrower outward channel about two inches thick through the cortex."

"God, that's huge."

"I know. That's why epilepsy and a few other problems wouldn't surprise me. In fact, I don't understand how that man was living normally. It doesn't take much of a lesion to be lethal. But the thing about this was that it seemed to be healthy tissue. I mean it was not dead or metastasized or sclerotic or anything. Just very unusual."

"Dr. Lesser, would it be possible to get a copy of your report and one or two slides to take back with me?"

"The report is no problem but I'd have to get permission for the slides. I did make some photomicrographs. Maybe I could give you a couple of those, then send the slides later."

"That would be terrific."

"We'd be interested in knowing what your pathology profs down there think. As I said, we don't know what that tissue represents."

Lesser left and returned with a copy of the report and three photomicrographs in a large manila envelope.

"I wrote on the back the location and magnification. If anyone has any questions, they can call me. Here's my card."

Mark exited the building into dazzling light. He felt lightheaded. *Wait until Jared hears this. Unbelievable.* The data were beginning to come together.

CHAPTER FIVE

JARED TURNED THE BLINDS to reduce glare from the sun. Was it a mistake to invite Lou Fazzi? he wondered. The man was clearly knowledgeable about brain physiology and it would be beneficial to have such a talented scientist hear Jaime Valenzuela's opinion on the slides from the Fresno coroner's office. Jared had picked Valenzuela to study the slides because he was known for meticulousness in tissue analysis. Valenzuela was a professor of pathology and a former president of the American Pathology Association. He also had a specialty in radiology. With Valenzuela, Fazzi would be tempered, Jared concluded.

Valenzuela was the last to arrive for the meeting. Mark and Fazzi were already seated at the table in the division's conference room. Valenzuela walked in slightly stooped, clutching the autopsy report, a sheath of photomicrographs, and a yellow lined pad full of notes. Bushy eyebrows, joined together by a few wiry hairs over his nose, stood out on his leathery face. His Spanish accent was still prominent even though he had emigrated from Argentina long ago. Jared introduced him to Mark and Fazzi.

"So, Jaime, we are all awaiting your opinion on this thing," Jared said.

Valenzuela's dark eyes flashed and he nodded slowly. "Why didn't you give me this when my career was young and I needed some publications? Why do you give me this unbelievable stuff on the eve of my retirement, Jared?"

They all laughed.

"We take what Fate gives, and when she decides to give it, huh, Jaime?" Jared said. "Besides, she knew that your honesty and humility are at their peak now."

Valenzuela smiled. "That's why I like you, Jared. You're philosophical."

Fazzi looked at Valenzuela with an uneasy expression, as if to say, Get on with it, man.

"Okay, what did I find? I find that the Fresno pathology report is essentially correct. There is a large abnormal lesion." He stopped, looked behind him at the white board, then stood and drew a side profile of a human head in larger-than-life scale. Next to it he drew a profile of the back of the head. Then he sketched in the lesion from both views.

"It looks like this. It is roughly shaped like a hammer with a short handle. The big end is in the thalamic and limbic areas on both sides and the handle reaches up through the occipital and parietal cortex just above the ocular region. What is the lesion? It has enlarged cells of different kinds—but mainly neurons. Many of them are enormous—eight and ten times their usual size. I have seen before human neurons maybe one-half again normal size, but this big I've never heard of. The glial cells are also large. The Golgi cells reaching up into the cortex are especially huge. And these up near the cranium are tightly packed and layered."

"Those are pyramidal neurons, right?" Jared asked.

"Right."

"Are the neurons normal except for size?" Fazzi asked.

"Yes, Lou, as far as I can tell. The cytoplasm, neurotubules, lipids, filaments, axons—everything about them seems in correct proportion. Not all the neurons are oversized. There are some that approach normal size especially on the outer areas of the lesion. And that is interesting because the lesion blends in with the adjacent tissue so there is no clear demarcation. That's one reason this lesion doesn't appear to be overtly pathological. I found no obviously pathological tissue in any of the slides."

"And you say that neurons of this size have never been found?" Mark asked.

"Not in humans as far as I know."

Fazzi cleared his throat. "In other species like mollusks and fish," he said. "For example, goldfish and other fish have Mauthner cells which are two huge neurons that drive the motion of the tail to one side, then the other. Aplysia, sea slugs, have giant neurons about one millimeter in size."

"How big are the normal human neurons?" Mark asked.

"About one hundred microns—one tenth millimeter," Valenzuela said.

"The enlarged mitochondria, have you seen that before?" Fazzi asked.

"Not this dense and heavy," said Valenzuela. "I have seen it in damaged livers but not in the brain. Now, I do remember reading a report of a rare syndrome called Giant Mitochondria Disease. I seem to recall it was a genetic problem and it is on file at the Human Genetic Mutant Cell Repository in New Jersey."

"No kidding?" Mark said.

"I don't know anything more about it than that. Maybe I could dig up the reference for you."

"Do you think the lesion is of genetic origin, Jaime?" Jared asked.

"It would have to be. How else could it be explained? Probably some kind of mutation that was manifested late."

"What if it were manifested early—right from infancy?" Jared asked.

"How could it be?" Valenzuela gesticulated impossibility with his hands. "It would obviously be a malfunction that would destroy the host."

"Well," Jared said in lowered voice, "I didn't tell you this because I didn't want you to be biased in any way, but we are seeing the seven-month-old child of the man whose autopsy material you saw and we think the baby may have a similar lesion."

"Dios mio!" Valenzuela looked horrified. "Is it a vegetable?"

"The baby behaves completely normally," Jared said.

"No! How could that be?" Valenzuela asked.

"We don't know. That's partly why we called you to look at the father's lesion," Jared said.

"You'd better tell him about the voltages, Jared," Fazzi said.

"There is an abnormality of EEG in the baby," Jared said. "Two, in fact. One is a spike-wave pattern in the temporal lobes, suggesting a seizure syndrome. The other is extremely high voltages in the parietal-occipital area—voltages over four hundred microvolts."

Valenzuela screwed up his face. "This is medical history, no?"

"It looks that way," Jared said.

Valenzuela asked, "Do you think the voltages are coming from the lesion—the giant neurons?"

"That's the obvious association," Fazzi said.

"And the baby's head, is it normally shaped?" Valenzuela asked.

"It's larger than average, but not abnormally so," Jared replied. "The only unusual thing about the baby's appearance is that he has very large eyes. But not grossly above the normal range. His hearing may be especially acute as well."

"I'd like to see that baby," Valenzuela said.

"Yes, well, unfortunately the family lives up in Fresno. Mark, do you think Mrs. Shenko would come down for some additional tests?"

"I don't know. Probably, if she thought it was for Gregory's benefit."

"And let me add," Jared said, holding his hand out toward Mark, "that the Shenko case is Mark's."

Mark smiled self-consciously.

"Wouldn't it be important to get at least a CAT scan?" Valenzuela asked. "Then you would know if the baby has the same lesion as the father's, and how it compares."

"Yes," Jared said.

"I agree with that," Fazzi said, "but it really would be great to characterize those packed neurons and see how they're functioning, how they can produce that voltage. Let's face it, this is pretty incredible stuff."

Valenzuela laughed. "Yes, indeed."

"What kind of procedures are we talking about?" Jared asked.

"Well, to study those neurons, some indwelling electrodes would need to be placed," Fazzi said. "I think we could get them inside two or three of those giant cells. Hooked up to my electrophysiology rig, we could measure resting and firing potentials and see if we can determine what neurotransmitters are involved, how the whole network of them work together to produce that voltage—"

"Hold on." Jared's face had reddened. "I don't think invasive procedures are advisable. We'd never get it past the Human Subject Protection Committee."

"I think we could," Fazzi said gently. "After all, the epilepsy is life threatening."

The conversation stopped as everyone realized the sensitivity of the issue and who around the table had authority among the four. Eyes ended up on Jared.

Jared spoke calmly. "There are lots of procedures we could talk about—PET scan, functional MRI, behavioral tests, angiogram, more EEG's. Rather than go over them all now, let's think about what tests would make sense and send each other email about them along with their pros and cons. We have to recognize that in any test the clinical benefits to the patient have to be high. Then we can get together again and see what we can agree on. We won't be able to do everything under the sun in one visit." Jared frowned and tapped his pencil. "Needless to say, this case could generate some important papers and I'm not interested in getting any more people involved, so let's keep this to ourselves for now. Finally, let me remind everyone about patient confidentiality."

After Jared saw them out, he walked back into the conference room and slowly erased the artfully sketched drawings from the white board. Quietude replaced the exuberance of a few minutes earlier. As Nick's heads disappeared, a sense of misgiving came over Jared. Valenzuela and Fazzi were right—Gregory's lesion was a major scientific discovery. The story had arrived in bits and pieces, and today it was full blown with the attendant euphoria.

He sat down, loosened his tie and collar button, and glanced at the scribbling and doodles on his notepad. Research plan. What specific questions should be answered next? Using what techniques? What kind of clinical management? Jared realized he needed time to ruminate. He would not be able to avoid the pressure of all the decisions. He was in charge of the Shenko mutation, for better or worse, despite the fact that he'd assigned the case to Mark.

THE NEXT MORNING Mark relaxed in the Hospital Espresso/Deli, sipping coffee after seeing four new patients in the infant care clinic. Two things were clear to him: Jared was now comfortable assigning him new cases coming into the clinic, and Mark was confident that he could quickly get up to speed on a wide variety of presenting problems. For the past two days he'd hit the books on failure-to-thrive, cleft palate following repair, severe chronic diarrhea, and strabismus or non-coordinated eyes. Mark now understood that the principle running through all of the clinic's patients was how their condition affected their motor, language, and mental development. That is why, Lena had said, the division had two psychologists to test the infants on many different measures of developmental progress. Mark realized he should spend time with those psychologists at some point.

He glanced around the room, enjoying the hubbub of talk. Nurses in whites, eyes flashing, dissected other staff and whispered about cases that shouldn't be discussed in public spaces. Medical students with stethoscopes prominently tucked into lab coat pockets conversed quietly, trying to be casual. Mothers with babies, seeking acquaintance with cohorts, bravely told about their children's problems and sucked up sympathy and understanding.

For Mark, patient care was an uncharted adventure. The challenge of diagnosing patients was as real as what he had done with his PhD: trying to decipher the billions of TA and GC base pair letters of the human genetic code, working to map DNA fragments to one of twenty-three chromosomes, struggling to arrange the DNA sequences in correct order, and slaving to select out the small percentage of genes from the 97 percent of junk DNA. He remembered a description of the process in a New York Times article: ". . . the mental torture of doing a jigsaw puzzle in which all the pieces are virtually identical." And when a gene was finally determined, one still did not know its functions in the human body. That was a whole other painstaking search in the haystack. Of course another complication was that recent research showed some of the so-called junk DNA was actually functional. Maybe no DNA was junk. The research surprises were never-ending.

A large part of his new motivation, he realized, was the Shenko case. The recent developments involving Rose, Corinne, Lesser, Valenzuela, and Fazzi buzzed in his head. While the scientific aspects were especially fascinating, the human dynamics—the perspectives and feelings of the people—made an interesting drama. He pictured Corinne's pained, expressive face. More than anything, he wanted to relieve her of the baby's burden, to fully diagnose and treat the epilepsy, to make Gregory normal.

"Boo!" Lena slipped into a chair next to him. "Mark, what planet are you on?"

He laughed. "A planet called Wishful Thinking."

"I've been there before." She smiled.

"Can I buy you a coffee?" he asked.

"No, I have to get back. I just wanted to bring you some mail. I thought you might want to see this one."

The envelope had a Porterville postmark.

"I'm going back," she said, "but promise to tell me what it says."

"Okay, I promise."

Mark opened the envelope. A scrap of paper inside had a phone number on it. With it was a short, handwritten note that read:

> Dear Docter Sanlder,
> Zenya's number I gave you was wrong. Here it is. She knose you will call. Thanks for the 500 doller ckeck. The nabor boy will fix a new flor and pant the kichen. I liked talking and please come agin.
>
> Rose

No wonder his calls to Zenya had reached a fax machine. Mark stuffed the letter in his pocket and thought about what he needed to do for the rest of the day. Mostly a lot of reading. He decided to leave early and work at home.

THE DRIVE HOME was uneventful. He parked in the driveway and retrieved three beers iced in a bucket, a bag of pretzels, a handful of journals, and his smartphone from the house. He settled in a lounge chair beside the pool, opened an ale, and took a long swig before turning to an article on strabismus. When his watch showed six p.m. eastern time, he dialed the new number he had for Zenya. This time his call was answered on the second ring.

"Ms. Zenya Shenko?"

"Yes."

"This is Dr. Mark Sandler calling from Southern State University Medical Center in Los Angeles."

"Oh, yes. My mother told me about you. I've been expecting your call."

"Good. Is this a convenient time to talk?"

"Well, I have to get ready to go out for a class, but I can talk for a few minutes."

"Okay. Ms. Shenko . . . do you prefer Ms. or Miss?"

"Oh, please call me Zenya."

"All right. Since time is short, let me get right to my concerns. Zenya, your mother told me of the seizures your brother had as a child in Kansas, once near

Lawrence and once in Salina. Do you remember these? And do you know if he ever had any others?"

"No, those were the only times I know of."

"Was there anything else about his health or behavior that wasn't normal?"

"No."

"Did you ever have any seizures, or anything that makes you think you might have the same problem as Nick?"

"No."

"Have you ever had an EEG, a test of your brainwaves?"

"No."

"Well, we are thinking it might be a good idea for you to have one."

"Well . . . I don't know."

"What if I were to arrange it with a medical center in Key West or maybe in Miami, and it would cost you nothing, would that be all right?"

"I just don't know. I guess I would have to think about it."

"Well, I believe it would be a wise thing to do. And it's completely painless. Would you think about it and let me know?"

"Okay, I'll think about it."

Mark was surprised at her reluctance. He wondered if she were a difficult person.

"Zenya, your mother said you didn't get along with Nick. Why was that?"

There was a pause.

"I don't know. We just didn't like each other much."

"I see. Can you tell me anything about your mother's health problems, the arthritis, the headaches?"

There was a longer pause.

"She told you about the headaches?"

"Yes. They were quite bad."

"Well, she wasn't smart. I learned to stay away from him."

Mark hesitated. "You mean Nick?"

"Sure. Didn't she tell you Nick caused them?"

"Uh, exactly how was that?"

"Whenever he got angry, he could cause headaches in people. He did it to Mom and sometimes to me. I saw him do it to others too."

Mark felt his chest tighten slightly. "When he got angry . . . I see. What did these headaches feel like?"

"Well, the closer you were, the worse the pain. It hurt like in the middle of your head. It buzzed, and you got this feeling of being afraid. When it was real bad, you couldn't think and couldn't hardly move."

Mark suddenly found himself without words.

"Dr. Sandler?"

"Yes, please go on."

"Well, if you were within ten feet of him, he could get you real bad, but if you were beyond that, you could usually get away before it got bad, unless he chased you."

"How far away did you have to be to not feel it?" Mark said softly.

"Oh, about fifty feet."

"What if you were in the next room?"

"The walls didn't make no difference. It was how far."

A prickly sensation danced on the back of his neck. He wanted to keep going in an ordinary conversational tone but his mind began blocking.

"All right," he said. "Is there anything else you can tell me?"

"Not really."

"Okay, well I'd better let you go, Zenya, but I'd like to call you again . . . say next week?"

"That'd be fine. I'm usually home on Tuesday, Thursday, and Friday evenings."

"Good, it's been nice talking to you. Thank you for helping."

He sat stunned. Headaches. Headaches in Zenya, Rose, and Corinne. But not the usual kind. Very strange headaches. The condensation from the bottle was cold on his fingers. I've got to write this down, he thought.

AT NOON THE BELLS in the tower of the campus library gonged their familiar musical soliloquy. The human pace quickened on the brick-and-concrete walkways between buildings. Jared took out the bag lunch his wife had prepared. Although the work day was only half over, he felt exhausted because he hadn't slept much the night before. Yesterday's conversation with Mark still reverberated in his head. Mark's call to Zenya Shenko had yielded something that was too incredible to believe. Jared remembered reading about the headaches reported by both Rose and Corinne Shenko in Mark's report. He could see why Mark was excited at the prospect, but the idea was preposterous.

Jared had not, however, ridiculed Mark's hypothesis. Jared had instead proposed that Mark come up with an experiment to test it. Better that Mark should be let down by facts that would speak for themselves. Mark had been somewhat reluctant to agree to an experiment but soon realized the necessity. It was a clever plan—in a nice way, put up or shut up.

After lunch Jared started through the pile of paperwork Lena had left on his desk. He was surprised that the Brain Research Bulletin was on top. The BRB was a public relations piece put out by the Brain and Neurology Institute, mostly to keep outside donors informed of the great things going on. He picked it up and read the yellow note that Lena had attached: "Jared, you may be interested in the blurb by Dr. Fazzi under Research Notes on page 2." He quickly turned to that section. The bottom item read as follows:

LATE BREAKING . . .
An infant with an unusually large lesion in the brain has been discovered.

The anomaly could be the result of a never-before-seen muta-tion. This patient, who has an abnormal EEG with high voltage potentials but otherwise functions normally, may present an unparalleled opportunity for study of brain function at the synaptic and cellular levels. The research is being conducted by Louis Fazzi, MD, PhD, senior scientist of the institute, Jared Weymouth, MD of pediatrics and Jaime Valenzuela, MD of pathology.

"Shit. Damn it. He didn't even ask me," Jared muttered. He dialed Fazzi. "Lou, what's the big idea of putting that piece in the BRB?"

"I didn't think you'd object. Was something wrong with it?"

"Yes. I didn't want any publicity about Shenko. You should have asked me first."

"But it's not a publication—the Bulletin is just a throwaway."

"I know, but it goes out to a lot of people. And I didn't like it. We were to keep this quiet."

"Well, I'm sorry, Jared. I'll be sure to check with you on anything like that in the future."

"Be sure you do."

There was silence before Fazzi said, "Did you get the emails on suggested tests?"

"I did, and I'm glad we're all agreed on the CAT scan. But I gotta tell you, despite your and Jaime's recommendation, I'm opposed to electrode implants, at least at this stage of the game."

"Why?"

"It's risky and doesn't advance the baby's care."

"What risk are you talking about, Jared?" Fazzi asked.

"Possible viral infection, capillary bleeding, triggering of seizure."

"Oh, come on. Implants are done all the time without any problems. What viral infection?"

"Encephalitis, Jakob-Creuztfeldt, or any number of new bugs."

"We use sterile one-time electrodes right out of a sealed package, for god's sake."

"It can't be chanced."

"Listen, Jared. This baby is a once-in-a-lifetime research subject. It's utterly amazing that a human has somehow developed a voltage cell of the kind seen in eels—giant neurons seen in sea slugs. As improbable as that is, it's impossible to think these complicated structures are some billion-to-one mutation. There have to have been small mutations over time with selection occurring. But for what evolutionary purpose? This is momentous stuff. Jared, if this baby dies before we can study what this is . . . well . . . it just can't happen. Jared, trust me, this is Nobel material. And you can be the senior author. I don't care."

Jared made a noise in his throat. "Truer words were never spoken, Lou. You don't care. You don't care about the baby, the mother, Mark—who you left out of the blurb—or me. You just care about one thing—what can you get out of this. Lou, I don't see that we'll be able to collaborate on this case."

Fazzi paused for a few seconds.

"You're cutting me out?" he asked.

"I'm sorry, but yes. Gregory Shenko is Mark's and my patient, not yours. Go find some other subject to puff about in newsletters. Clear enough?"

Fazzi inhaled, then shouted, "Jared, you are a first rate asshole, and you will regret this!" The line clicked dead.

Jared got up slowly, wadded a paper, and threw it at the wastebasket. He was wide by six inches.

Chapter Six

Mark held his smartphone to his ear. The underwater lights in the pool made wave shimmers on the wall of the main house. The water still moved from his swim. Watching the patterns—bringing chaos theory to mind—Mark could sense the question coming.

"Did you remember that it's your father's birthday next week?"

"I know, Mom, but I'm sure he doesn't want to hear from me."

"It would be nice if you at least sent a card. At some point you hardheads are going to have to start talking. A card would help."

"Oh, I'm sure. He'll probably toss it away unopened."

"I don't think so, Mark. He's been asking about your situation."

"Then why doesn't he just call me?"

"Do you want him to?"

"I don't know."

Naomi Sandler broke out in a melodic laugh and Mark couldn't help chuckling.

"Aren't we all silly?" she asked.

"Neurotic and dysfunctional are better words."

"Yeah, okay."

"I have to go, Mom. Got to get organized for a very important patient coming in tomorrow. I'll get something off to Dad."

"Am I pressing my luck to ask that you email Rachel?"

"Yes, you are. Bye."

Mark poured over his notes, here and there revising the test he'd devised to follow the CAT scan. Jared had approved the plan with amused skepticism. Lena was willing to do her part. The question was how Corinne would react. Mark reworked the script he'd made to explain and justify the experiment to Corinne. Her cooperation was key. And if the experiment went without a hitch, what would happen then? Win or lose, the results would be big. Genius or chump. And if a genius, then the real trouble would begin. He sighed, gathered his papers, and headed to work.

LENA WAS ARCHED over her desk when Mark arrived.

She looked up and winked. "A little late, aren't you? Mrs. Shenko and the baby just left for the CAT scan. Dr. Weymouth's with them."

"I know. I want to go over the interview that you'll do with her when they come back."

"Oh, sure."

Mark sat down in front of the desk, enjoying Lena's perfume. "There is specific information I would like you to obtain. Mrs. Shenko has complained of headaches. I'm wondering if somehow these might relate to the baby. So your task is to try to get her to recall every time she's had a headache in the last four months. Try to pin down the day or at least the week. Find out where she was, if she was with Gregory, and where *he* was and what he was doing at the time. In other words, was he playing, sleeping, crying, or what? And find out how close to her he was, like how many feet away. If she wasn't with Gregory—her mother was babysitting, whatever—be sure to record that, too. Do you think you can get all that?"

"Sure. Do you think her headaches are psychosomatic with Gregory being the trigger?"

"Possibly. We just want to check out an idea. Probably they're not."

"Okay, I'll see what I can find out and write it all down."

"Good, thanks."

He headed over to the hospital CAT scan facility and was directed to the machine bay in back. Gregory was already in the machine, sedated, head propped in place with small pillows, being watched over by a matronly technician. The machine hummed rhythmically, red light on. He quietly greeted Corinne and Jared. She seemed glad to see him, despite her preoccupation with her baby and the machine. Jared told Mark that they would have the results that afternoon from Valenzuela. After some time of whispering and waiting, the scan was completed. Mark carried the sleeping child back to the division office, accompanied by Corinne and Jared. They parked Gregory—still sleeping—in his infant carrier next to Lena, and Mark took Corinne to the Espresso Bar.

"I'm sure glad that's over," Corinne said. She was wearing an olive, fatigue-style pantsuit with a large brass zipper that ran from neck to crotch. On her feet were low-heeled leather shoes, also olive colored. Her thick hair was pulled back tightly from her forehead into a pony tail. Mark noticed that her wedding ring had been moved to her right hand.

"Yeah, those machines are unnerving. But Gregory slept through all the noises. He's great."

She laughed. "Yeah, great while he's sleeping." She took a sip of the latte Mark had bought for her. "So Dr. Weymouth said you're supposed to tell me what comes next."

"Right. Well first, Lena is going to meet with you. She's going to get some details on your headaches. It shouldn't take but a half hour."

"Okay, but what does that have to do with anything?"

"Maybe nothing, but I'm concerned about it."

She eyed him quizzically.

"Then, when Gregory is awake and alert, we're going to do a little test. It will be an interesting one." He smiled broadly.

She lowered her eyebrows in a frown. "Interesting. Okay."

"Cory, we want to see Gregory cry when you're gone. We'll put him in a crib in one of the testing rooms with you, me, and Dr. Weymouth. Then you'll leave the room and shut the door. He should become afraid and cry. We want to observe him in that situation."

"But why? You've already seen him cry."

"We want to observe his neurological tone. If you will trust me, I'll tell you more afterward. It won't last long—five or ten minutes—then you can come get him."

She frowned some more, then finally smiled. "It will be hard for me, knowing he's crying. But, I guess if it helps you to help us . . . okay."

When it came time for the test, all three adults seemed nervous. In contrast, Gregory was happy and playful. Corinne carefully laid him in the crib and gave him a small stuffed giraffe. Gregory bobbed his head and cooed, mouthed the giraffe, and looked out at them between the crib dowels. He was on his back clad only in a diaper.

Corinne bent over and kissed his head. "You be a good boy. I'll see you very soon."

Gregory watched his mother leave. After the door closed he looked at Mark and Jared. He looked back at the door and his expression changed perceptibly. In a few moments he again looked at Mark. Then his lower lip pushed forward, his eyes squinted, and he started to whimper. He stopped, looked at the door again, then around the room, his large eyes searching. Then he began crying in earnest.

Jared glanced at Mark. "I don't feel anything, do you?"

"Not yet. Maybe he has to get angrier."

Jared smiled as if to say, 'Just give it up, Mark'.

After a minute of watching Gregory cry, Mark decided to try a different tactic. He told Jared he'd be right back. He returned with an ice cube in his hand. He leaned over the crib and held the cube against the bottom of the baby's right foot. Gregory screamed and his face turned livid. Then he began to screech in rage.

The pain hit Mark between the ears. It came in searing waves, buzzing and echoing. He grabbed his head. It was excruciating. Something terrible was happening, something he didn't quite understand. Trembling, he dropped to the floor and scrabbled over against the wall. Still it pursued. He put his finger in his mouth and bit down hard. He couldn't feel it, the pain in his head was too overwhelming. How could he stop it? It didn't seem to matter where he moved . . . He could no longer concentrate. Somehow he managed to crawl toward the door and the pain lessened. Then the screeching changed to bawling. He got up and staggered out the door, his head throbbing. Corinne hurried past him into the testing room. He heard her talking to the baby, soothing him. The crying began to subside.

Jared approached Mark from the hallway.

"Mark? Are you all right?"

"Yes, I think so. The pain has gone now." Mark moved his head back and forth and up and down as if trying to loosen a sticky joint. He peered at Jared. "Did you feel it?"

"God, did I. I was lucky to get away. When the first jolt hit, I ran out the door." Jared put his hand on his forehead and looked at Mark in amazement. "You really expected this to happen, didn't you!"

"Well . . ."

"Jesus. Do you know what this means?" Jared didn't wait for an answer but turned and walked away, shaking his head. "Goddamn!"

After Jared turned the corner, Mark went into the testing room. Corinne was sitting on a chair, breast feeding Gregory, tears running down her face. The baby had a peaceful look as he suckled peacefully. Corinne looked up at Mark, her eyes round with fear. He put his hand on her shoulder and squeezed gently.

"Are you okay?" he asked.

"*I* am. Are you?"

He nodded. "Please come to Dr. Weymouth's office when you're done." He gave her a reassuring smile as he left.

JARED WAS WRITING at his desk when Mark and Lena entered. Jared looked up and waved at a couple of chairs. "Please sit down. We want to know about your interview, Lena. Tell us what happened with Corinne's headaches."

Lena reported that each of the four severe headaches Corinne recalled was at a time when Gregory was crying or screaming and they were in close proximity. After Lena finished and left, Mark looked at the floor and said nothing.

"You were right," Jared said. "I thought it was impossible, but you didn't. Amazing. Congratulations."

Mark raised his head. "Thanks, I guess."

Jared nodded. "And now we have a real problem. The last thing we can do is let Gregory do that again in this medical center. I don't think we should do any more tests. All we need is for him to get upset, clobber some nurse or technician, and create a stir. Somebody might call the police. Who knows what could happen."

Mark stared at Jared, stupefied.

"I want you to be with Corinne and Gregory from now on until they leave for Fresno. I will help out, if needed. We're going to have to talk to Corinne. Her cooperation is essential. She will need to be very attentive to Gregory and not let him get upset. Until we think this through, I don't want anyone else to know about it but you, me, and Corinne. Lena will know about it too, of course, but that's all. The fewer, the better. Do you agree with what I'm saying?"

"Yes, sir." Mark's brow wrinkled. "What will you tell Fazzi and Valenzuela?"

"You mean why we're not going ahead with other testing?"

Mark nodded.

"I already told Lou we weren't involving him any more. I'll have to tell Valenzuela, too. Uh, I want you to see what Lou put in a newsletter about Gregory. He doesn't even mention you as the baby's doctor."

Jared's phone beeped. It was Lena, asking if he wanted to take a call from Dr. Valenzuela. He grabbed the receiver. "Jaime, were you able to look at the CAT scan? . . . Good, let me put you on speaker. Mark's here."

"Hello, Jaime," Mark said.

"Hi, Mark. Okay, I reviewed the scan. The quality is good. Basically, there are no surprises. The lesion is just like the father's, but larger, if you can imagine that. The packed neurons near the cranium are denser. Other than that, it's the same. Again, nothing pathological in appearance."

"That means it has to be genetic," Jared said.

"Did you see anything in the parietal area?" Mark asked.

"No. All other areas look normal."

Nobody said anything for a few seconds.

"All right Jaime, we really appreciate your taking time to study this," Jared said.

"Happy to do it. I'll take another look to see if there are any details I might have missed. But, that's the story for now."

"Thanks," Mark said.

"Oh Jared," Valenzuela said. "Lou Fazzi called me. I'm sorry about that BRB misunderstanding. I hope it's not . . . irretrievable."

"Yeah, well Jaime, it *is* irretrievable as far as Lou is concerned. But that has nothing to do with you. Let's have coffee tomorrow."

"Okay, sure."

Jared hung up. His left eyebrow twitched. "I think it's time to talk to Corinne. I'll need your help."

"Sure."

"Just join in the discussion. I only hope she doesn't think we're crazy."

"I don't think she will."

GREGORY HAD FINISHED feeding and was asleep in the infant seat when Lena delivered mother and baby to Jared's office. Mark watched Corinne settle into a chair, then told her about his conversation with Zenya, comparing what Zenya had told him to what Corinne had told Lena during their interview. Then he and Jared both described in detail the incident in the testing room. When they looked at her for a response, she was able to keep her composure for a few seconds, then tears spilled down her cheeks. She lost control and put her head in her hands. Mark stood up and put a hand on her shoulder. After a minute she regained her composure and looked up, red-eyed.

"You know," she said haltingly. "I kind of knew Nick could do that but I never really could admit it to myself. All those times . . . like when we were in Roeding Park and I told him I was pregnant . . . he called me a stupid bitch and started yelling. The pain hurt so bad in my head, and I couldn't think, couldn't move." She closed her eyes for a moment. "And now Gregory . . . God, how did this happen to me? Instead of marrying Nick, I should have gotten an abortion."

For a minute Mark thought she was going to lose it again. He patted her shoulder awkwardly.

She looked up at Jared. "But how can they do it? How can they *make* people have headaches?"

He shook his head. "I don't know. It must have something to do with the high voltages we're seeing in the EEG. Those aren't just headaches. Some kind of neuro-induction, maybe. We just don't know."

TOMOLO LAY AT AN END slip at B dock, one of several docks within the Santa Barbara marina. The beamy, thirty-six-foot sloop rolled ever so slightly from the wakes of other boats transiting the protected harbor.

The sailboat was named to honor *tomols*, the planked canoes that Chumash Indians had made and paddled between the Channel Islands and the mainland.

Tomol planks were hand carved and sewn together. Their seams were caulked with asphaltum, a sticky tar seepage found along the ocean beaches. The tomols were only one of many Chumash artifacts showing high-level skills in tool-making and artwork. Today, Chumash village names—Mugu, Hueneme, Sisquoc, Nojoqui, Lompoc, and the island name, Anacapa—still haunt the geography of the Santa Barbara and Ventura coasts where, two centuries ago, Spanish soldiers and mission fathers subjected the Chumash to harsh treatment, conversion, and genocidal European diseases.

At eight forty-five a.m. on a Saturday, Jared turned the key and *Tomolo's* diesel engine came to life. Twenty minutes later she nosed past the breakwater, past Stearns Wharf, and into open sea, rising buoyantly over each of the long, gentle waves rolling in from the northwest. There was almost no wind and she powered along under a limp mainsail, hoisted only to help stabilize her tendency to roll in the swells. It was slightly overcast, damp but warm.

Mark appreciated the fact that Jared had invited him on this little excursion to Santa Cruz Island. Ian Trevor, an anthropology faculty member, had been invited along as well. Mark watched as Trevor took off his shirt, revealing a tanned and trim upper body of thirty-some years. The man smoothed his blond beard and sat back against a cushion propped up on a lifeline stanchion.

"Why is it that leaving the harbor always feels so good?" he asked in a clipped British accent.

Jared's wife, Joan Weymouth, completed the foursome. She chuckled, her gray hair shaking, smile lines indented. "Because every time we leave the harbor, we're embarking on an adventure."

"We're escaping problems," Jared said from behind the wheel, tugging on his captain's hat.

"Well, whatever it is, it's a fantastic feeling," Ian said.

"Ian, don't tell me there isn't an anthropological reason. I thought anthropology could explain everything," Joan said with a teasing smile.

He smiled at her. "Well, the need for vacations is a culturally developed value of western industrial society. Obviously, this wasn't a problem for hunting and gathering societies because those groups moved around a lot. Their vacations were built into their lifestyles."

"See, I knew anthropology had the answer," Joan said.

"Are we going to have wind later?" Mark asked, looking at Jared.

"Yes, it'll come up in an hour or so. It gets pretty strong in this channel in the late afternoon and the seas can whip up to a nasty chop. That's why I like to head over early. Being rail down and taking spray isn't all that pleasant."

"Can we head directly for Pelican Bay?" Mark asked.

"I'm heading a little west of it now. Once we're in close, we'll downwind into the anchorage. We should make it in about three hours. That'll give us some time to go ashore if we want."

"Good," Mark said. "When you want relief from the wheel I'll show you how a Downeaster does it."

By ten the overcast had burned off and the sun beat down. Slowly the wind came up and by half past eleven they were on a reach, making five knots on the mainsail and a large jib. Mark took the wheel, trimmed the sails slightly, and was soon getting more efficiency from *Tomolo* than Jared had. Sandwiches, veggies, crackers, and dip were broken out along with cold beer and soft drinks. Jared and Ian set up a chess game, propping up one side of the board to counter the heel of the boat.

"Will we have to take down the jenny before long?" Ian asked.

"Not for an hour at least," Jared replied, moving chess pieces into place. "You'll be mated long before then."

"Listen to the man. How easily he forgets who won the last two games."

"Yes, but those are still under protest because you plied me with liquor, sir."

Ian chuckled. "Aha. I get white. Let's try a Queen's Gambit. I feel offensive."

"It's very hard, but I won't say anything to that," Joan said, stretching out on the leeward side of the cockpit.

Jared laughed, then studied the board with a serious look. "Ian, you know a lot about evolution. How often does a mutation occur that makes an observable change in man?"

Ian raised an eyebrow. "That's certainly out of the blue, but let's see. Mutation rates are a controversial topic. Lately the experts have come to believe that mutations in chromosomes and genes happen a great deal. But the problem is how many have occurred that are viable. There must have been a lot, considering that in about a hundred and fifty thousand generations we changed from a creature that stood only four and a half feet high with a cranial capacity of five hundred cubic centimeters and with massive teeth and mandibles to what we are today."

Jared grunted.

"The brain's seen the most development, though," Ian continued. "Our capacity is now thirteen to fourteen hundred cubic centimeters. As to viable mutation rates, I've seen an estimate that mutations resulting in inherited syndromes occur about one in a half million per generation."

"Those would be dominant and recessive syndromes, right?" Mark asked.

"Both. The recessive are not as easily determined. But why do you ask, Jared?"

Jared looked thoughtful. He moved a knight, then looked up. "So when you consider the total population of the world and all the babies being born, one in a half million means a lot of viable mutations taking place every generation, right? If that's so, why hasn't there been any significant alteration to the species since Cro-Magnon man?"

Ian moved a bishop. "It depends on what you mean by significant, I guess. There's been lots of change in our physical stature, pigmentation, facial characteristics, facility with language, brain function. The latter has brought about the biggest change of all—the development of culture. Now physiological evolution doesn't matter much, even though it is no doubt continuing, because the main thing happening is cultural evolution—learning all the changing memes."

Mark tightened his grip on the wheel as the wind freshened and the boat heeled further. The chess pieces slid across the board. Jared glanced at the knot meter. They were doing nearly seven and a half knots.

"I was wrong," Jared said loudly. "We should roll in the jenny and just sail on the main. We have a lot of sail up and if it pipes up more, we'll be too heeled. I'll get the jib roller. Mark, could you tend the sheet? Joan, you take the wheel. I'll start the engine so you can keep us headed up, honey."

The big sail rolled up nicely after Ian wrestled the tip back out of the water. Without the headsail, the boat stood up more, yet still made nearly six knots. It wasn't long before they could see the trees and sand beaches on Santa Cruz Island.

"What a great island," Mark said, admiring the view. "Where is Pelican from here?"

"It's still hard to see, but it's about a half mile down the coast." Jared handed Mark a pair of binoculars he'd pulled from a cockpit bin.

After a calm downwind cruise to the entrance of the cove, they pulled down the mainsail and Jared maneuvered the boat into the anchorage. The anchor was released and tested. Then they relaxed in the cockpit and looked around at the land.

"Want to stretch our legs ashore—maybe hike up to that point over there?" Ian asked.

"Good idea," Jared said.

"I'm game," Mark said.

"I'm going to stay in the cockpit and read," Joan said. "You guys go ahead. I'll keep an eye on the boat."

AN HOUR LATER, Ian, Mark, and Jared reached the point, two hundred feet above the ocean. It was clear and the mountains on the mainland sprawled, lavender and peaceful, beyond the cobalt iodine sea. Mark looked around at the rocks poking up here and there through the coarse grass. He also noted the small cacti scattered around. Might be advisable to watch where one sat.

"A fine view," Ian said. "Makes the climb worth it."

Jared stared at the ground. "Ian, have you ever experienced anything like ESP?" he said as he moved over and sat on a barrel-sized rock.

Ian stayed standing. "Another question out of the blue. No, I can't say as I have, Jared. I know other people who say they have, though. What about you, Mark?"

Mark shook his head, smiling, and found his own rock to sit on. Judging by the look on Jared's face, this little discussion could take awhile.

"What kinds of *things*, Ian?" Jared asked.

"Well, you know, a person all of a sudden gets a strange thought about somebody they haven't seen for years and finds out later that they'd had that thought at the exact time the friend had died in an automobile accident or something. Those kinds of stories are told all the time—and by reliable people."

"But you don't believe them."

"All I can say is that it hasn't happened to me," Ian said, sitting down on a rock near Jared. "This whole parapsychology business seems far-fetched, but I know that an increasing number of respectable scientists are studying psi phenomena. In fact, there was a survey in a journal a number of years ago. Questionnaires had been sent to professors asking about it and ten percent of the natural scientists who responded said they accepted extrasensory perception as an established fact. And about forty-five percent said it was a real possibility. Can you beat that? We're not talking about some crazy fringe group. But how does one know for certain unless he experiences it first hand?"

"Let's say that psi phenomena are real," Jared pressed, "by what medium are these signals conveyed?"

Ian guffawed. "The $64,000 question."

"Seriously," Jared said.

"Well, you and Mark know more about biology than I do. But look, a neuron can send a hundred millivolt signal the full length of its axon. That's pretty amazing. How many neurons in the brain?"

"A billion or so," Mark said.

"How many synaptic connections getting signals?"

"Trillions," Mark said.

"That's a lot of signals inside an oversized cantaloupe. When you think about that, is it so difficult to imagine that one hypersensitive organ can sense something of these signals in another? Different species have evolved some pretty complicated mechanisms to find and get prey, to avoid predators, and to communicate with one another. Look at dogs, their olfactory systems can detect smells in a few molecules per billion over several miles. How is it that some animals know an earthquake is coming? Animals—and I include humans—have evolved unusual means such as pheromones to influence others. There is a lot of *stuff* we just don't understand well."

"I'd have to agree." Jared nodded.

Ian turned up his hands. "Given the mind-boggling array of detection systems that have evolved, and the continual surprises that biologists turn up, I'm not surprised that many scientists think there is likely to be something to psi phenomena."

Mark wanted to jump in, but thought better of it. It was Jared's show.

Ian pulled on his beard. "Why all the interest in psi, my friend?"

Jared stood and took a couple of steps down the path. "I don't know. Just something I've wondered about." He made eye contact with Mark. "Enough speculating. Let's go back and have a swim."

Following them down the path, Mark knew there was no chance that Jared would be able to get his mind off Gregory. The baby and his strange power, which Jared had dubbed "X", had been all they'd talked about since the event in the testing room. And poor Corinne. Knowing that Gregory was able to cause headaches had made her a basket case. She had become hyper-attentive to the child, responding to every whimper, trying to head off any upset. Mark and Jared had been on the phone with her every day since she returned home, checking to see how she and Gregory were doing, reassuring her. Her confidence had slowly come back to the point that she wanted them to go on this weekend sailing trip and not worry about her and the baby. Mark had given her his cell phone number just in case.

"She's brave," Mark muttered to himself. "Scared and brave."

CORINNE PLACED GREGORY in his car seat and waved to her mother watching from the bay window. Corinne was glad to have begged off staying for dinner. She needed to study and there were two hours yet before dinner time. Thank goodness Gregory had behaved himself at her mother's. Probably the reason he had never raged at Grandma was that he seldom became frustrated around her. She was an attentive caretaker.

She'd forgotten to put the sunshade in the window again and the car's seat was scorching. Corinne tugged her shorts down to keep her bare legs from touching the heated vinyl. She wondered again why Dr. Weymouth didn't want her to confide in her mother about Gregory. After all, if she couldn't trust Mom, who could she trust? But then Mom would tell Dad. And Dad would probably want to get a second medical opinion or something.

Gregory began whining. She immediately pulled to the side of the street. "Okay, sweetie. Don't cry. I'm here."

The last thing she wanted was to get zapped while driving. Thankfully, it had never happened. Yet, that is. She was lucky that Gregory liked riding in the car. She adjusted his position in the car seat and gave him a toy to to play with. He quieted down and she drove on.

She glanced at Gregory and chuckled. Yes, he was becoming a little prince. Every whimper commanded attention. But as worrisome as he was, and as strange as the events of the past month had been, she felt a certain relief. Her headaches were Gregory's fault, just as earlier they had been Nick's. That made her own health problems less mysterious. Now she just had to focus on Gregory. Could she manage him? She hoped so. That was the essence of life, wasn't it— managing life's challenges? And she wasn't alone. She had help from the doctors. Dr. Weymouth was one of the best pediatricians in the country. He seemed to understand what she was going through. And Dr. Sandler was helpful . . . and trying hard to act like a doctor. He'd been willing to cancel his weekend away in order to be by the phone. She smiled.

Driving east on Shaw Avenue, she realized that for the first time in over a year—actually since meeting Nick—she had time to think about her life. She had made mistakes, and suffered for them, but she knew of others in worse situations. Some girls from her high school class had children without fathers and without support. At least she had some savings, plus the student loan money, plus financial help from her parents. Thank goodness for them. And her father was right: she should use her money to finish college. Then she could get a job to support herself and Gregory.

Stopped at a signal, she studied her reflection in the rear view mirror. She was still pretty. At some time in the future, when she was ready, she could remarry. There were bound to be some nice guys out there who wouldn't mind having a kid as part of the package. But would they want Gregory? Maybe he would be all straightened out by then. That wasn't being *too* hopeful, was it?

CHAPTER SEVEN

HORNS HONKED AS PEOPLE queued at the entrance to the parking structure near the medical center. An attendant standing near the open gate tried to move the cars along more quickly by pulling out the time-stamped parking stickers.

Alice Masterson flashed her press card that allowed her to park for free. She had read the item in the *Brain Research Bulletin* about an unusual infant and thought it might be an interesting story. Babies were always appealing. She had called Dr. Louis Fazzi about a possible interview. Instead of the brush-off she often received from researchers, he seemed eager to see her. He'd even found time in his busy schedule to meet with her without delay.

Her step was spry as she confidently strode down the hallway of the Brain and Neurology Institute. She wore a green turtleneck blouse along with a green-and-gold plaid skirt. She believed in wearing the right colors and as an "autumn" she found that dark green went well with her curly, strawberry-blond hair and brown eyes.

Medical science writing had been a default career choice after Alice had dropped out of medical school. She found out she couldn't stand needles, tissue, blood, and pressure. Her father, a cardiologist, had been deeply disappointed, but he'd been able to land her a trial job with the prestigious *Los Angeles Tribune*. And now—at age twenty-three and near the end of her first year on the job—she had recently been made a permanent member of the newspaper staff.

She gave her name to a secretary and was quickly ushered into a large office. A stout man who looked to be in his mid-forties turned away from his large computer screen and stood up.

"Ms. Masterson? Lou Fazzi."

"Hi. Please call me Alice."

As she expected, Fazzi had the surprised look older men typically got when they found a young, attractive woman in front of them—as if to ask how such a youngster could know anything about science.

"I read an article of yours on breast cancer. Quite well done," Fazzi said.

"Thank you," she said, sitting down.

"So you'd like to know about this strange little baby. Okay, let me give you the background."

Fazzi talked for about a half hour about the child's lesion, the EEG, and human brain physiology. Then he smiled. "And if we could just get this baby to come in, we could learn so much more."

"Oh, is there some problem getting the mother to bring the baby in?"

"There is a problem, indeed. And I've been thinking, Alice, maybe you could help with it." Fazzi smiled broadly.

"Me?"

"You see, the pediatrician treating this baby—his name is Jared Weymouth—he and I had a disagreement. The situation is that Dr. Weymouth won't let the child come into my lab now and have the needed tests. I'm concerned for Gregory—that's the baby's name. There is a very real danger that Gregory could have a seizure and die. So we should be trying to find out the nature of the lesion and the epilepsy. But that won't happen unless the mother knows that my expertise and my facilities are crucial to helping her baby."

"Why doesn't she know?"

"Weymouth and his sidekick, Dr. Sandler, aren't telling her."

"But what could I do?"

"Well, maybe you would be willing to talk to her. You could find out more information for your story and encourage her to come in to see me as well."

Alice felt ethical warning signals. But as she pondered the situation, she warmed to the idea of interviewing the mother. She could find out a personal side to the baby's problem. What was it like to be a mother of such a child? That would inject human interest into the story. Maybe the story could become a general feature, not just a science article. She might even get noticed by the news editors. She smiled.

"I think you could be a friend to Mrs. Shenko," Fazzi continued. "You are close in age. She might like talking to someone who knows about medicine but relates to her as a peer. You could possibly get a photograph for your story, but more importantly, you would be helping that child get the treatment he needs—maybe even save his life."

Alice nodded slowly and jotted down some notes.

"To show you how important this is," Fazzi pulled a checkbook from a drawer and set it on his desk, "I will pay your expenses to go up to Fresno. I also will give you money for Mrs. Shenko as an inducement for her to bring Gregory in to see me. I will cover the expenses for her trip down. And, of course, she will receive no bills for the baby's treatment."

The warning signals rang louder. Alice straightened in her chair. "Well, that's very generous of you. But she lives in Fresno? That's a long way from here."

"Not so far. Only four hours by car."

"But . . . why don't you just call her and ask her to come in? Why should I be an intermediary?"

"It would be touchy with Dr. Weymouth. See, I've never met Mrs. Shenko and even though her baby was tested in my laboratory, she may not know who I am. You would need to establish rapport and then explain the situation so she wouldn't ask Weymouth whether she should see me."

Alice winced. "That might be hard."

"Yes, but the matter's so crucial that we have to try, don't you think?" Fazzi turned up his palms with a beseeching look.

Alice tapped her pencil against her lips. "Why did you and this Dr. Weymouth have a disagreement?"

"It was silly. That information I put in the *Brain Research Bulletin* upset him. He didn't want any publicity about the baby. I guess he thought I was usurping his role. It was an innocent move on my part, just a misunderstanding. But now he's cut me out."

"Just over that?"

"Yes. I apologized, but he got his back up."

Alice shook her head and relaxed. "You doctors."

Fazzi smiled. "So will you help?"

"I'll see. Do you have her address? And what's her first name?"

"Corinne. Corinne Shenko. I'll get you her address and phone number. It's in the medical record. I really appreciate your interest."

"This is my job," she said with a smile.

"One other thing, Alice. The sidekick I mentioned—Dr. Mark Sandler—you might want to read up on him. He is a gifted young scientist who made seminal contributions to the Human Genome Project at the Whitehead. He turned down a tenure track offer from Harvard to work in genomics and comes here to work as a pediatric fellow with Weymouth. Worse, he pans the genome project publicly! Here are copies of articles from *Science* and *Nature*. I think you'll find it very interesting reading, maybe even story material."

~

FOUR DAYS LATER, Alice was again on campus, sitting at a table in the hospital Espresso Bar. A nurse friend of hers from pediatrics said Dr. Sandler came here often. In Alice's briefcase were clippings and a picture of Mark Sandler from the journals that had covered the scientific tempest.

After about an hour she spotted him. He sauntered in alone wearing an open lab coat with name tag. She smiled as he glanced at her. When he was about to leave, paper coffee cup in hand, she stood up.

"Dr. Sandler?"

He stopped. "Yes?"

She extended her hand. "I'm Alice Masterson. I wonder if you could spare a minute to talk to me."

He took her hand in a careful grip. She noticed him glance at the open *Lancet* journal on the table.

"Are you a doctor?" he asked.

She sat down and motioned for him to sit opposite her. "I'm a science reporter."

"Oh, well, I don't . . . what is this about?"

"I went to Stanford medical school one year and left, and then I took a job with the *Los Angeles Tribune*, thinking I could help science and scientists by doing high quality reporting—you know, articles that help people really understand medical and scientific issues, instead of the hack stuff one often sees."

"Whoa." He smiled. "That's commendable, but I'm just a postdoc. I don't have anything for you. I suggest you talk with some of the well-known researchers in the med school."

She gave her widest smile and again pointed at the chair he hovered over. "Actually, they already get plenty of coverage. I'd like to do a story on a young scientist—especially an interesting one." She winked.

"You know who I am, don't you." Mark sat down, obviously uncomfortable.

"I've read some of what has been written about you, and the letter you wrote to *Science*, but I don't know you. I mean, who you *really* are."

He frowned and shook his head.

"All I would ask," she continued in a softer voice, "is that you not prejudge me. I would be open minded."

He looked at her, puzzled. "Are you any relation to Harland Masterson?"

"My father."

He nodded. "I read his textbook."

She smiled. "So did I."

He smiled and nodded. "Well, if you've read anything about me, you can understand why I don't want any more publicity. I have a new career, and what's past is past."

"I do understand that. And if I did an article, I would work hard to keep it positive. That is—if you're willing."

Mark stood up and shook his head. "I have to go."

She pushed her card across the table. "Will you think about it?"

He picked the card up without looking at it. "I'll think about it."

"Before you go, please answer one quick question," she said.

"What?"

"Why did you wait for the Human Genome Project to be finished before voicing your concerns?"

"The Genome Project is not finished. Sure, they've announced that all the genes have been sequenced, and I was a part of the effort, but that is the tip of the iceberg. They now must find out what all the genes do, and what all the gene variations do. They must learn about all the proteins produced by the genes and what those million or so proteins do—a field called proteomics. I was working on this when I left."

She nodded and pulled something from her purse. "I see. Do you still believe this? It's an excerpt from your letter in *Science*." She read from a three-by-five card:

The Human Genome Project will reduce the human spirit down to biochemical reactions. DNA sequences should not take away the awe-inspiring mystery of our humanity. We need to have a reverence for our evolutionary progress, to trust all the mutations and natural selection processes that brought us here. Certainly we should have more faith in our biological heritage than in our scientific hubris.

"Are you still confident about 'all the mutations and natural selection processes'?" she asked.

He stared at her for a long moment. "There's a reason you selected those particular words, isn't there?"

She smiled. "I asked first."

"I'll think about your question."

She stood up and held out her hand. "I hope I'll hear from you, Dr. Sandler."

When he reluctantly took her hand, she firmly squeezed his fingers. He looked away as if embarrassed, then left.

Alice tipped the dregs of her latte onto her tongue. Had she hooked him? She wasn't sure. She *was* sure that there were vibes. She could understand his wariness. He had been a reticent participant in a public debate and had received some knocks. He had taken what he thought was a principled approach and was surprised by the ad hominem attacks. The reporter who broke the story had probably set him up—the old game of "Let's you and them fight." But, that's the system. Through controversy comes clarification and understanding of issues. Ideas and people must clash. Education of the citizenry is the higher good.

AFTER LUNCH, Mark met Jared on schedule for a review of the Shenko case. Mark could tell by the professor's twitching eyebrow that the man was not relaxed.

Jared tapped his fingers on his desk. "Mark, I want to warn you that a reporter called and asked about the Shenkos. You may be contacted too."

"Was her name Alice Masterson?"

Jared stiffened. "That's right. She called you too?"

"Cornered me in the Espresso Bar. Wanted to interview me about my career change. She didn't say anything about the Shenkos, though."

"I hope you didn't tell her anything or agree to an interview."

"No, I didn't."

"Good. I told her we don't discuss patients and hung up."

"Do you know how she found out about them?"

"She didn't mention Shenkos by name, just asked about the mutant baby. I wouldn't be surprised if she saw the BNB blurb. That's exactly why I didn't want that kind of publicity."

Suddenly Mark realized why Alice Masterson had selected that particular excerpt from his long letter in *Science*. She saw a connection to the Shenko case. That woman's no dummie, he thought.

"Mark, I've been puzzling over the situation with Gregory," Jared said, "trying to figure out what we might do. One approach would be to see if the headaches could be prevented in some way, such as through conditioning techniques. But this raises a question about whether the baby has any control over his X wave. Is it spontaneous or volitional? What do you think?"

Mark nodded. "I've been wondering that too. I think the answer relates to the nature of the mutation or mutations that caused the lesion. There are two basic possibilities: One is that the mutation is caused by a series of small changes over many, many generations, guided by natural selection—gradual evolution as Fazzi suggested. If this is so, the baby might well have some conscious control. Evolutionary forces would tend to select those individuals who could control it, like electric eels turning up their voltage at the desired time.

"The other possibility is that the mutation is saltatory, occurring due to a sudden change in the DNA. These mutations come about by happenstance, like the trisomy of Down's syndrome or most mutations that cause disease. If this is what created Gregory's lesion, I would think he is unlikely to have controllability."

"Is the saltatory change what you think happened?"

Mark nodded. "Two things make me lean that way. One is the seizure syndrome, assuming Gregory's and his father's are the same. I find it hard to believe that a trait could be selected for increased survival when it has such a bad disease coupled with it. The other thing is that if the lesion were evolutionary, it would have taken tens, maybe hundreds of thousands of years to develop. A group of people would have had to interbreed in relative isolation to achieve that. Otherwise, the mutation would have become more widespread through what is called genetic drift and discovered long before now."

Jared sucked in his lower lip, turned his chair, and stared out the window. After a few seconds, he whipped back around. "But how do you explain the fact that the lesion is so much like a power cell, a very sophisticated kind of biology? Doesn't that argue for lots of step-like mutations?"

"Well, it's clear that the mutations in just one amino acid of a gene can cause multiple changes in physiology and function. Especially if the mutation affects regulatory genes that influence key structures in embryological development."

Jared shook his head. "You wouldn't be suggesting that the same kind of change leading to fish voltages could happen all at once during the fish phase of the human embryo."

Mark tried not to laugh. "Well, not exactly, although that's an interesting idea." He forced a serious expression and continued in seminar mode. "Lou Fazzi would probably argue that the similarity between electric eels and Gregory is due to convergent evolution. He would say that eel voltage cell genes would not necessarily be found in Gregory, because homologous structures need not be encoded by homologous genes."

"You're losing me with all this genetic mumbo jumbo. What the hell is convergent evolution?"

"The theory of convergent evolution states that even though two species are widely apart in phyla, they could evolve a similar structure in response to similar environments."

Jared frowned. "But fish are in water and man is on land!"

Mark smiled. "Well, fish use voltages to get prey and repel predators. Might not Gregory's headaches achieve similar ends?"

"That's preposterous! Where do you get notions like that?"

Mark laughed. "You mean you never discussed stuff like that in grad school?"

"No, only PhD's have that kind of time."

As Mark laughed, Jared stood and began pacing back and forth in the office. At one point he pushed up on the balls of his feet. "If the X is not volitional, it could be hard sledding for Gregory and Corinne."

Mark nodded slowly, realizing that behind all of this discussion, Jared's thoughts—and concerns—were about the baby's future development.

Jared sat down. "I think we should bring Gregory back in and try to see if he has any control over the X wave. And while we have him here, I'd like Sylvia Auerbach to test him. She knows a lot about infant behaviors and might give us some insight. You've met Sylvia, right?"

"Yes, the short-haired psychologist who does developmental testing?"

Jared nodded. "She's very talented."

MARK LEFT HIS OFFICE late, having spent several hours on the internet searching the bio-medical literature. He had found nothing that seemed even remotely applicable to the Shenko mutation. Even the Giant Mitochondria Disease that Valenzuela had mentioned was entirely different. In Westwood he stopped at a deli and got a hot kielbasa, onion, and mustard sandwich to go, and then drove to Palisades Park at the west end of Wilshire Boulevard. He walked along the railing that zigzagged with the cliff's edge. The sun floated like a yolk above the ocean's horizon, framed by spindly palm trunks. He felt an eerie unreality, the loneliness of harboring momentous knowledge that couldn't be shared. The phone in his pocket rang and he walked over to a bench.

"Mark, thanks for sending that card to your Dad. He appreciated it."

"Good, Mom. I'm glad something works." Mark sat down, still watching the sun.

"Why, what's the matter?"

"Oh, things are difficult here. I can't believe how things are turning out."

"You don't like it there?"

"I'm under a lot of pressure. I thought that after the stress involved with HGP, pediatrics would be a piece of cake."

"You know you can come back here and stay as long as you want. Your dad said the company would like to have you if you don't want to be a professor."

"Dad asked them?"

"Probably not formally, but he's very high up, you know."

"Well, I'm staying here, at least for a while."

"Do you have any social life?"

"If you call meeting a reporter, a social life."

"Oh, no."

"Yeah."

"What happened?"

"A gal from the *L.A. Tribune* cornered me at a coffee bar at the medical center."

"What for?"

"You know, wanting to do an update on the infamous Dr. Sandler. She even read me a quote from my *Science* letter."

"Oh, dear. I'm sorry, honey."

He watched intently as the edge of the sun slipped over the horizon. No green flash. "It's okay. I'm not going to talk to her. She may write something, but there'll be no information or quotes from me."

"I can see why you're down."

"I don't understand why people don't get the fact that it's all over with. Give me a break."

"The media are terrible. No respect for people's privacy."

"Yup."

"I think you need an understanding friend."

"Mom, I know where you're headed. Just give it up!"

"Okay, sorry. I don't want to add to your stress."

"I might email her some time, but only when I'm ready. The more you bring her up, the less ready I'll be."

"Okay. I said I'm sorry."

"Say hello to Dad."

Mark sat in the twilight, watching the ponderous shadows gathering around him. He could imagine a breezy email exchange with Rachel, full of quips and surface stuff zinging wittily as if there were no emotional undertow lurking. Could he stand that? It would be painful.

ALICE WAS ON THE ROAD. The sky had been dark and threatening for miles—a rare summer storm. Finally, the rain came. It put her on edge.

She knew her anxiety was due not only to the storm. It had been several days since she'd tried talking to Mark Sandler. Part of her current unease was that she was getting closer to his patient, Corinne Shenko. For some reason Alice felt uncomfortable about the upcoming encounter. Was it because she knew she shouldn't be trying to broker a deal with Fazzi? What would Sandler think if he found out?

The car's GPS was easy to read and she wasted no turns. Alice found the apartment address, buttoned her raincoat, hoisted her umbrella, and made her way into the building. She took the stairs and found the door next to a couple of potted plants. She had to knock twice.

A woman holding a healthy-looking baby boy opened the door. She was in a bathrobe. "Yes?"

"Mrs. Corinne Shenko?"

"Yes, that's me."

"And this must be Gregory." Alice smiled, looking at the baby sweetly.

"Do I know you?" Corinne asked.

"Mrs. Shenko, my name is Alice Masterson and I'm from Los Angeles. I came to bring you a message from Doctor Louis Fazzi of Southern State University Medical Center. Also . . . I just wanted to meet you, because you have a story to tell. I should also say I'm a reporter. A science reporter."

"You're a reporter?"

"Yes, I'm with the *Los Angeles Tribune.*"

"Really. Well, come in, I guess. It's wet out there. Did you drive up from L.A.?"

"Yes, I left early this morning."

Corinne took Alice's rain gear and had her sit in the living room. "I'm sorry I'm in my robe. This place is kind of a mess." She turned down the stereo.

"Oh, that's quite all right. I came unannounced."

"So who is this doctor?"

"Dr. Louis Fazzi," Alice repeated the name. "He worked with your doctor—Dr. Weymouth is it?—when you first took Gregory to Southern State. Gregory was tested in Dr. Fazzi's laboratory. They did an EEG?"

"Yes, I remember that," Corinne said, nodding. "I never met Dr. Fazzi."

"Well, he is one of the top brain doctors in the country. Dr. Weymouth consulted with him about Gregory." Alice smiled and sat back on the sofa.

"Is that so. But why did he send you, Miss . . . what is your name again?"

"Alice Masterson. Please call me Alice. Let me back up and explain. Can I call you Corinne?"

"Just call me Cory." Gregory began twisting in his mother's arms. She sat him on a blanket on the floor. He started pounding on a small plastic piano and looked up impishly. Both Alice and Corinne laughed.

"He's darling," Alice said. "Anyway . . ." She went on to explain about seeing a short note in the *Brain Research Bulletin* about a baby with an unusual brain lesion.

"I didn't know anything about that," Corinne interjected, sitting on the edge of her chair watching Gregory.

Alice continued, telling how she'd met with Fazzi, about the disagreement between Weymouth and Fazzi, and that Fazzi felt very strongly that Gregory should be brought in for more tests in his lab. She ended with Fazzi's offer.

"Wow. You mean he would pay me one thousand plus expenses just to bring Gregory in to see him?"

"That's right. And I have half of it in my purse for you now."

Corinne's eyes widened. "Well, that's real trust. He must want me to come in pretty bad. I just can't believe they'd argue over that little business of the newsletter."

"I know."

Corinne frowned. "Do you know what tests Dr. Fazzi wants to do?"

"I don't know. You'd have to talk to him. I have his number for you." Alice handed over Fazzi's business card.

Corinne examined it and thought for a moment, then shook her head. "I'd better talk to Dr. Sandler about this first. Dr. Weymouth doesn't want a lot of testing."

"Why is that?"

"Uh, I can't say."

Alice raised an eyebrow in surprise. "Okay."

"And you came up here because you want a story? What kind of story?"

"Cory, I think that Gregory's problem is newsworthy." Alice leaned forward. "His condition seems like such an unusual thing. I have a feeling that people would like to learn about this brain lesion. And who knows, the publicity might help to uncover others that have the same problem. In that way you could be helping. I also think people would like to know how you as a mother are handling all this. What it's like and all that. We could put a picture of you and Gregory next to the article."

Corinne nodded slightly. "What would you say in the article?"

"I would describe the medical condition, say how it was discovered, what symptoms or problems there are. I'd interview you to learn how it's been for you—you know, having to deal with Gregory. Maybe put in some quotes."

"Would you have to put in anything about Nick's problem?"

"Nick?"

"My husband. He had it too and died from it."

Alice leaned back. She'd almost forgotten about the husband. "Oh, yes. Dr. Fazzi mentioned that. Well, sure, I think it would be important. It would show a genetic connection and the potential danger of the lesion."

Corinne ran a hand through her hair, as if trying to straighten some tangles. "It's kind of private," she said. "I don't know if I'd like everyone reading about all that. You know what I mean?"

"Sure, I understand. But maybe I could write the article and not mention your name." Alice sighed. "Except then the pictures might not make sense without names. Gregory is so cute, it'd be darling to have him in there."

Corinne looked fondly at her baby. "I know. I guess I'll have to think about all this, Alice. Why don't you give me your number and I'll call you."

They exchanged numbers.

"Would you mind if I took pictures now?" Alice asked. "That way if you decided to go with the story, I wouldn't have to drive up here again. I could just get the information for the story over the phone."

Corinne shrugged. "I guess so. But you wouldn't put anything in the paper without my permission, would you?"

"I'd be sure to talk with you before anything goes to print, Cory."

Alice pulled out her Pentax and took pictures of Corinne by herself, holding Gregory, and of Gregory down on the floor playing. The clicks and flashes fascinated Gregory.

"Tell me, what symptoms or problems does Gregory have?" Alice asked as she sat back down on the couch and put the camera back in its bag.

"Not much, really. He's got a temper. But he's pretty normal as far as I can tell."

The CD had ended and Corinne got up to turn off the stereo. Gregory had resumed playing next to the folded up playpen that leaned against the wall. As Corinne turned to come back, her sleeve caught on the corner of the playpen. The playpen fell over, landing on Gregory's back and rump. He didn't see it fall.

His screech was loud and by itself would have frightened anyone in earshot. But the pain was the kicker. It slammed into both Alice and Corinne, immobilizing them for several seconds as they screamed in unison. After Gregory switched to crying, Corinne opened her eyes and dropped down beside him. She pushed the playpen upright and lifted the baby into her arms, shushing him. When his screeching had turned into a bawl, the pain had immediately subsided. Alice stared at the pair, tears running down her cheeks.

Corinne stepped over and touched Alice's arm. "Are you okay, Alice? It's over, don't worry, you'll be okay."

For a minute, all Alice could do was look intently at Corinne and the crying baby. "What *was* that?" she finally said. "What on earth . . . ?"

"I can't talk now," Corinne said. "I have to feed Gregory and put him down. I would like you to go now." Corinne picked up the raincoat and umbrella and opened the front door, waiting expectantly.

Alice stood. "But Cory, what about Dr. Fazzi? What should I tell him?"

"Tell him I'll call him. Thank him for the offer. It was nice to have met you. Bye."

"Goodbye, Cory," Alice said, backing out the doorway. "I was very glad to meet—" The door slammed.

Alice stood there for a moment. Her head throbbed and her legs felt a bit shaky. She slowly put on her coat and turned to the stairs. Wobbling slightly on her high heels, she made it down to her car. Once inside she breathed deeply and took out her pad and pencil. She wrote down the whole conversation word for word, describing all that had just happened in detail. As incredible as the pain was, it had not diminished her exceptional memory.

ALICE SLEPT FITFULLY that night, even though she was tired from the trip. Her mind wouldn't let go of what had happened at the Shenko apartment. Halfway through the night it occurred to her that she had the science story of the decade! She would be famous. She would be able to work for any newspaper she wanted and name her salary. One of the conditions of any new job, she decided, would be that the science writers on staff—all those smug and horny men—would have to receive assignments from *her*. She chuckled and finally dozed off.

Alice connected by phone with Fazzi at nine forty-five the next morning.

"So how'd it go?" he asked.

"You're going to find this hard to believe."

"She's coming in to see me?"

"No. She wanted to think about that. She'll check with Dr. Sandler."

"Then that'll kill it."

"Not necessarily—she would like the money."

"Umm. Maybe I should offer more. So what won't I believe?"

"While I was there a playpen fell over on Gregory. He had a seizure for several seconds."

"How do you know?" Fazzi's voice was lower.

"He screamed uncontrollably. A scream like no baby I've ever heard. But that isn't the half of it. He . . . he somehow made Cory and me have seizures too. I was out of my mind for several seconds. The pain in my head was fierce. I know what I'm saying must sound crazy, but it happened. And Cory knew what it was because she got Gregory to stop."

"Well, Alice, maybe Gregory had a seizure, but you and Corinne couldn't have experienced the same thing. Maybe it was just sympathy pain."

"Dr. Fazzi, you don't have to believe me, but I know it was real. I *know*."

"Uh huh." Fazzi was clearly unconvinced.

"Corinne made me leave right away. She obviously didn't want to talk about it."

"Uh huh. So how was it left with her?"

"She's going to call and let us know what she wants to do. She'll call you about making an appointment, and me about whether or not she wants to go ahead with the story."

"She's allowing you to do a story?"

"I think she will."

"Congratulations. That's great. Do you need any more information from me?"

"I may need to call you as I get into it. I'll need more information about Gregory's father, Nick."

"I'll get you what you need," Fazzi said.

Alice knew when she hung up that Fazzi hadn't believed her about the head pains being induced by Gregory. That meant that the science editor wouldn't believe it either. He would ask what verification she had from medical authority. And she had none. But the story was true. And somehow it had to be published.

MARK'S HEAD NODDED to the side and he awoke with a jerk. The medical journal he'd been reading had fallen on the floor. He fixed a cup of instant decaf, sat down, and then the phone rang.

"Mark?"

His heart sped up as soon as he heard her voice. "Oh hello, Cory. How are you?"

"I'm sorry to return your call so late—I just got in from the library," she said.

Mark leaned back. "Where's Gregory?"

"He's asleep. My mother babysat."

"That's working well?"

"Yes, she loves to do it. Anyway, I wanted to tell you that a reporter came to see me—a young woman from the *L.A. Tribune*. She found out about Gregory from Dr. Fazzi. She said he wanted me to bring Gregory in to see him for more testing and he would pay me a thousand dollars if I did."

Mark's stomach clenched. The man was more of a jerk than he'd realized. "A thousand dollars? Damn."

"I didn't take it. I told her—"

"Hold on. Was her name Alice Masterson?"

"Yes, how'd you know?"

"She's contacted both Dr. Weymouth and me. Anyway, go on."

"I told her I needed to talk to you." Corinne went on to describe the visit in detail, including Gregory's display of the X trait.

Mark sat up. "My god! What did she do?"

"She was pretty shook up. I made her leave fast because I didn't want to talk about it."

"Do you think she knew what it was—that Gregory did it?"

"I don't know. Probably."

Mark stood and started pacing in front of his desk. "Is she going to write an article?"

"She said she won't without my say so. Should I let her?"

"No. No way. If she calls, just say you've changed your mind. As for Dr. Fazzi, do not go see him. I wouldn't even call him. He's more unethical than I thought."

"I wasn't going to. Don't worry. I could use the money, but I'm happy with you and Dr. Weymouth."

Mark relaxed a little. "That's nice to know."

"It's true."

"Cory, we do need you to bring Gregory down for one more visit."

"Oh?"

"I know you're tired of that drive."

"It's not so much the drive, it's just that every time I come down there, things get worse."

Mark felt a twinge in his gut. "Yeah. Well, we just need to do two more tests. These tests can make a difference in how we can help Gregory learn how to stop causing the headaches. After this we'll start making things better."

"Promise?" She laughed.

"Promise. And we can talk about how to handle reporters and other nosy types when you're here. So I'll have Lena call to set the date. Okay? "

"Okay. Bye, Dr. Sandler."

"You might as well call me Mark."

Cory laughed. "Bye, Mark."

He hung up.

CHAPTER EIGHT

ALICE HAD EXPECTED the turn down, but not the derision. Her editor had laughed at her. He had said that if she wanted to write science fiction she should try *Twilight Zone* magazine. This was the *Los Angeles Tribune*.

Back in her cubicle, she inhaled deeply. So! She had the choice of writing about a baby with a unique brain lesion, keeping strictly to medical facts, or not writing anything at all. Could she put together an article from the verifiable sources? She thought she had enough for a short piece, especially after talking with Dr. Lesser at the Fresno coroner's office. But a short piece would not get her the fame she craved. She needed more.

Corinne was not home in the morning, but Alice was able to connect that afternoon.

"Hello, Cory. This is Alice Masterson."

"Oh, hi."

"How is everything?"

"Fine."

"I haven't forgotten you. It's taken me a little while to get ready to write the article. Now I'm there. I even talked to Dr. Lesser at the coroner's office. He told me about the lesion your husband had."

"Oh?"

"It was interesting, though sad, about how your husband died and all. I'm so sorry."

Corinne was silent.

"Cory, in order to write this article I need to talk with Dr. Sandler. Do you think he'd be willing to see me?"

"I don't think so. He and Dr. Weymouth don't want an article written."

"But you do, don't you?"

"No, I've decided against it."

"But why?"

"I just have."

"Okay, but would you at least tell me what happened when Gregory screamed?"

"No, I'm sorry. I can't."

"How could he do that?"

"I don't know."

"It's scary, isn't it?"

"A little."

"Did it hurt you as much as it hurt me?"

"Look, I'm not going to talk about it. Please leave me alone. Don't write the article. Don't write any article that involves my baby or me. Okay?"

"Cory, I'm going to write an article. It will turn out better as far as you're concerned if you talk with me."

"You said you wouldn't write an article without my permission."

"I said I would talk with you first, which is what I'm trying to do."

"I don't want an article written."

"Why not?"

"I just don't. I have to go."

After a sleepless night, Alice called a woman reporter she knew who wrote for the *L.A. Voice,* a weekly newspaper.

"Well, Alice, how is life at the *Tribune* empire? Haven't heard from you in a while."

"Life at the empire is suffocating, if you want to know. That's why I called you, Kim."

"But I thought you liked all that hard-driving stuffiness."

Alice gritted her teeth. "I'm up to here with it. I want to write an article they won't approve."

"Oh ho! It must be something relevant. Or, is it an exposé?"

"Neither exactly, but it could be a biggie."

"And I suppose you want the *Voice* to print it under my name or something?"

Alice detected a slight undercurrent of jealousy. Don't react, she thought. She drew in a breath. "I want it under my name."

"That wouldn't sit well with the empire, would it?"

"I don't care."

"Oooh. You *are* pissed! This must be one helluva story."

Alice kept her tone confident. "I think it would be a coup for the *Voice*."

"She said modestly."

"Can you help me, Kim?"

"Well, I see you're serious. The best thing would be for you to come down and meet with Shaw. He's the new editor. Good guy. Willing to take a risk. Shall I set it up?"

"Yes. I'd really appreciate it."

"The price is lunch on that budget they give you."

"It's a deal."

ALICE LOOKED BRIEFLY at the picture of Gregory before she placed it in front of Bob Shaw. There was something about the baby's eyes. They were piercing and twinkling at the same time.

"Photogenic tyke, isn't he," Shaw said. "Mother isn't bad either. With these photos the piece would have appeal, no question."

Shaw thoughtfully stroked his square jaw with his thumb and forefinger as he studied the photo. Finally he set the photo on his desk and looked at her. "So you're willing to state in this article that you personally felt this epileptic trance and it came from the baby."

Alice nodded, trying not to hold her breath.

"Well, I'll go for this article if you write it in first person, and we put a disclaimer on it saying that it represents your view. I don't want it seen as a news article. And, I want you identified as a freelancer who also writes for the *Tribune*. Okay?"

Alice smiled. "Sure."

"And you won't blame us when you lose your job there. I might give you a freelance assignment now and then, but I don't have a spot for you."

"I'm not asking for a job. The only thing I ask is that if the *Voice* gets an award for it, I get invited to the ceremony."

He lifted an eyebrow. "If we get an award out of this, I'll make a job for you even if I have to take a pay cut."

MARK PULLED UP his email messages.

> Hi, Mark. I wanted you to know there's going to be an article on the Shenkos and you. Would you please meet with me? Alice.

"Oh shit." *How did Alice Masterson get my email address?* Mark wondered. He answered his own question: Through Fazzi. Or any number of other ways.

~

Lᴇɴᴀ ᴡᴀᴛᴄʜᴇᴅ Mᴀʀᴋ go by, headed for Jared's office. Jared's curses behind the closed door were so loud that twice she stood up, wondering if she should knock and put oil on the troubled waters. She didn't interrupt, however, and eventually the door opened and the two men came out. The older man's hand was on the younger man's shoulder.

"Mark, you've got a choice to make here. I know it's a real Hobson's choice— you're damned if you do and damned if you don't—but it's still your choice. I would have nothing to do with the woman. I'd let the article happen, take the blow, and move on. At least I wouldn't be making it worse. But, that's me. You do what you have to do."

Lena turned back to the paperwork on her desk, happy that she wasn't the one making the choice.

Aꜰᴛᴇʀ ᴡᴏʀᴋ, Mark met Alice at a popular west L.A. cafe. He found her in a booth and squeezed into the bench opposite.

"I appreciate your meeting with me," she said, smoothing wavy blonde curls back over her shoulders with a smile.

"I haven't decided whether it's stupid of me or not." He picked up the menu and stared at it so he wouldn't have to look at her.

She laughed. "I'm not going to bite."

"That remains to be seen, doesn't it?" Mark said through gritted teeth.

She ordered tea and he asked for the fresh-squeezed lemonade.

"Look," he said gravely, "I came here with a proposition."

"Well, most propositions I get are in a nicer tone of voice."

He didn't laugh.

The smile faded from her face. "But I see you can only be serious, Mark. What's your proposition?"

"Simply this. If you will not do any coverage on the Shenkos, I will give you a full-blown interview, answering any questions you want."

She looked up at the ceiling for a few seconds, revealing an exquisitely shaped neck and collar bones, then looked back down at him. "I can't do that. The Shenkos *are* the far more important story."

"Can you write something without mentioning their names or the names of anyone at Southern State?"

A wistful expression settled on her face. "I know this is tough for you, Mark. I really do understand your situation. So what could I do to help you? "How about this? If you tell me how that baby caused a seizure in both me and Cory, I will write a very positive article—about them, about you, about everyone at Southern State. Fair trade?"

Mark removed his glasses and rubbed his forehead. The waitress gave him a curious look as she set down their beverages.

"I just cannot talk about the Shenkos," he said.

"Why?"

"You know why—patient confidentiality."

"All right. One last counteroffer then. If you will answer one question about yourself, I'll give the article a positive slant toward both you and the Shenkos."

"What's the question?"

"Do you agree in concept first?" Alice sipped her tea, looking at him over the top of her cup.

"In concept, depending on the question."

She nodded and pulled a pencil and small notepad from her purse. She flipped several pages.

"Okay. Here's the two-part question. Part one: Won't knowing the human genome help in determining the genetic cause of an epileptic syndrome from an unknown brain mutation, and thereby help in developing gene therapy treatment for the disease? Part two: Knowing this, how could you as a doctor say that the Human Genome Project should not have been done? That we shouldn't have the benefit of fixing the epilepsy?"

Mark sat back in the booth and stared at her.

She raised her eyebrows.

"That is more than one question," he said in a low voice. "The premises in the question alone would take an hour's seminar. Gene therapy is very complicated and is not likely to work on epilepsy, even if you knew the genes involved. So far gene therapy has not worked very well on anything. Asking me to give some quick answer to that question is the kind of oversimplification that give reporters a bad name with scientists."

She grinned. "Touché. And avoiding tough questions is a classic defense of people who are unprepared to say what they believe." She cocked her head to the side.

He finished the lemonade. The tartness squeezed his tongue and he coughed.

"Alice, I will answer your question with a question. And it goes something like this. There is a lot of basic research focusing on cellular signal transduction, gene activation and disruption, programmed cell death, mitosis, nerve regeneration, stem cell differentiation, telomerase function, and other fundamental processes. Through this, all of which will be greatly helped by the genome project work, it is quite possible that the human life span may be extended by sixty or so years.

People in significant numbers could start living to a hundred and fifty. My question to you is this: Should we bring about this extension of human life with an even sharper growth in world population? Should we do it, knowing that the extended lives will not necessarily have reduced health problems? That the cost of social security and medical care for the aged may soar even more, placing an even heavier burden on workers and the economy? That the added worldwide resources consumed—more houses, cars, food and so forth—will be severe, negatively affecting species habitat and causing more heating of the planet and environmental damage? That we will create more congestion and make cities like this one even more unlivable, and that worldwide food distribution politics will not get straightened out, so that even more third-world famines and malnutrition will occur, and that the rich will get even richer by keeping their money longer, and conversely the poor, poorer? And that all of this amounts to a trade of more quantity of life for some in exchange for less quality of life for most, along with more damage to the planet and animal species? Should scientists, Alice, continue to do the research, including the post-genome projects, that will bring about these effects? What say you to that?"

"Talk about assumptions in a question!" Alice raised her finger. "Mark, I now realize what your problem is. You're not just against designer babies or some loss of mysterious human nature, you are against progress."

Mark leaned forward. "No, I'm in favor of progress—but your progress and mine have different definitions. So how do you answer my question?"

"My answer is that we should never stop research. Research is different from the political decisions that are the province of the society and our leaders. Scientists don't make—and should not try to prejudge—all the decisions that flow from their research advancements. We don't ask them to make the decisions, only to do the research."

"True. Scientists don't make those decisions. But you see, society doesn't make those decisions either. What politician, what individual person, would go against extending his or her own life? Or the life of loved ones? So the big, serious issues aren't faced. And in effect, the scientists do the research and thereby *do* make the decisions."

Alice smiled. "Well, you picked an interesting argument for your position. But, hey, I don't buy it."

"Fine. We all make our choices. And another choice I've made, with all due respect—and I do respect you, Alice—I cannot condone or participate in your article."

In one smooth motion, Mark rose, left money for the entire tab and tip, nodded to her and walked out.

~

SYLVIA AUERBACH removed the final draft of her research paper, *Intentional Behaviors of Infants,* from the printer. She would email it to the *Journal of Infant Development* that afternoon. For the first time, Jared Weymouth's name would not appear as a co-author. This paper was a major step in her burgeoning independence from her mentor.

Sylvia's PhD was in behavioral psychology. After receiving the degree ten years ago she had gone to work for Jared. Now at age thirty-nine, she regarded that move as the best decision she had ever made. Her increasing recognition as an authority on infant developmental testing and her appointment as assistant research professor, not to mention cutting her dark hair short and losing fifteen pounds, had brought her a new outlook on life. Her husband, even her teenagers, had noticed.

The door opened.

"Well, there she is, acting like she's awake when she's really sleeping."

"Oh hi, Lena." Sylvia turned her swivel chair toward the smiling woman walking through the door. "How'd you know I was sleeping?"

Lena sat on the desk opposite her. "Just a good guess."

Sylvia laughed. "So have the Shenkos arrived yet?"

"Not yet. Mrs. Shenko called and said she'd be a little late. Maybe around ten fifteen. Just wanted to alert you. I'd better go back before the phone gets loose. See ya."

Sylvia waved and began page proofing her manuscript. She thought about Corinne Shenko whom she had briefly met during the last visit. A sweet girl. And the baby was precious. Sylvia looked forward to conducting the Piaget test. Jared had said he mainly wanted Sylvia to observe the child, mentioning a possible seizure syndrome. She was happy to help.

FORTY MINUTES LATER she was sitting in the testing room, preparing for the test.

Corinne walked in holding Gregory who was trying to put a toy car in her ear.

"Good to see you again, Mrs. Shenko." Sylvia stood and smiled warmly. "Well hello, Gregory. You sure look ready for action."

"He's more than ready," Corinne said, laughing as she pulled the car from his hand.

Sylvia had Corinne sit at a small table across from her. Between them, covering the table top, was a gray felt board. Gregory was positioned on his mother's lap so he could reach out over the board.

"What is this test, exactly?" Corinne asked.

"Basically, it's playing little hide-and-seek games. We want to determine if the baby understands object permanence, the concept that something exists in time and space even when it's not seen. Recognition of object permanence is a key developmental milestone at around six to eight months of age." Sylvia smiled.

"I see," Corinne said.

Sylvia took a toy ladybug from a pocket in her loose-fitting dress. "Gregory has turned into a beautiful child," she said. "His eyes are gorgeous."

"Thank you," Corinne said, beaming. "He's certainly growing."

"Now, let's see if Gregory would like this little ladybug."

Sylvia placed the toy on the board halfway between them. Gregory looked at it for a moment and then lurched forward and grabbed the ladybug with his right hand. He moved back and put it in his mouth, humming and bouncing up and down on his mother's lap. His large blue eyes twinkled as he watched Sylvia.

"Well, you aren't the least bit afraid of me, are you, Gregory?" Sylvia slowly reached out, palm up, to see if he would give her the toy. He gurgled and put it in her hand.

"That is very unusual. Most babies don't like to give up the toy," Sylvia said. Again she put the ladybug on the board between them, this time farther from Gregory. He looked at Sylvia and smiled, then again leaped forward and seized it. He murmured as he sat back and mouthed the bug's antennae with an impish look. Corinne laughed with Sylvia.

"He's delightful," Sylvia said. "I think he's going to do very well on this test."

"He's in one of his good moods, for sure," Corinne said.

"This is just warm-up activity, but I don't think he needs much," Sylvia said.

Gregory began nodding while he hummed in high-pitched tones. Again he gave the ladybug to Sylvia who began explaining the nature of the test to Corinne. The next time it was placed between them, Sylvia playfully snatched it away just before Gregory grabbed it. He looked surprised momentarily, then closed his eyes and squealed with pleasure. He opened them wide to look at Sylvia. She felt a warm sensation in her back and hips. She breathed deeply and hunched her shoulders unconsciously to settle her breasts in her bra.

"I'll tell you, if this were a test for charm, he would get a perfect score," she said, shaking her head and smiling.

Gregory bobbed up and down and Corinne shifted him in her lap. Sylvia picked up three yellow cloths from the floor and spread them out in a row on the felt board.

"Okay, Gregory, let's see how smart you are." Sylvia showed the ladybug to Gregory and then very obviously placed it under the middle cloth. He cooed as he reached under the cloth and took the toy.

Again the warm sensation surged through Sylvia. With it she felt herself becoming aroused. She looked at Corinne. Gregory was rocking gently in his mother's lap, bumping occasionally against her breasts. Again he gave up the ladybug to Sylvia. He murmured in a low pitch. This time she pretended to put it under the cloth, but concealed it in her hand and kept it. Gregory smiled, then went for the cloth. He lifted it up. Seeing nothing he looked at Sylvia and squealed gleefully.

Sylvia was engulfed by the same sensation, only stronger, as if a warm bath were flooding her body. Her breathing became heavier. A dreamlike state took her. She looked at the wall aimlessly and felt moistness between her legs. Then she realized Gregory was on the table reaching for the ladybug. His chubby little hand pried at her fist, working slowly in toward the bug. Sylvia's breathing quickened more as she felt the tiny fingers burrowing sensuously. Her excitement rose and she closed her eyes. Her mind wandered as her body tensed and quivered with desire. Suddenly the expanding wetness in her panties triggered an urgent need to find a bathroom. She jumped up and rushed out of the room, completely unmindful of Gregory and Corinne.

In the lavatory, Sylvia quickly shut the stall door, pulled up her dress and sat on the toilet. She touched herself. Soon her back arched as familiar throbbing spasms took her body. She leaned her head back against the wall and enjoyed the diffusing pleasure. After a few long minutes the reality of the situation registered. "My god. Gregory." She pulled herself together, washed quickly, and rushed into the testing room.

Gregory had crawled back toward his mother but fortunately was still more on the table than off. Corinne had one arm around him loosely while she leaned back in the chair. Her neck was flushed red and her eyelids were heavy.

"Mrs. Shenko?" Sylvia said.

Gregory turned and smiled at Sylvia. Corinne sat up slowly.

"Yes? Did you go somewhere?"

"I . . . I had to go to the bathroom. Are you all right?"

"I guess I drowsed for a moment."

Sylvia realized that what had happened to her had apparently happened to Corinne too. Sylvia wrestled with what to say. Finally she blurted, "Mrs. Shenko, I don't know how to say this, but did you just feel sexually aroused?"

Corinne looked embarrassed. "Yes. It must have been Gregory." She put her hand over her eyes.

"Gregory?" Sylvia asked.

Corinne nodded, embarrassed.

Gregory pushed the ladybug toward Sylvia, cooing.

Sylvia moved back. "No, Gregory. My god, what happened here? How could he do that?"

"Dr. Weymouth will tell you. I . . ." Corinne shook her head back and forth slowly.

"Mrs. Shenko, you wait here. I'm going to get Dr. Weymouth."

SYLVIA RAN INTO JARED'S office without knocking. He was dictating at his desk. "Finished already?"

"Jared, what the hell is up with that baby?"

"Why, what happened?"

"Jared, I don't know how, but somehow that baby seduced both me and Mrs. Shenko."

"He what?"

"Seduced. You know, sexually."

Jared stared, saying nothing.

"Jared, I need an explanation. Corinne said to ask you."

"Why don't you sit down, Sylvia."

"Jared, do you or don't you know what's going on? Or am I losing my mind?" She sat down on the edge of a chair.

Jared frowned, shaking his head. "The baby appears to have an unusual power, Sylvia, but this is a new one. Is Corinne all right?"

"Yes, she's in the testing room with Gregory."

Jared got up. "You wait here. I'll bring her in. And I want to get Mark. We'd better talk."

When Jared returned his left eyebrow was twitching. Corinne, holding Gregory, was more composed than when Sylvia had left her. Mark wore a serious expression.

Jared took a notepad from his desk drawer. "Okay, Sylvia, why don't you start from the beginning and tell us what happened. Then I'll tell you what I know of Gregory's apparent powers."

"Powers? God, I'll say." Sylvia took a deep breath. "What happened? Well, this isn't exactly easy to talk about."

Sylvia told everything as if she were describing an experiment in scientific terms. The sexual aspects were discussed with cold objectivity. She blushed only at the point where she went into the bathroom and reached a second orgasm. She left out the fact that she aided herself. Everything else was accurate. Jared and Mark listened without saying a word or showing any emotion. When Sylvia finished, Jared nodded. Then he looked at Corinne.

"I gather that you reached orgasm, too, Corinne?"

She turned red and nodded. "Yes, it was like a dream. I knew what was happening, but I couldn't stop myself."

"What did Gregory do while Sylvia was out of the room?" Jared asked.

"He played on the table with the ladybug. Then he came back to me. And when he touched me, that's when, uh, it happened."

"Was there any pain?"

"No, it wasn't at all like the headaches."

"How did it feel compared with times . . . like when you've made love?" Jared asked, looking at Sylvia.

Sylvia snorted. "Oh, very intense. Probably as strong as I've ever felt it."

Jared half smiled. "That's amazing. It was enjoyable then."

Sylvia broke out laughing and Corinne joined. "This is ridiculous," Sylvia said. "Sure it was enjoyable."

Gregory laughed and pounded Corinne's leg with the ladybug.

"Cory, has this ever happened to you before?" Mark asked.

"You mean because of Gregory?"

"Yes."

"No, never. But you know, when it was happening, I had this image of Nick. There were times when Nick and I made love . . . it had the same dreamlike feeling."

"Really?" Weymouth said. "But that would make sense. If Nick had the headache power, he would likely have this one, too."

"What do you mean, headache power?" Sylvia asked.

"Sylvia, we did not tell you this, but Gregory has the ability to give people painful, seizure-like headaches when he gets angry."

"What? I just can't believe all this. How in the world . . . ?"

"Apparently these powers have something to do with the brain lesion. His father had the same powers, it seems."

"Oh god, Jared," Sylvia stared at her mentor. "How can this even be possible? You say that so calmly."

"I know. It *is* incredible. But Mark and I have felt the headache just as you felt the sexual thing. I've given some thought as to how the headache effect might happen. And now it occurs to me that the sexual part fits in with it. See, the lesion goes from the outer edge of the cranium down into the mid-brain area. It is at its largest through the limbic ring. This is a primitive part of the brain that evolved not long after the reptilian period—maybe with the earliest mammals. The limbic area controls appetite states and emotion. It could be that the lesion is somehow transmitting Gregory's strongest emotional states outside of him. Maybe the packed giant neurons transmit his brainwaves very powerfully. Anger and sexual drive are basic affective impulses. Structurally, it would seem to make sense. We know that the voltages on his occipital scalp are extremely high. I suspect they will be even higher when he is in one of these emotional states."

"But that would mean that his brainwave signals are intelligible and that somehow we are sensitive to them," Sylvia said.

Jared nodded. "That's right. We know that scientists have implanted amplifier electrodes in human brains that cause computer cursors to move. Surface electrodes can also do this. So brain signals detected in this way are clearly intelligible. In Gregory's case his large neurons must be the transmitters. And, somehow we can receive them. It raises an interesting notion. Maybe everyone has these powers and can transmit and receive to some minute degree. But in Gregory, because of the lesion, his powers are unusually strong and he can induce and overwhelm others' neuronal systems when close by."

"That's a real radical idea," Sylvia said.

"Yes, it is," Jared said. "We are dealing with a radical phenomenon."

"I can't believe that we're sitting here talking like this," Sylvia said. "Jared, why didn't you tell me about the headache power?"

"Because we're trying to keep the number of people who know to an absolute minimum. So far, it's been me, Corinne, Mark and Lena. And now you. Also, I wanted you to be unbiased."

"My mother doesn't even know," Corinne said.

Sylvia was silent. She realized that Corinne was a patient with a problem and Jared had been making decisions as her physician. The other questions Sylvia had would have to wait until she got Jared alone.

"We have discussed the secrecy problem before and we believe it is in the best interests of the child," Jared said. "And we must ask that you not tell anyone either."

"I understand," Sylvia said softly. But she felt strange. How could Jared handle all of this so matter-of-factly? It was . . . mind blowing. He and Mark were trying to keep the knowledge from others. Was that justified? They just assumed their secrecy served Corinne and Gregory's welfare. Yet, how could brain powers as significant as these be kept from society?

CHAPTER NINE

AS HE WALKED THROUGH the hallway the next day, Jared found it hard to breathe. He knew his blood pressure must be up. He ducked into an empty testing room and relaxed in a chair, eyes closed. Fifteen minutes later, feeling a little better, he went looking for Mark and found him in his office. Mark looked up as Jared stepped through the door.

"Hello, Jared. Have a seat."

"Hi, Mark. How's Corinne doing?" Jared settled himself in a chair facing the desk.

"She's staring a lot. I think she's depressed."

"Is she alone?"

"Lena's with her."

"Maybe the sexual incident was too much for her," Jared said.

"I wouldn't be surprised. You know, I'm having trouble believing that sex business, to be honest."

"Well, I have no doubt about it. Sylvia and Corinne couldn't make up something like that. It's not just one person's imagination. It happened to both of them. Besides, it makes sense that if Gregory can project anger through brainwaves he might also be able to project lust."

Mark looked at Jared strangely. "Well, I'm worried about Cory."

"Me too. I think she's going to need help taking care of Gregory," Jared said.

Mark didn't say anything.

"What's needed is a person who could spend a certain amount of time seeing Corinne and Gregory almost daily. Someone who, when Gregory raged or did the sexual thing, could discourage it. The person would have to give Corinne lots of emotional support and teach her how to handle Gregory."

"So it would be someone who visits in the home?"

"Yes. It would have to be someone with some training or background in infant development. Someone like Sylvia would be good."

"Are you assuming that Corinne would move down here?"

"Yes, we should convince her to do that." Jared looked at the doubt lining Mark's face. "Don't you think she would?"

"I don't know."

"Well, if she won't, then I don't know what we can do. I'm leery of trying to find someone in Fresno who can do what's necessary."

"When you say that Gregory should be discouraged from exercising his powers, how does one do that with an eight-month-old baby?"

"It will take ingenuity. It may be that some conditioning process will be needed. That's why it needs to be a trained person."

"You mean behavior modification techniques?"

"It may require that, yes."

Mark nodded, but Jared could see the questions in his eyes.

"See, Mark, the biggest reason for starting this now is to prevent Corinne from becoming discouraged and slipping into counterproductive behavior with Gregory. This can happen easily with difficult children. Gregory is going to need a lot of love while he learns not to use his powers. You can imagine what it'll be like when he begins to get into things and Mother spanks him. Toilet training might be a problem. And things will definitely get worse before they get better."

Mark nodded. "So how long will this training take?"

That was the key question, wasn't it? Jared took a deep breath. "I don't know. Maybe several years. I would expect that things could settle down after Gregory learns to speak well. And by age six he should be in control."

"That's a long time. How will you get a person to work that long at it?"

"I don't know."

There was a knock on the door. Lena stuck her head in and smiled.

"Hi, Lena, come in," Jared said.

"Is everyone ready for the EEG?" she asked, stepping into the room. "Gregory has his bonnet on."

"Yes, but we need to talk about this before we get into the procedure," Jared said. "Please get Sylvia and Corinne and let's meet in my office."

"Sylvia's there already. I'll get Corinne."

Jared and Mark headed down the hall and joined Sylvia.

"By the way," Jared said. "I've decided we should call it the Y power."

"The Y power?" Sylvia frowned.

"Yes, the rage is the X and the sexual is the Y."

"Did you come up with that because you're going to write a paper?" Sylvia asked.

"No, only so we can refer to them more conveniently. I don't want anything published."

"Don't look at me," Sylvia said. "If I wrote something, I'd have to discuss my own sexual reaction. That's the last thing I'd want in print."

Corinne and Gregory arrived and were greeted warmly. Jared watched Corinne's interactions carefully and decided that Mark was right. She did seem depressed.

"I want to tell you what our plan is," Jared said, looking at Corinne. "But first tell me, is everything all right with you?"

She smiled weakly. "I guess I'm tired. That test yesterday . . . and I didn't sleep well last night at the motel."

"Would it be better if we didn't do this EEG now? If you have any reservations about it, I would rather postpone the test and reschedule."

"We might as well get it over with."

"You're sure?"

"Yes."

Jared filled Corinne in on the planned sequence of events and what her role would be. When there were no more questions, they went into the testing room, and Corinne put Gregory in the infant seat. The baby twisted and fought against the straps and began whimpering. Corinne tried to quiet him as Jared hooked up the wires and started the polygraph and video recorder. Jared handed Gregory the toy giraffe. This quieted the baby for a minute, then he started pushing against the straps again.

"The electrodes are locked in and the EEG patterns are okay," Jared said to nobody in particular.

Gregory looked at his mother, lifted his arms toward her, and began to cry.

"It's all right, honey. You stay there," Corinne said, her voice cracking. Jared put a hand on her shoulder.

"Since he's unhappy already, let's all go out of the room now," Jared said.

They filed out and Gregory squirmed, trying to see where they went. He cried louder.

"Poor thing," Sylvia whispered.

Corinne put her hand over her heart. "It's so hard to do this."

The crying ceased for a moment. Then the giraffe bounced off a table leg and hit the floor. The crying resumed, but not as loud. A minute passed during which Gregory's cry changed in volume from low to high and back to low. Then it stopped altogether.

"Mark, I think we should use the ice," Jared said.

Mark, carrying a small plastic container, went into the room with Gregory. The infant watched as Mark removed the lid and took out a cube. Mark reached over the crib railing and held the ice cube against the toes of one little foot. Gregory kicked his foot and screamed. Mark jumped back, grabbing his head. The container and ice scattered on the floor. The pain struck everyone in the hall like a mild electric shock. Sylvia screamed and all of them moved jerkily.

Gregory stopped yelling and watched Mark warily. Jared caught Mark's eye and pointed at the EEG tracing.

Mark easily found the burst of high voltage on the paper. The parietal-occipital pens had been pinned against their upper stops. He turned a knob, decreasing the input gain. Then glancing at Gregory who was watching him, Mark put the ice back in the container and walked over to Jared at the door.

"So what do you think?" Mark asked.

"How high was the amplitude?"

"It pinned the pens. I turned it three-quarters of the way to full resistance."

"That should be more than enough. Okay, give him some more ice."

Mark took another ice cube from the container and went over to Gregory. As the cube moved toward the little left foot, Gregory screeched—before the ice touched his foot. It was a heavy blast that folded Mark to the floor like a rag doll. Screams in a strange chorus filled the hallway. Footsteps sounded down the corridor. Then it was quiet again. Gregory looked down at Mark with wide-open eyes. Mark began to move and Corinne rushed in. She quickly unstrapped her baby and took him in her arms. Jared and Sylvia followed and helped Mark up.

"Are you okay?" Jared asked.

"I think so." Mark shook his head. "It's getting better now."

Lena came back from where she had run. Tears ran down her cheeks. "Dr. Weymouth, you're not going to do any more, are you?" she asked.

"No, this is it." Jared couldn't blame Lena. The experience had shaken him as well. "Mark, you're sure you're all right?"

"I'll be okay. That was something. Like a slug between the eyes."

"It was bad out in the hall," Jared said. "I can imagine what it must have been like in close."

Jared stopped the EEG and video recorder. Gregory, happy to be out of the bonnet, cooed as Corinne continued talking to him.

"Is he okay, Corinne?" Jared asked.

"He seems fine. But I'm glad you stopped."

"We won't do any more. In fact, this may be the last time ever. This time was different from the others. I think we got what we wanted, but let's see it on playback to be sure."

Jared ran the tape back and then started it. Gregory was seen throwing the giraffe. Everyone watched the small monitor in silence. Even Gregory watched when he heard the sound of his crying.

They saw the ice cube touch Gregory's toes. The kick of his foot and his scream were in perfect synchrony. His faced jerked upward, his mouth opened, and his eyes closed. Sylvia winced as the speaker blared. Moments after Mark's hand left the scene, Gregory's face returned to alert composure while he obviously watched something.

"See that?" Jared said, excited. "He knows he did something."

After a minute, Mark's hand and the ice container appeared again on the left side of the screen. Gregory's face registered fear. His prominent eyebrows tightened and his mouth opened. When the man-sized hand and the ice cube neared Gregory's left foot, his face exploded into a quivering rage. The screech overloaded the TV's audio, causing a deep buzz interrupted by intermittent flapping of the speaker cone. Gregory's face was red but became composed when he stopped screeching. He looked ahead and then down.

"Did you see that? Gregory screamed before the ice touched him," Jared said. "And he stopped it very fast, just like before. Then he looked to see what happened."

"What does that mean?" Sylvia asked.

"It means it was premeditated."

"Premeditated?" she said. "Are you sure?"

"Yes, I'm sure. Gregory anticipated that Mark would touch him with the ice, so he screamed before it happened. It was a preventive, defensive action. This means that the X power is not just a sensory reflex. He can will it."

Everyone looked at Jared. His right eye twitched. "This makes it a different boat," he said.

"But Jared, what about the Y power?" Sylvia asked.

"You mean, was that premeditated?"

"Yes, was it?"

"I don't know. Maybe something stimulated him. Maybe he did it on his own. If he has voluntary control of his rage, it would be logical to assume he has self-control over the sex power, too."

Jared looked at Corinne and his face softened. "Will you come into the office with me and Mark? We need to talk."

"Okay. Should I bring Gregory?"

"Of course. And uh, Sylvia, would you mind playing back the videotape in slow motion to see if there is a startle pattern just before the X power begins? I want to be sure I'm right about the voluntary capability. If there is in fact a startle pattern, then that would support the reflex hypothesis."

"All right." Sylvia's voice showed irritation.

In the office, Corinne had a faraway look on her face. Gregory was docile on her lap.

"Gregory looks sleepy," Jared said.

"Yes, he's tired."

"And you look like you could use some sleep, too."

"I'm sure I could." Corinne's voice was so soft he almost didn't hear her.

"Well, we won't talk long." Jared kept his own voice crisp. "But I think it's important to discuss our future planning. In a way we've reached a milestone. I said that I didn't think we should bring on Gregory's powers any more. I mean that. The problem from here on out is to get him to learn *not* to use his powers. Testing him like this any further would just encourage that use. I think we know enough. We now must work on his normal development."

Jared looked at Corinne, hoping for a response, but she remained silent.

"What I would like, Corinne, is to arrange for a specially trained person to spend time with you and Gregory on a regular basis—at least every other day to start with. This person would come into your home two or three hours at a time, during periods when you interact with Gregory the most, like at meal times and perhaps when you give him a bath and put him to sleep. She would get to know Gregory very well, play with him occasionally, but mainly watch him and try to help you understand how to lead him to develop normally. And especially, to show you how to teach Gregory not to use his powers."

"Who would do this?" she asked.

"I don't know for sure. I'm hoping to find someone willing, probably a psychologist."

"Would she live in Fresno?"

"No. And that's the important question I wanted to bring up. In order for me to know how things are going with Gregory and be able to meet regularly with this person, I would like you to move to L.A. I think that's the only way I can be assured of getting a good person who can help you while I make sure everything goes right."

"But I can't move down here. I mean, I have to finish school . . . and my parents."

"I know it would be a burden, but we would pay for the moving expenses. Mark and I will help you transfer to Southern State or Cal State Northridge so you could finish your college. I'm sure you could get your credits transferred."

"I don't know," Corinne said, shaking her head.

"Look, I know this is a surprise, but I think it's important for Gregory's sake. Why don't you think about it for a couple of days? Talk to your parents. I'll be happy to speak with them if you want me to."

Corinne didn't say anything. She looked over at Mark.

"Will you seriously think about it?" Jared asked.

She nodded, her eyes glistening with tears. "Wouldn't it be too late to transfer for the fall quarter?"

Jared nodded. "Probably. Maybe you could take some extension courses this fall."

"Couldn't we wait for winter or spring quarter?"

"I don't think so. We need to get this started right away," Jared said in a gentle voice. "Don't decide now. Get a good night's sleep and call Dr. Sandler or me tomorrow after you get back home. You'll probably have other questions."

Corinne nodded. She took a handkerchief from her purse and wiped her eyes.

"Mark," Jared said, "why don't you take Corinne and Gregory back to the motel now?"

After they left, Jared asked Lena to see if Sylvia could come in. He made a note to talk to Lena about finding Corinne an apartment.

Sylvia sat down but did not return his smile.

"So, was there a startle pattern?" he asked.

"No," she said in a curt voice.

"That means it was clearly premeditated." He clasped his hands behind his head. "Is something wrong?"

"Yes. I'm angry."

"At me?"

"I don't know whether it's you or this whole crazy problem."

"What exactly is bothering—"

"All right," Sylvia said, letting out an explosive breath "I guess I'm bugged that you asked me to look at the tape while you and Mark talked with Corinne. I know that she's your patient and you want to maintain privacy, but I'm feeling left out. You knew about Gregory's powers long ago and you didn't tell me until after the Piaget test when you had to. I always thought we had a partnership. After you, I'm the senior person around here, am I not?"

Jared leaned forward, hands on his knees. "You're right, Sylvia. I probably should have told you about Gregory earlier. Frankly, I've been caught up in trying to keep this thing secret. A lot of people know about Gregory's lesion but don't know of his powers. Lou Fazzi and the others aren't aware of the powers. Corinne's parents don't know. Her doctor in Fresno hasn't been told. So it's not that I have singled you out. Obviously, you are very important to me . . . you're my research partner. I meant no offense by keeping you in the dark. And I know that sexual thing must have been disturbing. I had no idea that could happen."

"Oh, it's not that. But why is Mark in on this so much?"

"Because Mrs. Shenko is more or less his case—part of his training in infant development. And Mark has been the one to make the discoveries. He first found out about the lesion. He hypothesized Gregory's X power after talking to Zenya Shenko, Gregory's aunt. He designed the experiment to verify the X power when Gregory gave us headaches the first time. Also, he has developed a good rapport with Corinne—more so than I have."

"Okay, that all makes sense. But, I don't know. What about science, Jared? How can we let this incredible finding be put under wraps? I mean, that sexual power— have you thought about it? The implications are enormous. Here is a baby who, when he grows up, may be capable of seducing women without them being able to resist. How can we take it upon ourselves to keep that from the rest of the world?"

Jared looked down at his hands and slowly cleared his throat. His words were measured. "I appreciate what you are saying. That issue bothers me too. And I think you know I would like nothing better than to pursue full-scale research on Gregory if he were an animal or anything other than human. We will continue research, but on a limited scale. We're going to keep in regular contact with Corinne and Gregory and observe his development through home visits. As for humanity's right to know, I think that is opposed by Gregory's right to privacy and his right to develop normally if he can. When he matures, he may wish to reveal all of this to the world, but I think he should have the choice. As his doctor I have to protect his rights. His father apparently had the same powers—maybe not as strong—and the world got along fine without knowing about them. Okay?"

Sylvia nodded slowly. "You said home visits. How are you going to make home visits in Fresno?"

"I have asked Corinne to move down here."

"You have?"

"Yes. I don't know if she will, though."

"Who would do the home visits?"

"I don't know. I'll have to think about that."

"I see."

"Regardless of who makes the visits, I would need your help regarding the kind of behavioral information we should collect and how to interpret the data. Also, on how to manage Gregory."

Sylvia shifted in her chair. "I would like that," she said. "But what good is it to collect the data if they can't be published?"

"Someday they probably will be published. It would be a labor of love for years, however. Still, it's worth it, isn't it? If and when something is published on Gregory, it will probably be one of the most widely read scientific documents in the world."

"Yes, it would." Sylvia put her feet down. She smiled. "I feel better."

"Good. I don't want you mad at me. It's bad enough to have made an enemy of Fazzi."

Sylvia forced a laugh.

CHAPTER TEN

AS FALL APPROACHED, the days became shorter and the countryside drier. Santa Ana winds blew in from the Great Basin and upper Mojave Desert, sucking moisture from the dry southland chaparral and making it perfect tinder. Dwellers in canyons and on ridges became nervous when the devil winds blew. Once the winds took hold of a stray flame, an inferno could sweep across hundreds of acres in minutes, devouring houses like a ravenous carnivore rampaging among rooted rabbits.

Mark's house was far enough into Santa Monica's residential neighborhood that he did not worry about the Santa Anas. His worry was the out-of-control Shenko case. And the aspect he worried about most was the Y power. If Gregory could truly exercise such a power, it revealed an evolutionary quirk that was hard for him to accept.

He had a call to make. A call that could help shed some light on the so-called Y power. He dialed and the phone was picked up immediately.

"Hello, Zenya. This is Dr. Mark Sandler. How are you?"

"Oh hello, Dr. Sandler. I'm just fine."

"It's been a while since we talked, so I thought I'd check in to see how things are."

"Well, thanks. Things are going pretty good, but it's been raining. We get these summer squalls and the humidity is terrible. I have to wear uniforms. If the rain doesn't drench me, the humidity does."

"I know what you mean. I've been in Florida during the summer before. You should try to get stationed in Southern California—the weather's great."

"Well, I put in for San Diego, but they might give me sea duty."

"Well, I hope you get San Diego."

"Me too."

"Zenya, I wonder if you've by any chance changed your mind about having an EEG."

She didn't hesitate. "Not really. I'm sorry, but I just don't like the idea—nothing against you though."

"I can understand that, but you know there is absolutely no pain."

"I know."

"What if we paid your way to Los Angeles? You could visit your mother in Porterville."

"I'd like to see my mother but I don't want to go back to Porterville."

"What do you have against Porterville?"

"Let's just say it wasn't a happy time for me there. I'm trying to forget it."

"And Nick along with it?"

There was silence for several seconds.

"Zenya, are you there?"

"Yes. I suppose you know I hated Nick."

"He gave you those headaches."

"Yeah."

"And he did other things?"

Again, there was silence.

"Zenya?"

"I don't think we should continue this conversation."

"Zenya, we know about Nick's sexual powers."

"How the hell do you know that?"

"From Cory, Nick's wife. Look, I'm not trying to pry. You don't have to say anything if you don't want to."

Mark heard a muffled sound.

"Zenya?" The sound stopped and he heard her take a deep breath.

"I'm okay. I could say a lot about what Nick was like, Doctor, but I just couldn't stand telling you. I've never told anybody except my mother, and I don't want to tell anyone else. Do you understand?"

"Yes, I do. I'm sorry to upset you."

"It's okay. Look, there's a TV program I want to watch."

"All right. Thanks for talking with me."

"Bye, Dr. Sandler."

Mark eased the receiver into its cradle and slowly shook his head. The thought of Nick using his powers on Zenya both titillated and chilled him. Then images of an older Gregory and Corinne flashed into his mind. God, what a nightmare it could be. No wonder Corinne was depressed.

Maybe it was time to get his mind off the Shenkos. He picked up the Sierra Club's Angeles Chapter bulletin that Lena had given him and turned to the schedule of summer outings. There were a lot of day hikes listed in the Santa Monica Mountains. He found a list of backpacking trips and noticed that a few were in the Sierras. He remembered the many trips he and Rachel had made to the backcountry of Maine, sneaking away from Boston when their schedules permitted. A trip to the Sierras would be wonderful, but how could he fit it in? And the upper elevations turn cold in the fall, with early snowstorms always a threat.

He turned on his laptop and checked his email. There was only one message, and he froze when he saw the originator line. It was from Rachel. He knew that sooner or later this might happen, but it was sooner than he wanted. After a minute he found the courage to pull up the message.

> Hi, Mark. Your mother said you were stressed with work these days, so I thought I would say hello. I know that the past year has been hell for you. You clearly deserve some recuperation. So here's hoping things lighten up at your job.
>
> I also hope that what I'm going to say will serve to lessen the burden. As a part of my psychological training I've had a number of therapeutic sessions that have helped me immensely. I want you to know that I bear no bad feelings toward you. I think our breakup had a beneficial side by helping me look at some hangups and to grow in a healthier direction. We had a lot of good times and that's the way I'm looking at it. I feel good about life right now and have no regrets. I only wish you the best. Take care, Rachel.

It was not breezy or humorous. In fact, the email was not at all what he would have expected. He knew he had to answer, and decided to reply immediately before he became paralyzed.

> Dear Rachel. I appreciate very much your message. I'm really glad you are happy and enjoying your job. Congratulations. Yes, it's been a tough year for me and right now I don't see a light at the tunnel's end. But I'll survive and eventually get to a better place too. I am remembering some of the good

things we had, such as our camping trips. I hope to take a
few days off and get up in the Sierras soon.
Thanks for your thoughts. Cheers, Mark.

Only after sending the reply did Mark start to agonize. Her message seemed sincere, but was there disingenuousness buried in her words? Could a person so easily recover from the kind of hurt he'd caused? Was she unconsciously trying to hurt him back?

He knew from his mother that Rachel felt he had bolted out of fear of commitment. Yet, how could he commit when his chosen career was in a shambles? How could he commit when the religious issue—how to raise their kids— was unresolved? She'd just assumed he could get comfortable with conservative Judaism. Arguing about eating pork was silly. Maybe it was all silly. Maybe he had found small problems and raised them to a level of insurmountability because he was afraid. Afraid of what? Responsibility? Losing freedom? Did he fear intimacy?

Deep down he knew there must be something. None of his relationships with women had gone very well. It just wasn't realistic that the problem was always with them and not him.

ON HIS WAY to work the next morning Mark got coffee from the Espresso Bar and took it to his meeting with Jared. Lena gave him an unusually big smile as he went into Jared's office.

"Come on in, Mark," Jared said, closing the book he'd just been looking at and setting it aside.

"Am I too early?

"No. Anything new?"

Mark told Jared about his conversation with Zenya.

"Hmm. That sounds worrisome, doesn't it?"

"Yeah. I think I should talk to Rose Shenko again. See if she has anything that might shed light on the 'Y' thing."

"Probably a good idea."

"I've also been thinking about Corinne. About the problem of getting her to move down here. I don't think she will."

"I sense the resistance there too. If she won't move, I don't know what to do. Maybe we could involve her parents, try to get their support."

Mark pushed his glasses higher on his nose. He felt nervous, but decided to throw it right out there. "I have another idea. How about if I go up there and do the visiting?"

Jared looked at him and frowned. "You mean you'd want to visit them in her home up there? Drive back and forth?"

"I could be up there a few days at a time. I'd take a small efficiency apartment near hers—stay for two or three days, then come back for two or three days."

"What about your other cases?" Jared frowned harder.

"Well, I wouldn't be able to do as much, see so many patients, make all the seminars. But isn't Shenko more important right now? Couldn't this still fit in with my program?"

Jared's eyebrow began to twitch. "I was thinking the assignment was more appropriate for a woman."

"I've thought about that. If the fact that I'm a man presents a problem to Corinne, then it would be off. But maybe that wouldn't matter to her."

Jared nodded slowly. "I suppose the rapport is there. But how long could you do this? We need her down here because it could take years."

"I'd do it only until we got her to move down—more than likely just through the fall semester."

"Still, that's a lot of driving, Mark."

"I don't mind the driving. That isn't the major objection I thought you'd raise."

"What's that?"

"That I don't have the training for it."

Jared laughed. "It crossed my mind, but I think you could be brought along. Maybe you'd be better because you don't have preconceived notions and theories to cloud your observations." He shrugged. "You would no doubt learn a lot. But I'd like to sleep on it. Let's discuss the Fleischer case."

As Mark started recounting his last two clinic visits with the "failure-to-thrive" baby, Lena knocked and popped her head into room. "Dr. Weymouth, I'm sorry to interrupt but there's a man on the phone asking for information about the baby who was written up in the article."

"What article?" Jared asked.

"I don't know. He said the baby with epilepsy from Fresno. Wouldn't that be Shenko?"

Jared and Mark looked at each other.

"Let me talk to him," Jared said, grabbing his phone. He listened for a minute. "The *L.A. Voice*? Is that a local newspaper? No, we don't know anything about it. We don't give out information on patients. I can't help you. Sorry, goodbye."

Jared's eyes smoldered as he twisted around. "That damned reporter," he growled. "Lena, do you know of a paper called the *L.A. Voice*?"

"Yes, it's a throwaway on the stands. You can get them in Westwood."

"But I wonder why that paper instead of the *Tribune*," Mark said.

Jared shook his head. "Would you mind going out and picking up a few?" Jared asked. "We'd better see what that busybody wrote. See what the damage is. Shit. Excuse the language, Lena."

IN LESS THAN twenty minutes all three were reading the article which began on the front page under the title, "Infant Discovered with Rare Brain Mutation," and subtitled, "Baby Gives Reporter Epileptic Seizure." There were accompanying pictures of Corinne and Gregory.

"This Alice Masterson did some homework—I'll say that," Jared said. "Fazzi, Valenzuela, the Fresno pathologist, Corinne, even a co-worker of Nicholas Shenko's. She made the rounds."

"It says you and Mark refused to comment," Lena said.

"Yes, she doesn't say it was because of patient confidentiality. She prefers that we sound uncooperative."

"Did you see the part near the end where she experienced the seizure?" Mark asked.

"I'm getting there. Mmmh." A moment later Jared chuckled. "Pretty good description of it, I'd say. But look how it ends: 'Some specialists at SSU who are aware of the case are now worried that needed medical procedures are being withheld. There is disagreement about how the child should be treated. The mother feels she and the baby are receiving good care. The baby presents something completely new to medicine and probably new to society. Should the case be handled confidentially in the manner of "business as usual" by two pediatricians? Doesn't the child deserve more? And don't the rest of us deserve to know what's really going on?'"

"There's a separate article on you, Mark," Lena said.

"Fortunately on an inner page," Mark said, grimacing at the sight of his name

"Thank god she didn't put in the Shenko names," Jared said.

"Yes, but the pictures are there and the home is listed as Fresno," Mark said.

"But the L.A. Voice wouldn't be distributed in Fresno," Lena said.

"No, but it's possible someone might recognize them and make the article known up there to somebody," Mark said.

"I don't like this one bit," Jared said. "This is an ill wind. We're just lucky it wasn't in the Tribune. Mark, I think you'd better tell Corinne. And, uh, go ahead and make plans for the visitations in Fresno as you proposed. Lena, get ready for phone calls from friend and foe."

LATER, AT HIS FAVORITE deli in Westwood, Mark sat down with a salami-and-artichoke heart sandwich and read the short sidebar article Alice Masterson had written.

Heretic Genome Doctor Cares for Mutant Baby
Dr. Mark Sandler, a noted researcher from the Human Genome
Project at the Whitehead Institute in Boston has turned up at
Southern State University. He is now a post-doctoral fellow
in the pediatrics department working with Professor Jared
Weymouth providing care for problem infants, including the
baby with the brain mutation. (See page 1.)

Eight months ago Sandler shocked the biomedical research
establishment by denouncing human genome research as
ill-advised and likely to lead society into playing God through
genetic manipulation. In a letter appearing in a leading research journal, he said "we should have respect and faith in
our human mystery and in the evolutionary processes that
created us," including mutations such as may have occurred
with the Fresno baby. Sandler declined to discuss the baby
and his mother for reasons of patient confidentiality. He prefers not to comment further on the controversy he engendered
by criticizing the Human Genome Project.

When Mark returned to his office, he felt uneasy. Things were happening fast. Yet there was no choice but to swim with the flow. He dialed Corinne's number. She picked up after two rings.

"Cory? I'm so glad you're home."

"Hi, Mark. Why? Have you been worried?"

How was he going to explain this to her. "Well, I haven't been able to reach you for a couple of days. How are things?"

"Things with Gregory are fine, so far. I guess you want to know if I will move down there."

"That's right."

"Well, I've made up my mind not to move until after the fall semester. I hope that doesn't cause problems."

"It doesn't. If you don't want to come down now, that's okay. We have another plan."

"What's that?"

"I'll come up there and do the visits."

"What? How could you do that?"

"It's an easy drive. So, until you decide to move, I'll be the person that visits you and Gregory like Dr. Weymouth described."

"But what about your job there?"

"I'll commute. Spend a couple of days up there, then come back here for a few days. Dr. Weymouth will consider this a part of my training."

"But, where would you stay up here?"

"I'll get a small apartment near yours."

"But isn't that expensive?"

"Dr. Weymouth has a sizable amount of donated research funds. He'll help with the rent. Do you know if there are any efficiency units in your building? Any that would be vacant?"

"There are a few. I don't know about vacancies. The manager would know."

"Can you give me his number?"

"Now?"

"If you don't mind."

"Okay, just a minute."

A good feeling came over Mark as he waited for her. She seemed to be accepting the idea, or at least not rejecting it out of hand. She came back on the line and gave him the name and number of the apartment manager.

"Good, thanks. I'll call him."

"But Mark—you're a man. How can you do this? Weymouth said it would be a woman."

"It will be strictly business. The important thing is what *you* think. If the idea bothers you, then we won't do it."

"I suppose it's all right. I mean, don't get me wrong, I know I need help with Gregory and I certainly appreciate all you've done for me."

"Well, then. Let's try it, Cory. You can always stop at any time."

"When do you plan on coming up?"

"By the end of the week if I can line up a place."

"So soon?"

"There's no sense waiting, Cory. Besides, I want to bring you the article that Alice Masterson wrote. It appeared today in a local newspaper."

"No! Really?"

"It has pictures of you and Gregory, but doesn't mention your names."

"Oh wow. What did she say?"

"It's not a bad article, but she knocks me and Dr. Weymouth. She mentions Dr. Fazzi and says there is disagreement over treatment between us doctors."

"Uh oh."

"Yeah. Hopefully, there won't be more articles. Anyway, I'll call you before I leave."

AFTER HANGING UP, Corinne sat down at the dinette table. She was disconcerted by the conversation with Mark. The article wasn't what was bothering her. It was that Mark could be a major intrusion. She would lose her privacy. She knew she needed expert help with Gregory, but Mark wasn't a psychologist or even a pediatrician. At least he agreed to call the whole thing off if she decided it wasn't working.

She put her hands in the tepid dishwater and groaned. Her back ached. She decided to go to bed early. Gregory had better behave himself.

CHAPTER ELEVEN

JARED LOOKED OUT AT the moving pine branches. There was definitely an ill wind blowing, he thought. At some point he might need to batten the hatches. He returned to his computer screen and read the email exchange that Mark had forwarded.

> Hi, Mark. How did you like the *L.A. Voice* articles? You're probably wondering what happened with the *Tribune*. They rejected the story so I got it into the *Voice*. Please let me know if I was too rough on you. Regards, Alice

> Alice, we're glad for one thing—that you didn't put in patient names. No comment on the main article. As to the article about me, I thought it was a bit pejorative. But I didn't expect better. Mark.

> Mark, I just learned that my article shamed the *Tribune* into action. They've talked to Dr. Fazzi and will put out something soon. Believe it or not, I tried to be fair. So I hope you will talk with me from time to time. It could be mutually beneficial, certainly more so than with any other reporter. And by the way, thanks for the tea and conversation. Sincerely, Alice.

Jared realized that one hatch needing to be battened was Mark. He had that flaw that was seen also in psychologists, social workers and Protestant ministers—a belief that things could be made better by talking. Jared would have to tell Mark and Corinne not to talk further with Alice or anyone about Gregory. Period. Jared scribbled a note. The last thing needed was for Gregory to become a medical celebrity.

Within two days the wayward wind freshened. Jared saw the *L.A. Tribune* science section piece as he ate his morning cereal. The headline said: "SSU Scientist Confirms Baby's Unusual Brain." In the article Lou Fazzi had answered questions about the lesion, the high voltages, the epilepsy, and the father's death. As Jared perused to the end, the final question and answer stood out as if underlined. "There has been a report that the infant can cause seizure activity in others. Could this be possible, Dr. Fazzi?"

"I've heard that story. There is no evidence of this that I know about. It is extremely unlikely. But I would say it is not outside the realm of biological possibility."

Jared closed his eyes. *Damn.* If only he had not taken Gregory for the EEG in Fazzi's lab.

As Mark drove by the oil fields around Bakersfield he saw that a few of the rusty pump rockers were moving, but most were stilled, looking like iron mules hobbled upright in death. He remembered reading that this desolate ground had yielded black gold for the Superior Oil Company which had provided wealth for the Keck family. Now the Keck Foundation of Los Angeles was a primary funder of advanced technology projects such as the Keck telescope on Mauna Kea and a biological imaging facility at the Whitehead Institute. The metamorphosis of decayed plants and dinosaurs from deep beneath Bakersfield into human biomedical research in Boston struck him with irony. But it was no more ironic than an eccentric playboy businessman providing an institute that would become the second largest benefactor of biomedical research after the National Institutes of Health. Universities vied for Howard Hughes funds, selecting the best scientists they could find, such as Dr. Louis Fazzi, to nominate for Hughes investigatorships.

The engine sang as Mark pushed the little Saab over the rolling hills between Bakersfield and Porterville. He was late for his meeting with Rose. But the urgency was his, not hers. She probably never expected anyone to be on time. When his dusty car pulled into her driveway, she walked out on her front porch with a smile and a wave.

"Hello, Doctor."

"Hello, Rose. Good to see you again."

"Glad you're here. Come on in 'fore the flies do." She was wearing the same dress and sweater as before, but he noticed her hair had been done.

She proudly showed him the kitchen.

"What a difference!" he said. "Much brighter."

"Yep. So, thanks Doctor. I like doin' the dishes now. Ain't that somethin'?"

They moved to the outdoor back patio, taking chairs from the kitchen. The warm sun forced her to shed the sweater.

"Guess what?" she said. "Zenya's movin' to San Diego. Got a desk job at the naval base."

"Oh, that's terrific. Now you two can see each other."

"Probly not. She won't come up here and I ain't got no money to travel. But maybe I could save some up, if I didn't hafta see the doctors all the time."

Mark nodded thoughtfully.

"Now, I want you to tell me what's gone on with Cory's baby," she said.

Mark brought her up to date with the X and Y, including his recent conversation with Zenya. When he looked up, Rose was staring forward, tears rolling down her wrinkled cheeks.

"I'm sorry. I know this is upsetting," he said.

He handed her a handkerchief from his pocket. She patted her eyes and cheeks.

"I didn't believe her," she said, looking out at the weeds.

Mark shifted in his chair.

"Who?"

"Zenya."

"About what?"

"About who done it with her when she got pregnant."

"When Zenya got pregnant? What?"

"She said Nickie done it and she liked it at the time, but I thought it must'a been Bob."

"Who's Bob?"

"He was my boyfrien'. He pro'bly would'a married me, but I threw him out."

"Rose, when did this all happen?"

"Zenya was fourteen. Poor baby." Rose sniffled and used the handkerchief again.

"Did she have a child?" Mark asked.

"Yeah, but it was stillborn. Midwife said it was shriveled up. Woman wouldn't show it to Zenya. Just wrapped it in a rag an' took it away."

Mark shook his head. They sat silent for a minute. Finally Rose stood and put her hand on Mark's shoulder.

"Want some coffee, Doctor? I'm gonna get me some."

"Sure, thanks."

She returned with steaming mugs. Mark pulled up a weathered redwood bench to set them on.

"Cory called me," she said. "Said she would bring my grandbaby to see me. I hope I kin love that child. I want to. I jes' don't know." Again she started tearing up.

"I think it would be good for you and Cory to talk."

"Yeah. I need to help her understan'."

"I think when you see Gregory, you'll find him more than lovable."

Rose smiled. "Yeah, if he's like Nickie, he'll be a charmer."

Mark grimaced. Gregory was a charmer all right, but with any luck he wouldn't turn out anything like his father.

"Doctor, please do me a favor."

"Sure, what?"

"Don't tell Cory about the sex stuff between Nick and Zenya."

"You don't think she can handle it?"

"Not that. It's jes' she don't need to be told. Won't be good for nobody."

Mark nodded slowly. "Okay, Rose."

"Thanks."

They talked on about harmless subjects for a while. Just before he got up to leave, Mark made out a check to her for $250.

"Good Lord. What's this for?"

"Travel money . . . so you can visit Zenya in San Diego and Cory in Fresno. But it's for nothing else. Okay? That's your favor to me."

Rose got up and took Mark's face in her hands and kissed him loudly on the cheek. "You're a wonderful boy. Your mama must be right proud of you."

Mark laughed. "I only wish."

In Fresno, Mark was caught up with logistics. There were no apartments available in Corinne's building, but he found a furnished efficiency across the street. He purchased sheets, a blanket, kitchen utensils, and enough food to stock one half of a cupboard and a shelf in the refrigerator.

His next task was working out an arrangement for visits with Corinne and Gregory. He was not surprised at her reluctance to be obligated to a schedule. She raised potential problems such as receiving last-minute invitations to dinner from her parents and visiting friends for unplanned lengths of time. To ease her concern he agreed to a contingency clause: if she and Gregory were not home at the time of a scheduled visit, Mark would assume something had come up and postpone meeting them until the next scheduled visit. And he would bear no resentment. Corinne was to live her life as normally as possible and not feel bound by the schedule if there were more important things to do. Once the contingency clause was worked out and accepted, Corinne agreed to five visits each time Mark was in Fresno: two mornings, one noon, and two evenings, the latter to include dinner and play time before bed.

The visits started on a Wednesday. Mark observed lunch and the time afterwards until Gregory took a nap. The second visit, planned for the next evening, was missed when Corinne stayed at her parents for dinner. But Mark had been forewarned. A visit Friday night was added to the schedule as a replacement. Mark decided to cut the schedule short that week and on Saturday, drove back to Los Angeles. At his meeting with Jared on Monday he talked about the uncertainties he was feeling about the visits.

"What happened at the first visit?" Jared asked.

"I went there at lunch time and just watched her feed Gregory and put him down for his nap. He's on soft foods now."

"Did anything go wrong?"

"No. She talked to me and offered me a sandwich, but I didn't know if I was supposed to be involved that way."

"Did you tell her that?"

"Yes, and she was surprised. It was a little awkward. She became self-conscious, especially when I wrote in my notebook."

"Uh huh. What happened the second time?"

"It was Thursday during breakfast time. Cory had to feed Gregory fast, get him dressed, and take him to her mother's so she could get to class by nine. You know, she was rushed and I ended up helping feed Gregory and I carried him to her car. I wrote my notes later from memory."

"Were you satisfied with the notes?"

"I think I remembered things—probably not all. I guess I'd like you to read them and tell me what you think."

"I will. Did you have any more visits?"

"The next morning, Friday, I observed breakfast again. It was more leisurely because her class started later. And I observed dinner."

"How did that go?"

"Fine. I barbecued shish kabob."

"And the observation?"

"Well, I played with Gregory on the rug in the living room. We had a pretty good time. Corinne was in good spirits too."

"So I take it you have evolved into a more participatory role with Corinne and Gregory?"

"That's right. But is that what I'm supposed to do?"

"I don't see anything wrong with it as long as you and she are comfortable that way. And as long as you can record the interactions reasonably well."

"I'm trying. I'm following the method in the Benson article you gave me. I want you to tell me if I'm covering what I need to."

"Leave the notebook with me and I'll meet with you before you go back. Let me ask—did you see any behaviors that were abnormal? Any of the powers?"

"No. No powers. He seemed perfectly normal to me."

"Good." Jared rubbed his forehead. "Did you show her the *L.A. Voice* article?"

Mark laughed. "She was amused. I think she likes the attention."

Jared shook his head. "That's the one reservation I have about bringing her to L.A. She might be too susceptible to a lot of media exposure."

ALICE MASTERSON SELDOM DRANK. At parties she sometimes took white wine. Tonight she poured a third of a glass of Jack Daniels from a bottle left in her cupboard by a former roommate. The syrupy, medicinal taste made her cough. But soon she felt her stomach warming.

She hadn't really thought they'd fire her. Onstine, the head of the features department, had been selected for the deed. He made no specific reference to the *L.A. Voice* article, but she knew he'd read it. They all had. She remembered his saying something about maturity and good judgment being expected of *Tribune* reporters. He suggested she try to get more experience at a less exacting newspaper. She attempted to argue, but he refused to respond. It was a "done deal."

She was glad she hadn't cried as she removed her personal possessions from her office desk. She thanked the well-wishers, mostly the women support staffers who came to sympathize and say goodbye. One was angry, saying it was a jealous maneuver on the part of her fellow science writers who did not like competition from an upstart—especially one who did not genuflect to them.

Alice dreaded phoning her father. He would consider the *L.A. Voice* piece a stupid thing to have done. He would see it as the same kind of mistake she'd made leaving medical school and would ask why she hadn't talked to him about it beforehand. Why couldn't he understand that she needed to make her own decisions? She wondered what her mother would say if she were still alive. Alice blinked away the sudden tears along with the mental image of that always-smiling face.

The next day, while she was making a salad, the building entry intercom buzzed. She held down the button. "Yes?"

"Miss Alice Masterson? The reporter?" said a male voice.

"Yes, who are you?"

"My name is Lawrence Carter. I'm sorry to ring you without an appointment. I tried to contact you at the *Voice* and they told me to call the *Tribune*. And the *Tribune* told me you no longer worked there. So I took a chance with the phone book and here you are."

"I see. What do you want?"

"I'm a reporter too. I thought your article in the *Voice* was superb, and I wanted to talk with you about it."

"Well, thank you. Who are you with?"

"I report for a Christian association newspaper."

"Oh, uh huh."

"I realize this may not be a good time, but perhaps we could make an appointment?"

"Well . . . oh these buttons are impossible. Wait there, Mr. Carter, and I'll come down, but only for a minute."

She found a late-twentyish man of medium height in an ill-fitting, dark three-piece suit. He had a large smile and a two-day old shadow.

"Miss Masterson, I'm pleased," he said, extending his hand smartly.

"How do you do, Mr. Carter." She found his grip too strong. "So you liked the article?"

"Very much. I consider myself a devotee of modern science, though I don't have a science background. I'm a believer in the gospel, actually, but I enjoy reading about science. And I want to tell you that I found your article very interesting. *Very interesting*. It was well written, if I may say so. You have real talent. I guess that's why I expected someone older. If it's not too rude to ask, why did you leave the *Tribune?* Are you moving to the *Voice?"* Carter had stared into her eyes the whole time he was talking.

"I'm not going to be working for either of them. I'm going to freelance for a while. But thank you for your kind words. I put a great deal of effort into that piece. What in particular did you like about it?"

"I especially liked what you said about the public having a right to know about this child. You spoke bravely—a rare commodity in reporting these days. If what you said is true, the child has something quite out of the ordinary. No question—strange. Of course the doctors won't tell us what it is. Without you the public would never have known about this."

Alice nodded. "I had cooperation from a few doctors, but not from the ones who know the most. They told the mother not to talk with me."

"Makes one suspicious, doesn't it?"

"It did me."

"Doesn't it seem awfully unusual that this human genome scientist, Mark Sandler, suddenly shows up to care for this mutant baby?"

Alice frowned. "Well, I think that was coincidence."

"Maybe, maybe not. You know these scientists have a world unto themselves. Creating babies in test tubes, cloning animals, mixing human and animal genes in cells—they just go along, oblivious to what society thinks about all this." His voice rose. "They're haughty—so cocksure of themselves." He paused. "Pardon me. Sometimes I get carried away on this subject."

Alice decided it was time to go in. The man was too "off line," as Kim would put it.

"Well, thank you for letting me know you liked the article." She moved toward the door.

"Are you going to do any follow-up?" he asked.

"I don't know. Probably not for a while, anyway."

"Sorry to hear it. You know, my paper would like to have some coverage on this baby. Would you mind if I put in an article about this? I wouldn't use any of your language, of course, just sort of paraphrase, and I'd be sure to cite your article."

"Sure. Go ahead."

"And if I wanted to get more information from the mother, would that be at all possible?"

"Well, she doesn't want any contact with the press. I couldn't give out her name or address."

"She goes to the university up there in Fresno, right?"

"Uh, she's in college, but . . ."

"Well, you know, sometimes people will talk to Christians when they wouldn't say a word to just plain folks. Do you know if she is a Christian?"

"I really don't know. I'm sorry, but I have to go in."

"Is her first name Christian?"

"I wouldn't know—Corinne, whatever that is."

He shook his head.

"What is the name of your newspaper?" Alice asked.

"*The Christian Force*. I'll send you a copy of the article if I write one."

Alice nodded.

"Are you a Christian, Miss Masterson?"

"I suppose so."

"Well, you shouldn't suppose about it. It's the only salvation there is."

Alice nodded. "Well, thank you, Mr. Carter."

"Good luck to you, Miss Masterson."

He saluted, then turned quickly and strode across the street to a Bronco truck with large tires. Alice could see another man, muscular and baby-faced, sitting behind the wheel looking at her. His hair was closely cropped and he wore a large, round, brass-colored earring. As the truck pulled by, Alice made out words on a sticker in the back window: ONWARD CHRISTIAN . . . something. The driver smiled and waved. Reflexively, she waved back.

~

THE NEXT DAY Alice drove down to the Tribune building. Mary, a receptionist, recognized her and nodded at the guard to let her in. Alice took the elevator to the research department, said hello to the reference librarian, and sat in front of a computer terminal. She typed the words, "The Christian Force." None of the responses indicated a publication or organization. Next she tried "Onward Christian Soldiers." There were four articles in the past three years but two caught her attention. She submitted the dates to a clerk. He brought out the newspapers and she took them to the reading room.

The first article described the midnight bombing of an abortion clinic in Hollywood. Nobody was hurt. Police said there was little evidence to go on. They had questioned members of anti-abortion groups including one called Onward Christian Soldiers. A spokesman for OCS vehemently denied any involvement.

Alice closed her eyes. "Oh, god," she whispered. She was almost afraid to look at the second article, which was published a year before the first one.

This one was front page: Five Gunned Down in Angeles Forest. She quickly read the copy. Three women and two men, reportedly devil worshipers, were shot around an open campfire as they apparently conducted pagan rites. Figurines of the devil were found stuffed in the mouths of the slain. The police were questioning a possible witness and also members of an organization called Onward Christian Soldiers. A spokesman for the group, Lawrence Carter, said the killings were God's will, but denied involvement by anyone in the organization. He said, "Onward Christian Soldiers is an easy target for law enforcement because we believe in fighting evil, and make no bones about it, but we use the pen, not the sword."

Alice's stomach churned. Her nose began running and she pulled tissues from her purse. After a minute she pulled out her notebook and began writing.

MARK RETURNED TO FRESNO, pleased that Jared had said his notes were well written in both substance and style. Jared's only suggestion was to reduce the description of uneventful activity.

When Mark knocked on Corinne's door he heard folk music playing. She was still singing along as she answered the door.

"Hi, Mark, come in." She had on cut-off Levi's and a red T-shirt with CSUF across the front. Gregory was in his playpen in the living room, seeming to listen to the music.

Mark unloaded a bag of groceries. "Mmmh, does that spaghetti sauce smell good."

"Doesn't it? I put everything in it I could find," she said.

"Okay, I'm in charge of the salad and the dressing. I hope you like Roquefort because the stuff I make is really strong."

"I love Roquefort," she said.

"How's the beer department? I'll split one with you."

"Really, Mark, you can have a whole one." She handed him a can from the refrigerator. "Besides, I'm going to have wine. But first I need to tell you about the reporter."

"Alice Masterson?"

"Yes. I got a weird message from her on my machine yesterday. I left it on so you could hear it." She hit buttons on the answering machine.

> Cory, this is Alice Masterson. It is Monday, nine a.m. The reason I'm calling is to warn you that you might possibly be contacted by a guy named Lawrence Carter. He's with a religious group called Onward Christian Soldiers. They are fundamentalist and . . . well a little strange. They believe in fighting evil and stuff. They have been in the papers. Anyway, Carter came to my door saying he read the article and wanted to know how to reach you so he could write an article about you and Gregory for their religious paper. I don't think he's dangerous, but you should be wary. I didn't give him your address, but if he somehow finds you, I wouldn't trust him. I'm going to check into this guy and his group more and I'll be in touch. And, uh, I wonder if you saw the article I wrote. If not, I'll send you one. Please call me. Bye.

"Her voice . . . she doesn't sound like she's joking," Mark said.

"I know, but it's too crazy. Could it be real? Maybe she just wants to be able to talk with me again?"

"Mmmh. She's clever, that's for sure. But it's the type of thing that shouldn't be ignored, just in case. Let's play it again."

Corinne stiffened. "You mean I should be worried?"

They listened once more.

"I'll talk to her," Mark said. "Don't call. Let me handle it. I'll contact her when I'm back in L.A."

Corinne nodded. "Okay."

They fed Gregory. Except for pushing a half-full dish of pudding off his high chair's tray, he was well behaved. He laughed at Mark's bird-like whistling when Mark carried him into the living room.

"Just put him on the rug, Mark. There's really nothing he can get into. He's probably tired of the playpen."

"How were your classes today?" Mark asked, after they started their dinner.

"Great. In Anthro we had a guest lecturer—an anthropologist who has done some digs in the Olduvai Gorge. I think it would be neat to go on an archaeological expedition in Africa."

"Yeah, that would be interesting. You know, Dr. Weymouth has a good friend at Southern State who's a professor of anthropology. His name is Ian Trevor."

"Really? I read an article by him, and one of his books is on our reading list. He's a cultural anthropologist."

"I went sailing with him and the Weymouths. Nice guy. Funny."

"Really! I'd like to meet him."

"Maybe we can arrange that the next time you come down. Have you filled out your application to SSU for the winter quarter?"

The smile left her face. "Not yet."

"There's not much time left."

"I'll get it done."

Mark helped with the dishes and took out the garbage. She put a bottle on to warm up before they moved into the living room. Corinne fetched a diaper, talcum powder, and Gregory's pajamas. Gregory was in a playful mood. Mark made a stuffed puppy come alive, attacking the infant from different directions as Corinne changed him on the floor. She joined in the frivolity, burying her face in Gregory's tummy and blowing with a loud *brrr* sound. Gregory squealed with delight and tried to grab his mother's hair. As the puppy dived and darted, Corinne bobbed up and down, mouthing different spots on Gregory's protruding belly.

Suddenly Corinne sat up with a surprised look. "Oh, he's doing it."

"What?" Mark said.

"The Y thing." She closed her eyes and sat motionless. Gregory continued to laugh and grab at her.

"The sex thing?" Mark asked. "I don't feel it."

Corinne crossed her arms over her breasts as if she were cold. She opened her eyes wide, looking straight ahead. Her breathing quickened.

"Okay, Cory," Mark said, "divert his attention to something else. Quick."

"Ohhh," she moaned, closing her eyes again.

"Hurry, Cory, get his bottle or something."

Gregory pounded on his mother's leg, laughing. Corinne reached out and grabbed Mark's shirt in a tight grip.

Mark realized he'd better do something fast. He tried to pick Gregory up, but as soon as he got to his knees with the infant he was pushed off balance when Corinne seized him tightly around the waist with both arms.

"Mark . . ." she moaned.

He fell forward, twisted, and landed on his side to keep from squashing Gregory. The boy continued to laugh and gurgle.

"Please . . ." she said, almost inaudibly.

Mark felt her move on top of him, straddling his leg. She thrust herself against his thigh, slowly at first, then faster and harder. He winced as her fingernails dug into his shoulder. Gregory, cradled in his arms, pushed the puppy at Mark's face.

"No, Gregory. Stop it," Mark said loudly. Gregory looked at Mark inquisitively, then cooed. Mark felt Corinne quicken her pace and he could barely keep from crying out as her nails gouged deeper. Better to hold still and prevent her from slipping off and hitting Gregory. He endured the pain from her nails and the dull pounding of her pubic bone on his upper leg. After a long minute she moaned loudly several times and he felt her body quiver. Then she slowly relaxed. When her grasp loosened, he gently rolled her off his side, away from Gregory. He carried the baby into the kitchen. Corinne sighed as she lay limply on her back, eyes closed.

Mark removed the milk from the water but the bottle was too hot, so he put it in the freezer compartment. Then he dressed Gregory for bed. He put the child in his crib and gave him the cooled bottle. Meanwhile, Corinne had gone into the bedroom and closed the door without a word. Mark heard muffled crying. After a minute, he went to the door.

"Cory?"

"Go away." Her voice was muffled.

"May I come in?"

"No. I don't want to see you. Go home, please."

"I need to talk with you. Are you all right?"

The sobbing slowed, but Corinne didn't answer. Mark turned the door knob. He pushed slowly into the dark room.

"Please go, Mark. I'm okay, but I don't want to talk."

As his eyes became accustomed to the dark he saw her sitting on the edge of the bed, head in her hands. He walked over and stood a few inches from her bare feet.

"What happened is nothing to feel bad about, Cory."

She started crying again.

"Please don't be upset," he said.

"Go away," she sobbed.

He reached out and smoothed her hair back from her forehead. He took a tissue from a box on the night stand and tucked it into her hands. She swiped at her nose.

"I feel horrible," she said hoarsely.

"There's no need to." He gave her more tissues. She took them without a word, but refused to look at him.

"I'm so ashamed."

"Why? You had no control over that. There's nothing to be ashamed of." He took her hand and slowly pulled her up. "Come here." He put his arms loosely around her and she leaned her head against his chest.

"How could you lie there and let me do that?" she asked, calmer.

"It happened so fast—I was trying to keep Gregory from getting hurt."

Corinne sniffled and he stroked her hair lightly.

"I feel like some kind of animal—doing that while you watched."

"I wasn't watching."

"Yes, but you felt it. God, what you must think . . ."

"I think more of you than ever," he said softly. He tightened his arms around her.

"Mark, I don't want you to visit anymore. It isn't going to work."

"This is not the time for that kind of talk, Cory." He began rubbing the small of her back. After a minute he felt her lean into him more. Then she hugged him. After several minutes her fingers moved to the back of his neck. She turned her face upward and they kissed open-mouthed. Their bodies pressed tightly and they held the kiss for some time.

"I'm okay now, and I think you should go," she said softly.

"All right."

"Thanks for being . . . nice to me."

"It was easy."

He saw her smile in the dimness.

"I'll be back tomorrow morning to observe breakfast," he said.

She breathed in deeply. "Okay. Thanks."

As she saw him to the door, they looked in on Gregory. He was asleep with the puppy cuddled next to his cheek.

CHAPTER TWELVE

O N THE WAY TO WORK Jared thought about San Miguel Island, west of Santa Barbara. Two summers ago, he, his son, and a nephew had anchored at Cuyler's Cove. Jared recalled the azure water, the dark lava boulders on the white sand bottom, the orange, yellow, and blue wildflowers waving against the red-brown cliffs. He remembered hiking for hours on the island mountain, observing seal and seabird colonies and watching the panorama of light shadings on the bays and landforms as the sun played hide-and-seek with billowy clouds.

At that time he'd imagined that there was no such place as Los Angeles where people ran helter skelter in search of the good life, no such place as Southern State University where scientists searched incessantly to find the nature of life. All that had no meaning when he was on San Miguel. There, natural biology and the physical environment just existed in austere beauty.

Today, he would participate in a synthetic drama about a child who embodied one of nature's experiments. If that child had been born into a Chumash Indian tribe on one of the Channel Islands three hundred years ago, he and his traits likely would have been incorporated into the natural order of things. Maybe he would have become a chief or a shaman. He would have fitted in, no questions asked. But today at Southern State there would be questions. Nothing could just be accepted.

The meeting was held in the president's conference room in the administration building. A twenty-foot-long table with a polished bird's-eye maple finish and leather side chairs dominated the room. A royal-blue wool carpet set off the table from the walnut paneling. Navajo rugs hung on the walls.

Jared arrived next to last, with only Bernie Konheim, director of the Brain Research Institute, yet to show. Gaylord Reese, Vice-Chancellor, sitting at one end of the table, welcomed Jared in a voice befitting a 250-pounder. Jared took a seat opposite Kurt Fonkels and nodded at Fazzi, Valenzuela, and the chair of the Academic Senate, Ray Cameron, whose trim physique, wavy dark hair, and sculptured face always reminded Jared of a movie star, instead of an academician. Jared nodded a greeting to Wilfred Adler, chair of the Human Subject Protection Committee.

"Well, I think we can get started now," Reese said. "Dr. Konheim will be a little late, but asked that we not wait. I sent you copies of Dr. Fazzi's letter. Also in the last few days you should have received a copy of Dr. Weymouth's rebuttal. We are here to discuss the issues raised, but let me say that this is not an official hearing of the university administration or of the academic senate. It is not a grievance meeting and minutes will not be taken. After the discussion, Ray Cameron and I will take things under advisement to see what, if anything, should be done."

Reese looked around at each person. His firm glance was met by silence.

"I must say I've not seen a problem like this in my eighteen years at the university. But I'm sure, as intelligent and collegial people, we can discuss this openly and fairly. As you know from Dr. Fazzi's letter, he proposes an electrode implantation procedure on the baby, Gregory Shenko. And I ask you to keep these names confidential. The baby and his mother are under the care of Dr. Weymouth. Dr. Weymouth declines to have the baby participate in such a procedure. Perhaps the best place to start is to ask you, Jared, why you won't allow such a procedure."

Jared frowned at Fazzi, then turned to Reese. "I won't allow such a research protocol because of the Hippocratic Oath I took a long time ago. The applicable portion says: 'I will prescribe regimen for the good of my patients according to my ability and my judgment and never do harm to anyone. To please no one will I prescribe a deadly drug, nor give advice which may cause his death.'"

"What the hell is this?" exploded Fazzi. "We come here to discuss a serious matter and are treated to homilies."

For quite a few seconds the room was quiet.

"Well, I would not consider the Hippocratic Oath a homily," Fonkels said. "It goes to the heart of the matter. Jared is putting his patient's welfare first and that's as it should be."

"But doesn't he think we all abide by the Oath?" Fazzi said. "Are Jaime and I supposed to be ogres proposing something against the baby's welfare? We're not talking about death, after all. This kind of argument is insulting."

"Hold on," Jared said. "I meant no insult. I told both you, Lou, and Jaime, just as I told Kurt, why I am against the electrode implantation. I also explained this in my letter you all received. How many times do I have to say it? That procedure has a high degree of risk for the baby and will not contribute anything to his health or well-being. Therefore, it should not be done."

"But Jared, you agreed that an angiogram might be appropriate at one time," Fazzi said. "That's invasive."

"Yes, and I have since thought better of it."

Fonkels said, "Jared, isn't the problem really that you have developed some animus toward Lou?"

Jared's eyes flashed. "Yes, I've developed some *animus* toward Lou. He wrote an abstract about our EEG findings on the baby and had it published in the *BNI Bulletin* without my approval."

"But wasn't that an honest misunderstanding?" Fonkels asked. "There was no harm done. That kind of thing is typical when collaborators get their signals crossed. I believe Lou apologized for that. Why have you made such a big thing of it?"

"And then in July," Jared went on, "Mrs. Shenko was contacted by a reporter that Dr. Fazzi sicced on her. My patient did not want any publicity, yet the reporter wrote a negative article anyway, no doubt with Lou's cooperation and encouragement."

"That was the *L.A. Voice* article?" Cameron asked.

"Yes. It was an invasion of privacy and Lou was behind it, making unprofessional remarks about me and my fellow, Dr. Sandler. That article did not help the image of this university."

Fazzi shook his head.

Cameron nodded. "Jared, I read the article. Tell me, is there anything to what that reporter said about the baby making others have epileptic fits?"

Several around the table chuckled.

"C'mon, Ray, you aren't serious," Fonkels said.

Cameron shrugged. "Well, one doesn't know what to believe about this stuff anymore. Remember when we were ready to believe fusion in a flask?"

"True," Reese said.

At that moment, Bernie Konheim entered the room. After greetings and an apology for his tardiness, he settled into a chair next to Fazzi.

"Dr. Reese," Adler said, "I think we have here a collaboration that went sour. Without assessing blame, perhaps it should be looked at in that way and the whole thing dropped."

"Yes, it would appear so," Reese said. He and others looked expectantly at Fazzi who sat red faced, saying nothing.

"Excuse me, Dr. Reese," Konheim said. "I know I have arrived in the middle of this, but are you saying that Drs. Fazzi's and Valenzuela's protocol for in-dwelling microelectrode recording does not have merit?"

"Yes, Dr. Weymouth's judgment is that the research proposed will not directly benefit the baby and he will not accede to the procedure while the patient is under his care," Reese said.

Konheim pressed on quietly. "Yes, I have carefully read Jared's letter and I agree that there are some risks. But as Lou has set forth in detail, these risks are minimal. And even granting for the moment that there may be no benefit to Gregory—which I don't really believe because the child is probably endangered by the lesion—there are great benefits to mankind that would result from the study. And I believe these outweigh the minimal risk to the baby."

"That's right," Fazzi said. "Dr. Weymouth looks only at Gregory, but what about the interests of mankind? Dr. Adler, aren't the benefits to society important in considering human subject protocols?"

Adler cleared his throat. "Yes, protocol applications have to describe all the risks of the research to the subjects, the benefits of the research to the subjects, and the benefits of the research to humanity and knowledge."

"See," Fazzi said, "the benefits to Gregory and to humanity are what make this procedure deserving of approval."

"But I don't think the benefits to humanity were spelled out in your letter," Reese said. "The research doesn't promise to cure any disease. What are the benefits?"

"The benefits," Fazzi said softly, "are that we will learn a great deal about the physiological characteristics and mechanisms of neurons. Neurons are the key to brain function. In their vast quantity and complex interactions they create intelligence and allow memory, language, culture, and civilization. When we learn how neuronal networks operate, we will make great medical progress. In my opinion, Gregory's lesion could teach us more about neurons than we've learned in years."

"If you want to talk of disease, mental retardation is a very real problem affecting millions of people," Konheim said. "Neuronal malfunction is no doubt one of the important causes of retardation, not to mention epilepsy which Gregory himself appears to have. There's also Parkinson's and other diseases."

"Yes, but we're still talking about very basic research," Fonkels said. "Let's not get carried away. Learning about Gregory's giant neurons won't be a panacea."

"The point is," Konheim said, "there is only one Gregory. It would be different if there were other subjects we could study, but there aren't. The last thing we want to do is harm Gregory or interfere with Jared's doctor-patient relationship. But what alternatives are there? This is a unique opportunity for medical science. This is the kind of research we must do to advance medicine. SSU will never live it down if we let this one get away."

Reese scratched his neck. "You have made good arguments. I understand your points. And I understand Jared's point of view. Doing potentially harmful procedures on Gregory to benefit humanity comes down to the good of the individual versus the good of society. But we are a society predicated on individual rights, so utilitarianism . . . the greatest good for the most people . . . can only be carried so far on this."

Reese sat back and crossed his legs. "Ray, do you have any questions?"

Cameron pulled his chair in closer to the table. "Yes, I do. Jared, I understand that a highly regarded psychologist on your staff, Sylvia Auerbach, is familiar with the Shenko case. What does she think about the baby's condition and what is her opinion on whether there should be brain studies of the kind Drs. Fazzi and Valenzuela recommend?"

Jared's eyebrow began twitching. "I haven't talked to her about it."

Cameron's face wrinkled. "Well, what do you think she would say if she were here?"

"I have no idea."

"Really?"

Several people around the table shifted in their chairs.

"Jared," Cameron continued in his well-modulated voice, "do you know anything about this baby's condition that has not already been described—anything that we should know to help us in our deliberation?"

"If I did, I wouldn't tell you."

Everyone stared at Jared. Electricity suddenly charged the air.

Reese jerked forward. "I'm sorry, I don't think I heard you correctly, Jared."

"You heard me correctly."

Fonkels frowned and shook his head. A smirk crept across Fazzi's face.

"Why wouldn't you tell us?" Reese asked.

"For reasons of patient confidentiality."

"But Jared," Fonkels said, "we're all trying to be collegial and reasonable about this. If you could modify that stance, it would be helpful."

"I'm sorry, Kurt, but that's where I come down."

Reese looked intently at Jared for a minute, then straightened his papers, picked up his briefcase, and put the papers in it.

"Well, Jared, do you have anything more you wish to say in this matter?" Reese asked.

"No. I thank you for hearing my point of view."

"Anything further, Ray?"

"No, I think I understand the issues. Let me know when you want to talk about it."

Adler and Weymouth found themselves walking together on the sidewalk after the meeting.

"Dr. Weymouth, I think you had them up until Cameron's questions. But who knows what they will do on this now."

"I know. I appreciate your support."

"Good luck."

Eight days later Reese's response came in a letter to Dean Fonkels with copies to all who attended the meeting.

> Dear Kurt,
>
> I have weighed the issues raised in Dr. Fazzi's letter of July 13 and in the meeting held last week. Following are my conclusions, concurred in by Professor Raymond Cameron, chair of the academic senate:
>
> 1. The reasons for the research investigation proposed by Drs. Fazzi and Valenzuela are compelling. In my judgment the benefits to the subject and to humanity outweigh the minor risks to the subject.
>
> 2. As long as a patient has confidence in his or her doctor, that doctor must agree to any treatment or research plan involving the patient. A doctor's authority in care of a patient is fundamental and must be institutionally respected.
>
> 3. Dr. Weymouth's unresponsiveness to some questions was most troubling. Still, I do not believe that any official action concerning the issue is appropriate or feasible despite the current unsatisfactory state of affairs. In keeping with academic tradition, Dr. Weymouth should be persuaded to reconsider his position by the power of argument.
>
> Sincerely,
> Gaylord Reese, Ph.D.
> Vice-Chancellor for Research

The day after getting a copy of Reese's letter, Jared received a handwritten note from Dean Fonkels. It read:

> Re: Reese's letter, I respectfully ask you to reconsider your position.
> Sincerely, Kurt.

Jared balled up the note and tossed it into the wastebasket.

~

MARK MET ALICE at Dolores' restaurant, a famous west L.A. eatery. This time he sensed a different person across the table. Her hair was slightly askew and she wore lipstick but no make-up. She had on denim jeans and a yellow top.

"Is this a day off for you?" he asked.

"I've had a lot of days off. The *Tribune* no longer needs my services." Her lips curved up wryly.

"Because of the *Voice* article?"

She nodded. "But I don't regret it. I've been interviewing at other papers and that's going okay. I have offers from two small papers so far but they don't pay anything. Sooner or later I'll get something decent."

"Will you stay in L.A.?"

She chuckled. "Probably not. That will make your day, huh?"

Mark shrugged. "Sometimes it's good to make a change."

Alice smiled. "Yeah, I guess you would know. I'm hoping to find something in northern California. People up there are more receptive to creativity."

Mark and Alice placed their orders. Alice settled back into the booth.

"So to what do I owe the honor of this date . . . using the term loosely," she said.

"You owe this honor to the message you left on Corinne's answering machine."

"Oh, that." She nodded slowly. "So you've talked to her. Did she like the article?"

"She liked it but thought her picture could have been better."

Alice laughed. "Beautiful people never think they look good enough."

"I wouldn't know."

Alice laughed again. "Doctors don't have to be beautiful."

"Thanks. Of all the things you've said about me, it's nice to hear something kind."

"Oh, come on. Quit pouting."

Mark smiled. "So what is this about Onward Christian Soldiers?"

"Well . . . Onward Christian Soldiers is a strange group. I don't feel good about them. I talked with a Methodist minister friend of mine in the Valley and he said they are a stepchild of a fundamentalist church in Canoga Park with a big congregation—mainly blue collar. The Soldiers are affiliated with this church but kept organizationally distinct. It's kind of a quasi-militant arm that reflects the aggressive bent of the church founders. Rather than turning off the member-ship, the existence of the OCS seems to attract new members to the church. The Soldiers have marketing appeal, but the church keeps them separate, just in case they become an embarrassment. My minister friend thinks the Soldiers probably don't do nasty stuff, just posture that way."

"What kind of nasty things are they supposed to do?"

"I have a couple of clippings you should look at." She reached into her briefcase.

Mark read the two *L.A. Tribune* articles.

"God, this is bad stuff—could it be them?"

Alice shrugged. "The crimes are real. But there is only conjecture that OCS was involved. No real evidence."

"Those devil worshipers sound bizarre," Mark said.

"Yeah. L.A. has it all. Criminals, psychotics, porno, SM. There's a lot of anger around—inner cities, gangs, militias, anti-abortionists, road rage, climate change activists—you name it. Plus, the new millennium has religious fundamentalists all heated up."

Mark nodded, worry lines showing.

Alice continued, "Your university world is pretty narrow, if I may say so. Still, I don't think Lawrence Carter is somebody for Cory to worry about. I just felt she should be warned in case he tries to find her."

"Alice, this is the kind of thing that Dr. Weymouth wanted to prevent. This is why we wanted confidentiality for Cory and Gregory. If you hadn't written that article, we wouldn't . . ."

"No, no. Look, one can't base actions on all the possible negatives of every situation. Who could have known about the OCS? I didn't. They're probably harmless. But we can't let fear rule even if they aren't."

Mark glared at her. "Well, thanks for the warning, but if something bad happens . . ."

She reached out and put her hand on his. "Look, I'll continue to find out what I can about them. I'll tell you anything I learn. You know that I don't want harm to come to anybody."

He nodded, quickly finishing the last bite of his sandwich.

"I have to get back," he said.

She smiled. "I'll let you know where I end up. I'll email you."

"I hope you find a good place, Alice."

"Thanks. Give my best to Cory. And give that baby a hug for me."

AFTER WORK THAT EVENING Mark had a headache and swam five more laps than usual. He tried to rest after pulling himself out of the pool, but his head continued to throb. He downed some aspirin and took a walk around the neighborhood. He was still brooding over his conversation with Jared a few hours earlier.

Jared had described his meeting with Reese, Cameron and the others, calling Cameron a "crafty sonofabitch unworthy of a faculty appointment" and Fazzi a "pompous asshole." When Mark told of his meeting with Alice, Jared had said, "You are her fool! She could be making up the Christian Soldier business just to continue pumping you for information."

Only when Mark reported the incident in Corinne's apartment with Gregory's Y power did Jared become more thoughtful. "Mark, you have to intervene more when the X or Y comes on. Shake Gregory. Shout. Take him outside, do whatever you can do." Their discussion had ended with Jared saying that they were in danger of losing control of the Shenko case. "I'm counting on you to manage things better, Mark."

As Mark walked, he caught glimpses of the ocean between trees and rooflines. He came upon a man and a boy, the latter around eight or ten shooting baskets in a driveway. He stopped to watch. The boy had the ball and moved directly at the man who had a hand up high in the air. The boy feinted left, then dribbled behind his back and drove right, pushing up an awkward, looping shot that swished through the hoop. The boy shouted jubilantly and the man laughed. They looked at Mark who clapped his approval.

The boy cackled, pointing a finger at the man. "Dad can't guard me."

Mark said, "You're quick."

"Yeah, I can fake him."

Dad said, "Let's see you do it again, hot shot."

Mark moved on. Back in the house he felt a little better. He made some tea and drew the steaming fragrance into his nostrils. He'd managed but one hot gulp when his phone rang.

"Mark, where have you been? I've tried you for days!"

"Hi, Mom. I was out of town for a few days. How are you?"

"Doing what?"

He took a deep breath and let it out slowly. "I had to visit a patient."

"Is this the woman and baby in Fresno?"

"Yes, the epilepsy baby. We can't get them to come down here, so I'm going up there."

"That seems a little unusual," she said.

"Yeah, well, this case is strange. But we're trying to help the mother, and I'm learning a lot on this one."

"I hope you don't drive at night."

"I'm a careful driver. Don't worry. So what's happening with Dad?"

"Guess what. He wants us to come out and visit you."

Mark was momentarily silent. Had he heard right? "Really? When?"

"We could come in a week or two. We'd go to San Francisco for a couple of days, then down to your place. Do you have room for us in your apartment?"

"Uh, sure. You could sleep in my queen bed and I'll sleep on the couch in the living room."

"That would be nice."

"Two weeks from now might work. Next week I'm going backpacking for a few days."

"Oh good. You need some vacation."

"Have you heard from Rachel?" Mark asked.

"Yes. She told me you two exchanged emails. That was nice, Mark."

"Things seem to be going well for her."

"She is . . . a strong person."

"I know."

"I really like her a lot."

"I know."

Mark and his mother settled on a weekend date for the visit. She promised to call again with the arrival time so he could pick them up from LAX. When the conversation ended, Mark sipped the lukewarm tea. The visit would be difficult for him and his father. But the reconciliation had to happen sooner or later. Was it auspicious that the father was coming to the son?

THE SSU FACULTY CENTER was a rustic, steep-roofed building that would look good surrounded by snow. Sylvia always enjoyed rubbing her fingertips against the interior cedar-planked walls. As she waited in the lobby for Ray Cameron, she felt tingly. When he had asked her to join him for lunch, he said he had some news. She spotted his tanned complexion among the throng of paler faces surging in. He grinned and hugged her, then put his hand in the small of her back and guided her to a reserved table at a far corner of the open-ceilinged dining room. They both ordered the halibut special and glasses of the house Chardonnay.

"Okay, the first news is," he said, "I've been selected for President of the NPA. Got word this morning. It'll be announced at the SF meeting in a week and a half."

"Oh, Ray, that's terrific! Congratulations. But, I didn't think you were the president-elect."

Sylvia was a member of the National Psychological Association, the primary professional association for academic psychologists. She knew what a prestigious honor it was to be president.

"Joe Sparks, the president-elect, had a heart attack two months ago and bowed out. So as first vice president, they approached me."

"That's marvelous."

"Thanks. I hope to energize the organization and get it to focus on some issues."

"They won't know what hit them," Sylvia said, grinning.

He laughed.

Only when they were finished with the fish did Cameron bring up the subject she hoped was on his agenda.

"You know, we had a faculty meeting yesterday. Your appointment was discussed, and I followed up with Atkinson this morning." He smiled. "And, I have good news and bad news. Which do you want first?"

Sylvia swallowed quickly. Atkinson was the chair of the Psychology Department and would be the one to determine if an offer could be made to her.

"Give me the bad news, Ray."

"No, I'll give you the good news. The faculty supported your appointment and Atkinson is willing to make an offer."

"Okay, before I wet my pants, what is the bad news?"

"The offer will be tenure track, but assistant professor, not associate."

Sylvia took a deep breath, slightly chagrined, but she knew instantly in her heart that she would still take the offer.

"Well, that is news, all right," she said.

"The consensus of the faculty was that you have great potential, but you need a research program separate from Jared's and a few more solid publications before you can be considered for associate. They would go for a promotional review in six months, however. And,"—he laughed—"and if space doesn't have to be taken away from any of them, they'd approve your appointment as assistant professor."

She laughed. "That figures."

He smiled. "Look, don't see this as negative. There is a small lab and window office available. And Atkinson has start-up funds to offer, plus full salary. This gives you the opportunity for independence and possibly tenure in six months."

She smiled. "Ray, I'm not looking a gift horse in the mouth. If they'll pay me as much as I get now, I'll take it."

"Well, you'll need to negotiate salary with Atkinson. But I think it's great, Sylvia. Just great."

She laughed, then winked. "Thanks for all your help. I know your input made the difference."

Cameron beamed. "Now, want more news?"

Sylvia nodded and fought the euphoria ballooning inside her head. She realized Cameron was talking and she wasn't listening.

". . . that Shenko case?" he asked.

"I'm sorry, Ray, I . . . zoned for a minute. What did you say?"

He chuckled.

"I asked if you knew about the meeting we had on the Shenko case."

"Jared told me a little about it—that you asked him what I thought about Lou Fazzi's research proposal."

"And that Jared had no idea what your opinion might be?"

She sipped her wine. "I'm glad I wasn't there."

"Why?"

"It would have been hard to answer."

"But you do have an opinion?"

Sylvia cleared her throat and lifted her gaze above Cameron's thick hair.

"I'm reticent about invasive brain procedures. I guess I agree with Jared that there might be harm in that. However . . ."

"You disagree that the benefits outweigh the risk?"

"I would need a lot more information to be convinced of the benefits. But what I also wanted to say is that I think the Shenko case needs more expertise, more consultants to help evaluate the baby."

Cameron leaned forward and spoke quietly. "Sylvia, Jared clearly was not telling us everything he knows about Shenko. Do you know what he was hiding?"

She put her hand on her forehead for a few seconds. "You're putting me on the spot."

Cameron searched her eyes.

"I just don't understand why this is so secretive. Jees, it makes me think that the reporter might be right—the kid can cause seizures. I know that can't be. But . . . *can* it?"

She couldn't help a sly smile.

"So it *is* true? And that's why you think other experts should be brought in?"

She nodded slightly.

"Oh my god!" Cameron's exclamation brought looks from people at nearby tables.

"Shhh. Look, Ray, this has to stay just between us."

"You need to level with me, Sylvia."

As they ate their desserts and had refills of coffee, Sylvia told Cameron all she knew about Gregory and his powers. She recounted in detail her experience during the Piaget test. Cameron asked question after question and Sylvia did her best to answer them.

"This is just incredible!" he said finally.

"Yes, it is."

Suddenly Cameron laughed.

"What?" she asked.

"I know how you could publish one paper and instantly become eligible for promotion to associate."

Sylvia gasped. "I couldn't. It's Jared's . . ."

"I know," he said, laughing more.

Chapter Thirteen

THE PHONE MESSAGE was short. Mark said he was passing through Tulare and would see her in about an hour. Corinne glanced at her watch and realized she had a half hour before he knocked on their door. She lowered Gregory onto the living room carpet and gave him his favorite picture book. He opened it and began pointing and gurgling with enthusiasm, trying to say words for the animals. Satisfied that he wouldn't cry, she moved back into the kitchen, unbagged the groceries, and put away everything not needed for dinner. She took the toilet paper and her new order of birth control pills to the bathroom. Then she changed into her olive jumper, dabbed on her favorite perfume and returned to the kitchen to begin preparing the food.

By rote she snapped string beans, browned meat for the chili, and tossed a salad. How would he act when he walked through the door? Like nothing had happened between them? She still felt the hug and kiss that had mended that awful night. Had he done it just to comfort her? She thought not. There had been passion, and it had seemed to surprise them both. The next morning they obviously felt the lingering tension, even though looks were averted and nothing was said. She pushed back a wayward curl. Maybe that strange evening would slowly fade as an unwanted dream. Her rational side hoped so. It was too soon to get involved with another guy. College and Gregory were all she could handle. And maybe Mark was too old for her anyway. And besides, as a doctor, he certainly could do a lot better. Yet why was he so caring with her and Gregory? And why had that kiss almost carried them away?

"Duh, Cory," she said to herself.

Gregory squealed when the doorbell rang. She shushed him and opened the door.

Mark broke into a large grin. "Hi, Cory. Something smells awfully good in there."

"Hi, Mark. Well, you said you liked chili."

"I do. And I also like that jumper on you." He picked up Gregory and twirled around with him.

"Thanks. I like to wear it 'cause it's easy to get out of in case Gregory throws up on me."

Mark looked at her and winked. "Or for whatever reason."

She laughed and felt her cheeks flush. She looked at Gregory. "You'd better not get him too excited."

"I won't. Has he behaved himself?"

"Yes, but I have to tell you about him and Mom."

"No! Really?"

"It wasn't too bad. I'll tell you later. If you'll entertain the squirmer, I'll get dinner finished."

"And I'll tell you later about Alice and the religious guys. That's not too bad either."

"Oh, good."

Corinne mixed a honey-mustard dressing, opened a jar of pea and carrot mush for Gregory, and set the table. She smiled as she listened to Mark and Gregory playing. She almost didn't want to announce dinner.

"Okay, you can bring in the squirmer," she called.

Mark slid Gregory into the high chair and helped Corinne feed him. When the baby was finished and happily playing with toys, Mark and Corinne settled down at the table and filled their plates.

"Are you still planning to go backpacking tomorrow?" she asked.

"Yeah, the car is loaded with all the gear. I have to stop at a market in the morning."

"Where will you go?"

"To a place called Mott Lake, about ten thousand feet . . . it's up near the crest. You go east from here on 68, past Huntington Lake, way back to the end of the road, and park at a lodge next to Florence Lake. They ferry you across the lake to the trailhead. From the west side of the Sierras it's about as close to the high country as you can get before you start hiking. That anthropologist friend of Dr. Weymouth's, Ian Trevor, told me about it. He loaned me his topo maps and an all-weather tent."

"I know where it is. My parents had a cabin at Huntington Lake for many years."

"Interesting. Do you like to backpack?"

Corinne made a face. "I went backpacking with my dad a few times when I was a girl, but I can't say it's a burning desire now."

Mark laughed.

"When will you be back?" she asked, suddenly realizing she was going to miss him.

"Monday—five days from now."

She nodded. "It could be getting pretty cold at that elevation."

"I have down gear. And there should be dry wood for fires. Anyway, tell me what happened between Gregory and your mother."

Corinne laughed. "Well, you know, I never thought Gregory had done anything to her 'cause she never said anything. But when I picked him up today, she asked if I had ever gotten bad headaches when Gregory yelled."

Mark stopped eating and looked at her.

"So I asked her why she was asking. She told me she'd had it happen twice, the second time yesterday."

"What happened?"

"The first time she didn't know what it was. She thought she had a sudden migraine. And it just stopped after a while. But yesterday was a lot worse. She was feeding Gregory and he went into a rage. She was filling his water bottle when he let loose. So she panicked and accidentally spilled the water on him." Corinne started laughing. "And he stopped, just like that."

"I'll be damned." Mark clasped his hands.

"I know. Maybe we should keep a cup of water around."

"It's worth a try." Mark paused. "Has she ever experienced the Y?"

"Well, I hope you don't mind, but I decided to tell her everything. And no, she hasn't experienced the Y. She's sure curious about it now." Corinne giggled and Mark laughed.

"So what does she think about all this?" he asked.

"She thinks it's crazy and unbelievable. But she won't stop babysitting. She said, 'He's my only grandchild and I love him.' Isn't that sweet?"

Mark's face softened. "Yeah. He *is* a good kid. Just has a couple of problems. And that almost makes him more lovable."

Corinne was surprised by her sudden tears. She felt Mark's hand on hers and she squeezed tightly as she blotted her eyes with a napkin.

"I'm sorry," she said. "I don't know why you're helping us so much. But please don't . . ."

"Please don't what?"

She shook her head. "Nothing."

He pulled the napkin away and looked into her eyes. "Cory, I'm going to be here. I'm seeing this through with you."

She smiled through the tears and excused herself. She ducked into the bathroom and splashed cold water on her face. When she returned, fully composed, she noticed that he had cleared the table and placed the dishes in the dishwasher. She served ice cream, cookies, and coffee, and they sat down and worked quietly on their desserts.

"Okay," she said, "You can tell me everything you learned about those religious guys."

Mark told her what Alice had said about her meeting with Lawrence Carter and the information she had obtained about Onward Christian Soldiers. He stopped and shrugged."And that's about it."

Corinne rolled her eyes. "I thought you said it wasn't bad. Those guys are crazies. It doesn't sound good at all." Her look was a rebuke.

"They *are* zealots—no question about that. But there's no evidence that they've done anything like the stuff in the articles. Anyway, I doubt that Carter could find you. He doesn't even know your name."

"But if he had my name, finding us would be easy."

"Are you listed in the phone book?"

"Under Nicholas Shenko. And there are only two Shenkos."

Mark nodded. "Yeah, I guess he could find you if he really wanted to."

"So what should I do?"

"Just be wary. Keep your doors locked. If he shows up, don't talk to him. Let me know right away so I can deal with him."

She looked at Mark. He was so earnest, she felt like hugging him. Instead she started clearing the dessert dishes.

"Okay, I'll try not to worry about this until something happens, which it probably won't."

While Mark played with Gregory, Corinne cleaned up the kitchen. She prepared a bottle for Gregory and with Mark's help, changed the baby, put him in his pajamas, and laid him in his crib. In a few minutes the bottle slipped from his grasp and he dropped off to sleep. She kissed him gently, then walked into the living room.

"Free at last!"

Mark smiled. He was laying prone on the carpet, elbows propped in front of him, looking at a topographical map. "Would you like to see where I'm going?"

"Uh huh." She stretched out next to him and watched with interest as he traced the trail from Florence Lake up to Mott Lake. They talked about elevations, other lakes, animals, and campfires. She could feel his hip against hers. At one point their stocking feet touched.

After a pause in the conversation, Mark leaned in toward her and inhaled. "What perfume is that? I really like it."

"*Allure*. I decided to wear it instead of my other one, *Repel*." She smiled slyly.

Mark laughed. She wasn't sure what he said next, but she felt herself pulled into his embrace. Their lips met and she grabbed him tightly. The kiss was as enveloping as before and she soon felt lost in his arms. Their bodies tightened against each other, the kisses deepened. After a time she pulled the jumper's zipper down to her navel. His hand slipped inside and he made an animal sound. Soon she felt him tugging at her jumpsuit, and she twisted out of it. He wrestled out of his clothes as she caressed his bare skin. Passion took them, and before long she felt the rhythmic hardness of her rump against the floor. When the gentle storm passed, she took his hand and they padded into the bedroom and slipped under the sheet of the queen-sized bed.

"Do you want to stay the night?" she whispered in his ear.

"More than anything."

AFTER STUFFING HER two soft-shell suitcases in the trunk, Alice glanced up at the Santa Monica Mountains. She could dimly make out the mauve, humplike shapes. A thickening blanket of smog and haze was slowly choking off the view. I'm not going to miss this, she thought.

She looked through each room one last time, picked up her coat and purse, and tossed the door keys on the kitchen counter. She had almost closed the front door when a jarring ring echoed through the empty apartment. She paused, then went back to answer it. No reporter can resist a phone call, she mused.

"Hello?"

"Is this Alice Masterson, the journalist?"

"It is."

"Ms. Masterson, my name is Raymond Cameron. I'm a professor of psychology at Southern State. I would like to talk with you about the Shenko baby, if that is possible."

Alice sighed. "Professor, at any other time I'd love to talk with you about that, but I'm moving to Sacramento today. I'm just heading out the door."

"Taking a plane or driving?"

"Driving."

"Well, perhaps Southern State is on your way. I'd like to treat you to lunch and give you an exclusive story opportunity. There is going to be a major news break on Shenko."

"How do you know that?"

"Because I'm going to break the news."

"You? When?"

"Next week."

"I see. Okay, I could meet you in a half hour, but not for lunch. Is there somewhere we could meet outside?"

"Do you know where Rodin's *Walking Man* is, near the sculpture garden?"

"Yes, fine. I'll see you there. I have blond hair and am wearing a white blouse and denim pants."

AS ALICE APPROACHED the replica of the famous torso and striding legs, she saw a handsome man in a gold turtleneck leaning against the statue, his hand on a powerfully muscled bronze thigh. She also noticed a petite, dark-haired woman standing in the statue's shadow.

"Hello, Alice," Cameron called. He introduced the small woman when Alice drew near and together they walked down a path to an L-shaped bench located amid sculptures spread throughout the grassy knolls and valleys of the garden.

Alice smiled at Sylvia. "Are you also in the psychology department?"

"I was recently appointed there, but before that I worked for several years in pediatrics with Jared Weymouth."

"Oh, you know Dr.Weymouth. Did you come in contact with Mrs. Shenko and Gregory?"

"Yes, and actually—"

"Before we discuss anything, Sylvia, let me back up and see if we can get some ground rules established here," Cameron said.

"Sure, Ray."

Alice felt like she was on the verge of something important. Thank goodness she'd answered the phone. She pulled a notepad out of her purse.

"Alice, since your time is short, let me be brief," he said. "And please don't write anything in that notebook of yours." He reached down and picked up a fallen maple leaf. "I am the president of the National Psychological Association which has its meeting next week at the Moscone Center in San Francisco. As part of my inaugural speech—which will be open to the press—I am going to announce that the NPA will study the ethical issues posed by the existence of Gregory Shenko and his strange powers. And, I will briefly discuss the powers."

"Is there more than one power?" Alice asked.

"There are at least two," he said. "You've experienced one. In fact, you wrote about it. The other you probably do not know about."

"Can you tell me what it is?" Alice asked, looking at Sylvia.

"Not today," he said. "But if you can attend the NPA meeting and cover my Friday noon speech, Sylvia will meet with you beforehand and tell you all about it.

So, the ground rule is that you will not publish anything nor talk to anyone about this ahead of my speech. In return, you will get advance information and be in the exclusive position to write most knowledgeably about the issue."

Alice looked away and her eyes came to rest on a nude statue of a black, Rubenesque female reclining with legs slightly apart. The figure's voluptuous breasts and pliant stomach folds sagged slightly. Alice winced and forced her eyes back to Cameron's friendly gaze.

"Why are you giving *me* this opportunity?"

"Because you are a good science writer. You already know a great deal about Gregory and his mother . . . also Weymouth and Sandler, and Fazzi. There is likely to be a lot of confusion and sensationalism when this breaks. We want to be sure that there is some good reporting taking place."

"And, we hope you have the same ethical concerns we do," Sylvia said.

Alice nodded. "Well, I do believe the public has a right to know about Gregory. But what do you say to someone like Dr. Sandler who asserts patient confidentiality, saying that Gregory has a right to avoid the glare of publicity?"

Sylvia and Cameron exchanged looks.

"There are competing rights," Sylvia said. "In this situation, the rights of the community outweigh the rights to individual privacy. Typhoid Mary did not have a right to be unknown."

Alice smiled and then looked at Cameron. "Will I be able to get in with a press pass?"

Cameron handed her a large envelope he pulled out of his briefcase. "Take this. It contains a program, ID badge, parking pass, and ticket to the luncheon, as well as instructions on where to meet Sylvia at ten that morning."

"You're really organized."

Cameron nodded. "We'll see you there."

Once on the 405 freeway heading north over Sepulveda Pass, Alice allowed her elated feelings to burst forth in several loud squeals. Finally! The break she needed. *Won't this gall Onstine and all the* Tribune *hotshots!* As she calmed down and settled into the fastest lane, she wondered what the age of the youngest person to win a Pulitzer was.

JARED DROVE SOUTH on Lincoln Boulevard to Venice Beach. He turned west, eventually finding an empty space in the large parking lot. Walking along an alley-sized street where cars were not allowed, he looked for the distinctive second-story deck that provided a view of the ocean. People and dogs passed by. He could hear the low roar of the breakers. Warm marine air massaged his nasal passages. Music and voices wafted out of open doors and windows as he passed. He liked the youth and vitality bubbling from the close-packed beach neighborhood. Spotting the familiar house, he climbed sandy steps and knocked on the screen door.

"Hello there, Jared. You made good time. Come in and let me build you a drink." Ian Trevor had on tan corduroy shorts, a blue knit polo shirt, and cordovan sandals.

"Hi, Ian. Thanks, I need one."

"The usual?"

"Please."

Ian stepped into the kitchen as Jared moved into the living room. The room had become Ian's den. Floor-to-ceiling bookcases lined three walls. A beige carpet ran from wall to wall, setting off the dark leather furniture, a square glass coffee table, and tall, brass lamps. Primitive masks, woven baskets, and other artifacts sat on shelves designed to attract the eye. Jared eased back into an Eames chair. Ian brought in two single-malt scotches and a plate of caviar, sour cream, and crackers.

"Where's Joan tonight?" Ian asked, picking up a small-bowled pipe.

"Went to a movie with a friend. Said that was more attractive than listening to us talk business."

"So you meant it—you really have a problem?"

"A huge one. And I appreciate your letting me unload on you."

"Why not. With a scotch I can handle anything. I take it your current dilemma relates to this Shenko baby?"

"Yep. I don't know how much you know, but I can no longer keep this to myself. I . . . I need some help."

"Well, what I know is what I read in the *L.A. Voice* and *Tribune* articles. And Mark told me a little the other night—that the mutation is a genetic condition. He mentioned his discussions with the grandmother and the mother, whom I guess he's visiting a lot up in Fresno."

"Did he mention the baby's powers?"

"Powers? No."

Jared's eyebrow began twitching and he rubbed his forehead. "Mmh. Well, get comfortable . . ."

Jared spent an hour talking about Corinne, Gregory, the discovery of the powers, Jared and Mark's approach to pediatric care and confidentiality, the fight with Fazzi and Valenzuela, the meeting with Vice-Chancellor Reese, and the efforts of Alice Masterson. He told of the OCS religious group and finished with Sylvia's move to the psychology department.

"So, my friend, that's a short version of the story."

"My god," Ian said. "Incredible, just incredible."

"Incredible is right. So I'm not surprised you don't believe it."

Ian drew on his pipe and looked away for a minute. Then he shook his head and grinned at Jared. "Well, I *do* believe it. A, because it's coming from you, and B, it's too fantastic not to be true. How could anyone make that all up?"

Jared exhaled. "Thanks, Ian."

"But it is sounding ominous, like things are all escalating. So I can understand your being stressed."

Jared nodded. "It's just been one thing after another. I've never felt so inadequate in all my life."

Ian brought in the bottle of scotch, topped off Jared's glass, and then handed him a cracker with toppings.

"Jared, what is worrying you the most about all this? I'm mean right now."

"Right now? Well, that I have to meet with Kurt Fonkels and the president in a week. Kurt tells me that serious inquiries have been coming into the president's office—from the media, the faculty, people in the community, the board of trustees. The president knows about my refusing to cooperate with Reese and the committee. He's going to want some answers. Second, I'm very worried about Sylvia. She packed up and moved over to Psychology two days ago. She's been cool toward me for the last couple of weeks. I think she's thrown in with Ray Cameron and will tell him about Gregory's powers. Maybe she has already. For all I know, maybe Cameron has told the president."

"Uh huh." Ian drew on the pipe and thought for a while. "I agree the meeting with the president could be very serious. Definitely cause for concern. Are you worried at all about the religious guys and Corinne and Gregory's safety?"

"Not much. I know Mark is, but I find it hard to believe that fundamentalist weirdos would be obsessed with a little baby. And Mark can't be *that* worried because he's gone backpacking, as you know."

Ian drew in deeply and blew out a smoke ring.

"Ian, I feel like my life has had an injection of LSD this past year. One surreal event after another. And now it's like I'm in a hurricane at sea. I didn't see it coming, didn't prepare for it, and I don't know how to save myself and the crew." Jared bent forward. "For some reason," he continued, "I've felt that it was crucial to keep this thing secret. But maybe that was wrongheaded. Fonkels and Reese certainly think so. Sylvia thinks so. What do *you* think?"

Ian knocked the ashes from the pipe, picked up a tobacco pouch, and refilled the bowl with care. He tamped the tobacco and then lit it.

"I don't think you're wrong, Jared. But I understand why others do. An event such as this . . . Let's face it, this mutation is probably the most significant change the human race has seen since homo sapiens acquired language. An event like this is both alarming and fascinating to people. The Bill of Rights almost can't apply. It's like a new hominid has suddenly appeared on the earth."

"Really?"

"Well, if this kid can do what you say, yes."

"I guess I haven't seen him like that. So you think I should turn Gregory over to the slavering crowd?"

"No, I don't. But I think you're going to have to stop fighting the crowd head on—quit beating into that hurricane. You have to look after yourself. Otherwise you'll get hurt. And I for one, wouldn't want to see that."

Jared rubbed an eye. "So what should I do?"

"I don't know, yet. Let me mull it over for a couple of days. But one thing I'm sure of is that you should take a few days off. Get away, try to relax and calm down. Leave this to me. We've been friends for quite a while. I'm going to figure out a good way to go on this. Okay?"

Jared sighed. "Okay."

"Jared, I'm serious about you taking three days off. Take Joan and go up to Santa Barbara or down to Laguna Beach. Cancel all your appointments starting tomorrow."

"How can I do that?"

"Very easy. Call Lena and tell her you're not feeling well and you won't be in. And don't tell anyone where you're going. Just call me when you get to your inn so I can reach you if I need to."

Jared chuckled. "Okay, doctor."

"Now, are you ready for chess?"

Chapter Fourteen

Mark's Vibram soles left waffle prints in the dirt. His heavy pack pulled familiarly on hip and shoulder straps and squeaked occasionally when he took a large step up the switchbacks. He sucked deep breaths of thin mountain air and looked at the bark of the gnarly pines he passed. A pair of gold-mantled ground squirrels scurried away and scolded him as he walked by. A green-backed lizard darted over rocks, and a jay screamed a warning as it swooped from limb to limb.

At the top of a decomposed granite knoll, he watched a brown marmot sniff the air and skitter down a hole between boulders. He removed his wide-brimmed hat, wiped his sweaty forehead, and brought the canteen to his lips. His eyes followed the trail down to a distant, yellow-green meadow with dead snags and patches of skunk cabbage on either side of a clear creek. He felt the bone-deep joy that pristine mountains always gave him.

He reached into a side pocket of his pack and pulled out the deep-fried pork rinds included in the care package sent by Rachel. The note with it had said, 'Have a good trip. I'll be in SF attending the NPA while you're up there. Look my way and I'll wave. R.'

He put his foot up on a rock. Of course the message *was* the pork rinds. She was saying that her religiosity had slackened. He laughed, scaring off junkos feeding in nearby manzanita bushes. He pictured Rachel at a Vermont campsite a year ago, laughing at the flapjack he had accidentally flipped into the fire. He could feel her dark, shampoo-smelling hair against his face as they snuggled in the zipped-together bag. He straightened up, threw a stone, and continued on.

He spotted a duck, three small rocks stacked up as a trail marker. It could be the exposed vertebrae of a miniature snowman, he thought. He was making good time. In a couple of miles he'd come across a junction where this trail met the John Muir trail that snaked the length of the Sierras. He strode ahead, focusing on the ecology of his surroundings.

At the edge of a meadow, he stopped to take in the shadows and verdant coolness of a grove of red firs that nurtured mushrooms and ferns in the earth below the graceful boughs. Beyond the lush grass, out by a breeze-rippled creek, a thick stand of aspen cast a blinding reflection from their shimmering leaves. The moist smell of turgid leaves, fir branches, and wild lupin suddenly became Corinne's exotic perfume. And once again, her memory vividly filled his mind as it had numerous times since leaving the apartment. He smiled as he relived the unhesitant embrace, firm body, and deep kisses that had become all consuming to him that night. What was it about her? Was she the forbidden blond shiksa? He pictured Rachel and Corinne standing together, both beautiful and grinning. He waved gnats away from his forehead, then turned back onto the trail.

After some time, he spotted a U.S. Forest Service sign ahead and slowed his gait. He saw something in the center of the trail near the sign. An animal. After a few more steps Mark stopped and felt his heart quicken. The animal appeared to be a wolf, rear end down, shoulders up with legs straight, staring at him. Mark pulled his small binoculars from a pocket in his hunter's vest and brought the animal into focus. It was indeed a grayish wolf, tongue out to one side and teeth showing. The gray-green eyes stared unwaveringly at him. Large triangular ears pointed forward and huge paws picked up and set down nervously. Mark saw raised fur on the back of the animal's neck when it lowered its head momentarily. There was something on the wolf's back. It looked like a green pack with side pouches.

A bearded man with a pack and walking stick came into Mark's view. The man patted the animal's head and looked at Mark.

"Don't worry, he won't hurt," the man shouted. "C'mon."

Mark walked slowly toward them and stopped ten feet away. "Is that a wolf?"

"His name's Arnie. Half wolf, half German shepherd. He's domesticated. I've had him since a pup."

Arnie stood up and wagged his long tail. He came over slowly to Mark, sniffed, and allowed Mark to stroke his head and neck.

The bearded man wore ragged, cut-off Levi's with a rope through the belt loops, a faded plaid shirt, and a yellow bandanna around his forehead. His pack, an old green Kelty, had a cup, fry pan, and dirty socks tied on the back. Judging by the man's firm muscles and skin tone, Mark guessed his age between thirty-five and forty.

"Where are you headed?" the man asked.

"Up to Mott Lake."

"Mmmh. It's a pretty little place."

"Did you come from there?"

"No. Arnie and I've been up in Evolution Valley for a couple of weeks."

Mark nodded, not knowing where that was, but remembering the name on one of Ian's topos.

The man fingered his beard. "Don't see many people in here this late in the year. Where are you from?"

"Santa Monica."

The man frowned. "L.A. type. Huh." The 'huh' was a grunt.

Mark nodded somewhat apologetically.

"Are you fishing?" the stranger asked.

"No, just came for the scenery. To think some and clear my mind."

"Huh. To think. That's interesting."

Mark stepped tentatively around the wolf-dog. "Well, I'd better keep moving. So long."

The man stepped closer. "Uh, tell me, are they building more high rises down there?"

"In L.A.?"

"Yeah. We need to cram more in down there." The man grinned, showing a chipped upper front tooth.

"Well sure, there's more building going on all the time."

"Good, good. Got to keep all those goddamn people down there. Too many of 'em coming up here."

Mark saw the man's eyes brighten with the not-so-subtle challenge.

"Yeah, well, good luck," Mark said as he started up the trail. He did not turn his head.

The man laughed loudly. "Arnie, c'mon boy. At least *you* have a sense of humor."

It took only a quarter mile for the weird encounter to dissipate from his thoughts. But he struggled for several miles to rid his mind of Corinne and Rachel. Once into a rhythm, he found new energy and kept on the trail without further stops. He reached Mott Lake at sundown, exhausted. His hands and nose were numb from the increasing cold. He pulled on his parka and wool gloves and hurriedly fired up the Primus. His dinner was hot cocoa, raisins, cheese, and crackers. Once he had burrowed into his down bag, his aching leg and butt muscles could hold off unconsciousness for only a few minutes.

The next morning, hovering with coffee next to a crackling fire, he looked around at his environs. A blue-mirrored lake, scarcely a quarter mile across, nestled in a cirque between massive granite peaks. Dwindling snow patches on the slopes fed small creeks seeping down into slushy meadows forming the shore. White bark pines and a few mountain hemlocks clustered around the lake, apparently the only trees to survive at the timberline elevation. After a breakfast of hot cereal and dried fruit he explored the area, looking for a campsite and decided on an obvious one in a grove of trees on a small bluff where a nearby stream cascaded into the lake, bringing snow melt from higher alpine snowpacks.

Over the next three days, Mark meandered around Mott Lake, thinking about Gregory and all that had happened since Mark's arrival at Southern State. At 10,000 feet, his view of events seemed clearer, as a football fan high in the stands sees the action on the field better than the players.

Through happenstance, an unlikely web of people had made connections to an enigmatic baby. Mark wondered if any of them really appreciated the child's true import—that Gregory's very existence refuted the assumption that current mankind was the grand endpoint of evolutionary progress. Mark wondered if any of them fully realized that Gregory's traits showed that human biology remained in flux, that evolution did not head in any particular direction, did not move toward any ideal of perfection. Life could go any which way. And here, in one little child, was one direction it had jumped, quite possibly from ancient hominid forms.

In their rigidly biblical appraisal, Onward Christian Soldiers had come closest to sensing Gregory's meaning. But their apparent objection was narrowly conceptual; they had no direct experience with the child. Sylvia, through direct experience, had insight into the Y power's potential threat to women. But she seemed not to see the totality of the package. Corinne had experienced Gregory fully, but through a mother's biased eyes. He was her problem child. Even Jared, who knew the most about Gregory medically, seemed only to understand him as a handicapped child. That left Mark alone in his perspective.

What would happen if society were to fully understand Gregory's meaning? Could many people allow Gregory to be Gregory? Let him produce offspring, bringing more Nicholases and Gregorys into the world? How many people would take Jared's attitude—trying to control or modify the traits for both the child's and society's sake? The do-gooder approach. And what proportion, like the OCS, would be intolerant and demand that Gregory be immobilized or worse?

Aside from society's rights and wishes, what about Gregory's? Was he a citizen with rights to freedom and privacy as long as he did not violate any law? Should his evolutionary line play out? Who decided? Who were the fittest here? As Mark pondered all of this, he found himself conflicted. What did he really think about this baby? By nature, he preferred to be a recorder of the action, not in the middle of the fight. But he knew he could not opt out. He knew that society as a whole would never come to understand what Gregory really meant to the world. The child's fate would be determined by a few individuals and groups who would influence others. For better or worse Mark was one of those who might have the most say in Gregory's fate.

Shortly after midnight on the day he was to leave, light snow began falling. At four in the morning, in the white-blurred beam of his flashlight, he brushed off his tent and packed up in the biting cold. He was on the trail at dawn, bundled in his hooded yellow parka. The snowfall steadily increased, building up on the ground. As he moved down in elevation he worried that he might have to hole up in the tent and weather the storm. Even if he could get to Florence Lake, would the boat come in such foul weather? Mark steeled himself and barreled on, at times guessing where the trail should be, watching for blazed trees and ducks of snowy rock. At one point the flurries caused a total white-out and he bent over, back to the wind. A pang of fear came over him. What if this were a major storm, snowing him in for days? He wasn't equipped for that.

He wiggled his toes to generate warmth. Suddenly he sensed a lightening and glanced up. The snowfall was decreasing. He could see again. He moved on, and in another half mile the snowflakes all but stopped. Visibility opened up. With relief he lengthened his stride. At the next rise he saw Florence Lake. He pulled out his binoculars. Halfway across the lake, coming toward him, was the boat. Mark yelled, lowered his head, and broke into a run, hurtling down the mountain like a mule returning to the corral.

CORINNE PULLED UP in front of her apartment building. She found it easier to unload groceries and Gregory from the curb than from the close quarters of her parking stall off the alley. She found herself humming as she unstrapped Gregory from the car seat. She thought of Mark arriving for a dinner of pasta and the spicy meat sauce that he liked. They would have Chianti.

"Can I be of assistance, Mrs. Shenko?" The male voice was cheerful.

She stood up quickly and looked around. A few feet away on the grass stood a young, smiling man in an ill-fitting black suit and tie. He had a pen in one hand and a bible and notepad in the other.

"How do you know my name?"

"Allow me to introduce myself. My name is Lawrence Carter." He paused for a second, staring at Gregory in the car seat. The infant was shaking the stuffed puppy as he watched the adults.

Her heart thumped. This was the guy Mark had said to watch out for. He was right in front of her. What a dunce I am, she thought. Why hadn't she looked around before getting out of the car?

"I'm sorry, but I don't know you, Mr. Carter. I'm in a hurry and I don't need any help. So please be on your way."

"Please don't be alarmed. I'm a reporter for a Christian magazine. I read the article in the *L.A. Voice*. The story is fascinating. It was very well written. The pictures of you and Gregory were sensational. I just want to get some information."

"Yes, well, I'm sorry I can't talk to you about it. I have to go in and put my baby down."

"I understand. Some other time?"

She reached in and pulled Gregory up into her arms, then shut the door.

Carter picked up the grocery bag from the lawn. "When would it be convenient for me to come back, Mrs. Shenko? I wouldn't take much time. By the way, are you a Christian, if I might ask?"

Gregory stared at Carter and began to whimper.

"Mr. Carter, I'm sorry but I don't want any more publicity. I don't want you to come back. I'm sure you can understand that I just want my privacy." Corinne reached out her arm to get the grocery bag.

"I understand. But please tell me one thing. Are you a Christian?"

"Look, it doesn't matter whether I'm a Christian or not. I don't have to answer that. Please give me my groceries." Gregory's whimpers turned into a steady whine.

Carter kept the groceries. "Oh, but it certainly does matter." His voice was louder and the smile had disappeared. "It's crucial."

"I don't care," she shouted. "*Hand* me that." Gregory began to cry.

Carter shouted back. "You should care, because it matters whether Gregory is a child of the Lord's or not."

Gregory's face turned red.

"Give me my damn groceries now!" Corinne yelled.

Carter stepped close and finally put the bag in her open arm. As his sneering face got close to Gregory's, the shriek came—piercing, pulsated, and multi-toned. Carter's eyes went blank and he dropped down as his knees buckled, the bible and tablet spilling from his hand.

Corinne squatted low to maintain balance, trying to ride out the X. "Quiet, baby. It's okay, it's okay." As the withering buzzing slowly quieted in her head, she stood and walked unsteadily toward the entrance. Keep your balance, keep your wits, she thought. Gregory eased back into crying. Holding the groceries tight under her arm, she managed to turn the key, then pulled the door open with her toe, and looked back at Carter who was now up on shaky feet, bible in one hand and Gregory's puppy in the other.

"Hey! That's a devil's child," he shouted. "You'll be sorry!"

She got inside her apartment and locked the door. With Gregory still in her arms, she warmed a bottle in the kitchen, cooing at him the whole while. Then she put him down in his crib. Her body shook as she put away the groceries. She thought of calling her mother, but decided to wait for Mark before talking to anyone. She lay down on the couch and let her tears flow unimpeded.

A short rap on the door jarred her from a fitful sleep. She glanced at her watch and realized she had been on the couch for an hour. The rap repeated and her anxiety rose sharply. "Who is it?"

"Mark. I don't have the key with me."

She ran to the door, jerked it open and threw her arms around him, burying her face against his smelly shirt and breaking into sobs.

"Hey, hey. Hey there. Cory, what's wrong?" He rubbed her back lightly.

She slowed her crying. "Did you see a man out there, a man in a black suit?"

"No. Why?"

"That religious nut Lawrence Carter was here! I was unloading groceries from the car. And Gregory let him have it with the X."

"No! When?"

"About an hour ago. Oh, I'm so glad you're here." She squeezed him tighter.

"Did he hurt you?"

"No, he was trying to be nice, but he frightened me. Said Gregory was a devil's child."

"Is Gregory okay?"

"Yes, he's napping."

"Okay, wait here. Lock the door again."

"Be careful," she yelled as he disappeared down the stairs.

After a while he returned, carrying his pack and a duffel bag of gear. "I didn't see Carter or anybody." He dropped the pack and bag on the floor and took her hands. "So, tell me exactly what happened."

She wrinkled her nose. "Mark, don't you want to take a shower first? We can talk about Carter later."

He laughed. "Yeah, sure. If I can take a cold beer in with me."

She smiled and retrieved a pale ale from the fridge.

"And I need a kiss," he said.

She raised up on the balls of her feet and presented her mouth. The kiss lasted a long time.

"To the shower," she said, pointing.

She smiled as she heard him singing in the shower. She tiptoed into Gregory's room. His breathing was steady, and she figured he would stay down for a half hour more. In her bedroom she pinned her hair up on top of her head and shed her clothes. She tiptoed into the bathroom and stood next to the opaque shower curtain. She began singing along with Mark. After another stanza he stopped.

"You have a great voice," he said.

"Thanks. Yours is nice too."

"Only when I'm in the shower."

She pulled the curtain slightly and stepped into the back of the tub behind him. He looked around, but she pushed his head forward.

"Don't look. With all that grime, I just thought you might need help scrubbing your back."

He laughed. "You're amazing."

She took the soap and washcloth to his backside.

"I'm in heaven," he said. "When you're done, I get to wash you too."

She laughed. Finishing up, she circled her arms around him, placing her hands on his pectoral muscles. "My hunk doctor."

"Are you ready?" he asked.

"Okay." She turned around and soon felt the washcloth on her shoulders and his aroused hardness lower down. His free hand came around to one of her breasts. He kissed her neck. She closed her eyes and twisted her head back. His lips found hers and she pivoted slowly into his arms. The hot spray splashed over them as they moved together, their soapy skin rubbing smoothly with their undulations. After a while he reached down and lifted her up, locking his arms under her buttocks. They slowly joined. When external sensations and sounds eventually seeped back into her consciousness, she felt the water and heard Gregory's voice.

"I've got competition," Mark whispered, as he helped her untangle.

She smiled dreamily and rubbed her flushed neck. "You've got no competition, mister. Welcome home."

As Corinne tended the marinara sauce, she decided that Mark was a protector. And she knew she was falling hard.

Mark stacked blocks in the living room and laughed as Gregory gleefully leveled them like some godzilla loose in Manhattan. On the wall behind the baby, a TV news anchor dispensed national disasters between headache and gastrointestinal remedies. Suddenly, Gregory lunged for Mark's glasses.

"No way, José!" Mark grabbed Gregory, rolled him up, kissed his tummy, and put him back down. Gregory laughed and put his arms out to be picked up again. "Uh huh," Mark said, pulling the baby up and cradling him. "How's my little zapper? Huh? You zapped a zealot today, didn't you." Gregory giggled and twisted to be let down. Mark obliged, then pulled the little legs trying to crawl away. "What are we going to do with you? Anybody makes you unhappy, you just zap away.

You're an equal opportunity zapper." As Gregory slipped away, something on the news caught Mark's attention.

"Oh shit. Cory! Come here."

"What is it?"

Mark pushed up the TV's volume. "After this commercial."

The newsman reappeared. "Now we have an amazing report from San Francisco about a strange baby. Is it science or science fiction? Let's go to Marne Sabin at the Moscone convention center."

"Good evening. The National Psychological Association has been meeting here for the past three days. Two thousand academic psychologists have been exchanging research information, as is usual for such scientific meetings. But today, the new president of the organization, Dr. Raymond Cameron, a professor from Southern State University, shocked his audience by announcing the discovery of a baby with, for lack of a better description, supernatural powers.

"As a part of his inaugural remarks, Dr. Cameron stated that the infant had been examined by doctors at Southern State Medical Center. Based on information from authoritative sources, Cameron claimed the baby has the ability to induce sharp head pains, actually small seizures, in people in the baby's vicinity. The baby can also cause sexual arousal in some females. Cameron would not elaborate further. He indicated that a committee of the NPA will be formed to study the case and make a report at a later time.

"That's all the information we have now on this. But I'm sure you can understand the uproar among the attendees caused by the announcement. Some of the psychologists we talked with said it probably was a hoax, but others are withholding judgment. This is Marne Sabin at the Moscone Center in San Francisco."

Corinne and Mark stared at each other. He slowly reduced the TV's volume and Gregory's happy gurgling filled the momentary silence.

"Oh my god," she said, hand over her mouth.

Mark shook his head. "Amazing. On national news."

"Who's this Cameron?"

"A friend of Sylvia's in the psychology department. That's her home department now. She must have told him about Gregory. She's the authoritative source."

"Why would she do that?"

He shrugged. "I don't know. To get recognition. She obviously feels no loyalty to you, me, or Jared."

Corinne frowned. "I just can't believe this. What am I going to do?"

"Well, first let's not panic. Let's call Jared."

With Corinne at his side, Mark dialed the kitchen phone. At Jared's office there was no answer. At his home the line was busy. Mark hooked up his laptop and checked his email. He found no recent messages from anyone at SSU.

"Why don't we eat and I'll try him later," he said.

Corinne kissed him lightly on the lips. "Mark, I'm just so glad you're here. I don't know what I'd do . . ." She paused. "Wait. Aren't your parents coming to your house tomorrow?"

"Yes." He looked at her with frustration.

"Then you have to go back. Look, I can move in with my folks."

"Hold on. I don't have to go back. Let me think about this."

Corinne wasn't surprised that Mark didn't seem to enjoy the dinner, despite his complimentary remarks. He said little. They focused their attention on plying the baby with food and grabbing objects before they became projectiles. When they had finished, Mark dialed Jared's home again, this time getting a phone machine. He left a short message and Corinne's phone number.

"Maybe Jared is inundated because of the news report. If he gets my message, I know he'll call," Mark said.

"I guess I'm more worried about Lawrence Carter than the publicity," she said, wiping the table.

"Let's hope he went back to L.A."

She stopped and looked at Mark. "But for how long, now that he's experienced the X?"

"Yeah, you're right. That will feed their craziness."

She handed him a full garbage bag from under the sink. "Do you mind taking this out?"

She heard the squeak of the door opening and then a yell of surprise. She dropped her towel and ran to the door. Mark stood on the landing, looking down. She saw the puppy on the doormat, furry and blond. Little flies buzzed around, lighting on the body. It wasn't breathing. There was something strange. Two small horns stuck out from its head, affixed by an elastic band running above the bulging brown eyes. A paper was stuck to its belly with a hat pin. Mark pulled up the bottom of the paper to see the writing. She could see crude lettering in black ink. Mark stood up and stepped into the living room, closing and locking the door behind him. He put his arms around her.

"It's dead, isn't it?" she said.

"Yes."

"What did that note say?"

"Stupid words."

She raised her voice. "What did it say, Mark?"

"It said: 'Beast, beware His wrath.'"

"Carter and his cult did it."

"Yeah, nobody else would do that."

"The puppy looks like Gregory's."

"Those chickenshit bastards."

"Should we call the police?"

Mark was quiet for a minute. "I don't think the police are a good idea. I'm going to get rid of it in the trash bin."

"This is horrible. What should we do? I'm really scared."

"We need to get out of here. Let's pack up and drive down to my place."

"Right now?"

"Yes."

"Would that be any safer?"

"It's certainly safer than here. And we need to stay together."

"What about your parents?"

"I'll have them stay in a motel."

"I don't know, Mark. What about my parents? My classes?"

"Look, you and Gregory need to be away from Fresno right now. Call your parents and tell them you're going to take Gregory down for another check-up. Your classes will have to wait."

She nodded slowly. "Okay."

"Pack several days' worth of clothes for you and Gregory." Mark grabbed a flashlight from his pack and a garbage can liner from the kitchen. "I'll be back in a few minutes."

"I don't think you should go out there, Mark."

"We can't leave that dog body there. Besides there are other people around outside. I think those OCS types are basically cowards."

"Be very careful. Please."

After removing the note, Mark tossed the dead animal in the building's trash bin in the alley. Warily, he walked around, looking for suspicious persons and vehicles. He saw nothing obvious, but realized that there could be people in some of the vans and trucks parked on the street. When he let himself back into the apartment he found Corinne pulling baby clothes from a chest of drawers. He stepped into the bathroom and washed his hands thoroughly. Then he went in to Corinne and hugged and kissed her.

"We'll get through this," he said.

"I'll try not to be afraid. Just stay close."

The ring of the phone broke their embrace. Mark answered it and immediately recognized Ian's English accent. He signaled Corinne to pick up the extension in the bedroom.

"Hi, Mark. I'm over at the Weymouth's. Joan and I went out for a bite and just got back to find your phone message. It's been a bit daft around here today. That announcement by Cameron up at the NPA meeting caught us all by surprise. Did you hear of it?"

"We saw a report on the evening news. Where's Jared?"

"Right. Well, Jared is over at the university president's house now, having been summoned to explain about Gregory. There are four reporters and two TV crews outside on the street, waiting for Jared to come back."

"My god, really?"

"It's a bloody carnival. What's happening up there?"

"There are no media, but a religious zealot has threatened Gregory. It's scary."

"Oh shit. Is it that Christian Soldiers outfit?"

"Yeah. So, we're packing up now to head down there."

"Where to?"

"To my place."

"Not a good idea, Mark. There will be media people at your place too. This thing has exploded."

Mark blew out an exasperated breath. "What can we do?"

"Come directly to my house. You remember how to get here?"

"I think so."

"Do you have your cell phone?"

"Yep."

"Ring me when you are ten minutes away and I'll meet you in the parking lot. I've got a private garage where we can hide your car."

"Man, Ian . . ."

"I know. We can talk when you're here. Don't worry, I've got some ideas how we can handle things. You'll be safe at my place. So I'll see you in a few hours. Give my best to Corinne."

"She's on the line. Cory?"

"Uh, thank you so much, Dr. Trevor. But are you sure you want us there, I mean with Gregory?"

"Of course. We'll have a jolly time. I've even got some toys in a closet. And you have to call me Ian."

After she hung up, Corinne's eyes filled with tears. How could this be happening? She sighed and pushed her hair back. Now she had to call her parents. What was she going to tell them?

CHAPTER FIFTEEN

CORINNE JUMPED UP and snatched an ash tray from Gregory's grasp. He started crying and Mark sat up, suddenly alert.

"It's okay," she said. "He's just tired." She picked Gregory up and glanced at her watch. It was half past midnight.

Ian nodded. "Look, we're all exhausted, so why don't we go to bed now and we'll discuss things over breakfast."

"Have you heard from Jared?" Mark asked.

"He called a couple of hours ago. Had a pretty rough go at the president's. Reese was there and Fazzi for part of the time."

"Did he tell them everything?"

"Yes. I advised him to do so."

"That must have been hard for him. Will we see him tomorrow?"

"No, the plan I have in mind . . . well, he shouldn't know about it. The three of us can talk it over, then depending on what you think, we can decide whether to involve him or not."

"I see," Mark said, looking at Corinne.

Gregory was asleep in her arms. "I'm about to crash," she said."I can't think about this. Let's turn in."

"So you have your towels. Is there anything else you need?" Ian asked.

"No, everything is wonderful. Thank you, Dr. Trevor."

"Ian." He smiled at her.

"Ian," she said, nodding.

~

Early the next morning Lawrence Carter picked up his phone in North Hollywood. "Carter here."

"Mr. Carter, it's Harley."

"Harley, what's going on? I've been waiting, man."

"They split. Must'a left last night after I dropped the pooch."

"Where'd they go?"

"I dunno. I was watching her car out front from a distance, in case the cops came, and the doc, girl, and kid must'a took off in his car out in back."

"What happened with the puppy? Were the police called?"

"No action there. I found it in a trash bag in the dumpster this morning. He might'a put it there just before I saw him walk up and down the block. Nobody else saw the pooch, far as I know."

"Doctors are used to dead bodies." Carter chuckled. "But it probably scared her and so they took off. Anyway, now they know we mean business."

"Yeah. Then this morning an older couple goes in her place with boxes and takes stuff. The man drives her car away."

"Who are *they*?"

"I guess her ol' man and ol' lady. Kind'a looked like her."

"So the question is, where did they go? My guess is they are over at her parents. She needed her car and stuff, so had the parents go back to get it. But, I suppose it's also possible they came down here. Harley, you watch her parents' house for a day or so. I have the doctor's address and I'll check it out."

"Okay."

"Harley, the Lord wants us to find them. That baby is absolutely the worst evil we've found yet. The media people are on to this too. Police could get involved. So play it very carefully. If you see anything out of the ordinary, let me know. This will put OCS on the map, my man. Call me tomorrow around nine or sooner if you spot something."

"Right, Mr. Carter."

"God bless you, Harley."

"God bless."

Mark slid out of bed as soon as he heard Gregory make noise. The baby had slept in the infant carrier in the corner of their room. Mark swept him up, grabbed the diaper bag and a bottle, and closed the door softly behind them, hoping Corinne would be able to sleep longer. The smell of coffee wafting through the house drew him to a sunlit room where Ian sat at a maple dinette table, leaning over the *LA Tribune*.

"Good morning, Mark and Gregory. How did you sleep?" Ian's smile was bright.

"Just excellent. That mattress is great. Gregory and I decided to let Cory test it out a little more."

"That's good. Moms can always use rest. Coffee?"

"That'd be super."

"Coming up. And what for Gregory?"

"I'll warm a bottle. Should keep him out of trouble for a while."

Ian and the baby stared at each other.

"Boy," Ian exclaimed, "are you a handsome kid with those big blue, almond-shaped eyes."

Gregory smiled and cooed at Ian.

"Yeah, he's a charmer."

Ian laughed. He shoved the paper across the table and stood up to get the coffee. "When you're ready, Mark, you'll want to read the front page story. It's by that Alice Masterson, carried by AP."

"Shit. That cannot be good."

Ian grimaced. "She certainly covered the waterfront."

Mark glanced at the front page and saw the same picture of Corinne and Gregory that had appeared in the *L.A. Voice*. The headline quickly drew his attention.

BABY'S STRANGE POWERS CONFIRMED
WAS THE MUTATION NATURAL OR ARTIFICIAL?

"Hell, what do they mean—artificial?" Mark asked, closing the microwave door and dialing the machine into operation.

Ian put an oversized mug of steaming coffee next to the newspaper. "Apparently some people—even a few scientists—doubt the mutation could have happened naturally. They speculate some kind of DNA manipulation took place at the university. Especially so, since you have been involved."

"What? That's preposterous!"

"Of course. Even Masterson says so, but she's reporting some public reactions she's received. You know how stupid people can be about genetic science."

Mark read the article with Gregory perched on his knee. The men laughed when Gregory put his finger on Corinne's face in the paper. But that was the only laughter. As Mark read further he grew morose. When he reached the end, he slowly sipped the coffee and stared out the window.

Ian said, "I wouldn't be surprised if that article gets picked up by every major newspaper served by AP, and most of the medium and small ones as well."

"Probably so," Mark said, still unfocused. "It's just amazing how fast this thing got out of control. The ingredients floated around slowly for a while, and then, out of the swirling mix, there was a big bang."

Ian nodded. "It's a blockbuster. And the media will be swarming."

Gregory was on his back, sucking the last of the milk. Mark awaited the exasperated cry and the bottle hitting the floor. But this time, Gregory sat up and pushed the empty bottle at Mark's hand. "Eh. Eh."

"Well, look at that. You want more?"

Gregory smiled and bobbed his head.

Mark refilled the bottle, and Gregory bounced up and down with happiness.

"He's beginning to communicate with purpose," Mark said.

"Clever little guy."

"Yeah, and we're worried about when he begins to communicate even more clearly."

Ian smiled.

Mark gave Gregory the warm refill and placed him on the carpet in the living room where he could be watched, then reheated his coffee in the microwave. "So what happened with Jared and the president?"

Ian twisted the blinds closed. "I don't want people to see in." He leaned back against the counter. "I'll give you the bottom line. The president told Jared in no uncertain terms that he wanted his cooperation. He wants Gregory to be studied at SSU, with the research overseen by a group of top university scientists that would include Jared and Fazzi. The president wants to meet with you and Corinne right away. He wants you to head an SSU genome team that would map and analyze Gregory's DNA—the mutational parts. He's talking in terms of as much laboratory space, equipment, and scientific help as you need. You would be a tenured full professor. He mentioned a full scholarship for Corinne to attend SSU. He said Gregory would be enrolled in the university preschool and later in the experimental elementary school, again on complete scholarship. The president thinks this will be best for Gregory and everyone concerned. That's the synopsis of what transpired over a several-hour meeting, according to Jared."

Mark stared at Ian, finding it hard to absorb the information.

"I say, pretty amazing, huh?" Ian said.

Mark shook his head slowly. "Best for SSU is right. Best for Gregory?" He swallowed. "To spend his life being tested in a medical center? To be watched constantly in an experimental school? I can't believe this. Something for everyone, with a price. It would be like . . . a cloister." He peered at Ian, trying to sense an inkling of attitude, some inflection of body language.

"What does Jared think?" Mark asked finally.

"Jared is terribly conflicted. He's exhausted, doesn't know what to think right now. He's concerned about the three of you, each for different reasons. I think he feels that at this point you and Corinne must decide what to do. He tried to call you at Corinne's last night, but of course, couldn't reach you. I told him I'd heard from you and that all of you were okay. He doesn't know that you came down here."

There was a distant thump, like a clod hitting the side of the house. Ian smiled and nodded. "That means that Corinne turned off the shower. My pipes are talkative. It's my signal to start breakfast." He began setting the table.

Mark grasped Ian's arm. "You said you had a plan. Is that it—to take up the president's offer?"

"Yes, I have something for you to consider. And no, it's very different from the president's plan. Why don't we discuss it when Corinne's here?"

Gregory began whimpering. Mark pulled him from under a chair in the living room, and following Ian's suggestion, took the baby upstairs to the "lookout" room and sat down on a soft, cream-colored leather couch. The two of them gazed at the ocean breakers, one body enervated, the other enthralled.

After some time Mark heard quiet footsteps coming up the stairs. Corinne emerged, head first, smiling. Her hair was clamped in a bun and she wore her olive jumpsuit and the Chinese slippers.

"Are my two guys hiding? Oh, what a beautiful view."

"We're staying out of Ian's hair." He pulled her down next to him. She hugged him and tried to kiss Gregory on the cheek. He laughed and pushed her face away

"Thanks for letting me sleep. I feel a lot better."

"After today you'll probably need more sleep."

"Why? What now?"

"Ian has today's L.A. Tribune. You'll want to see your picture and the screamer's, of course."

"Oh my god. Really?"

"Front page. By our friend Alice. Also, ask Ian to tell you what the university president told Jared. Our future is all set."

She looked dubious. "I'm going down there. Are you staying here?"

"Yeah. Call us when breakfast's ready."

The lingering aroma of her perfume added piquancy to his melancholy mood. He wondered if this was what romance in wartime was like. Sweet and sour. He nibbled Gregory's ear and evoked a halfhearted squeal. She had said her "guys." He liked being her guy. He liked the family feeling they had. But any semblance of normalcy for the three of them was gone now. The options were all but nil. He wondered if she would like Gregory attending a university preschool. Maybe she would be happy at SSU on scholarship. She might like taking classes from Ian. And for himself—could he stand doing molecular genetics again? Mapping Gregory's aberrant DNA of all things? Mark drew in a deep breath. He knew that it was her choice. She had the most to gain or lose. For her the stakes were high. So he should just butt out of any decision making. God, he felt lousy.

He pulled Gregory close. "What do *you* want, Gregory? Could you tolerate little wires in that noggin?"

Gregory stopped chewing on a rubber cowboy and bounced it off the plate glass window. He laughed and hugged Mark.

IAN SERVED SOURDOUGH PANCAKES with maple syrup, a fruit bowl of sliced cantaloupe, bananas, and strawberries, small glasses of guava juice, and coffee. Gregory sat on a chair with two giant dictionaries serving as a booster seat. He was loosely secured by one of Ian's cloth belts laced through the rungs of the chair back. Corinne fed him applesauce from a jar and slipped in occasional pancake pieces. The conversation, dwelling on the Kwakiutl and other cultures of the Pacific Northwest, was mostly between Ian and Corinne. As he listened, Mark thought the discussion amounted to avoidance—fiddling while the city burned. The world was reading and wondering about Gregory, that pretty mother, and the young renegade doctor. Mark kept telling himself to be patient. At one point Corinne asked him if he was feeling all right.

"I'm focusing on these superb pancakes and trying to learn something about potlatch, in case I might need to practice it."

Only when they had finished with second helpings did Ian bring up the unavoidable. "Cory, I think you and I could talk anthro for hours, but we need to talk about some pressing things."

Color faded from her face. "I know. It's just a treat to be able to talk with you."

"Likewise."

Ian recounted what Jared had told him of the president's offer. She asked a number of clarifying questions, then eventually turned silent. Mark leaned forward.

"Okay, we know the president's plan. What's yours, Ian?"

"Well, I see two basic choices. One is to face the music. In other words, meet with the media and be honest and open. This path begets lots of public attention and interference in your lives for a long time, whether at the university or elsewhere. This road completely changes your way of life. You become public figures. That's one path. If, however, you want to maintain privacy and try to live normally, you would have to disappear and become someone else. That is my plan."

"What do you mean?" Corinne asked, a worried look in her eyes.

"I mean hide out—change your names, become someone nobody knows."

"Me and Gregory?"

"And Mark."

She looked at Mark. "But how could we do that?"

Mark frowned. "How could it work, Ian?"

"I know a person who, I believe, would hide you. He lives in a remote area of the state. You would assume new identities and go there and stay with him."

"But wouldn't people recognize us? How would we survive?" Mark asked.

"It wouldn't be easy. You would have to live secluded, and sooner or later you would have to get a job and pull that off. None of your family or friends would know where you are, and you couldn't stay in touch with them, except by mail coming through me. In your new lives, nobody would know who you really are, not even my friend. If you want to try it, I'll go into the details. We would need to move fast."

Mark and Corinne looked at each other.

Mark took her hand. "I would do it if you want to. It's your choice."

"But what do *you* want?" she asked.

"I want what *you* want."

Corinne stared at Mark, her eyes glistening. She looked back at Ian. Then she quickly excused herself to visit the bathroom. When she returned after quite some time her eyes were red.

Corinne spoke deliberately. "I know that if we go on as we are, even at the university, it will be miserable. We'd be hounded. My life would be worse than Lady Di's. And poor Gregory. Mothers would be afraid to let their kids play with him. He could never be a normal kid. I couldn't stand worrying about slimeballs like Lawrence Carter slinking around, knowing where we live. There would have to be bodyguards. And . . . and the experiments on Gregory"—she held in a sob—"I want to try your plan, Ian."

Mark rubbed her neck, amazed at her decision, proud of her resolve.

Gregory yawned and slumped into sleep. The adults smiled and automatically lowered their voices.

"Okay, good," Ian said. "Let's talk about details."

"What does Jared think?" Mark asked.

"Jared doesn't know about this plan. Like everyone else, he'll be surprised when you've disappeared. He'll probably realize I had something to do with it, but for his own sake, I won't acknowledge anything. He'll be under intense suspicion at the university and in the scientific community. He will have to say with complete honesty that he doesn't know where you are and that he had nothing to do with your leaving."

Mark and Corinne both nodded.

"Okay, then," Corinne said, "what do we do now?"

AN HOUR LATER, driving Ian's Isuzu Trooper and wearing his broad-brimmed boat hat and dark glasses, Mark pulled into a parking lot on Santa Monica Boulevard, roughly one mile south of his house. After getting the maximum amount of cash possible from a nearby ATM, he settled back into the driver's seat. He picked up his cell phone and dialed his landlady's number.

She was surprised. "Mark! Where are you? Your parents are here and there are all these newspeople waiting around. Trucks with antennas and stuff. I've never seen anything like it."

"Shirley, I'm sorry for all this. It's a long story."

"I know. I read the paper."

"Could you please do me a favor? Go tell my parents I'm going to call them on my home phone. Be sure nobody else will pick it up. And don't tell anyone that I've called."

"Of course."

"Whatever happens, Shirley, my dad and mom can speak for me. They have my authority. Okay?"

"Sure, Mark."

Mark leaned back against the headrest and closed his eyes. This was going to be hard. They didn't deserve it. But there was no other way.

"Hello, Mark?"

"Hi, Dad. It's good to hear your voice."

"It's good to talk to you, Son. Are you all right?"

"A little stunned, but fine."

"We're both on the line, honey." His mother's voice was tremulous.

"Hi, Mom. I'm sorry for all this mess."

"You don't have to apologize. When will you get here?"

"I can't join you because of all the media."

"Oh, no!" she said.

"Mom, please just let me talk. I don't have much time."

"That's fine, Son," his dad said. "We're listening."

Mark gave a terse report of events since his return from Mott Lake. He did not mention Ian, saying only that they had stayed the night at a friend's. He then said he and Corinne had decided to disappear for a while and they would be out of touch with everyone. It could possibly be for a long time. Mark heard his mother begin crying.

"Then what they are saying about the baby is true?" his father asked.

"Dad, I hope you understand, but I'm not going to answer that. Okay?"

"Fine."

"Listen, Dad, I need the pink slip to my car. It's in my file cabinet in the second bedroom, under Saab."

"Why?"

"Could you just do me a favor and see if you can find it?"

"Sure. Talk to your mother."

"Mark, Rachel's here," his mother said.

"She is? How did—"

"She heard about the baby at the NPA meeting and decided to come down with us. We rented a car and drove together."

"Huh."

"I have the pink slip in my hand," his father said.

"Good. Now, is it possible for someone to sneak away and bring it to me? I'm about a mile from you."

"I don't see how," his father said. "There are more than thirty news people outside with trucks and cars. They have our rental car blocked. If we go out, they start yelling questions."

"Maybe Shirley could bring it to me. Could you get it to her?"

"Yeah, maybe. I've got an idea. We'll get the pink slip to you, don't worry. So tell me where you want her to go."

Mark gave directions, then drew a deep breath. "Dad and Mom, I don't know exactly when I'll see you again, but I want you to know that I love you both very much. I appreciate all the help you've given me."

There was more crying. "I love you too, Mark," his mother managed to get out. "Please be careful."

His father cleared his throat. "Good luck, Son. You know you can always count on us. I'll send some cash along with the pink slip."

"And Dad, if you don't hear from me in a month, just cancel my lease and take all my stuff out. Shirley will understand."

"If that's needed, I'll take care of it. I hope that's not needed."

"Thanks, Dad. Bye."

WHEN MAX AND NAOMI Sandler stepped out on the porch, the throng came to life. The couple was quickly surrounded by reporters, microphones, and huge video cameras.

"Mr. Sandler, do you know where your son is?" one of the reporters immediately shouted. "What do you know about Gregory?" yelled another.

Max held up his arms. "Listen, we will talk to you but you have to stop shouting. Let's be orderly. I'll make a short statement and then we'll answer some questions one by one."

The crowd quieted. Stand-up microphones and a speaker system appeared. A semicircle formed. Rachel came out and quickly squeezed through the side of the gathering, heading away. One reporter ran after her.

"Who are you and where are you going?" he asked, getting ahead of her.

"I'm just a family friend and I'm making a food run. We're starved. I'll be back soon. You'd better get back there because they're making an important statement."

"But what's your name?"

"Rachel Applebaum."

The man wrote it down, waved, and went back to the group.

The gaggle pressed ever closer around Max and Naomi. Max clenched his teeth. Naomi's hand slipped into his. He took a deep breath and cleared his throat.

"For you who do not know, we are Martin Sandler's parents. We are here on vacation—we just arrived today—and we were supposed to meet Mark here. But the sudden media events surrounding him, Mrs. Shenko, and her baby, have precluded a normal private time with our son. We regret that we will not be able to see him. We don't have the kind of information that you probably want. We know that our son has provided pediatric care for Mrs. Shenko and her baby at SSU. We don't know any more about the baby than what has been reported in the media. So that's about all we can tell you. We're willing to answer a few questions."

Arms shot up and questions were shouted. One man in front was dominant. "Mr. Sandler, do you know where your son is? And are the three of them together?"

Max waved his arms for silence. "We do not know where they are. We had a call from him earlier and he said they were fine, and they are all together, yes, but he would not say where they were."

"Mrs. Sandler," a woman reporter yelled, "there are reports that your son and Corinne Shenko are romantically linked, that he stays with her at her Fresno apartment. Is this true?"

Naomi came close to the microphone. "I have no idea about that. If you find out something, I'm his mother and I would like to know." There was laughter.

"Mr. Sandler, are they hiding out? Are they afraid to meet with the media?"

Max smiled and hesitated a moment. "I don't know if they're hiding. But let's face it, you guys are pretty intimidating. Anybody in your spotlight loses all privacy. Most normal people don't want the stress of that spotlight, right?" The crowed chuckled.

"Did your son have anything to do with causing Gregory's mutations?"

"Absolutely not. That I *can* say. I'm a pharmaceutical scientist, so I know that bringing about mutations of the kind alleged—if indeed there is any credence to the reports, which I seriously doubt—is just impossible with our current state of science. Further, my son is adamantly opposed to any kind of genetic engineering."

"Are you against the Human Genome Project like he is?"

"No. He and I differ on that. But I respect . . . I do respect his position. That's it. Thank you."

Max and Naomi retreated into the house and locked the door amid further shouting. Soon after about half of the crowd left, including Lawrence Carter.

LOOKING WEST THROUGH the passenger's window, Mark observed a coastal fog bank rising in the distance. It resembled the tumbling top of a giant wave breaking in slow motion. He knew that Corinne and Gregory, and all the others engulfed by the fog, were experiencing increased humidity, reduced visibility, and temperatures ten to twenty degrees lower than people still in the sun. As the creeping cloud approached, he smiled. It struck him as a meteorological manifestation of Ian's plan to damp down the hot, buzzing media.

He saw Shirley's car pull into the parking lot and nose into a stall. After assuring himself that no suspicious cars had followed her, Mark traversed the hundred-foot distance between the vehicles and came up to the passenger side. The window rolled down and he found himself staring at Rachel.

"Mark, is that you?" she said, removing her sunglasses.

"Rachel! Yeah, it's me." He glanced at the driver. "Hello, Shirley. Thanks for breaking out of the zoo."

Shirley laughed. "You're very smart to avoid them. I haven't seen anything that crazy since the O.J. and Nicole mess down on Gretna Green."

"The media are something," Mark said, looking at Rachel.

Rachel squinted, trying to avoid the sun's rays coming from behind Mark.

"Were you able to get the pink slip?" he asked.

Rachel nodded. "Here. Also some cash from your dad." She put the DMV document and a wad of bills into his hand. Her dark red fingernails brushed his palm and an erotic ping transduced through his nerves. He looked into her eyes and thought he saw a longing. Maybe he saw what he wanted to see.

"Thanks."

"Sure."

There were so many thoughts. None seemed appropriate. Should he just go? No, he couldn't leave her without acknowledging something.

"Rachel, would you come over to my car so we can talk? Shirley, do you mind waiting for a few minutes?"

"Not at all. Take your time."

They walked together to the Trooper without exchanging words. Her low heels echoed on the pavement. As he held the door open for her, he noticed how lithe and attractive she was in black stretch pants and a flowery short-sleeve blouse that hugged her shapely shoulders.

He got in and removed his hat and sunglasses. "You know, this is all so unreal."

She nodded nervously. "Yeah."

"I didn't expect to see you."

She nodded. "I didn't expect to come down here. That NPA announcement changed things for everyone, I guess."

He glanced at her, but she looked only forward.

"So how do you think my parents are handling this?"

"Fairly well. We talked a lot about it on the drive down. They are rallying."

Mark nodded. "Good."

He looked at the grill of the BMW facing the Trooper and remembered his strongest impression upon arriving in west Los Angeles. All of the cars were clean, and every other one was a BMW or Mercedes.

"Mark, I want to tell you two things."

Their eyes met and he saw that old confidence he knew so well.

"I appreciate the incredible stress you must be under. And I admire your commitment to help this child and his mother. You are . . . brave." She smiled weakly.

"Thank you." He had an impulse to take her hand, but for some reason his hand stayed frozen on his thigh.

She looked away again, and from her profile he saw a layer of moisture filling her eyes.

"The second thing is that I know you feel guilty about what happened between us," she said. "I want to say that you needn't feel guilty because I was just as contributory as you. In some ways our breakup . . . was a good thing. Because I've had to look at myself. As a result I'm growing and making changes." She wet her lips with her tongue. "At any rate, for any hurt you did to me and still feel bad about, I forgive you. So just tuck that away. I forgive you."

Now Mark had tears. They seeped out of the corners of his eyes and ran down his cheeks. He coughed and rubbed at the wetness. She took his hand.

"Rachel, you're" —he looked up as if seeking help from on high— "you're truly a fine person. A real mensch. And I just didn't appreciate that when—"

She tightened her hand on his. "Stop. Please don't say those things or you'll make me feel bad. I know you have to go. Let's just stop here." She pulled her hand away and opened her door part way.

"So that's it?" he asked.

"Well, you can do me one favor, if you want to."

"What?"

"Come around the car and give me a hug."

He laughed and so did she.

"Sure."

As they stood facing each other in the bright sunlight, he tentatively put his arms around her waist. She pressed in close and put her face against his neck. He smelled once again the sweet scent of her hair and felt the familiar softness of her breasts. His hardness rose quickly.

He took a deep breath. "Rachel, I have to tell you . . . that I'm involved with Corinne Shenko. I'm likely to stay involved with her for a long time. You need to understand that. So, you should find someone. Get married, have kids, and be happy."

"I know," she whispered. "Just hug me."

She was now leaning back against the car, pulling him against her. As he became harder, she squeezed tighter and moved her hips ever so slightly against him. Slowly they felt themselves slipping toward uncontrolled desire.

"Oh, Rachel."

"Mmmh. Mark, let's just never forget what we had," she whispered.

"I could never forget."

She released him slowly and kissed his lips gently. "Thanks for the great hug. Good luck, Mark." She smiled, turned and walked quickly to Shirley's car, where she looked back and waved before getting in.

Mark sat in the Trooper for several minutes, head in his hands. Finally he turned the key in the ignition. He found an opening in the traffic and gunned into the westerly lane. Within three blocks he entered the fog. At Ian's house he found Corinne in the kitchen using hydrogen peroxide on her hair and eyebrows. Her beautiful red tresses lay on the kitchen floor.

He handed Ian the car keys. "How long do you think we'll be gone to get the car downtown?"

"I would guess about three hours. I know this Mexican area where you can pay cash for cars. I think we can get a decent van for about two grand."

"You have that kind of cash?"

"I keep money in a safe."

"Ian, I can write you a check."

"No sir. I'm paying for this plus giving you cash. Like I said, I'll be able to unload your car in a month or two down near Tijuana and get a lot more than that. Don't worry about it. There's more important stuff to worry about. One is that we need to buy a better car seat for the little guy."

On the drive downtown both men were silently absorbed for a long while. Finally, Ian cleared his throat.

"Mark, I was looking at Gregory. He really looks different from other babies. The large head, those huge eyes and hefty eyebrow ridges. He's strongly dolicho-cephalic, as my bone colleagues would say. Have you noticed that?"

Mark yawned. "What is that?"

"A long head. I'm not a physical anthropologist, but I've seen a lot of skulls. He looks, well, he seems to have an almost ancient aspect to his head."

"Really? I don't know. He doesn't look different to me. "

"Before you and Corinne leave, I'd like to take pictures of Gregory. Do you think that would be all right with Corinne?"

"Ian, my guess is that anything you do is all right with her. But you probably shouldn't call Gregory a Neanderthal."

Ian laughed.

Mark leaned back against the headrest and closed his eyes.

Chapter Sixteen

NEVADA COUNTY, CALIFORNIA is gold rush country—a section of the Sierra Nevada at the northern end of the Mother Lode. The county's two predominant cities, Nevada City and Grass Valley, nestle close together at 2,500 feet in oak, fir and pine forested hills on the western slope. Farther west is the fertile Sacramento Valley.

Nevada City, the county seat, is a Victorian symbol of its bright days both as a prospecting settlement and a cultural center of early California. Established in 1850, Nevada City at one time was the state's third most populous city. The population declined as the gold seekers found it was not so easy to get rich. But the little city has survived in much the way it was in the 1800s despite a recent influx of population and high technology industry in and around it. Today, tourists and a small population of city dwellers enjoy the picturesque old shops, churches, museums, playhouses and other monuments to an exalted era.

About twenty miles north of Nevada City on Highway 49 is the tiny community of North San Juan. Historically, it was the principal center for a series of villages and mining camps situated at intervals along the San Juan Ridge. Today, the town of about 250 people consists of buildings on either side of the highway, and houses on a few nearby streets. Increasing settlement has taken place in recent decades at scattered locations on the ridge east of the town, a rural area best known for the brown, red, and yellow "moonscape" valleys originally formed by the hydraulic mining that took place in the 1860's.

North San Juan was their destination. Ian had packed the customized, 1996 Plymouth Voyager for them that evening, and they left in darkness, making one stop in Brentwood before pulling onto the San Diego freeway. The stop was a

Starbucks where Mark logged onto the SSU computer one last time to send two email messages. The first was to Alice Masterson:

> Alice, I want you to know that our worst fears happened. Lawrence Carter accosted Cory and Gregory in front of her apartment yesterday and threatened harm to the baby. Everyone's okay, but we'll not be in touch for a while. Mark.

The second was to Jared:

> Hi, Jared. I'm sorry I haven't been able to talk to you. The hike was good. But yesterday, that religious zealot, Lawrence Carter, accosted Corinne and the baby in front of her apartment, threatening harm to Gregory. We're all okay, but we've decided to lay low for a while, avoiding OCS and the media. I don't know where we'll stay, or if and when I'll be able to talk to you. I hope you aren't too upset that we've disappeared. Good luck. Thanks for everything. Mark.

With the messages going through the university's computer system, Mark knew that sooner or later copies would end up on the desk of the university president. Mark hoped this might relieve some of the pressure on Jared. The president would know that Jared had nothing to do with the baby's disappearance.

Mark glanced at Corinne in the parking lot light before they headed out. He saw a punk rocker, her blond hair short and spiky, and her face dominated by rosy cheeks with sharp accents of eye shadow, mascara, and a dark-colored lipstick.

"Do you think I'm sexy?" she asked.

Mark laughed. "Yeah. I feel like I picked up somebody."

"My parents will freak."

Mark drove nonstop, heading north—first on I-5 and then Highway 99—always within the speed limit. He finally eased into a tree-secluded parking area behind an office building on Cedar Avenue in northeast Fresno, not far from Dr. Kalakian's office. Mark's watch indicated it was a few minutes before midnight. There, waiting in a nearby car, were Corinne's parents who had brought money and a cooler of food. After nearly two hours of conversation in the curtained van, the couples parted tearfully. Mark then drove north again until he found a dirt road into a fig orchard on the outskirts of the city. They locked up, crawled into the bed in the back, and slept until the sun woke them.

Under a fig tree, wiping sleep from their eyes, they gave Gregory cold milk and pieces of hardboiled eggs and muffins. As they looked down the rows of the leafy, squat trees, they realized that at this unlikely spot, they would leave their old identities. Corinne smiled, not quite ready for the transformation.

"What?" Mark asked.

"I think my dad liked you. Mom obviously did."

He smiled. "They were great. It went much better than I thought. The way they sneaked through the back gate to borrow the neighbor's car. Clever."

"Yeah, and my dad's mood was surprising. He's enjoying playing with the press. Telling that New York Times reporter that if Gregory causes seizures, he should be sent to Congress. Can you imagine?"

They laughed and bantered, and watched Gregory futilely try to grab an ant running across the blanket. After a while Mark looked at Corinne and raised his eyebrows. She nodded, then placed her dark glasses on her narrow nose and tied a small scarf around her neck. She was anyone but Corinne Shenko. Mark put on Ian's boat hat and sunglasses and cinched the large leather belt one notch on his patched Levi's. He might be a farmhand from Modesto.

"Let's do it, babe."

"Okay, dude."

They took Highway 41 to Oakhurst where they gassed up. Whenever they went into service stations or through towns, one of them held Gregory in the back of the van with the curtains drawn. Taking turns at the wheel, they wound northerly along the Sierra foothills on Highway 49, passing through the old mining towns of the Mother Lode—Sonora, Angels Camp, Mokelumne Hill, Placerville, Auburn.

When they reached Nevada City late that afternoon, Mark picked up a cold beer and soft drink at a market, and they found a secluded park-like area off the road at the edge of town. They drank and downed sandwiches from the cooler. With nobody around, they allowed a cranky Gregory to play on a blanket. When he tired of that, they pushed on. Continuing west and north on 49, they crossed the narrow concrete bridge high over the south fork of the Yuba River. After a few more miles they came to North San Juan. There Mark adjusted his hat low over his sunglasses and walked into a small hardware and variety store. A pot-bellied man stood near the cash register.

"Yessir, what can we do for you today?" he asked.

"I want some Kleenex," Mark said with a slight Texas drawl.

"Sure thing. Right over there on the shelf."

Mark grabbed a small box and stepped up to pay.

"By the way," Mark said, "do you know of a guy around here called Colliver?"

"Colliver? Hmm, nope. Never heard of him. Does he live in North San Juan?"

"I heard he did."

"I've been here twenty years and I know everyone in town. Nobody here by that name. How long is he supposed to have been here?"

"Don't know," Mark said. "A few years, I guess."

"Well, maybe he's somewhere up on the ridge. There's been more and more people settling up there and most of 'em I don't know. You could go up to the little store on the corner of Tyler Foote and Oak Tree and ask some of them hippies. Maybe they'd know of him."

They drove east on Oak Tree Road, climbing in altitude and passing occasional wooden frame houses amid the hills. The small corner store had a sign reading, *Mother Trucker*. Mark parked in the dirt between a pickup and an old, dented VW bug. Inside, a twentyish man with a blond ponytail smiled from behind the check-out counter. A young woman in dirty overalls was picking fruit from a bin. A balding man with a full beard stood near the front, drinking a bottle of red liquid with an unusual label. Mark stopped in the main aisle and looked around awkwardly.

"Help you, mister?" Ponytail said.

"Looking for a guy by name of Colliver. William Colliver."

"Colliver? Who could that be, Mortie?" Ponytail directed the query to the bearded man.

"It's Bill—the philosopher."

"Oh yeah, sure. I'm not used to hearing his full name. So you want to talk about right thinking with the philosopher?"

"Uh . . . I'd like to find him," Mark said. "Can you tell me how to get to his place?"

"For sure," Ponytail said.

THE VAN'S ODOMETER did not work so Mark and Corinne constantly watched for the pine tree root looping out from the bank and back, as the young man had said. In about ten miles, the tree and root appeared. Two rust-spotted mail boxes stood on one post next to the entrance to a dirt road. One had the faded name of Colliver on it.

Powdery dust rose in a thick cloud behind them as they negotiated the curvy, rutted road. Manzanita bushes covered the hillsides in between stands of pine and isolated oaks. After a short while they came to a fork. A wooden sign pointed to the right for somebody named Korsen. Underneath it another said, *PRIVATE ROAD HERE ON*. Continuing to the left, they found themselves dropping in elevation. After about two miles, they came to a wooden gate. Across the top plank was written: *PRIVATE PROPERTY - NO TRESPASSING*. Mark got out and looked around. Finding no lock on the gate, he unlatched it, swung it wide, and closed it after moving the van ahead.

"Mark, I'm a little scared," Corinne said as he got back in.

"Come on, now. There's no turning back. Remember, I'm Mike, you're Susan, and Gregory's Bret. Our last name is Harris. I'm a programmer and you're a secretary. Don't use the old names again."

She tried to smile. "Okay, Mike."

"That's an okay, Susan." He grinned.

After quite a while they came to a bluff and crawled in low gear down three long switchbacks to a narrow valley, noticeably greener than the environment they had passed. The road stopped in a grove of tall pines where an old log cabin stood. A massive stone fireplace anchored one end of the two-story structure. Next to the cabin four vertical logs supported a shingled lean-to that provided cover for a battered green jeepster and a stacked pile of firewood. In front and to the right of the cabin was an open area where logs and wooden chairs circled a firepit. A hammock was stretched between two trees nearby. Behind the cabin in a sunny area, clothes hung from a line between two fledgling firs. A few yards beyond, a little creek bubbled down a narrow rock-strewn bed. The low sun cast long shadows on the bucolic scene.

As the van's engine chugged off, the planked door of the cabin opened and a large gray dog, wolf-like in appearance, bounded out and took an alert but silent position about fifteen yards from the newcomers. A tall man dressed only in cut-off jeans sauntered out. His skin was tanned, highlighting the hardened muscles of his arms, legs, and chest. He had medium length hair and a thick brownish-gray beard. He crossed his arms and walked slowly to the driver's side of the van. At close range his skin suggested a body early in its fourth decade.

"My god," Mark said softly to Corinne. "It's the guy I met on the trail."

"And who might you be?" the man said as Mark got out.

"My name is Mike Harris. Are you William Colliver?"

"I am." Colliver squinted. "You look familiar."

"Uh, I think we met on a trail up above Florence Lake last week."

"Huukk." It was a loud, sucking snort. "The guy from L.A. Wanted time to think."

Mark nodded.

"So am I supposed to know you, other than that?"

"No, you don't know me. This is my wife, Susan." Mark pointed as she came around to join them, carrying Gregory.

"Hello," Corinne said.

Colliver nodded at her, then said to Mark, "How do you know my name?"

"Dr. Ian Trevor said I should try and find you."

For the first time Colliver's stern expression changed. "Ian Trevor . . . for god's sake. I haven't seen him in years. How the hell did he know where I was?"

Mark felt the wolf-dog nuzzling his hand and cautiously petted the animal.

"He didn't for sure, but someone told him you were up near Nevada City in a place with a Spanish name. I asked for you at North San Juan and they sent me to the Mother Trucker store. A fellow there told me where you were."

"Amazing," Colliver said, shaking his head. "That just shows a body can't get lost even if he tries. How do you know Ian?"

"He lives in Venice, and we met through a friend. I found out he was a college prof and we hit it off."

"Oh yeah, anthropology. I haven't seen Ian since his days as a beginning professor at SF State. I took every anthro course he taught. We'd go beer drinking . . . it was a great time." Colliver broke into a grin, the chipped tooth noticeable. Then he laughed, as if remembering some savored moment. Mark and Corinne smiled.

"And that's your kid?"

"Yes, this is Bret. He's nine months old," Corinne said.

"Good looking baby," Colliver said.

"We like him," she said.

Colliver smiled. "So you just stopped by to say hello and remember Ian to me, did you?"

"A little more than that," Mark said. "We need your help."

"How's that?"

"We're tired of the city and we want to make a new life. Ian said you would help us."

Colliver made a face. "Goddamn. All you people from L.A. I can understand your wanting to get away from that smogged-up abomination, but we just can't handle any more up here. You take our water, but that isn't enough, you have to come up here to live, drive up land prices, bring developers, and mess us up, too." His steely eyes were angry and unfocused.

Mark said nothing.

"Ian said we would learn a lot from you," Corinne offered.

"I'm sure you would," Colliver said loudly. He stared at her for a moment, then his face relaxed and he rubbed his hairy cheek. "Do you need work?"

"Not right away," Mark said.

"You have money then."

"Yes, some."

Colliver patted the wolf-dog's flank. "So you're looking for a place to stay."

"Right."

"Willing to rough it?"

"What do you mean?" Corinne asked.

"I'll show you exactly what I mean. Follow me. C'mon Arnie. Let's find out how serious these city dudes are."

Mark took Gregory and, with Corinne trailing, they followed Colliver and Arnie down a wide path roughly parallel to the stream. It was quiet except for the sound of the creek, their footsteps, and the birds chirping. After they traipsed about a hundred yards Mark spotted a small log cabin on the bank under tall sugar pines. The door and windows were shuttered. The bark on the logs was long gone, revealing worm holes in many places. The chinking material looked solid, however, and a shake roof appeared recent. There was a stone fireplace similar to, but smaller and more primitive than the one on Colliver's cabin. A pile of matted pine needles along the footing and up against the door suggested nobody had entered the cabin in quite some time.

Colliver leaned against a tree trunk as Mark and Corinne caught up. He let them have a good look before he spoke.

"It's small but cozy. You're welcome to live here for a while."

Mark and Corinne looked at each other questioningly. Gregory watched Colliver, apparently fascinated by the beard.

"It's in better shape than it looks," Colliver said. "A good friend fixed it up about four years ago. Repaired a lot of the chinking, put on a new roof, installed a septic tank, put in a toilet and sink, and a nice little cook stove."

"A gas stove?" Mark asked.

Colliver smiled. "Wood. There is no gas or electricity here. No radio, TV, telephones, cell phones, satellite dishes, or computers. None of that junk. And no goddamn people littering and fuckin' around. Just nature—fresh, clean, and sweet."

Mark smiled and looked at Corinne.

"How do you heat it?" Mark asked.

"Woodstove. There's plenty of wood to be had."

"What about lights?" Mark asked.

"Kerosene lanterns. But you don't need them much. You go to bed when it gets dark."

"Is there hot water?" Corinne asked. "And how do you keep food refrigerated?"

"Sure. You heat it on the stove. As to keeping food cold, you store it in the creek."

"But what about a hot shower?" she asked.

"There is no shower. You bathe in the creek as long as you don't get soap in it. Or, you can come shower at my place. My stove has coils and I can get hot water enough for a shower. But you don't need showers much." Colliver grinned.

Corinne looked at him skeptically.

"The place is perfect for you," Colliver said. "It has a double bed up in the sleeping loft and a bunk downstairs."

"Where is your friend who fixed it up?" Mark asked.

"Don't know. I've kind'a been waiting for him to show up, but now I have my doubts. I just hope he's still alive. He's one of the few good Wittgenstein scholars there are."

"What kind?" Corinne asked.

"Wittgenstein. He was a philosopher—a brilliant logical positivist—one of the Vienna Circle boys."

"Oh," she said.

"This cabin is older than mine, but in some ways it's better made. It's warmer in the winter. Built in the late 1800s . . . probably by some coyote."

"Coyote?" Mark said.

Colliver smiled. "During the gold mining days these mountains were crawling with prospectors. Many of them just dug without registering claims. They called these coyote mines. Gold fever is still alive up here. People come digging or sluicing now and then. But the coyote spirit means something else now. It has to do with right life on the land."

A blue jay flitted to a branch above Arnie, cocked its head a few times, then flew in a straight trajectory to a large bush fifty feet away. Gregory laughed and waved his arms.

"I think he likes it here," Colliver said. "It's a good place for kids."

"But there wouldn't be anybody for him to play with," she said.

"He could play with the squirrels. The deer would be his friends. They're more trustworthy anyway." Colliver winked at her. "So do you folks want it or not? If you do, we can move my friend's stuff out."

"How much?" Mark asked.

Colliver guffawed. "Just like an L.A. guy." He looked Mark in the eye and said, "The price is this—that you read the books and articles I give you and have intellectual discussions with me at least twice a month. Both of you."

"That's all?" Mark looked at Corinne.

"Oh, and you chop two cords of stove wood, one for me and one for you, before winter sets in."

Mark grinned. "It's a deal."

Colliver nodded thoughtfully. "Good. Now let's go have some wine and get acquainted. We'll get you settled in the cabin later. Park your tin-crap vehicle back in here behind the trees. I don't want to see it. One good snow and you'll not be using it. During the worst of it, even my four wheel with chains isn't worth shit. I'm making a food run to Nevada City tomorrow and I'll get you stocked up for a couple of weeks. By then, you might decide to head back to LaLa Land . . . which is just fine with me." Colliver shook his head. "God, I don't know how Ian can stand it."

AS THE NEW FAMILY settled in on San Juan Ridge, they had no inkling of the cacophony of stupid conjecture, solid reporting, misinformation, charges, and countercharges occurring in the media about them. National and foreign news teams swarmed in Los Angeles, Fresno, Porterville, Sacramento, Pittsburgh, Boston—wherever they could find people who had knowledge about the "mutant" baby or his care-takers. Everyone wondered how the easily recognizable couple and infant could disappear without a trace. The "sightings" from nearly every area of the country that inevitably followed all turned out to be wrong.

The story caught the fancy of every imaginable segment of the public. Gregory, Corinne, and Mark, along with their relatives, were the sudden topic of newspaper and magazine articles, radio talk shows, news programs, and TV specials. Rose Shenko said her grandson was nobody to worry about. Ray Cameron, Lou Fazzi, Jaime Valenzuela, and Leonard Lesser explained about the lesion. Leading neuro-scientists were asked if the baby's alleged powers could conceivably be true. Most, but not all, said no. Corinne's parents did not know where their daughter and grandson were, but they weren't worried. Mark's parents said that nobody should try to find their son because they didn't consider him a missing person. There was a massive national audience watching when the highly credible Alice Masterson and Sylvia Auerbach appeared jointly on a TV program. Many of the questions dealt with what it was like to experience the X and Y powers.

Four sought-after people who refused to be interviewed, however, were Zenya Shenko, Lawrence Carter, Rachel Applebaum, and Jared Weymouth. Lawrence Carter issued a statement denying that he ever threatened Corinne Shenko as Alice Masterson alleged. His news release averred that Onward Christian Soldiers was not a violent group. Jared made a statement that he would give a press con-ference at the university in about six weeks, but he would have nothing to say before then.

Formal reactions to the stories and interviews emerged haphazardly. One of the first statements came from the popular Reverend John Tugswell of the Church of the Airwaves. In a nationwide TV sermon he stated that ". . . if there is a child with such powers, he could not be the work of God; he could only be the work of Satan. This child should be sequestered." This theme was picked up by other fundamentalist church ministers. One even called for Gregory to be "mercifully sacrificed." Most leaders of organized religions kept silent or said that more information was needed before leaping to conclusions.

The president of the National Association for Women's Rights stated: "The reported sex power of Gregory Shenko does not augur well for women. If the report is true, it is something to be condemned by all women." One well-respected feminist said that the critical comments were inappropriate and that women needed to support Corinne Shenko who had a medically handicapped child on her hands. Political figures, by and large, were hesitant to comment, no doubt wanting to know more of their constituents' opinions.

The predominant public reaction was one of curiosity, titillation, and disbelief. Many women and teenage girls thought that the handsome Doctor Mark and the beautiful Corinne should get married. People enjoyed the salt-of-the-earth folksiness of Rose Shenko talking about her son Nick as "a good boy and a bad boy rolled up in one, like most boys." Middle-aged and elderly women enjoyed Corinne's mother telling how she threw water on her grandbaby to "stop those stupid little tantrums." Many men identified with Corinne's father who said, "It's all a tempest in a teapot. I'm going huntin' on the good days and spending the crummy weekends with beer and the 49'ers." Yet almost everyone was on the watch for an attractive redheaded young woman with a baby accompanied by a tall curly-haired man with wire frame glasses.

At the end of the fourth week, when no solid clues on the whereabouts of G-C-M surfaced, Alice Masterson announced that she would establish a website to coordinate information. The URL designation was www.whereisgregory.com.

IN THE FALL MONTHS North San Juan Ridge turns cool. The weather remains mostly sunny, but a few rainstorms drive in from the west, and deciduous trees and bushes start losing their leaves. During those months Mark and Corinne prepared for the winter. They had taken all of Colliver's friend's belongings out of the cabin except for a few books and a guitar. Corinne made the house as comfortable and useable as possible. She gave Mark lists of things to get on his occasional treks with Colliver to Nevada City—food, clothing, bedding, pots and utensils, soaps and cleaners, toiletries, towels, kerosene, ice, paper and pens, and toys and a back carrier for Gregory.

Corinne and the baby did not leave the compound that fall. When Mark ventured into town, he wore sunglasses and a hat. He let his beard grow. On Mark's first trip into town he brought back a *Time* magazine that carried an article about them, complete with photographs. They hid the periodical for fear that Colliver, who happened in daily, might see it.

Mark chopped wood every day. Using a dilapidated wheelbarrow, he hauled more than two cords from the site of a downed fir three-quarters of a mile away. He stacked half of it under a tree next to their small cabin, covering the wood with a waterproof tarp, and the other half in Colliver's shelter. Two weeks into this project, Colliver joined them one day for lunch, bringing some late season melon. They ate together sitting on a log that Mark had dragged to a sunny spot near the small cabin.

"Mike and Susan," Colliver said as he finished a peanut butter sandwich Corinne had made. "I think you're working too hard. There's plenty of time to get the wood chopped. I have some stuff I want you to read. Take time off over the next few days and lay out in the sun and read it."

Mark laughed. "Oh, this is part of the rent?"

"Yeah, you might call this the first installment." Colliver chuckled and handed Mark some stapled papers and a small cloth-covered book.

"Do we have to take a test on it?" Corinne asked.

"As a matter of fact, there will be an exam. Not the usual kind, but a good kind. We'll put Bret in that back pack, make a lunch, and go for a hike. I want to show you the land."

"That does sound like fun," Corinne agreed.

"We need you to begin establishing a bond to your environment—to exorcise the invader mentality that our culture puts into our heads." Colliver winked and pushed out his tongue slightly.

"Invader?" Mark said.

"Yeah, the idea that you can bulldoze rocks and trees, or lay waste to the countryside with hydraulic water streams, or kill off all the wolves. It's the idea of pillage and rape that man has carried down through the ages. When you don't live in an area and you come in with powerful tools, strange attitudes occur. A friend of mine calls it the invader mentality."

Mark frowned and nodded. He looked at the materials Colliver had brought.

"Susan," Colliver continued, "since you like anthropology, you might like the article on the Maidu people who inhabited this area before European settlers took it from them. On our hike I'll show you a large rock with round holes where they ground their acorns."

"That would be interesting," she said.

"There's also an article on the flora and fauna of the ridge. It was written by a gal who lives a few miles from here. On our hike we'll identify yellow pines, swordfern, lupin, incense cedar, California buttercup, blackberry and all sorts of things. Maybe we can spot some of our neighbor animals, too."

"What's this book about early California?" Mark asked.

"That's an account of what this country was like before the gold rush. It de-scribes the San Joaquin Valley, its great tule marshes, and teeming wildlife—things few people now know about. There were herds of antelope, elk, black-tailed deer, wild horses and grizzly bear, Bighorn sheep, wolves, giant condors, all kinds of waterfowl, geese by the millions, duck, quail, and eagles. Also, you could find otter, mink, and wolverines in the mountains. California was truly a wildlife paradise until white men came in and killed off most of the animals and birds in the 1800's. I'd like you to read that book."

"Okay," Mark said.

"Some day all those species should be brought back," Colliver said, thrusting a fist in the air.

Gregory had been sitting on a blanket on the ground, drinking from a bottle. He dropped the bottle and crawled over toward the log, then grabbed Colliver's pantleg and pulled. Colliver reached down and lifted the baby up.

"Come and see me, Bret. You and I should become friends."

Face to face with Colliver's hairy head was too much for Gregory. He began crying, squirming and looking toward his mother.

"Now, now, don't cry, little one," Colliver said as he tried to nuzzle the child in his arms.

The beard against Gregory's cheek did it. Corinne jumped off the log and rushed toward her baby, but not before Gregory let out a high-pitched squeal. She threw the apple cider from her cup and it splashed across the heads of Gregory and Colliver. The squeal stopped and she grabbed Gregory and brought him close, murmuring in his ear. Colliver bolted upright, shook his head, and looked around, then up at the tree limbs.

"Damn! What the hell happened? Something jabbed me in the head." He looked around on the ground.

Mark, who was now standing next to Corinne, said, "I didn't see anything, Bill."

Colliver wiped the cider off his face and beard. "Why did you throw your juice on me, Susan?"

"I'm sorry. I slipped and it spilled," she said.

"Spilled?" he said. "Hell, you were way over on the other end of the log. You threw it at us."

"I was coming to get Gregory. I'm sorry."

"Are you all right, Bill?" Mark asked.

Colliver rubbed his head. "Well, I don't feel any bumps or holes. In the mountains you always worry that some rifle slug will hit you from some fool shooting in the air a mile away. I'm all right."

A WEEK LATER they went on the hike. Corinne proudly identified a number of trees and flowers before Colliver pointed them out. Gregory seemed to enjoy the outing which covered nearly four miles by foot. He was alternately alert, making babbly sounds, or asleep. Mark was impressed with the amount of land that Colliver owned.

"How many acres is it?" Mark asked as they rested in the shade of a large black oak.

"One thousand and forty, including the Korsen property right up to the road. I bought it as a sort of repayment to nature."

"How's that?"

"My father left me some money when he died so I plunked a lot of it down on this property—paid in cash. See, my dad made his money as a real estate developer in the Santa Clara Valley. Now they call it Silicon Valley. It's turned into another abomination like L.A. All these nerdy assholes driving convertibles with phones stuck on their ears talking to their stockbrokers. Goddamn 'em anyway."

Mark frowned.

Colliver continued, "My great grandfather, who I was named for, was a hard rock miner. He came over from Cornwall in the 1850s."

"One of the gold rushers, huh?" Corinne said.

"Yeah, one of those early despoilers."

"Where was his mine?" she asked.

"He worked for the Wisconsin Mine Company in Grass Valley—a foreman down in the tunnels. Spent all his life listening for the Tommyknocker."

"What's that?" she asked.

Colliver laughed. "Depends on who you listen to, but my grandfather told me a Tommyknocker was a little elf that the Cornish miners believed in. He supposedly looked after them. If there was a cave-in, the timbers would begin creaking beforehand and that was the Tommyknocker telling them to get out."

"How interesting," she said.

"Not really," Colliver said. "Who the hell would want to spend his life working in a dark, dank hole to make someone else rich?"

OVER THE NEXT SEVERAL weeks when the weather was good they took hikes. Corinne especially liked the flat granite rock near the creek where the Maidu women ground acorns into meal, leached out the bitter tannin, and made the thick mush that they served in intricately woven baskets. She imagined that the rock was also a medicine place where the Indians took sun baths to cure their ills. Corinne, going there alone, found that the rock helped to relieve anxieties that increasingly weighed on her. Here they were—isolated and at the mercy of an eccentric who had a strange intellectual agenda. When would she see her parents and friends? And then there was Gregory. Fortunately, there had been no further X incidents, and Colliver did not appear suspicious . . . yet. But how long before he found out? And there was this strange rustic way of life. It was nothing like what she had expected. Maybe it was all a mistake.

Chapter Seventeen

Like a giant gull, the United Airlines jet banked around the bay, dropped fast over the downtown skyscrapers, and touched down with precision. Alice Masterson disembarked with a briefcase and light coat, then found a taxi. In a short time she was checking in at the registration table of the Society for Neuroscience meeting at the convention center. It was mid-November and San Diego was once again hosting several thousand attendees of the largest international scientific organization devoted to the study of the brain.

At the week-long confab countless posters, papers, seminars, symposia, and panels would be given by a bewildering variety of researchers: molecular biologists, biochemists, geneticists, physiologists, developmental biologists, pharmacologists, psychiatrists, biophysicists, cell biologists, psychologists, electrophysiologists, neurologists, bioengineers, behavioral neuroscientists, structural biologists and more. Each of these disciplines was fairly well recognized by the others, and for the most part, the content of the disparate presentations could be understood by everyone. There was one panel discussion, however, that had an unusual profession participating. On this panel there was a newspaper journalist.

Alice pulled open the program booklet to look for her session. She randomly glanced at a seminar title: *Drosophila CBP Co-activator of Cubitus Interruptus in Hedgehog Signaling.* She shook her head. She was familiar with many medical and scientific terms, but this was ridiculous. What did flies have to do with hedgehogs? Or with the brain? It sounded off color.

She looked at the throng milling around the lobby. One thing was clear: they weren't fashion plates. She saw some women in dresses, but most—probably the postdocs and graduate students—were in slacks or denim pants. While they dressed like ordinary people, she realized these were extremely bright, educated types who, no doubt, would consider her an air head. She got a sinking feeling that this could be quite different from the national TV interview.

She felt a slight tug on her arm. It was Sylvia. Thank goodness she had on a suit. At least Alice, with her navy skirt, jacket, and cream-colored blouse with ruffles, would not look totally out of place at the podium. They found a table in the food service area and sat down with coffee.

"So how are you handling celebrity?" Alice asked.

"All the letters, email, phone calls—I had no idea," Sylvia said. "If I had known . . ." She shook her head.

"You still would have done it," Alice said.

"I suppose. Once I agreed to Ray's NPA announcement, the die was cast. But, I didn't think that after his presidential speech he would step back. I didn't realize you and I would end up as the point people. I wanted to count on someone, now that Jared is gone for me."

"Is that bridge totally burned?"

"He sent me an email soon after the NPA meeting asking how I could have done this to him. I replied that principles have to supersede friendships. Since then I haven't heard a thing. I know he's furious and almost nobody talks to me over at the Pediatric Clinic."

Alice nodded and ran her manicured fingernails through her curls. "Oh well. Life goes on."

"Yeah. Anyway it's fun to come to a meeting like this. I went by some posters and saw one about a fat thermostat in the brain. It was from the lab of a well-known obesity researcher, Roger Conelly. The postdoc at the poster said that they had found female hamster pheromones that signal males to stop eating so she can get more food. From these pheromones they hope to develop pills that can change people's 'eat/don't eat' thermostats. He claimed there would be the Five Pounds Lighter pill, the Ten Pounds Lighter, whatever you needed. Pretty amazing, huh?"

"I want the Five Pounds Lighter on the Hips pill."

Sylvia laughed.

"So what do you expect with the panel today?" Alice asked.

"More of the same. They'll want detailed descriptions of X and Y, and then they'll ask a lot of pointed questions. Did you know that the other two panelists are Nobel laureates?"

"Yeah, I heard. You seem worried. Is that why?"

"No, not that." Sylvia stirred her coffee and watched the swirling liquid for a moment.

"What, then?"

"Something Ray mentioned yesterday. He said that he had not figured on Gregory disappearing."

"It certainly surprised us all."

"He said that if they don't turn up, there will be no way to test Gregory and certify the powers scientifically."

"But who can doubt the powers now?"

"Scientists like these at this meeting. They're skeptical by nature."

Alice frowned. "Well, sure. But Corinne, Mark, and Gregory will be found and soon. There is no way they can avoid being recognized by someone, somewhere. Do you know that I'm getting several thousand hits a day on my new website? My service provider can hardly keep up."

"I hope they do turn up."

In the program booklet the panel presentation was found on a loose, inserted page. The title was: *Anecdotal Reports Concerning Infant with Unusual Brain Lesion.* The event started at noon in the largest meeting hall. At 11:45 am, there was standing room only. Reporters with tablets could be seen. The moderator, Richard Goodstine, director of a highly respected neurobiology institute in Portland, Oregon, introduced the four panelists. With characteristic drollness he explained that this forum was inserted late into the program due to a sudden surge of member interest in the area of anecdotal research. The audience laughed. With a few more quips that provided relief to the palpable tension permeating the room, Goodstine explained the format. The panelists sat at a table on the dais. Dr. Auerbach would go first, Ms. Masterson next. Then Drs. Clyde Finlayson and Harold Newman would provide final commentary, pro and con. After each, there would be a Q&A period—written questions only.

As Sylvia spoke from the podium, Alice was struck by the controlled precision of her words. The quiet, measured voice with subdued inflection marked her as intelligent and respectful of the need to convey meaning without bias. Even Sylvia's portrayal of the Y power and its effect on her and Corinne did not betray any of her own feelings.

Alice inspected Sylvia's appearance as she spoke—no makeup, unobtrusive lipstick, minimally stylish hair, low-heeled shoes. Alice suddenly wished she had dressed down. As the last question was answered and applause echoed off the walls, she quickly wiped off her crimson lipstick before standing.

She placed her notes on the lectern and glanced out at the mosaic of clothing and faces. She began talking in the same quiet, precise manner as Sylvia. The words flowed as if she were writing a long article that would need no editing. She told of her encounter with Corinne and Gregory, her meeting with Lawrence

Carter, and all of her *tête à têtes*, emails, and phone calls with Mark. She found she did not need her notes. Word-for-word conversations with the doctor at the west L.A. restaurant came back to her. She embellished nothing, trying not to make herself or Mark look better from what had actually transpired. When she finally stopped, there was silence, then a slow buildup of applause even louder than that given Sylvia. Most of the questions that followed surprised her. For every question about Corinne or Gregory, there were two about Onward Christian Soldiers and four about Mark. Questioners seemed fascinated with the young scientist—what he thought, what he said, and how he, mother, and baby could have disappeared so completely. Alice had, however, expected the last question: *Where do you think they are?*

"What I say now is total opinion. As I mentioned, I think the encounter with the OCS people in Fresno was the precipitating event for their coming south. But I think that their utter disappearance from west L.A. could not have happened without planning—and without help from others. Who might have helped? Maybe his father. Maybe a friend. I don't think Dr. Weymouth was involved in it. And where are they now? If I had to bet, I would say Mexico or Canada. I think they obtained another vehicle, disguised themselves, and drove at night. This is conjecture on my part. In any case, I think they will be located soon. I'm getting many tips on my website. Sooner or later, someone will recognize them. So let me end with that. Thank you so much." The applause was again strong, and this time Alice turned loose her smile.

Dr. Finlayson was introduced next. He had drooping jowls and a slouch that belied his bright, alert eyes and boyish smile. He nodded at the warm reception.

"Thank you. It's difficult to be next after that act." He turned and nodded to Alice, then turned back to the audience. "But I have a few comments. I have followed the Shenko matter with great interest as I suspect many of you have. What on earth are we neuroscientists to make of this baby? Well, I think Gregory and his father represent something so important for evolutionary neurobiology and for science, that it will cause a paradigm change in society's thinking of who we humans are. Why do I say this? Setting aside the alleged X and Y powers, if the large lesion and high cranial voltages are correct, these developments alone are stunning. I know Lou Fazzi at SSU and I know colleagues who know Jared Weymouth. The word is that both are careful and responsible scientists. Therefore, I suspect what they have said to the media is correct and supportable. Two weeks ago, Dr. Weymouth and Dr. Jaime Valenzuela submitted a manuscript to *Science*. I learned just this morning that this paper has been accepted. I can't wait to see it. How about you?"

Finlayson's eyebrows danced to the quick applause. He looked at the panelists seated at the table. Getting smiles from the women and a frown from Newman, he continued.

"Not surprisingly, Weymouth's paper does not deal with the X and Y powers, or so I'm told. This indicates to me that there is not hard evidence for these phenomena. But I'm not discounting the anecdotal observations from our two distinguished speakers. After all, there is not hard evidence for human consciousness either, but I doubt few of us would dispute that it's real."

Laughter rippled across the room. Finlayson picked up a glass of water, sipped an inch, and then placed bifocals on his nose. For the first time he looked at his notes.

"What should we think about the X and Y claims? Let me share some of my thoughts. First, I'll respond to some science commentators who doubt that the lesion evolved for any functional purpose. One person even pointed to Tay-Sachs disease, which is caused by one DNA base change in a key enzyme. The argument is that one small mutation leads to the many phenotypic changes in Tay-Sachs children and that a similar small DNA alteration could be the cause of Gregory's complicated lesion. I disagree. I think just the opposite is correct—while there could have been an initial major mutation during a developmental stage, at some point many, many mutations were probably required to produce the complex functionality of the lesions in Gregory and his father. Those packed neurons have an uncanny resemblance to eel and fish voltage cells and as such, could only have evolved over a long selection period. Each incremental change must have yielded increasing value for survival. I would liken such development to the evolution of the eye, which is far more complicated than a voltage organ. The record suggests that a fully functional eye takes about a half million years to evolve. As eye development moved toward perfection, it brought increasing utility and survival benefits.

"To those who say that the voltage systems of water-based species are not likely to have evolved in a primate environment, let me point out that the eye evolved independently forty times in a wide variety of environments. To those who say that no other hominids have this, I say that we don't know that. Even so, except for recent findings on Neanderthal, it appears that no other hominids but man have wiring for symbolic language either. Further, the Homo species broke off from the gorilla-chimp line about seven million years ago. There would have been plenty of time to develop this system many times over."

Finlayson looked out at the audience as if surprised that people were so quiet. He expected maybe laughter or scoffing sounds.

"Now you may ask, What about physics? How could a minute voltage on a cranial surface of one head transmit across a significant distance in the air to another head and have any electrical effect? Obviously, this is the strongest argument against X and Y. But we all know the amazing inventiveness of biological systems, the incredible mystery of nature that Einstein mentioned. Gymnotiforms, or knife fish, in the fresh waters of Central and South America, rely on their ability to produce and detect weak electrical fields for sensing other fish in their muddy environment. These electrolocating fish do this by means of ampullary organs that excel at detecting weak electric fields. But that is in water. What about in air?

"Well, we know that homing pigeons and other animals have evolved brains that detect the earth's electromagnetic waves. We know that a radio frequency signal of only one milliwatt can be detected miles from its source. I would like to suggest that there may be a role here for resonance. Just as an opera singer can shatter a crystal goblet by a resonant sound wave, how surprised should we be to contemplate a tiny resonant electromagnetic signal being detected by electrically super-sensitive neurons? And once detected, how easy for the signal to then cause the neurons to hyperpolarize, in other words to activate? And how easy would it be for the resultant neuronal action potentials to release powerful neurotransmitter chemicals of one kind or another, causing seizure-like immobilization or intense opiate-like sexual stimulation and pleasure? We see just such voltage-chemical signaling and modulation in our everyday investigations of such neuronal cells, don't we?"

There were grunts and body movements in the audience. Many people nodded.

Finlayson paused for a long time, letting his last message sink in.

"Now, what about the objection that the X and Y powers could not have co-evolved with a life-threatening epileptic disease? This is known as a pleiotropic mutation, one causing multiple effects. If all of the offspring with such powers die early, this is clearly a drawback to survival success. But consider sickle cell anemia. It co-evolved to provide increased resistance to malaria. A *plus* and a *minus* can still be more of a *plus* for selective advantage. If the X and Y are as potent as they appear, they could more than counterbalance the epilepsy. And here, I might speculate. One would expect selection pressure for earlier sexual maturation in such individuals. This evolutionary change in the timing of development is called heterochrony. Early maturation would allow more time for insemination and offspring before early death from the epilepsy. It would be interesting to see if this is so with Gregory and his genetically affected forbearers.

"Finally, let me respond to some who say that the Shenko powers could not evolve because the development trend of human males and females—their *evolutionary psychology*, if you will—has been toward more egalitarian roles. Despite what has occurred in modern westernized societies, and despite what we may wish to be so, evolutionary processes carry no such intent. I quote the esteemed biologist, Richard Dawkins:

> Nature is not cruel, only pitilessly indifferent. This is one of the hardest lessons for humans to learn. We cannot admit that things might be neither good nor evil, neither cruel nor kind, but simply callous—indifferent to all suffering, lacking all purpose.

"Let me close my remarks by saying that Gregory Shenko's lesion and his alleged powers are entirely possible in that they are consistent with what we know about biology and evolution. I suggest we keep our minds open until we get more information."

"That was brilliant," Sylvia said to Alice.

"Yeah, very impressive. I would like to get a transcript of those remarks."

Clapping filled the hall for some time. Finlayson took a seat at the table and nodded several times at the response. Finally the other Nobel laureate rose and advanced to the lectern.

Dr. Newman's curly gray hair added an inch to his six-foot-four, bean pole height. Hollow cheeks, thin lips, and a long nose lent severity to his gaunt appearance. As he leaned forward with his suitcoat shoulder seams slipping down toward his elbows, he resembled a stork hunched up for the night. Newman seemed impatient with the applause and began speaking before it died away.

". . . and in my many years of attending these Society of Neuroscience meetings, I must conclude that this panel discussion represents an intellectual low point. The anecdotes about the so-called X and Y powers by two of our panelists were entertaining, but unless I fell asleep, there were no data presented. My esteemed Nobel colleague presented some fanciful notions, but unless I dozed off, he had no data. Dick Goodstine was charitably humorous. But I will not suffer such fools as gladly.

"Let me ask the other panelists and let me ask you: Are we still a scientific society? Or are we now the Society for Storytelling? Next year will there be a panel on Bigfoot? Or how about a panel on UFO experiences? I'm sure we could enthrall an audience twice this size if we find the right entertainers."

Laughter filled the hall.

"Am I being unfair? A little too reactionary? I don't think so. I should not have to remind anyone that the history of science is replete with hoaxes and pseudoscience. Only the careful evaluation of actual data separates the wheat of solid research from the chaff of junk science, reality from wishful thinking, sanity from Alice in Wonderland. In this case, Alice and her sister." Laughter by many in the audience followed the remark.

"Remember Piltdown Man? Now there was a good one. Leading scientists of the day found bones for the 'missing link' between apes and man in a gravel quarry in Sussex in the first decade of the 1900s. It wasn't until 1953 that Piltdown Man was proven to be a forgery. Part of the tragedy of hoaxes like this is that they hang on and waste everyone's time.

"How about the anatomist Jean-Baptiste Lamarck? His nineteenth-century theory that acquired characteristics are transmitted to descendants lasted well into the 20th century, repeated and repeated by scientists with nothing but anecdotal data. The Soviet Union blackballed scientists who did not subscribe to Lamarckian ideas. Incredible, but unfortunately true.

"More recently, there is the phenomenon of cold fusion. Despite the failed attempts to replicate the initial experiments conducted by capable people at many top programs in this country and around the world, this field keeps growing. If you look on the Web, you find information zealously presented as if cold fusion were a proven fact. As I say, these things tragically develop a life of their own.

"Closer to our field of neuroscience, think of the incredible damage of Sigmund Freud. I'll bet many of you in this audience were steeped in the myths of id, ego, and superego, and the oral, genital, and latency stages, and all of the rest of the baggage. Brain science is finally out from under this stench, though Freudian aroma can still be whiffed in some corners of our field. But look back at the incredible waste of training for many bright people in this crap. And the clinical disasters such as blaming parents for causing schizophrenia in their children with their poor parenting. What Freud did to psychology and neuroscience is a pretty sad story. Lots of anecdotes and inventive thinking led to the Freudian crap.

"Today, there is with us the notions of ESP—extra sensory perception, parapsychology, and all the related claptrap. Programs on this stuff have lodged in very good universities. Try as the proponents do to gain scientific credibility, they still have the hurdle of producing hard, convincing data which they cannot get over. The X and Y powers of Gregory fit into the rubric of ESP and the paranormal. This makes the claims about Gregory particularly insidious—at least to me. So I say to everyone who wants to entertain these extrasensory notions: *Show us the data. Show us the data. Show us the data. Please!* Before you say there are X and Y powers in some unfortunate baby and you alarm the nation, *please—show us the data!*

"If the data are not available, then the saying of Wittgenstein applies: *Daruber man kennt nicht, er mussen schweigend sein.* The translation: Whereof one cannot speak, thereof one must be silent. It's as simple as that, my friends. This is the Society of Neuro-SCIENCE, not the Society of Weird Tales. I thank you." Newman quickly turned and sat down.

The applause started slowly, built to a thundering crescendo, and became a standing ovation with hurrahs, lasting for a long time.

RAIN BLEW IN SHEETS against the west- and south-facing windows of the cabin. The first large storm of the season bent the trees and shook the bushes. Gregory kneeled on a chair and watched the tempest.

"That's rain, Bret. Can you say *rain? Rain?*" Corinne smiled at Gregory.

He looked at his mother and took his fingers from his mouth.

"Wane," he said, softly.

"Yes! Rain. That's right. Rain."

"Wane," he said again, laughing.

Corinne picked him up. "You're so cute." She hugged and kissed him. "Would you like to get ready for a nap? Huh?"

"Booh, booh," he said, getting excited and pointing to the picture book with kids holding umbrellas on the cover.

"He's really trying hard to talk, isn't he," she said, looking at Mark who was putting two small logs on the fire.

"Yeah. Yesterday he said 'Arnie' so perfectly that Arnie came over to him. Talking this early is truly amazing."

Corinne frowned. "Do you think that dog's safe around Bret?"

"He seems gentle. I've never seen him bristle, not even when Bret grabbed his tail."

With Gregory on her lap, Corinne read while Gregory pointed to pictures as soon she pronounced the words. Gregory made her read the book twice, saying "'Gain, 'gain," while Mark watched with fatherly pride.

When Gregory finally squirmed away, Corinne said, "Your turn next."

Mark nodded. "On a day like this he's got us where he wants us."

"It's sure cozy, isn't it?"

"Yeah. I have to be careful about making the fire too big."

She turned wistful. "This is our cute little hideaway where nobody can find us."

"Yeah. So far."

"Do you like it here?"

"Yeah. So far." He smiled.

"You're a goofball."

He winked.

~

THE CHANNEL ISLANDS floated in the ocean like slightly brown pancakes on a blue griddle. White-topped waves danced around them like crackling grease. The Alaska Airlines jet directly overhead made a course change and followed the flightpath into LAX. This time Alice was on her way to the main auditorium at SSU where Jared Weymouth would soon hold his press conference.

From the taxi's window, glimpses of her erstwhile city did not divert Alice's concentration from the event ahead. For her the issue boiled down to what Jared would say about the X and Y powers. Ever since the Society of Neuroscience meeting, the scientific community and those who followed science in the media had become divided. In one camp were those like Finlayson who thought the powers could be real and, if so, must have evolved. The larger group consisted of those like Newman who thought the X and Y were bogus and that the lesion was unrelated to any biological function except possibly the epilepsy. *Hoax* was the word most often used by the Newman school. The schism had set the stage for Weymouth's presentation. Excitement was high.

Alice found Sylvia and took the empty seat next to her in the third row of the orchestra section. The huge auditorium, including the balcony, was completely full. Two TV media crews were positioned near the front.

"Thanks for saving this great seat," Alice said.

"I got here an hour ago and then had to hold off some senior faculty. I said I was saving it for a VIP." Sylvia grinned.

"Well if anyone asks, I'm Corinne Shenko's sister."

A man emerged on stage and tested the sound system. Then a large colored slide appeared on the screen: *Press Conference, Southern State University.*

"Sylvia, do you think Dr. Weymouth will talk about the X and Y powers?"

"He'll have to. If not in his main presentation, then in the questions. If nobody else asks, I will."

Vice Chancellor Reese came out and explained that Dr. Weymouth would talk and present data in the form of slides and a video for about forty-five minutes. Then he would take written questions from the audience for about twenty minutes. The questions would be reviewed by a committee of three senior faculty members. Reese introduced Dr. Weymouth as a professor of pediatrics and head of the Division of Child Development.

Jared came out wearing a grey suit with a white shirt and a blue and gray tie. He reached the lectern in quick strides. He straightened his papers and looked out on the crowd for half a minute, smiling slightly.

"Good afternoon. First I am going to present the data that appeared in a recent *Science* article authored by myself, Jaime Valenzuela, and Leonard Lesser. I understand that reprints of this article were made available to you. Second, I will present some additional information including a video clip that was not a part of that article. Third, I will briefly discuss the so-called X and Y powers, and then take questions. Before I start, I want to say that I regret that Dr. Mark Sandler is not here to participate in the discussion. Much of the data is his. He would have been a co-author on the paper, perhaps lead author, but was not due to his unavailability."

Slides went up in succession on the large screen, and Jared explained data on various aspects—pathologic, genetic, pediatric, and electroencephalographic—in the case of Baby A. He never mentioned the names Gregory, Nicholas, or Corinne Shenko. The presentation was dry and technical and followed the article closely. When the last slide disappeared and the lights went up, Jared cleared his throat.

"Now I want to direct your attention to a video that will appear on the large screen and several monitors around the auditorium. It will run first, then I'll discuss it. And then it will run again."

Alice turned to look at a large monitor off to the side and then saw Fazzi one row away. He looked her way and they exchanged waves and smiles. He cupped his hands around his mouth.

"Can I see both of you afterward?"

She nodded.

The videotape appeared as a split-screen image. On the right appeared multi-lined EEG tracings across the screen. A hand with an ice cube came into view near the baby's foot. Gregory silently screamed in rage, the hand disappeared and the EEG tracings jumped several fold in amplitude, completely filling the half screen. After several seconds the videotape ended.

"What was shown was Baby A going into a rage when Dr. Sandler was about to touch an ice cube to the baby's foot. The baby had previously experienced the ice cube touching his foot, screaming in reaction, but on this occasion he screamed in anticipation. On the right you first saw the baby's extraordinarily high occipital EEG voltages in an active state of around five hundred microvolts. When the baby raged, the voltages jumped to the three thousand microvolt range. Let's look at it one more time."

After the repeat, Jared took a deep breath.

"Okay, let me summarize to this point. We have shown brain slice photomicrographs of the father's lesion. We have presented CT scan images of Baby A's larger lesion that is essentially in the same location and of the same shape as the father's. You have seen EEG data of the baby's unusually high occipital voltages in sleep state, active state, and a state of rage. In the latter state, you saw a huge jump in amplitude when the baby went into the rage. Such high EEG amplitudes in all states have never been seen before in humans."

Jared sipped some water. "Here are conclusions that I offer for your consideration. One, the lesion is of genetic origin in that it was passed from father to son. Two, it is a reasonable hypothesis, but not conclusive, that the voltages result from the lesion. Three, the EEG changes from sleep, active, and rage states suggest that the voltages reflect different physiological conditions, and this suggests that biological functions are being served."

Jared cleared his throat and looked out at the audience. "What could be the biological function of the lesion and the voltages? This remains unknown. I make this statement because I have no data to show that the baby has any powers, X, Y or otherwise. I repeat, I have no data to show the existence of any powers that the baby might have. That concludes my presentation."

As the applause came up, Sylvia leaned over to Alice. "That was so incredibly conservative, I can't believe it."

"Yeah."

The first few questions were about technical procedure, but then there was a question that caused Sylvia and Alice to listen carefully.

"Dr. Weymouth, did you not coin the terms X power and Y power? If so, what exactly led you to do this? And, do you personally believe that one or both of these powers are real?"

Jared laughed and the audience chuckled.

"This question was not unexpected. Yes, I coined these terms to describe personal sensations that I and others strongly perceived at times in the baby's presence. The X sensation was an intense feeling of hurt and dizziness in the head and the Y was an intense feeling of sexual arousal. I have personally experienced the X but not the Y. I cannot describe the Y sensations any differently or better than Sylvia Auerbach and Alice Masterson did at the Society of Neuroscience meeting a few weeks ago and on other occasions. Do I think these powers are real and do I believe these powers are caused by the high cranial voltages from Baby A? The answer to both of these is that *I don't know. I just don't know.* The sensations were wholly subjective. I have no objective data to support or refute these notions. Without objective data, I must conclude at this time that the powers do not exist. For that reason I will not speculate further about the nature of the powers or about what purposes they may serve."

After a few more technical questions, Reese abruptly ended the event. As the unsatisfied crowd made its way to the exits, animated conversations melded together. In an aisle near the front Fazzi walked in a tight circle, waiting for Alice and Sylvia. His face was flushed.

"Hi, Lou, how are you?" Alice said, extending her hand.

"I am so angry," he said, grabbing and releasing her hand.

"You know Sylvia, don't you?"

"Yes, hello. Can you believe what has just happened? Jared stiff-armed us. He sucked everyone into Gregory's X and Y powers and now he throws doubt on all of it with this . . . this sanctimonious objectivity. He's just made SSU a laughing stock. I'll tell you—the president is not going to be happy. And last week I learned there are no biological samples on Gregory. No blood was taken. Nothing. There is none up in Fresno either. So we can't even do DNA studies. Jared has been derelict and uncollegial. And there's going to be hell to pay."

The women said nothing in response. Fazzi looked at them and softened his glare and his voice.

"Sylvia, I would think that you should feel the same way as I do," he said.

"Well . . . yes."

"Sucked everyone in?" Alice said. "Before now, Jared never talked about the powers."

"But he was orchestrating the information through others. Why else would he have named them X and Y?" Fazzi said.

"I didn't think you believed the X and Y," Alice replied. "Now you do?"

"Oh, I believe there is something there. I'm convinced the lesion is the product of evolution. It couldn't have evolved unless those voltages contributed somehow to increased survivability. Maybe X and Y are real, maybe they're not, but something has to be operating. The point is that we have to do more research on Gregory to pin it down."

"But I don't see that anything can be done at this point," Sylvia said.

"Something damn well *can* be done. I would like you to come to a meeting with me, Ray Cameron, and Reese. Okay?"

Sylvia shrugged. "Sure."

Fazzi put his arm around Alice. "I'm sorry, Alice, but this is internal university stuff."

She smiled. "I'll find out about it sooner or later."

CHAPTER EIGHTEEN

MAYBE IT WAS the winter weather—most of the nation had been dampened with rain and snow. Maybe it was Jared's dry academic presentation—it hadn't appeared to reveal anything new. Or maybe the story had just run its course. Something had squelched public interest in Gregory Shenko. Whatever the cause, media coverage of the topic waned as a good many people swung to the view that the claims about the baby were exaggerated, if not an outright hoax. The capstone to the disenchantment was an answer given by the president at a White House news conference in the Rose Garden one week after Jared's talk.

"Mr. President, two congressmen and one senator have urged that the FBI be charged with finding the baby, Gregory Shenko. Will the FBI be directed to do this?"

The president chuckled. "I take it your question is serious. Well, the issue as I see it is: On what grounds should we try to locate this baby and his mother? I can't see any grounds. Nobody in my administration can find any reason for the federal government, or government at any level for that matter, to be involved. The baby, his mother, and the doctor have broken no laws. No relative has filed reports that they are missing persons or that there is suspected foul play. The majority of the scientific community doubts the reports about the baby's alleged powers. Even the university doctor who studied and cared for the baby is unwilling to say the powers exist. I'm not saying this thing is necessarily a hoax, but the sensational reports don't meet the test of common sense, at least to me. So no, I will not authorize federal personnel getting involved. The baby, the mother, and the young doctor are private citizens. Their freedom and rights, including privacy, have to be respected."

As the Shenko case faded from the public eye, the intensity felt by the participants subsided. Time again moved forward.

Mark sensed the change during his solo trips to Nevada City. The radio talk shows had moved on to other topics. *People* and other magazines in the stores no longer carried G-C-M stories.

"Does that mean Bret and I can come out of confinement?" Corinne asked as she stowed groceries in a high cupboard. "As much as I like Anthro, I've about O.D.'d on Ian's articles and books. I need to get out of here."

Mark embraced her from behind, his arms locking gently around her. He kissed her neck and whispered, "Would you be my date on a trip to town?"

She turned and hugged him. "You know just what to say to a girl."

"Is Bret asleep?" he asked.

"No. Another ten minutes or so."

"You're cruel."

"Can't you handle delayed gratification?"

"No and neither can you."

He interrupted her laugh with his lips.

ON THEIR FIRST joint trip to Nevada City just before Christmas, Mark stayed in the van with Gregory while Corinne went into the stores. She spent the most time in a shoe store getting new boots. Dinner was consumed in the van after she ventured into a take-out pizza place. Their last stop was the post office where she dropped off a large manila envelope addressed to a P.O. box in Santa Monica—the second such mailing since their arrival in Colliver's canyon. In the envelope were letters to their families that Ian would re-mail from L.A. There was no return address on these envelopes or any indication inside on the whereabouts of the senders. Family members knew they could send letters to the unnamed Santa Monica P.O. box and that eventually Corinne and Mark would receive them.

For a holiday dinner Corinne warmed a precooked turkey in Colliver's oven and made traditional trimmings. They exchanged cards and gifts—a bottle of cognac for Colliver, a Nordic-style sweater for Corinne, a rain jacket and woolen socks for Mark, and wooden toys for Gregory.

The first snow came in January. Gregory was taking a few steps at a time. The snow fascinated him and he frolicked in it despite the cold. "Snow, snow," he said. He laughed every time he fell over and looked to the adults for recognition of his funny game. They laughed and clapped.

The day after Gregory's introduction to the fluffy white stuff, Mark, Corinne, and Gregory bundled up and joined Colliver on a food run to North San Juan. The road was only lightly covered with snow and the Jeepster had no difficulty getting out. It was the first time since their disappearance that Mark, Corinne, and the baby were seen together in public—if a store with five people was considered public. They stocked up on fresh vegetables. Colliver had told them of the snows three years ago when he had been cabin bound for three weeks. The winter proved to be mild, however, which was not a disappointment for Mark who liked fresh meats and vegetables. They went food shopping at least every ten days.

From time to time visitors would call on "Bill the philosopher." Mark and Corinne at first avoided these contacts, opting for a hike or staying inside their cabin whenever they heard a car arrive at Colliver's. But increasingly starved for human interaction, they began calling on Colliver when his friends were there. They came to know a teacher and his wife who lived a few miles to the east and a poet named Warren who lived alone not far from the Mother Trucker store. Mark and Corinne were readily accepted by these friendly people who did not seem to think it at all unusual that the Harrises had come from southern California to live in a remote mountain cabin without plans or income. There were many such people on North San Juan Ridge. It was coyote land.

One Sunday afternoon in February Mark, Corinne, and the baby accompanied Colliver to a hootenanny at the teacher's house. There were fifteen people there, including the poet and Mortie from the Mother Trucker store. Guitars and five-string banjos nearly drowned out the singing, but the wine, good company, and blazing fire in the wood stove more than made up for the musical hodgepodge. Gregory played with toys and managed to conduct himself without incident. Mark talked to almost everyone and conversed at length with one younger man who had a scar on his face. Corinne befriended a young woman with a child fifteen months old. She and her husband had moved to the Ridge only a year ago and he had found a job as a bartender in Nevada City.

After the spaghetti and tossed salad dinner, the poet read some of his work and then an open discussion ensued, mostly between him and Colliver. The theme was "right thinking," the term Mark had heard at Mother Trucker. Everyone in the room seemed to enjoy the dialogue even though it was not easy to follow.

When Mark, Corinne, and Gregory arrived home, the cabin was freezing. Mark and Corinne zipped Gregory into two heavy sleepsuits and tucked him under covers in the makeshift crib next to the bed in the loft. In turn, Mark and Corinne jumped into their bedclothes, burrowing under a pile of wool blankets. That night Mark found Corinne unusually amorous and they quickly shed some of the blankets.

IN THE MORNING'S frigid air, Mark engaged in the ritual he found the toughest of their winter living—pulling on cold Levi's and a bulky sweater, easing down the ladder and getting fires going. His breath came out in clouds. Outside, icicles hung from the eaves. He shivered as he waited for the flickering kindling to catch the larger sticks of wood. He held his hands next to the flame, warming his fingers and palms, then piled on larger pieces. His face warmed and finally his chest as the flames started to roar. He moved into the kitchen next and made a fire in the cook stove. That morning there would be buttermilk pancakes. He clinked the griddle on the iron stove to make sure Corinne would be up soon. He could hear Gregory stirring.

"Wasn't last night fun?" she said, as they sat down at the table.

"Yes, I had a good time."

"Those people were all so friendly. And nobody seemed to wonder about us."

"Well, life isn't exactly easy up here, so everyone feels more connected with each other. Maybe it's the need to recover tribalism that Warren was talking about. I'll tell you, I thought I was an environmentalist, but Colliver and these people have ecology deep in their brains."

She laughed. "And Bret! I can't believe how well he behaved. Do you think he's learning?"

"Yeah, maybe the water dousing is working. But let's not count our chickens yet."

Gregory squealed as if knowing they were talking about him.

"Yes, you were a good kid," Corinne said, kissing him. "Who was that fellow with the scar you were talking to?"

"Didn't you meet him? His name is Ogden. Interesting guy—an ex-convict."

"No kidding?"

"No kidding. And I learned something from him. There is a place in Reno where I could get a birth certificate made up."

"You talked to him about that?"

"We were talking about beginning new lives, and he said that after finishing his parole, he started over with a new name and everything. He told me about this graphic artist who would do a birth certificate for two hundred dollars. With that you can get a driver's license and then a social security number."

"Are you thinking we should do that?"

"Only me. I think it's too risky for you and Bret—at least for a while. But if I could get one, then I would be able to register the van and get a job."

"What if you got caught?"

"Look, this whole business has risks. Same with the letters to Ian. We need a certain amount of luck. This guy Ogden says the bureaucracies are so screwed up they seldom catch anything. I think it's a risk worth taking."

She raised her eyebrows. "Honey, I'm sticking with you—freezing in the mountains or rotting in jail."

"What do you mean? It was hot in that bed last night."

She smiled, then turned serious. "Mike, are you . . . are you still glad we did this?"

"Sure. I think we should stay with the plan. Why, are you having regrets?"

"No. I guess I just need your reassurance."

He squeezed her shoulder. "Nobody can see very far ahead, but right now I'm feeling optimistic. I can see we're going to make a life up here. Besides, where else could I get so much time with a beautiful babe?"

AFTER BREAKFAST MARK put on outdoor gear and stepped outside. He kicked a ridge of snow and broke off an icicle to suck on. He walked slowly toward Colliver's, his feet sinking a few inches on each step. Fir-scented smoke from Colliver's chimney hung in the air. A muledeer suddenly bounded away through the brush, her pointed hooves momentarily suspended like a ballerina's toes during each leap. Mark watched her disappear over a rise.

"Come in," Colliver said cheerfully. "Gorgeous morning, huh?"

"Nice but cold."

"Come on over to the fire. Coffee?"

"Sure."

"So," Colliver said from the kitchen cove, "how'd you like the party?"

"It was fun. The people were nice. I liked the poetry and your dialogue, too, even though some of the ideas bothered me."

"Aha, good. What were they?"

Mark sipped the instant coffee and stood next to the fire. "Well, I can buy Schumacher's ideas about the need for intermediate technology—that simplicity and small scale technology create more satisfying work and more humane organizations. And I buy that it is also more ecologically compatible. But if we need such technology, I don't understand why you criticized science. Science itself isn't bad. It's the use to which it's put, isn't it?"

Colliver nodded, his hazel eyes darting. "That's right, but unfortunately science has been put mostly in the service of our mass production technology. It keeps the global economy and out-of-control transnational corporations going, putting us deeper in the hole. Look at pesticides and chemicals in farming. Sure, they increase our food production, but what has happened? The loss of our topsoil, poisoning of our waters, killing of our wildlife, breast cancer. Look at our vehicle and building mania. This got us large inhuman cities, freeways becoming parking lots. Is the world better off for all the new technology? Much of the third world population continues to starve. And there is global warming. If we don't stop the CO2, we will be doomed."

Colliver shook a finger as if shaming someone. "So the point is that science has been used to make a technology that solves one problem only to create worse ones in the process. Science is looked on as magic, as a kind of god that will somehow solve mankind's discontent. And the people are led into these Faustian deals because of the myth that science will always get us out of the mess."

Colliver's voice ratcheted up in pitch and loudness.

"The scariest thing now is biotechnology. All these doctors and nerdholes will have access to the genomes of people, animals, and plants and will start changing all kinds of species attributes, creating a goddamned different world. It's already begun. You don't know if a tomato is a tomato anymore. I mean, talk about playing God. Right?"

Mark looked at the fire, a miniature symbol of everything in flames. "Bill, I told Susan that I'd get back soon to clean up the kitchen. I'd better go. Thanks for the coffee."

Colliver laughed. "So the seminar is over? Okay. But maybe we can go for a hike when the sun's higher. It'll be pretty with the fresh powder."

Mark nodded. "Yeah, Susan and the screamer would like that."

He retraced his snowprints and looked in the direction of the doe he'd seen. She had not returned. Why did Colliver upset him so? Mark too had misgivings about science. Maybe it was that Colliver's opinions were so rabid. Or presented too rabidly. He was too often the preacher and seldom in the mood for just ordinary talk.

It was March and the azaleas had caught fire. Reds, pinks, purples, whites, and more reds lined the walks in profuse intensity as if attempting to cheer Sylvia Auerbach on her way from the parking structure to the psychology department building. It was a losing effort, for that morning she had an appointment with Professor Augie Weber, chair of the department's promotions and tenure committee. He had arranged the meeting to explain her unsuccessful review for promotion to associate professor.

Weber's head was completely shaved, revealing bumps and valleys in phrenological abundance. Bushy eyebrows and a bulbous nose protruded from a tanned, wrinkled face. A soft voice and wide smile were quick to counter the menacing aspect. He wasted little time on pleasantries.

"Sylvia, as you know we obtained outside letters from five leading people in your area, and there was consistency in their opinions of your work. All of them said you were making important contributions to your field, but only one of the five recommended promotion at this time. The other four felt that your two recent single-author publications were excellent, but not by themselves sufficient to establish your independence from the lab of Jared Weymouth. They think you show promise in this respect, and now that you are in a different department, you should have more time to demonstrate your own research direction."

Sylvia nodded at the blue eyes locking on hers with sincerity. "I guess I'm not completely surprised."

"And frankly," he continued, "the members of our departmental committee felt the same about this. So I need to tell you that your next review will be not later than four years from now. We are confident that this amount of time should allow you to get another grant and really establish a first rate program of your own."

"And I have to pass the next review—or leave?"

"That's correct."

She nodded and frowned.

Weber ran a liver-spotted hand across his pate and pushed forward his lower lip.

"Uh, one other thing. On this business about that baby, Gregory Shenko. To be completely fair, I have to say that the views of both the external and internal reviewers on this—fiasco is too harsh a word—this professional aberration, we all feel that the faster you can distance yourself from this business, the better off you'll be. Don't talk about it, don't write about it, stay away from it. Keep a low profile and stick to your knitting. Understood?"

"It sounds like this was a significant factor in my review."

Weber smiled. "Officially, no. Unofficially, it consumed most of the conversation at our meeting."

"I see. One last question out of curiosity. What if Jared and I had been able to prove the existence of the X or Y power and published it in a peer-reviewed journal?"

Weber's eyes danced and he laughed. He leaned far back in his swivel chair. "Well, you did not hear it from me, but if you had done that, you would have received an accelerated promotion to full professor."

She laughed. "I didn't hear it from you."

He leaned forward and wagged his finger. "The message is—forget about that baby, okay?"

"Okay."

At eleven forty-five that morning Sylvia left her office with a small suit bag over her shoulder and briefcase in hand. She was wearing slacks, a loose-fitting blouse, a heavy sweater, and soft-soled shoes. She made her way to the sculpture garden and found an empty bench in the shade of a large, twisted sycamore. After looking at her watch, she stretched out, head on her suitcase.

Dark thoughts circulated faster with her eyes closed. Patient referrals had fallen off precipitously since her move to Psychology. They would probably dry up completely in a few months. How could she get subjects without a continuing connection to the Child Development Clinic? Without more babies to study, how could she achieve the aims of her current grant, much less get another one? Without more research there would be no way to get tenure. Maybe she wasn't cut out for the competitive research game. Maybe she should move to a teaching college and go home every day at five. Her husband and kids would vote for that. She felt a surge of guilt. They had suffered a lot over the past year. She had become more of a celebrity and less of a wife and mom.

She hated the stupid refrain that reverberated in her head, but the metaphor wasn't far off. Without much thought she had entered a high stakes game, assuming she would be a winner. Then new cards were dealt and the bet was raised. Now her up cards were bad and her chip stack was down, as everyone could see. Part of the refrain from "The Gambler" flashed through her mind, something about holding them and folding them. The player next to her tapped on the table, then tapped on her shoulder . . .

"Hi, Sylvia."

She opened her eyes.

"Oh, Alice. Hi."

"Ready to go?"

"Sure."

Alice drove as fast as the early afternoon traffic allowed on the 405 South, known by most Angelenos as the San Diego Freeway. In contrast to Sylvia, Alice's mood was ebullient.

"I've got news!" she said. "I think I will be accepted in the neuroscience PhD program at UC Davis next fall."

"Oh? I didn't know you were applying to grad school."

Alice grinned. "Well, part of it's your influence."

"Uh oh. When did that happen?"

"After the neuroscience meeting, I decided—what the hell? So on a lark I went up to the Davis campus and talked to some faculty. And one thing led to another. My dad's pretty psyched. You know, if not an MD, at least a PhD, although he wouldn't say that."

Sylvia laughed.

"So how are things going for you?" Alice asked.

Sylvia told of her meeting with Weber. Despite the supportive words, Sylvia could tell that Alice felt embarrassed. Maybe this was one of those times she shouldn't have answered the *How is it going?* question honestly. Maybe she and Alice weren't as close as she had thought.

"Anyway, tell me again how the contact happened with Zenya," Sylvia said.

"She emailed me at whereisgregory.com. It was lucky I saw the message. For quite a while there I couldn't even begin to look at all the mail coming in. I paid a couple of students to read them and answer with canned responses. But the hits and messages are down to ten percent of what they were, so lately I've been reading them all. Her message was: *Dear Alice, Would you tell me where my baby nephew is, if you know? Thank you. Zenya Shenko.* I emailed her back saying that I couldn't talk confidentially via email. That I would like to see her in person, and could I come down and visit? She sent me her phone number and we talked." Alice hit the steering wheel with her hand. "Can you beat that?"

"Pretty amazing. Does she know I'm coming with you?" Sylvia asked.

"No, but I don't think it'll be a problem. She knows who you are. She said she watched our interview on TV."

"Do you think she just wants to know where Gregory is?"

"I don't know. She made it clear that the ground rules were no publicity or articles about her and nothing about her put on the website."

Sylvia nodded. "Are you really that worried about information on the website?"

"Sure. We don't dare put up unevaluated information. We list sighting reports only by general area, northeast, southwest, and so forth. We are being very careful because we don't want Gregory found by the crazies. I know that Lawrence Carter visits the site because he's sent me email a couple of times. I've never answered."

"What's happening with that bunch?"

"Onward Christian Soldiers has support from the Canoga Park Church, but even more financial support from other fundamentalist churches across the country, according to their website. Carter's internet service provider is now down in El Cajon, though I don't know why. But the OCS crazies are no doubt still around. Apparently Carter's controlling them from somewhere in the San Diego area. They're still looking for Gregory, I guess."

Sylvia grimaced. "So you think they're still a threat?"

"Yeah. Sometimes I think it's better that Gregory is in hiding."

Passing through Orange County reminded Sylvia yet again how things change. In her youth she had travelled through the Irvine Ranch with her parents, enjoying the citrus orchards and planted rows of green. Now it was planned cities and upscale suburbs.

"What exactly do you do when a sighting report is sent in to the website?" Sylvia asked.

"We ask for details—you know: description, exactly where seen, who with, license plate number, etcetera. We ask if the sighter can get a second sighting. Very few sightings hold up because the detail is not credible. If the sighting passes this review, or if there is a second sighting in the same area, I will go investigate. So far the *Bee* has covered my travel. I've been to Vancouver, B.C., Austin, and Vermont. None of them panned out. The woman in Austin was a spitting image of Corinne and she had a one-year-old baby. But she also had an older child and a short husband."

Sylvia laughed. "So where do you think they are?"

Alice smiled. "Even though Mark's Saab was located in Tijuana, I don't think they are in Mexico. Neither Mark nor Corinne speak Spanish. I think they're in the U.S. or possibly Canada. And I can only conclude that they've been sequestered by someone, maybe in a remote area. But how long can that last? They aren't monks. It'll get old. Sooner or later they'll have to rejoin the world. After all, it won't be too long before Gregory should be in a preschool."

"I can't wait that long," Sylvia said. "I need a research experiment done on Gregory."

Alice looked over at her, confused.

"Wake me when we get there," Sylvia said, leaning her head back and closing her eyes.

Bushes and tree branches swayed in a brisk breeze as Alice exited the freeway. Zenya's address was two blocks from the San Diego Naval Training Center. They had no difficulty finding the townhouse building. Before going up the walk, they stretched and smoothed out their clothes under a bright afternoon sun. Their hair flew in the ocean wind.

Zenya recognized both women, greeted them warmly, and showed them into the small living room of the two-story unit. She was wearing an aquamarine, toga-like outfit that went well with her slender frame. She brought in a coffee decanter and cups on a tray.

"It's so nice of you to have us down and take time off from your work," Alice said.

"No trouble at all. I didn't take time off. I get every other Friday afternoon off like this. 'Sides, I'm really curious about what happened to Gregory, Corinne, and that Dr. Sandler. Mom says you would know if anyone does."

"Well, as I said, I don't know where they are," Alice said, "but I'll tell you as much as I do know."

She discussed at length the circumstances of the trio's disappearance from all sources known to her. She wrapped it up saying, "So I really don't have any clues on their whereabouts, and I don't know anyone who does."

Zenya sipped her coffee, then said, "Maybe the guy that sold Mark's car knows where they went."

"Possibly. But nobody knows who that person is, other than his description as a white male around thirty-five. The Mexican who bought the car doesn't speak much English and he dealt with the man for less than twenty minutes. It was a cash transaction."

Zenya laughed. "Pretty smart, ain't they."

Alice and Sylvia laughed and said in unison, "Yeah."

The conversation turned aimlessly to Zenya's apartment, living in San Diego, working for the Navy, growing flowers, and sewing. Refills of coffee were poured. Sylvia wondered if Zenya was as bored by the conversation as she seemed. Alice eventually hinted that the commuter traffic had probably eased and they would need to get back on the road.

After Alice and Sylvia declined more coffee, Zenya leaned forward. "Tell me, did you get a lot of money for bein' on TV?"

Alice and Sylvia glanced at each other. Sylvia said, "Some, but not a lot."

"How much was it?" Zenya pressed.

"Well, we each received five thousand dollars plus our travel expenses," Alice said.

Zenya's eyes widened. "I'd say that's a lot."

Alice shrugged. "I guess. Why do you want to know?"

"Well, I'm kind'a short these days. My car broke down and they can't do nothin' for it. I need to buy another one."

Alice and Sylvia again looked at each other.

"Would you want to go on TV?" Alice asked.

"Hell, no! I don't want no publicity, no way. And you both agreed not to say anything to anyone about me, right?"

"Of course. This is all confidential, Zenya," Alice said.

"Good." Zenya set her cup on the saucer and leaned back. A twinkle appeared in her large brown eyes. The corners of her lips hinted at something.

"I'd be willing to trade some information for a little fee, let's say, but it'd have to stay secret," she said.

Alice smiled. "Well, that has possibilities. I haven't spent my TV money, yet." She turned to Sylvia.

"I'd be willing to use some of my money too," Sylvia said. "Depending on how important the information is."

"I think it's worth five thousand," Zenya said. "It's a part of this Gregory business."

Alice chuckled. Sylvia frowned.

"Will you tell us what it is and then let us decide how much we think it's worth?" Sylvia asked.

Zenya turned her head and looked at them from the corners of her eyes. "Would you go the whole five thousand if it was really, really somethin'?"

"Yes," said Alice.

Sylvia shook her head, then looked at Alice who was nodding slightly.

"All right," Sylvia said.

Zenya ran her long fingers through her short hair. "Okay, just lean back on the couch there and don't get scared. It won't last long."

She closed her eyes, took a deep breath, and grimaced, obviously exerting herself.

As Sylvia watched the strange effort of the thin woman across from her, she felt some dizziness. Her head became light, like those times as a child when she spun around and around on the lawn. The room began to tip and she grabbed the back of the couch. She couldn't focus on anything and closed her eyes. Her stomach lurched and a strong wave of nausea went through her. She was afraid she would fall on her side, but there was no place to fall. She heard Alice moan. Just as Sylvia thought she might get sick to her stomach, the queasiness stopped. She opened her eyes and found the room had righted itself. She looked down at the table and then up at Zenya, who was staring at her with a coy smile. A hand took hers and she looked at Alice who had tears on her cheeks. Sylvia look back at Zenya.

"Was that good enough?" Zenya asked.

Chapter Nineteen

Rays of amber-tinted sunlight filtered through the branches of jacaranda and magnolia trees, dabbing speckled shadows on Jared and Ian's faces. The pair sat in folding chairs they had tucked into a secluded pocket of Sunset Park. The men engaged in conversation that hardly rose above the decibels reaching them from a spirited after-school soccer game some distance away. The summer air was warm and Jared had removed his tie.

"Even though we've had reduced contact, I think our talks in many ways have been more meaningful, don't you?" Jared said.

"For sure." Ian propped his sandaled feet on the trunk of a jacaranda.

"Before I talk about the hearing, would you please update me on Mark, Corinne, and the baby?"

Ian lit his pipe and blew an oblong smoke ring that twisted into a figure eight before it disappeared. "They're continuing to do well. Mark is getting more freelance computer work and recently started part-time as a physician's assistant for a local doctor. Corinne is mostly looking after Gregory, but also reading everything I send her. I love her letters. Her observations and questions are at the level of a PhD student. The baby . . . he's getting to be more of a handful. They're making progress on extinguishing the X, but realize it will take time. Gregory is saying short sentences. And he loves books and being read to. Colliver got him a book about climate change for kids, and Corinne says that he can't get enough of it. He's advanced a lot from when we last met."

Jared smiled, trying to picture the trio at a cabin in the forest. "Gregory's language is developing amazingly early. That's good. That can only help with managing the powers. They're not tiring of that incredibly rustic life? The isolation?"

"Oh, they miss some things. Playing on the internet, talking on the phone, stereo music, hot showers, a refrigerator. But I get the impression that they like the pioneer lifestyle even though it's challenging. I sense from Corinne's letters that this new life seems meaningful to them in a way that their previous life was not. They've even made a few friends, so are less lonely than they were at first."

"Hmpf. I can't believe they could be happy that way for long. Living in the past may be romantic, but it can't be satisfying."

Ian laughed. "You and I are of a different generation."

Jared threw him a dismissive look.

"And, no doubt they are being influenced by my culturally atavistic friend," Ian added.

"So tell me the latest on the senate review of Fazzi's charges—speaking of anachronisms."

Jared's eyebrow began to move and he pinched it with a thumb and forefinger. "Well, you remember that the senate's committee on charges met last spring. After a lot of wrangling they finally decided by a close vote that Fazzi's charge is legitimate."

Ian nodded. "That really surprises me."

"Yeah, it did everybody."

"The policy violation was what again?"

"You know, the way I handled Gregory was not in keeping with academic standards—that as colleagues, professors have obligations to a community of scholars, that the university seeks to sustain an environment of sharing, extending, and critically examining knowledge and values, and professors must further the search for wisdom, blah blah . . . you know, all the highfalutin' language."

Ian raised his hand. "But wasn't there some specific code you are supposed to have violated?"

"Yes, the language is embedded in my brain. As members of the academic senate, faculty must perform research with honesty and integrity, strive to contribute to the body of knowledge in their discipline, and disseminate such knowledge appropriately. Fazzi charges that I subverted this faculty code by not conducting appropriate research on Gregory and that I hid data and information from colleagues rather than disseminating it."

Ian shook his head. "This kind of charge is absolutely unheard of."

"Of course. That's why the committee argued so much. They knew that what they did or didn't do would set a precedent for SSU and maybe all universities. The problem was that if they didn't agree that the academic senate's high-minded principles were serious, they would undermine the whole notion of the academy—centuries of believing in the *community of scholars*."

"Uh huh. So what happens next?"

"To nobody's surprise, over the summer the president concurred with the committee's decision. So now the issue has been referred to, of all places, a divisional committee on Privilege and Tenure, just the same as all grievances and disciplinary cases. It's like I sexually assaulted somebody. And this committee can recommend censure, suspension, demotion, or dismissal."

"Unbelievable. Do you think Fazzi and Cameron have been the senate's driving force behind all this?"

"Fazzi, Cameron, and Reese. And probably, behind the scenes, the president. Rumor has it that the Shenko business has been embarrassing for the university, and the president can't bear that it happened on his watch. He's looking for a scapegoat."

"Thank god it's in the hands of faculty. They'll exonerate you quickly."

Jared was quiet for a few moments. "*That* I'm not sure of. I learned yesterday that the committee will hold hearings and has asked several people to appear in addition to me."

"Who?"

"Lou Fazzi, Jaime Valenzuela, Kurt Fonkels, and Sylvia."

"I see."

"The way I read it, Fazzi is a minus, Jaime a plus/minus, Kurt a weak plus, and Sylvia a minus."

"Why is Kurt only a weak plus?"

"Well, remember the committee Reese formed when Fazzi complained the first time? After that hearing, Kurt asked me to cooperate with Fazzi and I didn't."

"Prior documented evidence of uncollegiality."

"Yep."

"Do you talk with Sylvia at all?"

"Nope. I'm sure she's mad at me because she's not getting baby referrals. And Cameron is now her shining light."

Ian was quiet for a few moments. "No matter what the minuses say, they will sound like jealous colleagues. Your reputation will count for ten pluses."

From Ian's uncritical response, Jared knew that his prospects were grimmer than he had thought. "I wish I could believe that."

"Just keep positive, friend."

"I'll try."

The men were quiet for a minute, listening to the sounds of birds and baseball admixed.

"Jared, can I change the subject?"

"Sure."

"I want to show you something anthropological."

From a cardboard tube Ian pulled out a large sheet of paper on which were sketched outlines of several heads.

"These are side views of the shapes of six hominid heads, ranging from *Australopithecus* to modern human. How would you arrange them from the most primitive to current Homo *sapiens sapiens*?" He gave Jared a pencil.

Jared stared at the heads. "What is the point of the exercise, Ian? To determine my ignorance?"

"I'll tell you when you're done."

Jared marked them slowly. "This is clearly modern man. This small one is most ape-like, probably australopithecus. This one might be next to modern, say Cro-Magnon. Maybe this big one is Neanderthal. The other two are primitive, somewhere in the middle. I don't know the different forms—Homo *erectus*, *habilis*, *heidelbergensis*, whatever. This one looks kind of like a combo of *erectus*, Neanderthal and Cro-Magnon."

"Very good. I give you an A plus."

"So what's the point?"

"One of the heads is Gregory's, resized as an adult."

Jared looked at Ian. "You're kidding!"

"Not kidding."

"And . . . not the modern one?"

"No."

"Damn."

"He's this one," Ian pointed at one of the heads. "The one you described as a combo of *erectus*, Neanderthal, and Cro-Magnon."

"I'll be go to hell. I know that Neanderthal is now seen as having been smart, as having had language, and as having interbred with Cro-Magnon. Some of us even have Neanderthal genes. But Gregory—those brow ridges and the big, sloped back head are really that prominent?"

"I traced it from a photo I took. The nose, mouth, and chin are modern. It's the orbital and cranial structure that look ancient. It's most noticeable from a side view."

"So what is your explanation, Professor Trevor?"

"I have no explanation. But I would like to know a lot more about Gregory's ancestry."

"Well, there are the notes about the grandparents and relatives that Mark got from Rose. Don't you have those?"

"Yes, and I've read them. The grandparents are dead, but there is a great aunt named Galina who could be alive somewhere—maybe in North Carolina.

"Well . . ."

"Do you mind if I nose around?"

"Only if there is no connection made to Gregory, me, or this whole thing."

"Of course."

"And if you find out anything, tell me first."

"Of course."

CORINNE FELT HER SHOULDER blades and buttocks press against the flat granite chunk she had named Medicine Rock. An unusually hot October sun warmed her bare legs and midriff. She allowed the muscles in her neck to relax and closed her eyes as her head sunk into a small foam pillow she had brought. Being away from Gregory was heavenly. She smiled as she pictured his hesitant look when she had walked away from him and Colliver. Colliver had rattled a rock in a tin can to distract the tottering boy who looked back and forth between the two adults. She had turned and quickly strode away, expecting to hear him cry.

"Bye, bye, Ma ma. See you latee."

She had turned, shocked. Gregory waved at her.

"Go on, we'll be fine," Colliver had said, laughing.

Yes, even though Colliver could be a pain, he was a godsend. Without him they wouldn't have made it. He had given them a home, friends, and a way of life. And now he was a babysitter. But more than this, he was a confidante. He knew who they were and had accepted and valued them the same as his beloved trees and mountains.

Corinne remembered the time two months ago when Colliver discovered who they were. It had been one of those days. Gregory had thrown another tantrum which was not doused with a half cup of water. She had managed to run out of the cabin. As she hunched down on a tree round, nervously listening to the screams emanating from the cabin, Colliver appeared.

"My god, Susan, are you guys trying to wake up the Indian spirits?"

She had started and said something incomprehensible.

"What's the matter? Is Bret okay?"

"Oh, he'll be all right. I can't stand his screaming so I came out here." She knew there was anxiety in her voice.

"Let me go in and see if I can calm the little chipmunk."

"No, Bill . . ."

Colliver strode into the cabin. The screaming slowed momentarily then started again with a vengeance. Colliver bolted out the door, his face in pain and his arm crooked around his head. He stopped a few yards past Corinne and looked at her with stunned amazement. "What the shit?"

She began crying.

"Of course. *Jeesus!* He's that baby Gregory and you are the Fresno girl. Mike must be the doctor. Well, I'll be damned."

She nodded, sniffling.

That evening after Gregory was down, Mark, Corinne, and Colliver had talked late into the night. Colliver was surprised that they had been afraid to tell him because he might not keep their secret. "After all, what are friends for?" he asked with feigned insult. Colliver didn't think that any of their mutual friends would betray them if they knew. "We're not city folks up here. We need each other." That night Mark and Corinne had slept soundly.

Corinne turned onto her stomach and looked at the frothy water tumbling through the rocks in the creek bed. Ferns on the bank waved gingerly in a hesitant breeze. A dragonfly hovered over the water, then zoomed away. In the distance a crow gave a haunting caw.

She wondered if Gregory's feistiness would ever lessen. The terrible twos. Bad enough in a normal child, but much worse having to deal with the X. These days a "No, Bret" was as likely to set him off as not. He knew the water glass was always ready and had recently defied it even when thrown in his face full force. And for some reason he was more willing to X her than Mark. Maybe she wasn't tough enough? The last time she had been X'd Mark had filled a cooking pot with water and drenched the child. She chuckled, remembering the disbelieving look on Gregory's face as water dripped from his curls to the floor. Still, as bad as he was, she loved the little imp.

Corinne smiled and thought of last month when Mark had taken a three-week vacation. This had allowed her to visit a few friends and shop more often. She had written long letters to her parents. There had been more hikes, sometimes with Colliver. However, most of the time was spent around the cabin. Mark chopped wood while she sat under the trees and read, keeping an eye on Gregory playing nearby. The togetherness made her feel they were a real family, even though she knew better. It was a nice fantasy, though.

A leaf crackled. She rose up and turned to the sound. It was Arnie.

"Hi, Arnie. Come here, boy."

He allowed her to caress the soft, loose fur around his ears. His curved mouth seemed to be smiling.

"Did Bill tell you to come get me? Huh?" She looked into the animal's yellow eyes.

The wolf-dog whined.

"Okay."

She returned with Arnie to the cabin to find Mark out front with Colliver and Gregory.

"Hi, hon, what brings you home?" she said, kissing Mark on the cheek.

"I decided to come for lunch and take the afternoon off. Who knows how many days like this we'll see for a while."

"Smart," she said, winking at Colliver. "Hey, how about if I make us salami and cheese sandwiches?"

"Sounds good to me," Colliver said.

Mark moved over to Gregory. The child was pushing a little wooden car under a pile of sticks.

"What are you doing, Bret? Is that a garage, huh?"

Gregory looked at the boot next to the car, then up at Mark's face. Gregory pushed against Mark's leg.

"Aren't you going to let me play?"

"No. Go 'way."

Mark squatted down and tousled Gregory's hair. The boy started to whine, pushing at Mark.

"You'd better leave him alone—he's cranky," Corinne said. "On second thought, he's probably hungry. Maybe you should bring him in and we'll feed him." She started for the cabin.

"Okay, squirt, what do you say," Mark said. "Want to eat? Let's go in and get something good." Mark picked up Gregory and slung him to his shoulder.

Gregory began yelling and kicking. "Down, Daddy. Down, down." Mark headed for the cabin and the yell turned to a loud screech.

"Ah, damn!"

Mark let Gregory slip heavily to the ground and stumbled away, holding his head. Colliver ran off in the opposite direction. Corinne rushed back out the door and over to Mark, now leaning against a tree forty feet from Gregory. The child beat his hands in the dirt, his voice pulsing in angry screams between breaths. Colliver came around to Mark and Corinne and the three of them watched the infantile behavior for several minutes. The tantrum did not let up.

"Bill, will you help me?" Mark said, motioning toward the back of the cabin.

"Sure."

"What are you going to do?" Corinne asked.

"Use the wash tub," Mark replied.

"Oh, no," she said.

The men picked up the large galvanized tub behind the cabin and carried it to the creek, where they let it fill in a deep pool. Then they muscled it up the slope, trying to keep the water from sloshing out.

"Oh, god. It's full," Corinne cried. "You're not going to use all that, are you?"

"Sure are," Mark said.

They set the tub down and Mark edged toward Gregory to see if the X was still coming. It was. He retreated and they waited. After several more minutes Gregory's screeching scaled down to crying. Mark signaled Colliver and they carried the water over to the prone boy who managed to look up just as they positioned the tub. He screeched, but too late. The downpour doused the scream like a campfire. The water hit Gregory's face, body, and arms in a steady stream, running off to puddle around him. When the last drops had fallen, Gregory was coughing and gasping for air. Corinne quickly grabbed him up, turned him face down, and patted his back. Soon he was sobbing in her arms, mud all over his face. Eventually he stopped and gave a pouty look at Mark.

"No water, Daddy. No water, no water," he yelled.

"No hurt head," Mark said, pointing to his and Corinne's heads. "No hurt head? And no water."

Gregory looked at Mark. "No water, Daddy," he said in a softer voice.

"And no hurt head, Bret."

They stared at each other for a few moments, then Gregory said, "Okay. No hurt head, Daddy."

Mark's jaw dropped. The adults all looked at each other.

Late that night, as Mark and Corinne were about to get ready for bed, they heard a knock. Mark went to the door. "Who is it?" he asked softly.

"Bill."

Mark motioned him in.

"Shh, the baby's asleep. Is anything wrong?"

"Shit, no. I've just been thinking and I wanted to share something with you guys. Is it too late?"

Corinne came down the ladder in her pajamas and lit a lantern in the kitchen area. They sat around the table and talked in low voices. Gregory, asleep in the living room, did not stir.

Colliver rubbed his hands. "Okay, it's about Ludwig Wittgenstein, whose name used to come up a lot in this cabin."

"What about him?" Corinne said, a slight edge to her voice.

"Well, his philosophy seems difficult to a lot of people. But when you boil it down, it's simple."

"Uh huh," she said.

The kettle was still hot and Mark made tea.

"One of his concepts is that goodness, or value, or meaning, is not to be found from the outside world. Thus his statement: *The world is my world.*"

"Huh?" Corinne said.

Mark sipped and lowered his cup. "Does he mean that everyone interprets his own reality?"

"In a sense. More to the point, it is that the world is what it is. Whatever we find is the way things are and we must accept and endure."

"Oh," Corinne said. "You're right, he's not profound."

Colliver laughed. "You're tough, Susan."

"Well?"

Colliver continued. "Wittgenstein's position was that living the right way involves acceptance—or agreement with—the world, or God, or fate, whatever you believe."

Colliver drank his tea and watched his protégés, letting the ideas sink in.

"Is that all?" Mark asked.

Colliver laughed again. "A little more. Wittgenstein felt that one who lived in this way would see the world as a miracle. In other words, he believed that there is no answer to the problem of life. The solution is the disappearance of the problem."

Corinne narrowed her eyes. "Is this about Bret? Are we supposed to say that he's not a problem?"

"No. It's about all of life, and only about Bret to the extent that he's part of our lives."

"It's kind of an Eastern concept, isn't it?" Mark said.

Colliver smiled. "Wittgenstein was a modern European—Jewish in heritage, Catholic in religion, and an engineer by training. He gave up an inherited fortune. Believed in doing things the bloody hard way."

"Well, Bill, maybe you should give up your money," Corinne said.

Colliver grimaced, then downed his tea. "I think I'd better let you get your beauty sleep, Susan."

"I don't mean to be unfriendly, Bill, but philosophy goes better at a decent hour, I think," she said.

"Thanks for stopping by and sharing, Bill," Mark said. "We'll think on Wittgenstein."

Colliver nodded. "I have a book that will help you, if you want. Thanks for the tea."

EVEN THOUGH SHE was a celebrity of sorts, Alice perceived the status change immediately. Moving into the student role from the world of work was a come down. Still, she was enjoying it. The uniform of T-shirts, jeans, and sandals wasn't so bad after all. Her classmates were warming to her after a period of awe. The professors, at first amused or skeptical, soon responded favorably to her serious-ness and hard work.

And hard work it was. Fortunately, her undergraduate biochemistry, genetics, and statistics began coming back. She found that she liked molecular biology. Basically it was playing Sherlock Holmes, only the intricate puzzles to be solved involved material you couldn't see, and the bewildering number of lab tests you had to master often didn't work. Then, more like Watson than Holmes, every so often you had to show everyone how dumb you were by explaining what you were trying to do. No wonder there was hubris in science. It was incubated by years of humiliation.

She tossed her briefcase onto the kitchenette table, consulted the Roladex, and dialed an SSU number.

"Hi, Sylvia, this is Alice. Can you talk?"

"Alice! I've been thinking of you. We haven't talked since before you started school. Have they buried you?"

"They're trying, but I love it. I had such great classes today, I had to call someone."

"That's terrific."

Alice and Sylvia chattered like long separated parakeets put back together. They brought each other up to date on their lives. Alice was excited to learn that Sylvia had visited Zenya twice since the three of them had met in San Diego.

"What's happening with her?" Alice asked.

"Well, she had to show me her new Honda Civic. It's a pretty metallic green. She's very happy with it and wanted to thank us. I'm supposed to pass that along to you. Of course I tried to learn more about her power—which I'm calling the X2. She told me it developed about the same time as her period. Or, at least that's when she discovered it."

"That's interesting."

"Right. She didn't want to talk about the sexual business with Nick and his using his powers on her. But she did say that she could counteract both his X and Y with her X2 when he was up close. She used her power to stop him whenever he tried his Y on her—except for a couple of times that she wouldn't talk about. And after a while, he left her alone."

"Wow."

"Yeah."

"Do you think the X2 co-evolved to protect that genetic line of women against the X and Y?"

"It's the only hypothesis I can think of—a defense against unwanted seduction and pregnancy."

"Incredible, isn't it."

"Uh huh."

"Worth the five thousand dollars?"

Sylvia laughed. "Rub it in."

"So what happened on the second visit?" Alice asked.

"Nothing. We talked about this and that. I just want to develop a friendship with her. I'm thinking I'll go down there every few months."

"Friendship for friendship's sake, or to get her to undergo testing?"

Sylvia chuckled. "Well, both. Getting her to agree to testing will take a while."

"And a chunk of money."

"That too, I'm sure. But she wouldn't do it unless there was also trust."

"Well, good luck."

Alice, shifting in the chair, loosened her belt and unbuttoned her jeans. She would need to get back to the gym soon, she thought.

"Did you happen to see the article in the *LA Tribune* published on the anniversary of Gregory's disappearance?" Sylvia asked.

"Yeah, I pulled it off the wire. Most of their info came from my website and my previous articles. They weren't about to interview me, though."

"It was pretty balanced, I thought," Sylvia said. "Except for the business about the academic senate review taking place with Jared."

"Yeah, I hadn't been following that. What's happening now?"

"Still moving like molasses."

"When will you meet with the committee?"

"Next spring at this rate. Or maybe never. Some of my department colleagues say I should decline to appear. But Cameron and Fazzi say my testimony is really important. So, I don't know."

"Why is it going so slow?"

"You know faculty, they deliberate *slooowly*. Now that there is public interest and scrutiny from faculty at other U's, this little committee is moving at a snail's pace, checking everything, trying to maintain consensus on procedure. In fairness to them, this is new ground and could set a precedent."

"Understandable." Alice reached back and unhooked her bra. "You know, Sylvia, I don't have the greatest track record with men. I end up going out with too many losers. Thinking about the X2 power—if I had that, it would be really useful. Just a little touch of that at the right time."

Sylvia laughed. "I know what you mean. But I think I would rather my husband have the Y and to heck with the X2."

"No!"

"I didn't say that. My sex life is fine."

Alice laughed. "You know, of all the people who email into the website, about two-thirds are women. And most ask if the Y power is for real and what it feels like. So, if you ever wanted to go on a speaking tour, you could probably make a lot of money."

"I may have to if I don't figure out how to make tenure."

"Are you getting any more infant referrals?"

"Only from one part-time doctor at the clinic and the babies are few and far between. I wish I had time to change to a new line of research that doesn't require babies. But I don't—at least not enough time to establish myself."

"You're in a tough spot."

"At least my termination will not be as dishonorable as Jared's."

AFTER THE TUB TRAUMA, Gregory never again used the X power on Mark or Corinne, a development that gave the two immense satisfaction. Because of this and his spurt in growth and language, three months later Corinne decided to take Gregory for a nursery school assessment. The day nursery school was held in a converted double garage in North San Juan. The school had a fenced yard with colorful play structures that could be seen from the main road through town. The teacher-owner, Mrs. Grace Harmon, had a welcoming smile and a gift of gab that put strangers at ease quickly.

"We place children according to their developmental level, not necessarily their age," she said. "Is Bret potty-trained?"

"Yes, he got out of diapers quite a while ago and is doing surprisingly well."

"That's wonderful." Mrs. Harmon bent down to Gregory's level. "Bret, would you like to come inside and play with some toys? The other children are outside and you'll have all of the toys to yourself."

"Yes. Can I ride the horsey?" He pointed to a rocking horse along one side of the large room.

"You surely may," she said.

Gregory started jumping up and down.

"Say thank you, Mrs. Harmon," Corinne said.

"Thank you . . . Mrs. Harm," he said, looking at the teacher and smiling shyly.

"Before you go, Bret, can you count to five?" Mrs. Harmon asked.

"One, two, free, four, five, six, seben, eight, nine, ten, leben, twelf, dirteen . . . uh, twenty. Can I go now?"

Soon Gregory was moving among the wonderland of toys, trying everything he came to.

"He's well behaved," Mrs. Harmon said. "More mature socially than most of our three year olds—but he would do fine in that group."

"But he's only two and a half," Corinne said.

Mrs. Harmon laughed. "That boy is older than two and a half. He could start kindergarden at age four."

Mrs. Harmon decided that Gregory should start in a six-child play group beginning in two weeks.

With that, the issues of a second car and a driver's license for Corinne became a prime conversational topic for the couple. They finally left Gregory with Colliver one day and drove to Reno, coming back with a birth certificate for Susan A. Harris, born in Chicago. For five hundred dollars they picked up a battered 1975 VW bug from the poet's brother, who said the Beetle was in good enough shape to get from Colliver's canyon to North San Juan and back every day. That same week Mark received a substantial raise and more hours working for Dr. Beamer, who found his assistant amazingly versed in the ways of medicine as well as computers. And not long after that, Corinne became a teacher's aide for several hours a week, assisting Mrs. Harmon with Gregory's play group.

One late spring evening as Mark and Corrine walked along the path from Colliver's cabin to their own, they stopped to look at bats darting in the last vestiges of twilight over the western hills.

"You never see that in the city," Mark said.

"Maybe Colliver's right not to have electric lights. You develop sharper night eyes," Corinne said.

"Yeah."

"Mike, do you have the feeling that we're putting down roots?"

"I can feel them sinking deeper each day."

"Are you okay with that?"

"Yeah. Yesterday I looked at the Whitehead Genome Project website for old time's sake. I thought about sending an email saying, 'You idiots are out of touch. Do you even know who Wittgenstein was?' But I didn't. Wittgenstein wouldn't have."

CHAPTER TWENTY

THE TOPS OF THE QUARTERING waves occasionally slapped *Tomolo's* bow as she grace-
fully lifted herself over each swell like a seaborne hurdler. Jared had the sloop
close-hauled to prevent any angling toward the beach. He took his eyes from the
taut-sheeted dacron and gazed at the boxy buildings of downtown Santa Monica
and then further west to the haze-enshrouded Malibu hills, all dotted with ocean-
view houses and condos. He had taken the afternoon off at Joan's suggestion.
She knew that a solo sail was probably the most relaxing thing he could do the
day before the Promotions and Tenure committee's last hearing—the one where
Sylvia would be questioned.

Jared couldn't decide whether he was amused or disgusted. After dawdling
most of the year, the committee had suddenly decided to have two rapid meetings:
a hearing with Sylvia in late May and an executive session in early June. At the
latter, the committee would reach a judgment. Jared would be present for Sylvia's
testimony but he would have to remain silent, as he had at all of the meetings
where witnesses had appeared. After she was excused, he would be provided with
only fifteen minutes to say what he wanted—rebuttal, new information, plea for
lenience, whatever.

He turned *Tomolo's* big chrome wheel to miss the Santa Monica buoy that
bonged haphazardly with the waves. Fat brown seals lay on the red buoy, raising
their heads only if boats came close. Jared wondered how the animals could
snooze on a rocking, clanging bed of steel. The bonging was like an alarm, forcing
his mind back to his predicament. Yesterday he had heard the faculty scuttlebutt
that Sylvia would drive nails into his coffin. With most of the testimony against
him, the P and T committee would feel obligated to make a strong statement for

preserving the academic community myth, which was more important than the myth of an individual faculty member's rights. It did seem that bad news was coming.

He and Joan had carefully reviewed their retirement program. They would be fine if worse came to worse. Still, he doubted there would be a dismissal. If the decision was between dismissal or demotion, he would resign. He had his pride. But he did have the right of appeal. Some friends advised him to go down fighting, that he would have a chance with the board if not the president. He didn't relish the idea. He preferred accepting his medicine with dignity. After all, it would be better than the beheadings of twelfth- and thirteenth-century scholars, or Galileo's treatment by the Inquisition.

Beating into the wind was a lot like pursuing a career, he thought. You faced water over the bow on some days and easy motion on others. Either way there was always the feeling of moving ahead. Retirement, however, was like coming about and sailing downwind. The sense of progress was lost because the following waves frequently moved faster than the boat. "May you have fair winds and following seas" would no doubt be said at his retirement dinner. So be it. He spun the wheel. It was time to head home.

THE MEETING WAS HELD again in the Tom Bradley Conference Room of the Faculty Center. Jared felt trepidation, waiting for the question period to begin. He held his eyebrow as a precautionary step and looked at each of the five full professors, all casually dressed. He glanced at the boney woman with the small tape recorder, the university's general counsel in the pinstriped suit, and finally at Sylvia in a simple green dress. She continued to avoid eye contact with him.

The committee chair, Roy Kazewski, a jovial, jowly man with white hair, was a member of the National Academy of Sciences and a leader in the field of protein structure and x-ray crystallography. As a longtime chair of the biochemistry and molecular biology department he was experienced at controlling meetings. He explained the procedure to Sylvia and stated that the committee was focusing on specific issues, namely whether Dr. Weymouth had withheld information from or misled colleagues, had not collaborated forthrightly, or had not appropriately sought new knowledge as a member of a community of scholars.

At Kazewski's invitation, Sylvia provided an overview of her past research work with Jared, her involvement with Corinne and Gregory Shenko, and her change to the Department of Psychology.

She ended with, "I am ready for any questions the committee might have."

Professor Claire Ryan of OBGYN led off. "Dr. Auerbach, did Dr. Weymouth ever keep information from you about the Shenkos?"

Sylvia joined her hands and leaned forward. "Yes, when he first asked me to test the baby, he did not tell me about the nature of the lesion or that the baby had exhibited the ability to cause seizures in others, what he called the X power."

"And do you think that was inappropriate on his part, with your being a long-term research collaborator?" Ryan asked.

"Uh, no. Not at all. In this instance it was very appropriate."

There was a pause and some shuffling. Jared caught his breath.

"Well then, how was that appropriate?" Ryan asked.

"As he explained to me later, he wanted me to be unbiased in my testing of the infant. I possibly could have been influenced by Gregory's history if I had known more. Or, I might have been frightened or nervous."

Professor Solomon of the Department of Medicine interjected. "Wait a minute. Are you saying then that Dr. Weymouth's interactions with you were fully appropriate concerning your collaboration on this case?"

"Yes. They were fully appropriate."

"But that is not what we had heard," Solomon said with exasperation.

"From whom?" Sylvia asked.

"That doesn't need to be answered at this point," Kazewski said quickly. He nodded at Professor Jacque Taché of the Brain Research Institute.

"Dr. Auerbach, is it not true that Dr. Weymouth told you and others at one point that he wanted there to be no further testing of the so-called X and Y powers, that nobody should know about them, and that nothing should be published about them?"

Sylvia smiled thinly. "Let's take those separately, Professor Taché. Dr. Weymouth did not want invasive procedures such as in-dwelling electrodes or an angiogram, and I concurred that those were not advisable. He did not want to further stimulate the alleged powers, but he did want continued behavioral research, and he wanted me to be heavily involved in this. For reasons of patient confidentiality he did not want the Shenko case discussed outside our group, which is normal procedure for the Division of Child Development. He did publish on the lesion with Jaime Valenzuela. He did not want to publish on the X and Y powers because there were no data to support these notions, as he has said elsewhere."

Professor Barbara Nishi of the Department of Physiology began chuckling, her hand in front of her mouth.

"Dr. Nishi, do you have a question?" Kazewski said.

"I'm just thinking that it sounds like Dr. Auerbach and Dr. Weymouth had a good working relationship, contrary to what we were led to believe."

"Did you have a question?" Kazewski again asked Nishi.

The woman nodded. "Okay, a question. Dr. Auerbach, we heard that you differed with Dr. Weymouth about whether the public's right to know about the child outweighed the child's right to privacy. Someone said you gave the example of Typhoid Mary. Please comment on this."

"Before you answer that," Kazewski said, "and we want you to answer it, let me say something. Matters such as human subject approval, patient confidentiality, the right to privacy, or the public's right to knowledge, are not the issues we are focusing on. The committee will not ignore them, but they are ancillary to our decision-making. It should be kept in mind that collaborators are normally expected to be capable of maintaining confidentiality about research subjects and honoring their right to privacy. Okay, you may answer."

Sylvia shifted in her chair and frowned.

"The answer is that Jared and I did have opposing opinions on Gregory's and Corinne's right to privacy and still do," Sylvia said. "I came to believe the public should know about the child's powers. And as you know, I took steps with Ray Cameron to publicize information about Gregory at the NPA meeting and afterward in the media. I'm sure Jared did not approve of my actions. But, colleagues should be able to continue collaborative relations even with disagreements. In other words, to agree to disagree and move forward."

"Aha! Exactly," said Taché. "But Dr. Weymouth did not do that with Dr. Fazzi. They had a minor misunderstanding and then Jared cut him out completely— in a very uncollegial way."

Taché glared at Jared who looked away. Sylvia glanced at her former mentor and their eyes met for a second.

"Dr. Taché," Sylvia said. "I don't know the details of what happened between Jared and Dr. Fazzi. However, I would suggest a point for your consideration. Jared and Dr. Fazzi had never collaborated. They had never published together. So there was no successful history. A serious misunderstanding early in a relationship is hard to get beyond. We all know that collaborations can't be forced. I don't think Jared's collegiality can be judged on one potential collaboration that went sour. He has collaborated happily with quite a number of colleagues at SSU and at other universities throughout his career."

"But what about you and Jared?" Professor Larry Larsen of the Department of Surgery was a big man with a deep voice. "Hasn't your relationship ended because of your disagreement?"

Sylvia cleared her throat with difficulty.

"There's a glass of water behind you on a table," Kazewski said softly.

"Thank you." Sylvia turned and took some water.

Jared wiped his forehead with his handkerchief.

"My relationship with Jared has continued, though it is understandably not as close as it was when I was in the Division," Sylvia said. "I continue to be referred some infant patients from his clinic. My recent publication in the *Journal of Infant Development* was challenged by a letter to the editor, and this was not long after I had appeared on TV. I sent a copy to Jared asking how I should answer. He sent me several thoughtful paragraphs. Let me say that I know if I walked into Jared's office today to talk about joint research interests, he would act like a friend and colleague. In fact, I plan to do this soon because I have an idea about designing an experiment that could physiologically substantiate one of Gregory's X and Y powers."

Jared tightened his face, trying to stem the flow. He pushed his handkerchief against his eyes, but couldn't control the burst of feeling. His choking gave way to sobs. He heard the sound as if it were from someone else. He wished he could vanish.

Conversation stopped. Everyone looked at the pained soul slouched in his chair, his body racking involuntarily.

"Let's take a ten-minute break," Kazewski said.

Sylvia, teardrops moving down her cheeks, hurried over to Jared, and put her arms around him.

THE VAN'S LOW GEAR whined in pain as Mark eased down the switchbacks. He loved this last stretch of the drive home, with its glimpses of the cabins amid the proud pines and the thick creekside verdure. Soon Arnie would bound up the road to meet him and then prance alongside the van, as if daring the steel monster to get away.

The day had been unusually good. Doc Beamer had become a believer of Mark's prowess with medical websites. Mark had plugged in the woman's symptoms: blurred vision, dry mouth, and difficulty in speaking and swallowing. Beamer thought it some kind of poison—rattlesnake or spider—but Mark came up with botulism. Sure enough, the woman had eaten some home-canned vegetables. An ambulance had whisked her from Beamer's office to intensive care at the regional hospital. A doctor from the hospital later called to say she was recovering and to congratulate Beamer on the rare diagnosis.

Corinne met Mark at the door in shorts and halter. He embraced and kissed her strongly.

"Well, you're in a good mood," she said, pushing away.

"Where's the squirmer?" Mark asked.

Gregory rolled out from under his bed. "Ha, ha, ha."

Mark grabbed him up and hugged him.

"How's my little pumpkin head?" Mark asked, tickling Gregory who squirmed and laughed. "Although I have to say you're getting a lot bigger."

Gregory banged his fists on Mark's head. "You're a punkin' head, Daddy."

"Bret's a little hyper because he knows we have to talk about something with you," Corinne said.

"What's hyper, Mommy?"

"Never mind. Let's have dinner now, then we can all talk, okay?"

Mark looked at Corinne, trying to discern how serious the problem might be. "Okay, Mommy."

She served skirt steak, cooked carrots, wheat bread, and a small salad. During dinner Mark told her about the botulism case and other news from work. Gregory spilled his milk and then quieted with embarrassment when Mark scolded him. After a dessert of blackberry pie, Gregory climbed up on Mark's lap, waiting for his mother to clear the dishes.

"So what happened today?" Mark asked.

Corinne leaned back against the sink, hands on hips. "Bret got on this tricycle that another boy, Jimmy, had been riding and Jimmy came back and tried to push Bret off. Bret started yelling at Jimmy and pushed him back. And then Jimmy screamed and ran away. He went to the teacher saying that his head hurt."

Gregory put his thumb in his mouth and leaned back against Mark.

"Was anyone else near Bret?" Mark asked.

"Yes, a little girl was right next to them but didn't seem to have any problem. And I was about ten feet away and I didn't feel anything."

"Maybe Jimmy bumped his head on something."

"I was watching and it didn't look like it. This has happened a couple of times before and each time I didn't think it was the X because nobody else near Bret was affected. It always happens with just one child and always when Bret is angry at that child."

Mark encircled his arms around Gregory. "So what are you saying, that Bret has learned to aim at just one person?"

She nodded.

"I find that hard to believe." Mark turned Gregory around to look into his face.

"Bret, did you hurt Jimmy in the head?" he asked sternly.

"But he . . . I had the bike. And he pushed me."

"What did you do to him?"

"Nothing."

"Did you hurt him in the head, Bret?"

"I didn't hit him."

"But did you hurt him with your head?"

"But he . . . He was hurting me."

"Bret!" Mark grabbed Gregory's arms tightly. "Did you hurt him in the head? Answer me."

"I didn't do it hard."

Mark and Corinne exchanged a deep look.

"Bret, listen to me," Mark said. "You are never to do that again to anyone. I don't want you to do that any more. Do you understand?"

"Yes."

"I mean it, Bret. If I ever hear of you doing that again, you will be in deep trouble. Is that clear?"

"Yes, Daddy."

Gregory then said, "Daddy, can I change the subject?"

"What is it?" Mark asked.

"Could I have a new book about global warming?"

"What?" Mark asked incredulously. "You already have a book."

"Yeah, but that's a baby book. I want a grown up book."

"Why all this interest in global warming?" Mark asked.

Gregory pointed to the top of his head. "I can tell that it's happening."

"What do you mean?" Mark said.

Gregory looked directly in Mark's eyes. "I can sense it."

Mark looked at Corinne, who raised her shoulders as if to say, *beats me.*

"Okay, go read your other new book. Mommy and I want to go outside for a while. I'll give you a horsey ride in a few minutes."

"Oh, good."

Outside, Mark looked at Corinne.

"Shit!" he said with clenched teeth. "Just when we thought we were getting ahead. Now he can direct the X at individual people. And he says he 'senses' global warming. Do you believe that? There is just no way he could detect those conditions."

She took his hand and they walked slowly down the path toward Medicine Rock as the sun began to set.

"Bill said on their walks he could zap specific animals without Bill's feeling it," Corinne said. "So maybe individual people is not too surprising. The global warming thing is out of the blue. But I do know this—Mrs. Harmon says he's now reading at the third grade level, head and shoulders above everyone in her pre-school. She thinks he should skip kindergarten and first grade and start second grade soon."

~

IN THE HOSPITAL espresso bar Sylvia took a small empty table in the corner. She expected to be nervous; instead she felt upbeat. It had been that way for the past week—ever since the P and T committee had released its report. She hadn't wanted to meet with Jared before then, even though he had invited her to coffee the day after the hearing, and even though the head nurse at the clinic had called to say they had an office for her to use in reviewing cases for her study.

Jared walked in, waved at her, bought a cup of coffee, and came over and sat down. The smiles were broad and the eye contact strong before either said anything.

"Thank you," Jared said earnestly. "Thank you for rescuing me."

She smiled. "I just did what was right."

"But, you didn't have to do it."

She shrugged. "I hear the report has gone to the president. Do you have any idea what he will do?"

Jared savored his coffee, then smiled. "I got an email from him a half hour ago. He said he would accept the committee's recommendation that no action be taken against me. He accepts their finding that there is not convincing evidence of any wrongdoing."

"Marvelous!" She reached across the table and squeezed his hands.

He nodded and laughed. "Yeah."

"I think the majority of faculty were on your side and he came to realize it," she said.

"I think so, and that is gratifying."

"So," she said, "will your life get back to normal?"

"Slowly. But I can't get this behind me until you tell me something."

Her forehead wrinkled up. "What?"

"Why you did what you did at the hearing."

She looked away for a moment, then smiled. "Well, there were several reasons. One is that you had treated me well for ten years. How could I overlook that?"

He nodded.

"Another is that the charge was basically unfair. Fazzi was trying to destroy you. All the high-minded language about the community of scholars couldn't sugarcoat his venom."

Jared laughed.

"A third reason," she said, "is that right now I'm in the same situation you were in. I'm withholding information on a potential research subject that would be of great interest to others."

Jared's jaw dropped. "You are?"

"Yes."

He roared with laughter and Sylvia joined in.

"And finally . . ." she said. "Finally, there is the selfish reason that I want to continue collaborating with you."

"On Gregory or in general?"

"Both. I meant it when I said I have an idea for an experiment when Gregory comes out of hiding. The only condition is that I be senior author on any publication."

Jared looked at her seriously. "Fair enough. Do you want to tell me about your idea?"

"I'll write it up and send it over in a week or so—marked *privileged communication*." She winked.

"Good. So does that Alice reporter think that Gregory is going to become available?"

"Not necessarily. By the way, Alice has started in a neuroscience PhD program at UC Davis."

"That's interesting. But it would take a helluva lot more for her to be redeemed with me."

"Well, stranger things have happened."

Jared gave Sylvia the cross sign for warding off evil. They both laughed.

As Sylvia got up to leave, Ian walked up.

"Well hello, Ian," Sylvia said. "I haven't seen you in a long time."

"Hi, Sylvia, Jared. I've been hiding."

"I guess," she said. "I have to leave, but one of these days we should have coffee."

"That would be good," Ian said.

They waved as she left. Then Ian and Jared sat down.

"Were you looking for me?" Jared asked.

"I went to your office and Lena said I might find you here. I take it that things are all okay between you and Sylvia?"

Jared smiled. "Couldn't be better."

"That's great. Maybe I'll take her up on the offer of coffee."

"I think you should. So what's up?"

"I've got information on Gregory's great aunt, Galina Shenko."

"Really?" Jared sat forward.

"Yeah. Let me tell you what happened. I have this former postdoc, Bill Tang, who is on the faculty at Chapel Hill. He owed me a favor and I asked him to look in major city phone books in North Carolina for her name. Well, there wasn't anything in current directories, but he went back five years and found her listed in Durham. One weekend he drives over there to her address—an apartment building. She wasn't living there, but he goes around to the neighbors. A lady knew this Galina, but said she lost her memory and was put in a nursing home there in Durham. So Bill talks this neighbor into going with him to pay Galina a visit. He calls me from the home and says Galina is in pretty bad shape, doesn't remember anybody, not even her friends. Early onset Alzheimer's."

Jared shook his head. "What a shame. For her and us."

"Yeah, but let me finish. I asked Bill if he could find out about her physician so we could see if a CAT scan or MRI was ever done. And he got me the doctor's name and number at Duke."

Jared laughed. "Pretty clever, Ian."

Ian smirked. "So today I got this letter in the mail." He handed it to Jared.

"From the doctor?"

"No, read it."

Jared pulled out the letter and a thick lock of grayish brown hair fell on the table.

"What the hell is this?"

"Galina's hair."

"What?"

Ian laughed. "Bill spent some time with Galina, combed her hair . . . and clipped a little, I guess."

Jared looked suspiciously at Ian. "What are you planning to do with it?"

"With your permission—I repeat, with your permission—I have a friend up at Berkeley who does mitochondrial DNA analysis."

Jared touched his eyebrow. "The mitochondrial Eve stuff. Everyone's African ancestor."

"Exactly."

"What would you expect that to show?"

"Probably nothing. It's a very long shot. And mtDNA dating is still controversial. But what the hell? Why not give it a go? I don't have to tell my friend anything other than asking him to do the analysis. I'll pay the fee he charges."

Jared tapped his chin and looked up at the ceiling. "Well, okay. But again, no linkage to the Shenko case or to me. And I'm the first to know the result."

"But of course."

"What about the MRI on Galina?"

"Right. I talked with the doctor and he remembered Galina but said there was nothing unusual on the scan which I think we can safely conclude means no lesion."

"Well, if there is no lesion, I don't understand the point of doing a mitocho-drial analysis on Galina."

"We're looking at dating the maternal line."

Jared shook his head. "Explain it to me if you get any results worth talking about."

Ian laughed and slapped Jared on the shoulder.

IN FRONT OF THE CABIN the little boys in trunks and cut-off jeans moved about like jumping beans. They screamed, ran, squatted, poked, hopped, and laughed. From the cabin doorway Corinne looked at the bodies through squinted eyes and saw a collage of blurry limbs that reminded her of modern ballet. It was beautiful.

"It's my birthday, so I get to go down the rock slide first," Gregory shouted.

There were jeers in response.

"I'm oldest, so I go next," a brown-skinned boy yelled.

"I don't care, I'm playing water wheel," said another boy.

Mark rose up from tying a boy's shoes. "Hey, listen up! Everybody got their water wheel and towel? We're going down now to the creek single file, following Mr. Colliver."

"Yeah, kids," Colliver said in his deep voice. "Anybody acts like a twerp and I'll feed him to the bears."

The kids screamed and jumped. Gregory growled and flashed his teeth, bear-like.

"You, too, Bret," Colliver said.

Derisive laughter.

"What's a twerp?" a blond boy asked.

More laughter.

"A twerp is someone who doesn't know what a twerp is," Colliver replied.

Louder laughter.

"Okay, head 'em out," Mark yelled.

"What are we, cows?" Gregory said.

The unruly dance moved down the path with Arnie prancing out on the flank.

Mark and Corinne exchanged waves.

"Have fun, guys," she yelled. "Work up an appetite for cake."

Back inside the cabin she smiled to herself. How had Gregory turned so quickly into a boy? She continued food preparation for the barbecue. His rapid development continued to amaze her. And the best part was that he had become more social and was now maintaining friendships with other boys. No, the best part was that for many months he had not used his X power, at least not when she or Mark were around to observe. The big issue now was starting him in second grade. Mrs. Harmon had talked with the elementary school, shared some test results, and thought they would accept him with her recommendation. Clever Mark had suggested getting Gregory a birth certificate with a date earlier than the real date. But then they'd have to tell him he was actually older than he thought. She wasn't sure that was a good idea, although Gregory would think it "super." He was more than ready for school. She hummed as she formed the hamburger patties.

The boys dragged back in ones and twos with Mark and Colliver bringing up the rear. None of the gang was too beat to down burgers, pop, and chocolate cake even though the Happy Birthday song to Gregory sounded anemic. The birthday boy summoned enough breath to knock out the four candle flames in one blast. After the cake was eaten, Corinne brought out the presents the boys had brought. Gregory ripped off the wrapping paper. There was a penlight, a miniature tom-tom, a squirt gun, a bag of candy—quickly broken open—and a computer game CD. Gregory looked at it curiously.

"What's this?" he asked the boy who had given it to him.

"A CD game, silly. For your PC. It's really fun."

"We don't have a computer." Gregory looked at the boy, then at Mark.

"Huh? You don't?" the boy said.

"We don't have any electricity."

All of the boys looked at Gregory. One said, "That's weird."

"Don't you watch TV?" asked the blond boy.

Gregory looked at the ground and shook his head slowly.

"Tell me something, boys," Colliver said. "Would you rather go swimming in the creek or watch TV?"

"Swimming," most of the boys said.

"Sure. Would you rather see a real bear outdoors or a pretend bear on your computer screen."

"A real bear."

"Sure you would. Well, that's what Gregory gets. Real life, not fake life. Isn't he lucky?"

"Yeah," some said, but not convincingly.

Long after his friends had gone and Gregory had bedded down for the night, Mark, Corinne, and Colliver sipped wine in front of Colliver's cabin. A kerosene lamp hanging from a tree branch threw dim, flickering light.

"As advanced as he is, I still wouldn't put him in school yet," Colliver said. "He's just turning into a little hiker. Let him see more nature this year. I'll hike his legs off. He'd be better off with that than in a crowded classroom. There's plenty of time for school."

Mark picked up a pine cone and threw it toward the creek. The stillness was broken by crackling bounces. "You've been great with him, Bill, but he wants to be with other kids."

"Whatever we do," Corinne said, "we need to move to a house with electricity. I want him to have a computer. I don't care about a TV. But he just can't be computer illiterate."

"Oh, god. Go ahead, do what all the lemmings do," Colliver said with disgust. Mark gave Colliver a sharp look.

Colliver frowned. "Shit, I can't believe this . . . after all our discussions." He gulped his remaining wine. "I think I'll turn in before I say something totally obnoxious."

THE NEXT MORNING as he stepped out the door on his way to work, Mark found an envelope on the threshold. He called Corinne and together they read the handwritten note from Colliver.

> Mike and Susan,
> I was out of line last night. Maybe I just don't want to see good friends leave. I understand about Bret. I'm off backpacking for a couple of weeks, but there is something I neglected to mention. The Korsens are moving to Arizona because of his health. You are welcome to move into that house. It has two bedrooms, electricity, shower, hot bath, all the American Dream stuff. It's closer to the road and the school bus goes right by, which I know Bret will ride. The house needs work: roof, flooring in kitchen, plumbing, painting, etc. If you're willing to fix it up, there would be no rent. You would pay only utilities and taxes. You'd still have to talk philosophy (just kidding). I told the Korsens that you might be by to look it over.
> Cheers, Bill

That evening after dinner Mark began packing an overnight bag, planning to leave before sunrise to attend a two-day conference for physician assistants in Oakland. Dr. Beamer had suggested he attend and had agreed to pay all expenses. Mark would ride with a fellow from Grass Valley.

"I stopped by the Korsen's yesterday," Mark said. "They told me to come by any time. So I thought we could go look seriously the day after I'm back."

"What'd it seem like?" Corinne asked.

"I didn't go in. It's about 1400 square feet, I'd guess. Pretty run down."

"Do I get my own room?" Gregory shouted from the floor where he was reading the new book on global warming that Mark had given him for his birthday.

"Hush. We don't even know if we're going to move there," Corinne said.

"I want to," he replied in a whiny voice.

"We'll see, sport," Mark said.

"When are they moving out?" Corinne asked.

"In two months. They're going to a retirement center in Scott's Valley. They complained that Bill never would repair anything."

"That figures. Well, the timing would be right if we wanted to start him in school," she said.

"I want to go into second grade," Gregory said.

"We know," Mark said. "We'll talk about it when I'm back. Now Bret, I'm leaving before you get up tomorrow and I'll be gone for two days. Bill is gone too. So you are the man. You have to take care of Mommy and do whatever she says. Is that clear?"

"Yes." Gregory came over and put his arms around Mark's upper legs. "Why do you have to go?"

"I have to go for my job. But I'll be back before you know it."

Corinne came close and whispered in Mark's ear. "I think he's nervous because this will be the first time you've ever been gone."

"Mmhh," Mark murmured.

At preschool the next day, Corinne thought that Gregory played and interacted normally. But when they came home she noticed that he was clingy and wanting to talk to the point of being silly. She gave him frequent hugs. After dinner she sat down with Ian's latest article. Gregory came over and put his head on her lap.

"Mommy, I want to sleep with you tonight."

Corinne ran her hand across his forehead. "You're not doing very well, are you? Okay, you can sleep with me, but you have to go to bed at your usual time. I'm staying up for a while to read."

"Oh, good."

"I expect you to be asleep when I come to bed."

He nodded. "Okay."

Corinne read for an hour, then wrote a short letter to Ian, commenting on his article supporting the theory that the first humans in the Americas arrived on the west coast in boats. She closed with a note about the birthday party and told about Gregory using the X on individual people and also his claim to *sense* global warming. She ended it with, "As usual, your materials save me from boredom. Thanks. Yours, Susan."

She brushed her teeth, put on a nightgown, blew out the wicks, and climbed the ladder in the dark. Sliding under the sheet, she listened to the regular breathing of the sleeping boy on Mark's side of the bed. She adjusted her pillow and closed her eyes, realizing that she was very sleepy. As she relaxed with eyes closed, she pictured Ian reading her letter. The image gave her a warm feeling. Then she felt Gregory snuggling against her.

"I thought you were asleep," she whispered.

"Mommy, I want to be near you. Something outside scared me."

"I didn't hear anything, but I know you have super hearing." She gave him a hug. "You can stay here for a minute, then you have to move over to your side. I want to go to sleep."

"Okay." He stroked her arm.

She lowered her eyelids and soon felt herself drifting off. Deep breaths came as her body relaxed. She was somewhere on a beach. Then Ian's bearded face came into view. She smiled at him. He smiled back and walked toward her. His shirt was open, revealing bleached chest hair against a dark tan. She took a deep breath and his cologne filled her nose. His arms came around her and she felt tingles of excitement. He kissed her on the neck and pulled her against him. Familiar waves of desire licked at her. It was vaguely like Nick. Her breath came faster. She wanted his touch and moved her body into him. Waves licked stronger. His hands caressed. The sensations built urgently, beyond the stopping point. She let the waves take her, laying back, opening. Her fingers were between her legs. She was thrusting, now lost to everything . . . and then the non-stop flashes spread over her like an aurora borealis. She heard herself groan. Ian slowly faded away. Far-off sounds of crickets seeped into her consciousness.

Gregory shifted. "I love you, Mommy."

She thought: My god! Gregory.

"Do you know what happened, Bret?" she said, her voice husky.

"You . . . you were shivering."

"Uh huh."

"Are you okay, Mommy?"

"Yes. Let's . . ." she sighed. "Let's just go to sleep now."

"Good night, Mommy. I love you."

"I love you too, Bret."

Late on the next day Mark arrived, tired but in good spirits. Gregory was already asleep and Mark and Corinne kept their voices low so as not to wake him. She offered Mark some food but learned that he and his companion had stopped for dinner on the way home.

"Did Gregory behave himself?" Mark asked.

"He was an angel."

"That's good."

"Mark, I really want to get him into school. I don't think it would be good for him to be hanging around here so much for another year. I think we should take the Korsen's house."

"That's fine with me."

"And I'm thinking I'll find a full time job."

"That's fine, too."

Chapter Twenty-One

THE DAWN CHORUS of birds rose to a clamor outside her window. Sylvia listened appreciatively for a minute, then got up quietly so as to not wake her husband, dressed in the walk-in closet, and filled her thermos cup from the automatic coffee maker in the kitchen. She drove to the university and arrived in her office within thirty minutes. As the sun glowed radiantly below the rim of the mountains, she fired up her computer to finish off her thirteenth research paper since joining the department over four years ago. After three hours of timeless concentration, she wheeled slowly around to a knock on her door.

"It's open," she said.

"Hi, Sylvia. I thought I'd personally deliver this." The department chair's administrative assistant smiled and put an envelope in Sylvia's hand.

"Thank you, Emily. I think I know what it is."

After Emily waved and closed the door, Sylvia quickly opened the envelope and read the letter that congratulated her on her appointment to associate professor with tenure. She took in a deep breath and then emailed her husband. Next, she dialed the phone.

"Well, Alice, do you want the good news or the good news?"

"You got the promotion?"

"Uh huh. Signed and sealed."

"Oh, that's wonderful, Sylvia. I'm so happy for you. But there is other good news?"

Sylvia chuckled. "You may not believe this, but I think Zenya is willing to go for the experiment."

"No! What made her change her mind?"

"She wants a bigger car, as befitting someone heading the support office of an admiral, and she wants to fix up her condo."

"Oh my god. How much?"

"She hasn't said, but twenty thousand would not surprise me."

Alice sucked in loudly. "Sylvia!"

"I know. We're just going to have to raise it, that is, if you want to be a co-author of the paper of the century."

"I don't know. But let me tell you my good news, too."

"Tell me."

"My final experiment came out great, and I can wrap up my thesis and defend in two months. My advisor thinks it could be published in *Neuron*."

"That's terrific, Dr. Masterson."

Alice laughed. "Also, I've got a postdoc already lined up at the Vollum Institute in Portland . . . in a really good electrophysiology lab run by a senior scientist named Craig Westerby."

"That's at the med school up there?"

"Yeah, it's separate from the med school but part of Oregon Health and Science University. It's on this hill overlooking the city, and you can see Mt. Hood. The lab took me rafting. Really neat people. It's such a beautiful area."

"It's great in the summer, but take your rain gear."

Alice laughed again.

"What are you going to do with the website?" Sylvia asked.

"I'll keep it going. It hardly matters. The information coming in these days is nil. I just can't believe Mark and Corinne haven't surfaced. Do you realize that Gregory is six and must be in school? I don't know how they could have done that."

"Yes, it is amazing. I think Jared knows things, but he keeps mum. By the way, he likes the design of my experiment for Zenya but says it will be complicated to arrange the EEG machines. You remember Clyde Finlayson, the Nobel laureate? What would you think if we involved him too? He's really sharp and on our side."

"You think he would want to?"

"I think so. I'm going to call him. You'd come down for a meeting, wouldn't you?"

"For sure."

LONG GRASS AND WILDFLOWERS were everywhere on San Juan Ridge. The ground was moist from periodic showers, but on this day the sun was bright. School was almost out. Gregory had done surprisingly well in second, third, and fourth grades, pleasing his teachers and Mark and Corinne. With summer approaching, the time was conducive to frolicking and horseplay as school children were dropped by the bus at stops along Tyler Foote Road.

Gregory, now seven, got off at the stop one third mile from the turn-off to Colliver Canyon. Several children dispersed from this point. Gregory walked with his friend, Carlos Reyes, a third grader. One of the other boys getting off, a fifth grader, was disliked by most of the children. He pulled girls' hair, bullied smaller children, and acted like a smart aleck. After the bus left, he lived up to his reputation. Moving to the high side of a clearing he pulled up handfuls of long grass with dirt clods hanging on the roots and began throwing the missiles at the other children. One socked Carlos in the shoulder, spewing dirt on Gregory. Most of the kids scattered under the barrage, but Carlos and Gregory dropped their books and began throwing the grass clumps back at the attacker.

At this time, two leather-jacketed motorcyclists on Harleys with thin wheels forked out to the front came down the road side by side. The fifth grader threw, Carlos ducked, and a large grass clump smacked the nearest rider on the side of the face as they went by. The boys stopped and watched as both cycles braked and circled around.

"Run!" the troublemaker yelled. The boys bolted. Gregory followed Carlos who stupidly ran parallel to the road in full visibility of the cyclists. One of them shot past and parked thirty yards ahead of Carlos. The other got off behind them and began running in pursuit. Seeing a brawny fellow closing in from the front, Carlos turned up into the brush on the hillside. Gregory followed but was yards behind.

Hearing footsteps closing on him, Gregory stopped and squatted down behind a bush. But his booted pursuer spotted him.

"You've had it now, you little shitass," he yelled.

When the man was within ten yards, Gregory stood up and let loose a hair-raising screech. The man went down heavily, sprawling into the brush next to Gregory. Further behind, the other cyclist came around a tree and paused, eyeing his friend on the ground.

"What happened, Dirk?" he shouted.

Gregory let loose again, this time silently, and the second man's knees buckled. He sagged down on his side, holding his head. Gregory fled up the hill. After several minutes of running, he hid behind a large oak and kept stark still as he listened. After a long while he heard a motorcycle start up. Then the other cycle started and both roared off.

With his heart pounding, Gregory moved down toward the road. He heard Carlos shout his name.

"What happened to you?" Carlos asked.

Soon the two were talking animatedly. They found their books, then headed off cross-country in the directions of their homes.

TWO WEEKS LATER, Dirk Rogers dialed an El Cajon number.

"Onward Christian Soldiers," the voice said.

"Yeah, I'm trying to get a hold of a guy named Lawrence Carter."

"This is him. Who's this?"

"I'm Dirk Rogers . . . you don't know me . . . it took me a while to get your number. This is about that kid that has the weird powers—you know, the boy you're supposedly lookin' to find."

"Gregory Shenko. Yeah, what about him?"

"A buddy and I were out riding our Harleys and we both got blasted when we were chasing a couple of kids up a hill. We think one of 'em musta been him."

"No kidding. Where was this?"

"Uh, well . . . before we give any info, we'd like to know what your group could do for us. My buddy, Carl Gaston, and me are outta work and we need money."

"I see. Tell me, Dirk. Are you and Carl Christians?"

Dirk chuckled. "Well, even though we're members of a bike club called "The Sun Devils," we both wear crosses under our shirts."

Carter laughed. "The crosses are what count. Good, good. I think we can do business. So what money do you have in mind? And where do you live?"

"We both live in Modesto. We don't know exactly where the kid lives, but we think we can probably find him again, say around a month or so after school starts. As to the money, I dunno . . . at least five thou for each of us. Half up front, and half after we locate him. Which brings up a question: What do you guys plan to do if we find out where he lives? What's the game plan?"

"All right, Dirk, what I'll need to do is get approval from the OCS Board—on the amount of money, how much I can do up front and how much when you can give us the kid's location. The amounts you say sound reasonable to me. As to the game plan . . . I'll also need to check with the Board on that. But give me your contact info and I'll call you back in a week or so. Boy, I still remember getting zapped when that kid was a baby. What did it feel like?"

"Like gettin' hit in the head with a bat. Except it also felt zingy."

Carter chuckled. "Yep. That's what I remember too. Okay, give me your address and phone number, Dirk. And Carl's too."

THE UNSEASONAL, wind-borne rain transformed summer into fall in a matter of minutes. The drops slanted northeasterly, blowing against the front of Mountain View Medical. Puddles gathered on sidewalks. Mark watched the meteorological mischief from his new office—one befitting MVM's medical administrator. In some ways, he thought, the weather seemed symbolic of his life recently: warmth turning to chilliness.

He had to admit that, against the odds, the Harrises were succeeding in hiding. He had received recognition and recently, a raise. Corinne enjoyed her job as a librarian. She had slowly let her hair become red again. Gregory had just started in the fifth grade, was doing well, and had friends. Colliver was as cantankerously companionable as ever, despite going nearly apoplectic at the remodels over the summer. Their house had a new roof, new paint, a refurbished kitchen, curtains, comfortable furniture, a telephone, refrigerator, stereo, washer, dryer, and a computer. No TV, however. To top it off, they had friends and an active social life.

Yet, with all of this (or because of it all?), a cool cloud had descended. Mark felt it most with Corinne. Her need for affection had fallen. Sex between them had decreased. And when it happened, the ardor was less. He didn't know why. Maybe they had been spending too much time fixing up the house and not enough time on hikes and in conversation? Too much time on their jobs instead of at home? Or was it him?

And Gregory? His development in all areas—physical, cognitive, social, emotional —seemed normal except for the X-ing of birds and squirrels, which according to Ian, Jared thought was acceptably boyish. Neither Ian nor Jared believed that Gregory could *sense* climate change, however. The Y power was non-existent. There had been no evidence of seizure-like activity since the eye-rolling as an infant. But there was something about Gregory that made Mark uneasy. Was it that the boy was too clever by half? Why did Gregory have a much better relationship with Colliver than with Mark? Had Mark been too much of a disciplinarian? Maybe he had seen the boy as a medical problem to be managed instead of a son. Mark grabbed the phone and punched a speed dial button.

"It's me," he said. "What do you think about this storm? Should one of us pick up Bret from school?"

"I just heard a weather report," Corinne replied. "The storm will lose its punch. I'm sure Bill will meet Bret at the road as usual."

"Oh. Well, good."

"Honey, I have to work late again," Corinne said. "We're in the middle of the book relocation project and I'm the one who knows where they go. Do you mind getting dinner going? There's that chicken that just needs heating and there's string beans and salad material."

"No problem."

"And if I'm not there by seven, please go ahead. I'll eat later."

"Okay."

"Thanks, sweetheart. Gotta go. See you tonight."

Mark eased down at his computer. He clicked up a national news website and saw an item reporting that the Human Proteomics Project was making good progress. *We soon will have the entire instruction manual for humans*, the university scientist asserted.

"Those idiots," Mark said to himself. "That's what they said about the Genome Project. Knowing the proteins doesn't mean knowing what they do. Hype and fundraising bullshit."

He brought up whereisgregory.com and looked at the same old pictures of himself and Corinne. Gregory was still shown as a baby. Nothing new, he thought, as he perused the pages. *Wait. Alice Masterson got a PhD in neuroscience? She's going to Portland for a postdoc?* Amazing. Not only was his life changing, it looked like the rest of the world was changing too.

He pulled up the office email program. No interesting messages in his in-box. He didn't feel like working. Was it time to do it? Send her a message from the past? What the hell. *Just do it*, as Nike says. He composed a message using the name Bob Smith, a fictitious employee whose email account he had recently created. As he addressed the message, his fingers seemed slow and unsure.

> Dear Rachel,
> Are you still there? This is your old high school bud, Bob Smith. I got your email address from our class reunion book. I haven't seen you since your college graduation when you threatened to push me into the fountain reflecting pool. Remember that? Give me a shout for old time's sake.
> Bob

It was after six on the east coast and Mark didn't expect a reply. But he checked his incoming mail an hour later. And there it was.

> Hi, Bob. Good to hear from you! Of course I remember you and me at the fountain. Hindsight indicates I blew a good opportunity then. So what are you doing these days? As you probably know from the reunion blurb, I'm still doing psychology stuff here at the big U. I live in a nearby condo with my sweetheart, Jeff, who is in the frisbee business. So let me know what's up, Bob.
> Rachel
> P.S. Jeff is the greatest Labrador.

Mark grinned, thought carefully, then sent another message.

ONE WEEK LATER, Gregory squeezed into the back seat of the Volkswagen. Corinne and Mark took the front seats, Mark behind the wheel.

"Now remember, Bret," Corinne said, "you behave yourself tonight. No asking for food and no roughhousing on the furniture. And if you use the bathroom, be sure to flush the toilet."

"Okay, but is it all right to watch TV?"

"Only if Nina lets you. You do whatever she says."

"Didn't she babysit me before?"

"Yes, about two years ago. You'll remember her when you see her."

"Oh, I think I know her. Is she short with kinda long brown hair?"

"Yes."

"And . . . and her brother has the model airplanes?"

"That's right. But you won't be in their house. You'll be in the Olivers' house. We're going with the Olivers to a poetry reading in Nevada City and we'll be back about eleven."

"Do the Olivers have any kids?"

"No. Just you and Nina will be there. If you get tired, you can lay down on the couch."

"How come I can't go to Nina's house to look at the models?"

"Because you can't, Bret. They live quite a ways away," Mark said. "So don't pester her about it either."

When they arrived, Mark took Gregory up to the house. Nina opened the door. She was petite for her twelve years. She wore Levi's, a sweatshirt, and loafers. She said hello to Mark then smiled at Gregory.

"Hi, Bret. Remember me?"

"Yeah. Hi."

The Olivers and Mark said goodbye and gave last minute instructions. Nina and Gregory went into the family room.

"Bret, we can play some games or watch TV, whatever you'd like."

"What kind of games?"

"There's Parcheesi, or cards, or checkers."

"Uh, I'll play you checkers," Gregory said, seeing the board already set up. They sat on the carpet, the board between them. Nina let Gregory choose his color and move first.

"How do you like school?" she asked.

"It's good."

"What grade are you in?"

"Fifth."

"Uh huh."

Gregory looked at her. "What grade are you in?"

"Eighth."

"That's almost high school, huh."

"One more year then I'm in high school."

"You don't look that old."

"Gee thanks, Bret."

"Well, I mean you're not very big. I'm almost as tall as you."

"So, you're big for your age and I'm small for mine. That's the way God made us." She smiled.

Gregory smiled. After a few more moves it was clear that he would lose.

"Nina, do you know any jokes?"

"I'll have to think. Do you know any?"

"Say your name."

"Nina."

"Okay, what's this," Gregory said, pointing to his nose.

"Nose."

"Okay, what's in my hands?" They were cupped like a bowl.

"Nothing."

Gregory laughed loudly. "Nina knows nothing, get it?"

She smiled. "Ha, ha, real funny."

"Do you know any knock-knock jokes?" he asked.

"Do you?"

"Oh wait. Uh, will you remember me a year from now?"

"Is this a joke?"

"No. Just answer."

"Sure, I'll remember you a year from now," she said.

"Will you remember me a day from now?"

"Sure."

"Will you remember me an hour from now?"

"Of course."

"Will you remember me a second from now?"

"Yes, Bret."

"Knock, knock."

"Who's there?"

"You didn't remember me." Gregory howled.

Nina laughed in a high-pitched warble. "Pretty cute, Bret."

"I got another one. Are you good at spelling?"

"Pretty good."

"Okay, how do you spell eyecup?"

"E Y E C U P."

"No, I mean spell 'I' like big I."

She looked at him suspiciously, a smile playing at her dimples. "I'm not going to spell that, Bret."

"Why?"

"It's dirty."

Gregory laughed. "No, it's just two words."

"Right, uh huh."

"I C U P," he spelled. "What's wrong with that?"

"It's not nice. That kind of talk belongs in the bathroom."

Gregory laughed. "Everybody has to pee. There is nothing wrong with going pee, is there?"

"No, but it's not polite to talk about it."

"But grown-ups tell dirty jokes."

"Well, that's for grown-ups."

"Don't you know any dirty jokes?"

"Yes, Bret, but I don't tell them."

"But you must have listened to them."

Nina smiled. "Look, do you want to play any more checkers?"

"No. Can we watch TV?"

"Okay, let's see what's on." Nina scooted over and turned the set on, and then took off her shoes. A show about wild animals came on.

"Let's watch that," he said.

"Okay." Nina moved back and leaned against the couch.

"Can I take off my shoes too?"

"Sure, but leave your socks on."

Gregory took off his shoes and wiggled his toes. "Look, my feet are bigger than yours."

"I don't think so."

"Sure, look." He moved in front of her and put one foot bottom-to-bottom against one of hers. They were the same size.

"See, they're the same," she said.

"No, they're not." Gregory tried to push his foot higher.

"Hey." She grabbed his foot and tickled it with her fingernails.

Gregory giggled and tried to twist away. She held tightly for a few seconds, then let go. Quickly he took her foot and tickled it. She laughed and pulled loose.

"You're really ticklish," he said.

"So are you."

"Are you ticklish under the arm?" As he said it, Gregory went for the target on her left side. She tried to defend but his fingers got there and did their work. Laughing, she jerked sideways but his other hand fumbled for the other side. Suddenly she was face down, squirming.

"Bret," she shouted, laughing more. As she caught and stopped the second hand, the first managed to find a new spot. Gregory had leverage as he leaned over her. His hands moved all around, hitting high and low, her sides and the small of her back as she writhed.

"Bret, stop it," she screamed. There was no mirth in her voice.

He pulled away and she sat up.

"Okay, enough's enough," she said. Her sweatshirt had ridden up showing the white of her bra. She quickly covered herself.

"All right," she said. "Let's settle down and watch TV. Come sit back against the couch."

He moved next to her. "I'm sorry, I didn't mean to hurt you."

"You didn't. But a person can only be tickled so much."

"Do you want to tickle me?"

"No, let's just watch TV," she said, still catching her breath.

They watched in silence for a few seconds. Two lion cubs were playing with their mother. A commercial came on.

"Nina, would you do me a favor?"

"What?"

"Scratch my back?"

"Okay, sit in front of me so I can still watch."

He moved in front, sitting on the floor between her knees, back to her. She slowly rubbed his back, occasionally scratching gently with her nails. After several minutes of rubbing, her breathing thickened.

"Bret," she said after a minute, "that's all. I don't want to do this any more."

"No, please a little more. It feels good."

"All right, just one more minute."

She continued rubbing. Gregory pushed back a couple of inches, touching against her inner thighs. After a minute Nina stopped rubbing. Her breathing was loud and fast. She put her arms around his chest and hugged him. She moved against him with a slight rocking motion. He pushed back rhythmically. Her grip became tighter and tighter. Gregory didn't say anything. Finally she gasped. He didn't move, but continued to watch the screen. After a minute Nina let go, got up and sat on the couch. Gregory turned and looked at her. Her face was red and she turned away.

"Nina, want to play Parcheesi?" he asked.

"No."

"Checkers?"

"No, I just want to sit here, Bret. You watch TV."

He pretended to watch.

After a while she said, "Bret, do you know what happened when I was rubbing your back?"

"You got sexy?"

"Uh . . . you could say that. But I don't want you to tell anyone, okay?"

"I won't. It didn't bother me any. I kinda liked it."

Nina suddenly laughed.

"Did you like it?" he asked.

"Yes, but it was a surprise. I didn't know it would happen."

"Want to do it again?"

"Oh, no. Thanks, but that was enough."

"Okay. If you do, just let me know."

Nina laughed again. "You're a funny kid, Bret. I mean you're nice and I like you, but . . . When did you learn about sex?"

"I've seen animals do it. And my parents told me about it a while ago. When did you learn about it?"

"I guess when I was about your age. Well, probably not as young as you are."

"Want to hear another knock-knock joke?" he asked.

She smiled. "Okay."

"Knock knock."

"Who's there?"

"Boo."

"Boo who?"

"Please don't cry." Gregory laughed loudly. Nina joined.

"Still want to play Parcheesi?" she asked after a minute.

"Sure."

She got the Parcheesi set and sat down on the floor again.

COLLIVER LOOKED at his watch, then said, "Come on, Arnie. It's time to go down to the road and meet Bret." Arnie bolted out of the cabin and pranced alongside Colliver, knowing exactly where they were going. They had done it so many times.

As Colliver and the wolf dog walked up the switchbacks, Colliver thought of his conversation with Gregory that June day when Gregory had not come down Tyler Foote Road as usual after getting off the bus to meet with him and Arnie. He had come from the direction of the cabins. Colliver realized something was strange when Gregory said he'd explain, but then asked Colliver not to tell Mark or his mother. Gregory had then told in detail of the episode with the two motorcyclists, including that he had zapped both of the riders with the X, out of fear that they would beat him up. Colliver had remembered seeing the bus and later the leathered guys on the Harleys go by. It wasn't until much later that Gregory came to the driveway and road intersection from the wrong direction, having gone cross-country to avoid the possibility of seeing the motorcyclists again.

Colliver's subsequent lecture, he hoped, had sunk in for Gregory. He warned him that there were people who wanted to find the boy and do him harm and that he had to be extremely careful in using his powers because, as in the motorcycle incident, that was one way that strangers could know that he was the mutant kid who had disappeared. Colliver worried that such fellows—or others—could show up again, this time with guns. Colliver said it was probably all right that Gregory had used the X in self-defense in this one instance, but he needed to watch out for people he didn't know showing interest in him and to be sure not to give them reason to suspect who he was.

"Okay, I understand," a chastised Gregory had said. Colliver hoped so.

The sun was bright and the tree leaves sparkled as man and wolf dog reached the edge of the road, waiting first for the bus to pass, then to spot Gregory and Carlos walking toward them. Soon the engine of the bus could be heard and it appeared around the curve. Colliver got ready to wave at the driver. But something was different. A kid's hand was waving out an open window. It was Gregory's.

Through the open window, Gregory shouted: "They're behind in the black car." And he pointed to the rear.

Four to five car lengths behind the bus was a black Chevrolet with two fellows in the front seats. Colliver waived at them vigorously. The car braked, then slowly backed up to the side of the road opposite Colliver.

Dirk rolled down the driver's window. "Is everything okay, mister?"

"I was just wondering if you guys needed any help. You look new to this area."

Dirk smiled and stepped out of the car. "Well, actually we wonder if you know of a couple of kids that ride that bus, one is a Mexican and the other has an odd-shaped head. We owe 'em some money."

Colliver nodded, but then noticed a bulge and part of a pistol handle sticking out of the guy's right front pant's pocket. "Yeah, I used to know of them. I'll tell you what. I got some beers down in a creek about a half mile from here and you two look like you could use some refreshment. Why don't you take me down to my cabin—just a half mile—and I'll tell you what I know. This here's Arnie, my half wolf dog, and he won't hurt anyone."

Dirk smiled and looked over at Carl who had stepped out of the car. "Sounds like a winner, huh Carl?"

"Sure does. Thanks a lot, mister."

"You can call me Bill."

"And I'm Dirk and my buddy is Carl."

They all shook hands. Colliver got in the car and they drove down to his cabin. He knew that the car would be a warning to Gregory, should he come back looking for Colliver instead of going home to the Korsen place. When Dirk and Carl were comfortable in outdoor chairs, Colliver fetched three pale ales from the creek and opened them.

"Ahhh, this is great," Dirk said, after swigging one.

"Yeah, hard to beat a Sierra Nevada," said Carl.

"So, Bill," said Dirk in his low voice. "Did you ever hear about that baby with the strange powers? The one that disappeared with his mother and a doctor from L.A. years ago? It was all over the news."

Colliver screwed up his face. "Yeah, I think so, but I'm kind of a hermit and don't keep up with the news very much.

Dirk and Carl laughed. Dirk continued, "Well, we think that the kid with the unusual head we met, just might be that baby . . . of course, grown up a lot and now in school."

Colliver shrugged. "Well, I do remember those boys passing by once in a while on the road last year. But I think the white kid has moved away, 'cause I haven't seen him this year—just the Mexican. The reason I go down there is to wave at the bus driver who I've known for years. Also, to stretch the legs of Arnie here." Hearing his name, Arnie wagged his tail.

"Maybe the family was afraid of us finding them and moved away this summer, Dirk," Carl said, looking at his friend.

"Maybe," Dirk said. "But, do you know where they lived, Bill?"

"No, I don't," Colliver said, then pointed at Dirk's pants. "I notice you're carrying. I like guns, got rid of most of 'em when I came here though, but still have an old Remington 30-30 hanging up inside." Colliver pointed to his rifle hanging on the wall just inside the doorway.

"Do you hunt?" Dirk asked.

"Sometimes. I own a lot of acreage and there's deer and all kinds of wildlife around," Colliver replied. "Do you guys like to hunt?"

"Yeah," said Carl. "I have a gun collection . . . mostly target shoot, but I'd like to hunt more."

Colliver nodded. "Well, who knows, maybe we could work something out. But as to that boy with the weird powers, did he do something to you?"

Carl looked at Dirk.

Dirk took a swig. "Let me tell you what happened, Bill. But first, do you have more beers?" After Colliver retrieved three more from the creek, Dirk told the story in about the same way that Gregory had, but spent more detail in describing what the X had felt like.

"Wow," Colliver said, showing amazement. "And it was the same for you, Carl?"

"Yep. I seen Dirk on the ground, then suddenly my head nearly exploded with a ringing noise. When I was finally able to get up, Dirk was beginning to move, but the kid was long gone."

Colliver cupped his chin. "Well, I'll be damned! If it happened to each of you separately, must be something to it. But I have to say that I've never heard of anything like that before, with that kid or any kid around here."

Dirk swigged. "Well, after that happened, on the way home, I remembered about that baby who had disappeared. And it clicked for me. When I got back to my place I got on the computer. I learned that nobody had ever found the kid. He and his mother and the doctor just disappeared into thin air. But it makes sense. The boy would be around six or seven now."

Colliver nodded. "Interesting, though the white kid seems older than that."

Carl petted Arnie who had sidled up to him.

Colliver pursed out his lips. "But if what you say is right, maybe the kid was acting out of self-defense. Maybe he thought you were going to beat him up. Was that your intent?"

Dirk and Carl both laughed. "Yeah," Dirk said, "I was going to pound the SOB for throwing the clod at us."

"Well, okay," Colliver said, "so it wasn't exactly a fair fight, was it?"

Dirk was surprised. "What are you getting at, Bill? One of those kids had it coming."

"Yeah, but do you know which kid actually threw the clod?"

Carl shook his head. "No. But it hit me in the side of the face. It could have caused an accident. They were all doing it. Once we turned around, they all ran. I guess I don't see your point."

Colliver leaned forward. "My point is this. If this particular kid hadn't thrown the clod, if he thought you were going to beat him up anyway, and if he had this weird power as you describe to immobilize you temporarily, wouldn't it make sense for him to do it in self-defense? It would be better than using a gun, wouldn't it? In some states, not this one, there are laws allowing guns to be used in self-defense. If he'd had a weapon, both of you might be dead."

Dirk and Carl looked at each other.

"Well, I suppose," Carl said. "Are you trying to say he did us a favor?"

Colliver smiled. "Well, I think any judge would say that if this went to court."

Dirk raised his voice. "But the point is, this kid ain't natural. There are people who say he ain't made in the Lord's image." Dirk pulled the cross out from under his shirt, letting it dangle from around his neck.

Colliver nodded. "Oh, I see. Are you fellows believers?"

Again, they looked at each other. "Well, sure," Dirk said. "I mean we don't go to church, but you know, we do believe. Don't you, Bill?"

Colliver took a sip of the pale ale. "Here's the way I see it. Supposedly the Lord made all of creation, including the animals. If this boy has some strange powers, the Lord must have made him that way. Oh, and now I do remember reading an article about that baby. Seems to me the real father had an epileptic seizure and died young, and the kid probably has this too. So you might say the Lord will cause this kid to die early, like his real father. Something is messed up in his brain. So the Lord will exact His kind of justice. Just like he must have allowed you two to live, instead of being shot—you know, if the kid had a real gun."

Dirk screwed up his face. "Man, you sure are some kind of strange."

Colliver laughed. "Well, we're just talking. Who knows, maybe the Lord is talking through me, but I have to say I don't go to church either."

Carl smiled. "Well, Bill does make a point. What happens on Earth is the Lord's will."

Dirk shook his head. "I dunno. I think it's time to go. Thanks a lot for the beers, Bill. Give me your phone number and we'll call you about hunting."

"I don't have a phone, Dirk," Colliver said, smiling.

"You don't? Wow, you *are* weird."

"I get along fine without one. And I don't get any of those solicitation calls, either. Look, like I said, I'm kind of a hermit."

Carl laughed. "So how can we reach you?"

Colliver wrote out his mail address on a paper and handed it to Carl. "It's simple, write me a note and drop it in the mail. Be sure to put your return address on it."

"Okay," Carl said, pocketing the paper. "I will drop a note saying when we'd like to hunt."

"That would be great," Colliver said, as all three walked to the car, Arnie tagging along.

"And if I were you," Colliver said, "I'd just forget about the episode with that kid in June. No harm, no foul."

"Actually, I agree," Carl said. But Dirk shook his head. "Except we won't get some money."

"What do you mean, Dirk?" Colliver asked as they stood by the car.

"This religious guy named Lawrence Carter was going to pay us two thou each for telling him where this Gregory kid can be found.

"But we still don't know," Carl said. "He's probably gone."

Colliver held up a finger. "Yeah, and look at it this way. If you boys come huntin' here, that is easily worth more than two thousand each . . . being able to go on a private land like I have. Plus I'll provide meals and all the beer you can drink. But my requirement is you don't tell this Lawrence guy about this. I clearly don't want to see him coming around. He sounds too religious, even more a weirdo than me."

Carl and Dirk nodded and laughed as they got in the car.

Colliver waved as the car turned around and headed out. Colliver then realized, despite his promise to Gregory, that he would have to gather the family together and talk through all this, even though he thought the chances were good that Carl and Dirk would not talk with Lawrence Carter. They might want to come hunting, however. But at least he would have a couple of days warning by mail.

THE GRAYISH-BLUE BASE of the monolithic cloud contrasted with its lavender and orange top, still catching the sun's final rays stealing over the coast mountains. To Alice, the scene was majestic. She smiled inwardly, feeling fortunate to have spent time in a place like Portland where there was real weather. Sometimes dreary, sometimes gorgeous, but most times the weather was interesting. She tossed her suitcase in the backseat, got behind the wheel, and soon had her car speeding toward the Portland airport. As beautiful as Portland was today, she was looking forward to Malibu's monotonous sun. She'd even found her swimsuit.

She thought of Jared Weymouth whom she would meet for the first time. Would he still dislike her? Sylvia had said not to worry. As a budding scientist her spots had changed. And Nobel laureate Clyde Finlayson would be there. She would also meet that anthropologist friend of Jared's, Ian Trevor. Sylvia said he was as clever as they got. They all would spend the weekend at a private beach house. And Sylvia would pick her up at LAX. Alice pushed on the accelerator. She couldn't wait.

THE NARROW, TWO-STORY house stood shoulder-to-shoulder with others well above the high tide line. On its ocean side, the modern structure had a deck at the lower level and a large room with floor-to-ceiling windows upstairs. As if ordered for Alice, the sky was blue, the water cool, and the sun and sand hot. She alternated between swimming and lying on her towel. Late in the afternoon her stomach stirred. It was time to go in.

She found Jared on the deck.

"Hello, Dr. Weymouth." She felt embarrassed that he was fully clothed and she was in her bathing suit.

"We finally meet," Jared said as he held open the gate for her. "I'm glad you could make it down."

"Thank you. I'm glad to meet you too at long last. In some ways I feel like I already know you."

"Yes, well, we have been through a lot. I'm delighted to hear about your career in science. Sylvia says very good things about you."

Alice blushed. "Thanks."

After showering and changing, Alice entered the big upstairs room. Everyone was there. The men stood up and she greeted Clyde Finlayson, said hello again to Jared, and was introduced to Ian Trevor. Before everyone could sit down, Sylvia had them move to the large table where the food was waiting. Alice made sure she sat next to Jared.

Sylvia held a wine glass high. "Here's to Jared for arranging this house."

"Hear, hear."

"It pays to have grateful, well-off patients," Jared said.

When dinner was finished, they moved back to the comfortable chairs in front of the view window. The sun was sinking behind clouds on the far horizon. The flotilla of boats had thinned to two sloops, their sails barely drawing in the waning wind.

Sylvia thanked them for coming, then said, "I don't need to tell you how terribly important it is that everything we talk about does not go beyond this room. Not to anyone. Anybody have a problem with that?"

Everyone shook their heads solemnly.

"Good. Now Jared, you wanted to say a few words."

"Yes. I thought I'd update you on Gregory. While my source is not first hand, I have information that he is doing well in all respects. He is developmentally and intellectually very advanced and has been skipped two grades." Jared looked at Finlayson. "Clyde, this would tend to confirm your point about heterochrony."

Finlayson nodded and smiled. "Yes, very interesting."

Jared continued. "His powers have been successfully socialized. Thanks to Mark and Corinne, the X and Y are no longer a problem for himself or others. So I think that this major achievement justified the family's disappearance and all of the grief that happened to them and others." Jared pointedly looked at Alice.

Everyone but Alice smiled, knowing the dose of problems Jared had received.

Jared continued. "There was a recent claim by the child that he could 'sense' global warming, to use Gregory's surprising language, but nobody gives this any credence. He does like reading about climate change, however, and maybe this led him to make the claim."

"How old is the boy now, chronologically?" Finlayson asked.

"He turned seven, but acts nine to eleven," Jared replied. "Perhaps not as significant as the boy's developmental success, but in a way more important, is that Gregory has had no seizure episodes, at least not any seen or reported by others."

"That is great news, Jared," Sylvia said.

"For sure," Finlayson agreed.

"We're clearly not out of the woods. As I say, he's only seven," Jared said, "but it's a good sign so far. The next big test is likely to be adolescence."

"Which for him may be earlier than usual?" Alice asked.

"Quite possibly—good point, Alice." Jared nodded. "Anyway, that's all I wanted to share. We can move on to Zenya."

Sylvia wheeled in a small white board from another room.

"So let me tell you about Zenya's X2 power—that's the term I gave it—and how we discovered it," Sylvia said. "Alice, you feel free to chime in. Then I'll explain the experiment that I am proposing to set up in about six months in San Diego with Zenya and three normal subjects. Your critique and suggestions are needed. The purpose is to see if we can record EEG data that can substantiate the X2 and show that it causes measurable neurophysiological effects in others. If this is proven, then it would obviously give strong support to Gregory's X power."

Finlayson chuckled. "Talk about going for the gold . . ."

Sylvia smiled and the others laughed.

"I love it," Finlayson said. "Continue."

The rapt conversation about the X2 power and the proposed experiment continued late into the night. Thoughout the discussion Finlayson kept coming back to why the X2 power would have evolved. Protection against male use of the X and Y powers did not fully satisfy him. Concerning the proposed experiment, Ian said it was critical to have an innocent cover explanation for the normal subjects.

"On that score, how about this?" Finlayson said. "Tell them it's a playing card experiment to test telepathy. And I'll recruit Harold Newman to be one of the subjects. I'll be the card guy. That'll teach him not to be on any more panels at neuroscience meetings."

Everyone roared with laughter. "Any axe to grind, Clyde?" Jared said.

"Not an axe, more like a lance."

There was discussion of the logistics and who would do what. After coffee ice cream with chocolate syrup, Sylvia brought up the budget.

"We're going to need to pay Zenya and the volunteers, lease the EEG and video equipment, and pay a small room usage fee to a biotech company. I figure it will come to $40,000. So how can we get the money? Jared has offered $5,000 from his private donors account. That leaves a lion's share to raise."

There was no response for a minute. Then Finlayson cleared his throat. "I'll provide the rest. Hell, it will be worth it just to get Harold."

Alice clapped, quickly joined by the others.

"Not out of your own pocket, I hope," Sylvia said.

"I have a no-strings award from the Kollenberg Foundation. I've been wondering how to spend it. You've heard of the McArthur genius awards? This is called a half-genius award."

With the plan set, everyone turned in for the night, agreeing to reconvene for breakfast at eight. Ian had a remaining topic for the morning.

Following breakfast, they again settled in front of the windows. Ian, wearing his corduroy shorts, asked Jared not to say anything, then clipped the paper with the drawings of five heads onto the easel. After agreeing on the order from modern man to Australopithecus, the group was shocked to learn Gregory's position in the sequence. Ian then told the story of finding Galina Shenko, obtaining a sample of her hair, and submitting it for mitochondrial DNA analysis.

"Before I tell you the results," he said, "let me refresh you on the concept of everyone's common ancestor, the so-called Mitochondrial Eve. She has been consensus dated to about one hundred and fifty to two hundred thousand years ago in Africa, and is the common genetic relative to all modern females—those many around the world who have been tested so far. The sample is large and from all races and continents."

Ian put up a diagram that looked like a tree with one long and several short limbs coming upwards from a squat trunk. He marked points on the longest branch as he talked.

"Here's Lucy, or *Australopithecus afarensis*, three million years ago, and *Homo erectus*, one point eight million years ago. The earliest Homo erectus came out of Africa and their fossils are found in Africa, Asia, and Europe. *Homo heidelbergensis* —forerunner to Neanderthal and Cro-Magnon—is here, about seven hundred thousand years ago. Eve is about here, two hundred thousand years ago, still back in Africa. All modern *Homo sapiens* allegedly come from her and they left Africa about forty to fifty thousand years ago. So mitochondrial DNA data support the Recently-Out-of-Africa theory of modern human descent."

Ian looked around at everyone. "Now, how did Galina Shenko's mtDNA come out? There were five times more mutations in it than had been seen before in any modern human. My expert friend said there had to be a mistake in this sample because it would date her ancestor back to about six hundred thousand years—in other words, more than three times as old as Eve."

Sylvia gasped.

"Hm mmh mmh," Finlayson muttered.

"Just for comparison purposes," Ian said, "the Neanderthals who roamed Europe during the mid-to-late Paleolithic, from five hundred to thirty thousand years ago, have DNA that has been dated back to a divergence point from the Homo *heidelbergensis* line at about five hundred thousand years ago."

The group remained silent, trying to digest the meaning.

Finlayson recovered. "Something's not right. If modern human mtDNA is a big upside down pyramid funneling back to Eve, there should be an even bigger funnel going back to the first Galina. And that means there should be even more present-day women walking around with the older Galina-type mtDNA."

Ian smiled. "That's right, but there aren't—at least that have been sampled so far. So Galina's line is more like a narrow pipe going straight back to the Galina Eve, not a broad upside down pyramid."

Finlayson raised his finger. "But a pipe is mathematically impossible because there would have been missed daughters and steady intermixing of Eve-like modern mtDNA into the Galina line down through the generations. Therefore, her mtDNA would not show such differences to most modern women."

"Exactly," Ian said.

"So either the test is wrong or something else is going on?" Finlayson said.

"Yep," Ian said, beaming. "And that's what we have to figure out."

Alice raised her hand. "If the test is right, would it shoot down the Recently-Out-of-Africa hypothesis of human ancestry?"

"It could," Ian said. "But the Galina Eve could in some ways support the African Eve concept too. If Galina is an extremely minor line that somehow survived in parallel, the Recently-Out-of-Africa crowd was clearly dominant."

"Didn't the Shenkos come from Russia?" Sylvia asked.

"That's right. We looked up immigration documents on file and they list a village in the Carpathian Mountains of western Ukraine."

"So what do you make of all this, Ian—the Shenko powers along with the mtDNA testing?" Jared asked.

"There clearly is something unusual going on," Ian said. "All these things would not just happen together by chance. As to Galina's mtDNA test, the results might be due to an artifact. I will have her hair tested by someone else. If the second test comes up with a similar date, then I guess we can think much more seriously about this. It just may be that Gregory is a different kind of hominid."

"Wow. Very interesting. Well done, Ian," Finlayson said. "And well done to you, Sylvia and Alice, for the information on Zenya. Boy, this all makes me feel like a postdoc again." The group laughed.

Sitting next to Jared as he drove toward LAX that afternoon, Alice wondered if Sylvia really had been called to a meeting at the university. Or was it a ploy to get her and Jared together, one-on-one.

"Tell me, Alice," he said, braking in the stop-and-go traffic, "don't you think it strange that there haven't been any true sightings of Gregory, Mark, or Corinne in all this time?"

Alice winced. "Sure, but the best chance was early on when interest was high. The more time that passed, the more they were allowed to solidify their new identities. Then the public slowly lost interest."

"Are you happy they haven't been found?" He glanced at her.

She smiled. The acid test question. "Yes. Maybe it surprises you, but I realize now that it turned out best for Gregory to be raised out of the public eye. I'm not a reporter any more, Jared."

Her tone was apologetic.

Jared shrank slightly. "I'm sorry. I hope I didn't offend you."

"You didn't. And I won't ask you or Ian to tell me where they are."

Jared turned to her with surprise. "But I don't *know* where they are."

"Ian must. How else could he have obtained the drawing of Gregory's head?"

Jared grinned and nodded and decided to change the subject.

"I know of Dr. Westerly, your mentor. He is a leading expert on the cellular mechanisms of seizures."

"That's right."

"Did you choose him because of Gregory?"

"No, it was a coincidence. But I've found the subject interesting. I've learned that epilepsy and seizures are complicated. The exact cause is not known. Seizure onset is unpredictable—it can be from a bump on the head, emotional stress, tumors, some developmental or hereditary anomaly that comes into play with growth, or a combination."

Jared nodded. "Dr. Westerly argues strongly that the inhibitory circuits of neuronal firing are what get disrupted."

"Yes. In a seizure, neuronal bursts, normally kept regulated by inhibitory circuits, accelerate out of control."

Jared's eyebrow moved slightly. "Do you think that Nick's and Gregory's lesions are the cause of their epileptic syndrome?"

"I don't know. I'd say it's the obvious hypothesis."

"Yes, I would think so." Jared got off on Century Boulevard and headed west to the airport. "Alice, your training up there is first rate. Have you given any thought about where you might like to do your next postdoc?"

"Not really, why?"

"Well, Southern State has a lot to recommend it."

She smiled. "I hadn't thought of that."

Chapter Twenty-Two

THE TOPS OF THE TALL FIRS in downtown Nevada City waved back and forth in the wind as if to say, *Hello down there.* "Hello guys," Corinne said as she walked past the jaggedy bark of their stolid trunks. The fall air was nippy and she zipped up her fleece jacket. Down the street she caught sight of the restaurant. Soon she was seated in a booth near the blazing fireplace in the center of the Bistro Café. Taking the supervisory position at Corrigan's Bookstore on Broad Street had put her within a short walk of places like the Bistro where she and Mark could meet for lunch. She signaled as he came through the oversized plank door.

"Hi, honey," he said, leaning over and pecking her cheek.

"Hi, you."

After they ordered, he handed her an envelope, already opened. "You'll want to read this from Ian."

She took several minutes on the four-page letter, said *Wow* twice, and laughed twice as she read. "That must have been something. But I don't get where Zenya was in relation to the others."

Mark laughed. "It was clever. What they did was to put her in one room next to a wall. In the next room, right against the same wall were three unknowing volunteer subjects, two women and one man, and he was this Nobel guy, Dr. Harold Newman, the one who had said that Gregory's powers were all a hoax. Remember him?"

"Yeah, at the NPA meeting where Alice and Sylvia spoke."

"Right. So they had Zenya in one room and the three subjects in an adjacent room all wired up for EEG's and had video cameras on everyone. The volunteer subjects didn't know about Zenya. They were told it was a telepathy experiment.

This other Nobel guy, Clyde Finlayson, was located across the room from the volunteers and was staring at playing cards to see if they could pick out the card he was thinking about. Then Zenya, on the other side of the wall, gave off what they're calling the X2 power."

Corinne laughed. "And they all got sick to their stomachs with Newman throwing up. That was pretty mean."

Mark laughed. "I would have liked to have seen that. But the amazing thing was that every one of the volunteers gave off unusual but similar brain waves when it happened. Their waves were exactly in synch with Zenya's high voltage X2 wave. There were real-time clocks on the EEG machines and video cameras for accurate records. The timing was exact. What an experiment!"

"So this proves the X2 power is real?"

"Beyond a doubt. Who could question those data, all obtained on video?"

"Boy, if I were those volunteers, especially Newman, I would be mad. Such deception."

"Well, Ian says they had been warned that they might feel ill, and all volunteers signed consent forms. They had to keep the real nature of the experiment secret because they didn't want any power of suggestion to occur. Hell, they paid them one thousand dollars apiece. I guess I would go through brief vertigo for that kind of money."

Corinne laughed again, then turned serious. "So I guess they want to publish this and include both Nobel guys on the paper. But what happens if they do? Won't the media go crazy? Start hounding Zenya? Won't people start thinking Bret's X and Y powers are real too? We already had those motorcycle guys who came and hunted on Bill's property. We had to hide out in our house with Bret the entire time." Corinne laughed. "Bill was sure pissed when they shot that buck and hauled it away. But he did it to keep Bret safe. I'm just worried that if this research gets published, people will start looking for us again."

"Yeah, that worries me too. I guess that's why Ian asked what we thought of them publishing it. I don't know, Suz. Should we say 'no'?"

The waitress brought large bowls of beef stew, a specialty of the Bistro, and they ate quietly for a while.

"The worst that could happen is that we are found," Corinne said. "And you know what, I'm beginning to think maybe that wouldn't be so bad. We could see my mom and dad, visit your family. Let's face it, Bret is eight already."

"Going on twelve."

"Right. Do you know that he looks at girls? We were in the market yesterday and he was looking up and down this sixteen-year-old blond?"

Mark laughed. "I know. As long as he doesn't do the powers, looking is okay, I guess."

"And he's big and muscled for his age," she said. "Girls think he's older."

Mark grinned. "You sound like a proud mother."

She kicked him under the table.

"Ow!"

"It's not funny," she said.

Mark took a swig of beer. "Well, I don't care if they publish it either. Let come what may."

Walking back to the bookstore, Corinne found it interesting that neither of them cared much whether their life changed. Perhaps that was to be expected, given the state of their relationship. It wasn't bad, just unexciting. Gregory was the only glue at this point. Maybe that shouldn't be so surprising, she thought. If it hadn't been for Gregory, they wouldn't have gotten together in the first place.

SYLVIA ARRIVED AT Ian's house before Jared who was coming in from San Francisco that morning. She hoped his plane had not been delayed. A light fog hung in the air, but she didn't think visibility was bad enough to stop incoming flights. June in L.A. was often like this.

"Come in, Sylvia." Ian smiled broadly.

"Hi, Ian."

She moved into the study, admiring the artifacts on display. Ian brought in coffee.

"Well, Ian, I can see your line now. Where others say, 'come look at my etchings', you say, 'come see my atlatls.' How could a girl refuse that?"

Ian chuckled. "I used to say, 'come see my bones,' but that didn't work very well."

Sylvia laughed.

"Do you think Jared will be late because of the fog?" she asked.

"No, he just called. He's on Lincoln Boulevard; should be here any minute."

"Oh, good."

They sat down. "I've been meaning to say for some time, Sylvia, that since your masterful handling of the P and T committee and the renewal of your joint research with Jared, he's got a new lease on life. I've not seen him looking so well in a long time."

"Thank you. It's gone both ways. And don't you think that Gregory's success, from Jared's viewpoint, has had a lot to do with it?"

"Definitely."

"Also," she said, "I suspect he had a secret agent who helped him through the rough stuff." She eyed Ian knowingly.

He smiled. "Jared's an old friend. I did what I could."

Within a few minutes Jared rapped on the door and they all decided to head for the beach. They took low beach chairs, a hot thermos of coffee, and a bag of fresh rugallahs Jared had bought at a Venice bakery. It was a weekday morning and there were few people on the sand. The noise of the waves and the jets overhead overrode the usual city sounds.

"Has everyone signed off on the draft article?" Jared asked.

"Finally," Sylvia said.

"I understand that Clyde is an Academy member and will submit the article to *Proceedings of the National Academy of Sciences*," Ian said.

"He said he could get it in quickly once I gave the word," she said.

"What title was decided on?" Jared asked.

"Synchrony of Anomalous EEG Patterns in Four Human Subjects."

Ian laughed loudly, causing Jared and Sylvia to join in.

"That must have been Harold's choice," Ian said. "It's a little like calling the bombing of Hiroshima, *Anomalous Urban Effects from a Fissionable Object*."

A young Latino in cut-off Levi's walked onto the beach near them, a frisbee in hand and a brown-and-black mutt running in circles around him. With a smooth arm motion he lofted the disk high in the downwind air. The mutt dashed off, positioned itself perfectly, then leaped to snag the purple plastic. Then the dog ran to the top of a dune and began chewing his prey. The young man ran toward the dog, calling desperately.

"It was all perfect until the last act," Jared said. He turned back to Sylvia. "So you'll go ahead with *PNAS*?"

"Well," she said, "I thought we wanted to know Mark and Corinne's reaction before we decided. Have you heard from them?"

Jared looked at Ian. "Did you hear anything, Ian?"

Ian retrieved a folded-up, typewritten paper from his shirt pocket. "I'll read you what Corinne said. This is an excerpt from her recent letter:

> Mark and I have no objection to publishing the experiment with Zenya. We hope that she will be able to handle the attention when her identity as the key participant becomes known, as is likely. We think the media and the scientific world will quickly make the connection to Gregory and this will spark an intense effort to find us, no doubt, through you, Jared, and our families. It'll probably be worse than that

motorcycle-guy scare. But we have discussed this and do not think it would be terrible if we were found. Maybe it's time for Gregory to face the world. He's nine and very mature for his years.

Ian looked up. "That's it."

Sylvia caught her breath. "Oh dear. She says *yes* but means *no*."

Ian nodded. "Yeah, that's my reaction."

"My gosh. I didn't . . . I guess I was hoping that Zenya's identity wouldn't have to be revealed. But maybe . . ." Sylvia stopped and looked at Jared for help.

Jared cleared his throat. "The problem is, what would you say to scientists who ask about the details of the article, who want to know more about Subject A giving off strange brain waves that apparently affected Subjects B, C, and D? What if someone wants to replicate the experiment? Are you going to keep the videotapes secret? Zenya's identity will ultimately come out. One thing will lead to another."

Sylvia shook her head slowly. "I guess I was so caught up in the experiment and getting the paper done that I wasn't thinking about the aftermath."

"It's understandable," Ian said.

"But if we don't publish, won't we be in the same situation as before— keeping important research from the scientific community?" she asked.

Jared laughed. "I'm happy to turn over that responsibility to you, Sylvia."

"Thanks a lot. Seriously," she said.

"That's right," Ian said. "And there is a second problem. The second mtDNA dating on Galina's hair came out at 550,000 years. That means the Shenkos are a different species."

"Oh, my gosh," she said.

"My god." Jared said. "So, it's real?"

"Yes. And the scientist in charge of the lab wants to know where the hair came from."

"What are you going to tell him?" Jared asked.

"I'm not going to respond."

Sylvia looked dubious.

"If you want my opinion," Ian said, "I think we should put everything on hold for a while. We're not going to get scooped. We don't need to rush either of these publications. We could wait for a year and then reassess."

As the fog lightened, the horizon of Santa Monica Bay lengthened. An oil tanker anchored off El Segundo suddenly emerged, its low hull showing it was full of the oil it had brought to the shore refinery.

"Do you think Clyde or Harold would care if we delayed?" Jared asked.

"I think Harold would be all the happier the more we delayed," said Sylvia. "I don't know about Clyde. I will talk to him. He's put in a lot of money. But after all, it's my decision."

Two days later, Sylvia forwarded Jared and Ian the following e-mail message.

> Sylvia,
> I don't care about publishing it right now. I don't need publications. What I care about is satisfying my curiosity. This whole thing has me up nights. What I would ask is that you arrange for me to talk with Zenya. I would like about two hours of her time. I would make it worth her while.
>
> Yours, Clyde.
> P.S. Tell Ian thanks for the update on the second mtDNA test. It's great. We might as well blow up anthropology as well as neurobiology.

Nearly one year later the article remained on hold and no effort was being made to ready it for publication.

THE AFTERNOON OF THE DAY after Ian received a rare call from Corinne found Jared and Ian in a privately chartered Cessna 210 enroute to Nevada County Airpark, the nearest airport to Colliver Canyon. The engine noise made conversation difficult, but they leaned their heads together and raised their voices enough to be heard.

"Did Mark say where at school it happened?" Jared asked.

"It was in a hallway or some place in the building, but not the classroom."

"How long did it last?"

"About a minute. She said Bret—Gregory—seems fine now. Of course Mark and Corinne are worried sick."

Jared nodded.

Ian looked down at the quadrangular fields going by. Looking toward the Sierras he spotted lakes and river canyons. He especially enjoyed the little towns that looked so perfect from an altitude.

"Thanks for arranging the plane and pilot, Ian."

"What?"

"I said thanks for arranging this."

Ian waved. "No problem. It was the fastest way to get there."

Colliver met them at the small airport in Grass Valley. Standing next to his 4-passenger used pickup, he waved as they approached the parking area. Jared patiently held his luggage as Ian and Colliver grabbed and pushed each other like friendly old hounds reunited after a long time apart.

"Bill, this is Jared Weymouth," Ian said finally.

"Glad to meet you, Jared. I've heard a lot about you."

"Likewise, Bill. Thanks for picking us up on short notice and putting us up."

"Pleased to do it." Colliver grabbed the doctor bag from Jared's hand and shoved luggage into the back of the vehicle. "This must be one of the most distant house calls you've made."

Jared laughed. "The second farthest. One time a wealthy Mexican business-man flew me to Mexico City for a second opinion on his child." Jared screwed up his face. "Interesting. That little boy's problem was also a seizure."

Colliver delivered them to the Harris' house and Mark and Corinne ran out to greet them. Gregory watched the bittersweet reunion from the deck. After a while Corinne brought her wary son down the steps and introduced him to Dr. Weymouth and Mr. Trevor.

Looking at Jared, Gregory blurted, "Are you going to examine me?"

"Yes, a little later," Jared said, producing a model airplane kit from his bag. "But, first things first." He handed the kit to Gregory. "This is similar to the plane that Ian and I flew in on today. We thought you might like to build it."

"For me?"

"Yes, but only if you promise to put it together," Ian said.

"Oh, that'll be easy. Thanks a lot!"

The adults chuckled as Gregory ran into the house. Mark brought down chairs from the deck and the group sat in the shade of two tall incense cedars enjoying their aroma. Corinne served iced tea and snacks.

"Thanks for coming so quickly, Jared," she said.

"I wish it hadn't taken this event for us to get together," he said. "But it's good to see everyone, especially that fine strapping boy. If I didn't know better, I'd say Gregory looks at least thirteen. I mean Bret. I have to get these names down."

Corinne smiled. "You can call me Corinne, I don't mind."

"No, Bret, Susan, and Mike Harris it is," Jared said. "I'll get it."

"Do you want to examine Bret now?" Mark asked.

"In a while. Let's let him get a head start on the airplane. If you don't mind talking freely amongst us, what I'd like to hear about is the seizure—how it happened, when, where, and all that."

"Well, it happened at about nine this morning at his school," Mark said.

"Who got the call?" Jared asked.

"I did," Corinne said. "At the bookstore."

"From whom and what did they say?"

Corinne explained that the school nurse called to say that two policemen saw Gregory fall in the hallway. They tried to help him up but he was out, and they could not wake him. They carried him to the nurse's office. The nurse said he was stiff as a board and only when she put a cold compress on his forehead did he come to. He was groggy for a while, then slowly got back to normal. He didn't remember falling or being carried.

"Policemen?" Jared said.

"Apparently they were there to meet with the principal about school security," Mark said. "Bret had just been excused from his class to go to the lavatory and they met in the hallway."

"Do you think Bret was afraid of them?" Jared asked.

"I wouldn't think so," Mark said. "He's met policemen before."

"Has anything else happened in Bret's life recently—bumps on the head, falls, strenuous exercise, stress of any kind?" Jared asked.

Corinne shook her head. "Bill, on your hikes, has anything happened?"

"Nothing I can think of."

"Mmm," Jared said. "Did the nurse say his eyes went back up into his head?"

"No, but she said his eyelids were quivering . . . kind of opening and closing quickly," Corinne said.

"Uh huh. When he started talking was his speech slurred?" Jared asked.

"She said he started speaking normally. Wondered how he got there. Didn't remember the policemen or his fall. He stayed with her, talking until we got there."

Jared thought a minute. "It sounds like a brief but complete outage. Well, all right. Why don't I go in and see Bret now." He got up.

"Should I come with you?" Corinne asked.

"No, just stay here. I'll call if I need anything."

Jared spent about an hour with Gregory in his room while Ian told Mark, Corinne, and Colliver the latest on Galina's mtDNA and its significance. As longer shadows crept around them, an unspoken heaviness seeped into the conversation. When at last Jared rejoined them, he saw dour faces.

He smiled. "Do you know that he's almost got that airplane finished? All those pieces? Incredible." He looked at the worried faces and realized they wanted doctor talk.

"I examined Gregory and we talked for quite a while. He seems as normal as he could be. He acts like nothing is wrong and believes that nothing is wrong. His explanation for what happened is that he must have tripped going down the stairs and hit his head. He thinks he was looking at the policemen instead of at the steps."

Mark held up his hand. "The problem with that is there were no stairs where he was. The nurse said the police saw him collapse after they rounded the corner."

Jared smiled. "You and I know there was a seizure—probably a generalized tonic-clonic type. But Bret is not ready to believe anything like that. I think that we should not confront him with it at this point. And, my view is that it is too soon to give medication. Dilantin, Tegretol, Barbita, all of them have potentially serious side effects and require careful monitoring. I think we should watch Bret over the next few months and see if there are any further symptoms. He can go on normally except that you should not let him do dangerous things, such as swimming, climbing trees, riding his bike."

"What about baseball and soccer? He plays after school," Corinne said.

Jared thought for a moment. "I think those are okay. You should alert his coaches and teachers to be watchful, however."

"What about hiking?" Colliver asked.

"That's all right. But not to the point where he would get extremely fatigued."
Colliver nodded.

"Now," Jared continued, "I didn't talk to him about his powers, but I think it is important that he not use these. Do we need to talk with him about these or has he stopped them?"

"I've not heard of him using his powers for quite a while," Mark said. He looked at Colliver. "Bill, has he zapped any birds or animals recently?"

"Not for a while—at least while he's been with me. He's more in a talking phase—wants to know the why of things. Why do I live differently from everyone? Why don't I get electricity and use a computer instead of a typewriter? God, he can be insufferable."

Everyone laughed.

"Well, all of you should make sure he never uses his powers. I don't know that they would trigger a seizure—they didn't in the past—but it is a precaution," Jared said. "Also, try to avoid situations where he would get emotionally upset. I know that's not easy."

"I lectured him recently that he's never to use the powers, and if he ever does, to let me know," Mark said.

"That's good," Jared said. He sensed that their mood had improved.

As the sun dropped low, they agreed to meet for barbecued lamb at Colliver's cabin, Gregory included. Colliver headed out to get the charcoal started and to drop the luggage at the coyote cabin. Corinne and Ian decided to walk the trail from the house to the Colliver compound by way of the Maidu rock. Mark and Jared stayed at the house to talk for a while and then they'd bring Gregory.

THE TRAIL WAS NARROW. New tree branches and deer brush rubbed against Corinne and Ian as they went by. Shafts of sunlight lit up pollen dust and spider webs as they sauntered slowly over the soft forest ground.

"How are you doing other than this seizure thing?" Ian asked.

"It's hard to think of anything but Bret and his seizures right now. I'm so worried that it might be the same as Nick's."

Ian nodded. "Uh huh. That's understandable."

"But that's not what you asked. Let's see. Aside from Bret, I'm doing reasonably well, I guess. I have a fairly enjoyable job, but not a career. I have a family, but it's not quite for real, you know, since we're not married. Bret acts like an ordinary kid most times, but is far from it." She took a deep breath. "Sometimes it feels a little like being in prison, writing all these letters to you and my family on the outside. Know what I mean?"

"Yeah."

"And now the mitochondrial DNA stuff. I mean, seizures are one thing, but to think your kid is some kind of early hominid throwback . . ." She shook her head. "Anthropology is great when it's out there or back there, but when it's here in your house . . . I don't know. It makes me feel weird."

"I can understand."

"I never used to think anything about his heavy eyebrows. Now they stick out every time I look at him. Seriously, Ian, do you think there could be Neanderthal in his background?"

Ian smiled. "Who knows? If not Neanderthal, maybe ancient Homo erectus. A number of new genetic studies suggest Neanderthals interbred with premodern humans to a minor degree while coexisting with them for thousands of years. Our DNA evidence tends to confirm this."

"So Neanderthal wouldn't account for Bret's physiology?"

He shook his head. "I don't think so. Not by itself. Frankly, I don't know what to think about Bret. Part of me says that it is not uncommon for ancient traits to show up in anyone now and then. The term for it is *primitive retention*. One example is hirsutism—people with hair all over their bodies. Another example is someone born with a stub of a tail. It makes me want to head for the Ukraine to try and find others with Bret's appearance."

She chuckled. "Always the anthropologist. So what do you think about Bret's powers?"

He laughed. "Well, I think Bret has some ancient mutations that evolved prior to Neanderthal and Cro-Magnon for purposes that enhanced survivability. And in the breeding of his line with modern man, the Shenko heritage took the best of the Cro-Magnon while keeping the best of the old traits. They were able to have selective breeding."

Corinne shook her head slowly. "That makes sense, I suppose."

Ian's brow creased. "And Susan, I'm of a mind now to believe that Bret just may be able to sense climate change . . . as he claims. You see, during the four hundred and fifty thousand years or so of his line, there were several ice ages. Only in the last ten thousand years have we had such a nice warm period. And scientists now know from the ice cores that climate has changed suddenly and rapidly many, many times in the past hundred thousand years. Such changes must have affected hominids' ability to live. So any climate detection advantages for moving to better places for food could have been selected. I doubt that Bret can sense minute changes in temperature, but maybe he can sense CO_2 in the air. That's what Clyde Finlayson thinks. Maybe we should call this the Z power."

Their footsteps echoed softly as they dropped in elevation. Corinne, out in front, suddenly stopped and pointed. Ian followed her finger and saw a buck with a large spread of antlers standing on a ridge. The proud animal looked in their direction, flicked its tail, then disappeared into a copse of trees.

"The bucks seem to know this is protected land. We see a lot of them," she said.

"He's magnificent."

She looked at Ian's face not far from hers, his eyes bright with wonder.

"Ian, is it okay that we not talk about Bret?"

"Whatever you want. I'm following your lead, lady."

She laughed.

AS CORINNE AND IAN headed for Medicine Rock, Mark and Jared settled in chairs on the deck with cold bottles of beer.

"Good beer," Jared said.

"It's Sierra Nevada pale ale. I discovered it in L.A. when I first arrived. It's made in Chico."

The men looked out at the forest vista. The sun was well below the trees, providing a twilight aura.

"That was nine years ago," Jared said. "A lot of water under the bridge since then."

"And some over the bridge."

Jared laughed. "Yeah, both of us have paid some dues. I don't have any regrets, but I expect you do. This kind of wrecked your career."

Mark took a long draught. "Yeah, it's lasted longer than I thought."

"Mark, you can come back to pediatrics. I am thinking about retiring in a couple of years. I could get you established with a faculty spot. That's the least I could do."

Mark nodded slowly. "Thanks. Maybe it is time for us to come out of the closet. Bret should have more of a relationship with his grandparents. And if the seizure thing is serious, we should be closer to specialized care. Tell me, Jared, do you think the seizures will become dangerous as happened with Nick?"

Jared's eyebrow moved.

"Hard to say. This was a serious but minor seizure—not a horrible one. Each person is different. If this happened only once every year or so, that's not so bad. In some ways an occasional serious one is better than frequent small blank outs every day. I can tell that Bret's a fighter. And very bright. Do you know his IQ?"

Mark smiled. "He was tested last year at 165. And he's skipped three grades."

"Unbelievable. And he's not behind socially?"

"No. People think he's mature for his grade. Sometimes I feel he condescends to act like a kid for our sake."

Jared laughed. "Well, he'll need that maturity if you go public."

"Yeah, and I think Susan and I will need a lot of maturity to deal with him when he finds out even more of his background. I expect he will challenge the hell out of us."

Jared nodded. "That's par for the course. But you never know."

The next morning Gregory was allowed to go with Colliver, Ian, and Jared to see the Cessna take off. After the plane had become a speck, Colliver and Gregory returned to the compound where they were joined by Mark and Corinne. That afternoon they all went for a leisurely hike and picnic. Gregory insisted on bringing his new model airplane.

By the end of the week, Gregory was back in school and Mark and Corinne were at their jobs. Before leaving work on that Friday, Mark sent the following e-mail message.

Hi, Rachel,

My nephew is back in school now. There have been no other episodes since the one Tuesday. It's a wait and watch situation now. Our fingers are crossed. This event triggered much discussion. We now have a plan to visit relatives both in CA and on the east coast during the next few months. We may

meet the east coast people in Wash. DC to give the nephew a chance to see historic sites and the Smithsonian. (He's into airplanes and space travel.) Wouldn't it be great if there were an opportunity to see you? I'll keep you posted.
Bob

Chapter Twenty-Three

ZENYA LEFT HER COST accounting class at nine-thirty p.m. and walked across campus to her car. She had parked it on a side street near Cal State University, San Diego. The evening was warm and stretching her legs felt good. Receiving an A on her mid-term had buoyed her mood. If she could maintain an A in the course, the admiral would probably let her take other "managerial" courses. These might help position her for a promotion to chief petty officer.

The residential street was quiet as she reached her Volvo and removed the keys from her purse. A car moved slowly up the street behind her and began blinking its high beams. She turned to see what the driver might want. The headlights went out and suddenly a strong hand came over her mouth and pulled her back against a large muscled body. She felt the cold metal of a gun barrel jam against her temple.

"Stand still and keep quiet or I'll blow your head off. Don't try to use your head thing either. If I feel a twinge of anything, I pull the trigger."

The slowly moving car stopped alongside and the passenger's door swung open. There was no interior light.

"Get in and stay quiet," the man said, pushing her down into the three-passenger front seat. The driver grabbed her arms, bent them behind her and wrapped heavy tape around her wrists. The first man leaned in and put tape around her ankles. He pushed her further to the middle, slid in beside her and slammed the door. The driver stepped on the accelerator and the car shot forward.

As they pulled onto the I-8 freeway east, light from overhead floods came through the windshield. She noticed out of the corner of her eye that the driver had on a suit and tie. She tried to steal a look at the man on her right, but he grabbed her neck.

"Close your eyes," he said. He pasted a piece of tape over her eyes.

"What do you want with me?" she said, her voice quavering.

"We want to talk with you," the driver said.

The car changed lanes and sped up.

"What do you want to talk about?"

"About the experiment described on the Paranormal website chat room. It said a woman's brainwaves caused nausea in three volunteer subjects. It was posted by a UCSD psychology student who participated. I recently had the opportunity to talk with that young lady. Very interesting what happened there."

Zenya was quiet for a moment, then said, "So you know who I am."

"Zenya Shenko, daughter of Rose Shenko, sister of Nick Shenko, aunt of Gregory Shenko."

Zenya swallowed hard. "Are you . . . that religious guy who scared Corinne and the baby some years ago?"

"Yes, you might say that modern day disciples of God are religious guys. We might as well formally meet, Zenya. Lawrence Carter is the name. And on your right is Harley Johnston, both with Onward Christian Soldiers."

Zenya tried to wiggle her arms to increase the blood supply to her hands. The gun pressed against her ribs.

"Keep still," Harley said.

"If you just wanted to talk, how come you kidnapped me?"

Carter laughed. "We didn't think you'd give us the time of day otherwise."

"Where are we going?"

"To a little cabin about an hour away. Why don't you just be quiet and relax until we get there. You can think about what you can say to convince us you are a righteous, God-respecting person instead of the devil's creation."

Eventually Carter turned off the freeway and drove on roads for some while, turning several times. She felt the grittiness of gravel under the tires and then the dips and bounces of a rough dirt road. When the engine cut off, there was quiet. She could sense no light.

Harley pulled the tape from her eyes and unwrapped her legs.

"Okay, get out."

It was nearly pitch black. She was guided into a small house enshrouded by trees. When the lights went on inside, she saw a soiled carpet, old furniture, dust on tables and chairs, and through a doorway, two empty beer bottles on a kitchen counter. Old-fashioned Venetian blinds were closed tightly over the windows. Her feet were taped again and she was gently pushed into a soft upholstered chair.

Carter sat down on a nearby couch. There was a bible next to him. He held a notepad and pen. Behind her, Harley sat on a straight back chair, the automatic pistol still in his hand.

Carter stared at her for a minute. "Now, Zenya, I'm going to ask some questions. Your job is to tell the truth, and only the truth. The Lord will be listening carefully and I will be instructed by Him. When displeased, His wrath can be severe. Do you understand?"

"Yes."

What followed was an interrogation lasting nearly an hour. Carter asked about Gregory and his whereabouts, Rose and Nick, Zenya's childhood, the X2 power and the experiment, Zenya's contacts with Mark, Jared, Sylvia, and Alice, Zenya's job and friends—especially boyfriends—and finally her belief in God and attendance at church. She told more or less the truth. She omitted Nick's use of his powers on her and her adolescent pregnancy. She claimed strong religious beliefs and heavy involvement in a neighborhood church, even though she had gone but a few times. She made up having had two long-term boyfriends, but said she was not seeing anyone now. She sensed Carter's keenness for anything sexual. When the questioning wound down, Carter wore a sardonic look.

"Zenya, I don't believe that you and Rose *don't* know where Gregory is."

"It's the truth. I don't know and my mother said she doesn't know."

"Uh huh." Carter looked at her with suspicion. "Well, Zenya, what should the Lord do with you?"

"Mr. Carter, if you take me back to my car, I'll never say anything about this to anyone."

Carter smiled. "It is a sin to lie, Zenya. What do you think, Harley?"

Harley frowned and shook his head.

"Zenya, you say you are a Christian. But the Lord can see through masquerades."

"Wait. To show you I'm sincere, there is one other thing you didn't ask about," she said.

"What is that?" Carter said.

"I could only whisper it to you 'cause I don't think the Lord would want it mentioned out loud."

Carter smiled and got up. He cautiously bent his ear down near her face.

She whispered: My boyfriends tell me I have another power that I'm not even aware of. And that's when I have sex with them they have orgasms much more powerful and longer than normal. They go kinda wild with ecstasy. And, uh . . . if you wanted, I could show you too, but we'd have to do it in private." She smiled at him and let her hand touch his thigh unobtrusively.

Carter stepped back. He looked into her eyes, then down at her body. He was quiet for a moment, then spun around slowly.

"Harley, the Lord is talking to me. He wants me to find out more about the devil's ways. I am to go into a room with this creature."

"Yes, sir."

Carter walked over to Harley and spoke in a low voice. Then he came back to Zenya and undid the tape around her ankles and hands. "Go in that room." He nodded toward a door.

She entered a small room and saw in the dimness a mattress on a double bed, a chest of drawers, a chair, and a window with the blind closed tight. Carter came in behind her. Harley brought up a chair and sat just outside the doorway. Carter tossed Harley the car keys. "Stay alert, Harley." Carter shut the door, making the room dark except for a sliver of light coming in at the bottom of the door.

"The Lord looks favorably on your cooperative spirit. But if Harley hears me call, he'll move fast and ask no questions. So don't think of trying anything. Take off your clothes and get on the bed."

She removed her clothing and heard him hastily doing the same. The springs squeaked as she got on the smelly mattress. She felt his body land heavily next to hers.

"Okay, come here," he said.

She gently put her arms around him and began kissing his neck and mouth. He hungrily embraced her. Soon his breaths came faster and she felt his turgid member against her leg. He moved on top of her, shaking with excitement. She guided him to the right place and opened to his hasty thrusting. After a rhythm was established and she felt he was near ejaculation, she pulled his head down against hers and blasted powerfully with her X2 wave. He jerked and tried to pull his head away. She held on, took a deep breath, and let go again. His penis softened and fell out. He grunted, twisted, and pushed hard against her shoulders, trying to get his knees up. She locked her arms around his back, stayed with him and released the X2 as strongly as she could. His arms buckled and he flattened on her, gasping. Suddenly he retched, spewing foul-smelling stuff onto the pillow near her head. Once again she let him have it. Now he began thrashing without purpose. After a few more blasts his body sagged limply with slight quiverings of arms and legs. She kept the X2 going as she imagined Shenko women had done against attackers for many millennia.

With each wave, Lawrence Carter's hyperpolarizing brain neurons became flooded with biochemicals and died by the hundreds of thousands.

～

NOT QUITE TWO WEEKS later the southland clouded over. The ozone count rose sharply in the Los Angeles basin.

The Super Shuttle dropped Alice at an address on DeMille Drive in Los Feliz, an old neighborhood northwest of L.A.'s downtown. For a minute she stared at the two-story, Spanish-style house. It had thick stucco walls and a red-tiled roof. Large sycamore, elm, and pine trees provided shade on an expansive front lawn. Clusters of sago palms graced the centers of colorful flower beds. Decorative ceramic tiles faced each of the front steps leading to an interior, arched porch.

Suitcase in hand, she negotiated the steps to the dark-stained door with wrought iron hinges and dropped the heavy knocker twice. She remembered that Sylvia's husband was the legal counsel for a major studio, but she thought this home looked like a producer's—some latter day DeMille choosing to live down the street from the master's old mansion.

"Miss Alice?" The attractive, middle-aged woman had gold on a front tooth and a Mexican accent. "I'm Carmen. Miss Sylvia went to the store and she come back soon. Please come in."

Alice was shown into the living room where she eased down on a leather-and-chrome chair. The terracotta tile floor had small, cobalt-colored tiles providing accent every few feet. Covering the center of the room was a Persian carpet with an intricate blue, purple, white, and saffron design. Heavy beams across the ceiling had flowery designs painted on their lower sides. A leaded glass window looked out on the backyard where an oval swimming pool nestled in a sumptuous environment of leafy plants, bright flowers, and statuary.

Carmen reappeared with a newspaper. "Miss Sylvia ask me give you this."

"Oh, yes. Thank you."

"Make yourself home. You want something to eat or drink?"

"No, thank you."

Alice looked at the front page of the *L.A. Tribune* that had come out two days after Zenya's death. She saw side-by-side photos: a small cabin in some trees and a young Lawrence Carter and Harley Johnston together in front of a church, smiling. She read the headline and subtitle:

WOMAN DEAD AND RELIGIOUS MILITANT IN COMA
SLAIN WOMAN IS GREGORY SHENKO'S AUNT. BOY WITH
ALLEGED POWERS STILL MISSING AFTER TEN YEARS

Tears filled her eyes as she read the long article. She put the paper down, leaned back in the chair, and cried softly into her hands.

"Oh, Alice!" Sylvia rushed into the room. They hugged with emotion.

"Isn't it awful? I feel so horrible about Zenya," Sylvia said. "What a nightmare—shot so many times."

Alice nodded. "Why did those bastards go after her? Do you think Carter found out about the X2?"

Sylvia shook her head. "Who knows? Maybe one of the volunteers leaked it. For all their research, the *Tribune* didn't say anything about her power. But if somebody didn't leak that information yet, they soon will."

Alice wiped her eyes with tissues from her purse. "Have you had any calls from the media yet?"

"Several, but I'm not talking to them. Have you?"

"A reporter from the *Tribune* and one from *The San Diego Union* called. I told them I knew Zenya and that I was in mourning and not available for comment."

Sylvia nodded. "We should get going. Are you okay?"

"Yeah, after I use your bathroom. Your house is so beautiful, I'm afraid to walk around."

They got in Sylvia's Lexus and soon were heading north on the I-5 toward Bakersfield. Once she had reached cruising speed, Sylvia broached the topic that had kept her awake every night since the initial reports of the abduction and killing.

"Alice, Jared called this morning from San Diego. He was able to talk with Lawrence Carter's doctor and to see Carter in the hospital. The man is technically not in a coma, but he's basically a vegetable. Can't talk, can't direct his eyes, can't swallow food, can't move any muscles except for a slight jerk of his left leg and some wiggling of a couple of fingers."

"Incredible. What about the other guy?"

"Well, you know that Harley was picked up walking on a road about ten miles from the cabin. He still had the gun in his hand and the car keys in his pocket."

"Yeah, I read that in one of the early reports."

"Okay. Well this detective told Jared that they asked Harley why he didn't get away in the car. He said that he couldn't remember how to start it. And he couldn't remember what had happened at the cabin. So his mind was messed up too, but not nearly to the degree of Carter's. Harley's shirt was torn and some of the buttons were on the floor near Zenya's body. The police figure there was a physical struggle just before he shot her. They found powder burns on her body."

Alice looked down. "She went down fighting."

"Yes, she did. But I just don't understand how she could have destroyed Carter's mind. Did you talk to Clyde about this?"

"We talked quite a long time. Nobody knows for sure what's wrong with Carter's brain, but the standard things are being ruled out. One is a stroke. I heard that the medical tests showed no blood leakage or clots in his brain. Alzheimer's? It never happens that fast. Trauma? There are no bumps to his head or body. Anoxia? There is no indication of a cut-off of oxygen or blood supply. So what's left? One of the news articles I read said some of her head hairs were on the bed and on his body, and some of his pubic hairs were found on her. They had to be having sex or about to. With their heads that close together Clyde thinks her X2 waves could have penetrated with devastating effect. I understand that her autopsy showed a brain lesion nearly as big as Gregory's."

Sylvia nodded. "But how could the X2 wave that we felt kill neurons?"

Alice nodded. "My hypothesis, and Clyde buys it, is that the X2 wave produced gross dysregulation of a major brain chemical called glutamate, and there were runaway firings of his neurons. The term for it is *excitotoxicity*. Glutamate is the prime neurotransmitter for synaptic transmission in the brain. Its disruption could have happened in major CNS areas—cerebellum, hypothalamus, cortex, everywhere glutamate-using neurons operate. Research shows that excitotoxicity causes seizures at one level, and in great excess, death of neurons, even to the point of killing an animal. Glutamate is a toxic acid that must be tightly regulated. Quantities too high or too low in synapses cause neuronal cell death. If the glutamate pumping molecules on cell surfaces don't operate correctly, excess glutamate pours into synapses and neurons start dying massively, just like in a stroke. And there is a *rollout effect*—one neuron going bad can cause others to go bad and so on."

"God, I wouldn't have thought the body had such toxic stuff."

"Who would have thought that the brain had opiates? Acid in the stomach is so powerful that it burns holes in the lining if not carefully regulated. There are many ways the body's chemicals and voltages can go out of whack. Look what a tiny bit of spider venom can do."

"But do neurons die that fast?"

"In seizures, runaway neurons immobilize the body very quickly. In stroke, neurons die in two to twelve hours. It wouldn't surprise me that the X2 power causes cell death faster than in strokes. And nobody got Carter to a hospital until the next day."

Sylvia frowned. "It's hard to believe that the X, the Y, and the X2 would produce such different effects."

Alice nodded. "You know what I learned the other day? Individual hearing cells tune their excitability to one certain frequency. When you think of such incredible specificity in biology, it's not hard for me to believe that these waves evolved different tunings for different effects."

Sylvia smiled. "You know what?"

"What?"

"You're getting too smart."

Alice laughed.

The Porterville Congregational Church had a windowed cross with colored panes above the entrance and a much larger metal cross at the roof's peak. As they joined others moving up the front walk, Sylvia pointed at a small van with a dish antenna down the street.

"I see it," Alice said. "CBS."

"At least they had the decency to park a block away."

"I don't think they should be here at all," Alice said.

There were about ninety people in the cushioned pews when the service started. Rose, in a black dress and small hat, sat in front. Two women were on one side of her, and an elderly man in a suit was on the other.

The minister, a rosy-cheeked woman looking hardly a day over thirty, talked about Zenya's family, her upbringing in Porterville, and her accomplishments in the Navy. As the young cleric projected into the microphone, she exuded strong feelings and intimate knowledge. Alice wondered if she had been Zenya's friend. Her long robe and short hair shook as she painted pictures of Zenya's life. At poignant moments eyes in the audience became wet. Rose stifled sobs. Toward the end of her talk the minister paused, leaned forward, and lowered her voice to a conversational level.

"What are we to think of this tragedy? This painful loss? A vibrant, young woman that we all knew has been destroyed needlessly, her life taken by people believing they were acting on God's behalf." The voice rose. "What travesty! What sacrilege! Zenya was a child of God just like you and me. As was her father and Nick. As is her loving mother, Rose, and her nephew, Gregory. What arrogance! What audacity for anyone to assume that God would speak against those He created." The minister continued *sotto voce* again. "And, you know what I think? I think that God was so angry at this evil done in His name that he meted out punishment on the spot. The leader of this unholy conspiracy received immediate rebuke to his body and brain. The other was found wandering in the desert, a lost soul. They will be nothing. And Zenya's memory and good works will stay."

After a hymn was sung by another young woman, slides came on a large screen that lowered automatically. Pictures appeared of Zenya with her family and friends, including one with a young girl who looked very much like the minister. The last shot of Zenya's smiling face brought loud crying.

After the ceremony ended, all of the attendees gave heartfelt condolences to Rose outside, and then began heading for their cars. Rose asked Sylvia and Alice to join her in an anteroom near the foyer.

"I'm right glad you could come," Rose said, squeezing their hands. "Wasn't that a nice service?"

"Beautiful," Alice said.

"Very nice," Sylvia said.

"Tomorrow we'll put her in a grave on the side of a pretty hill. Near her daddy."

Alice and Sylvia nodded.

"I expect you wanna talk to me about what happened to that Carter, right?"

"Uh, yes," Alice said, surprised.

"I bet you want to tell me that it was Zenya that done that to him." Rose smiled slightly.

"We wondered what you thought," Alice said.

"Well, after all, I'm her Momma. I ain't dumb."

"Of course," Sylvia said.

"See, one time I tol' her she should flirt more with boys but she says she was different from other girls. I thought maybe she was gay, ya know, but she never went with women. Just kept alone. That time when Zenya got pregnant, Nick afterward told me she would never marry, that she had the same thing he did, but different. So even tho' she didn't want to tell me nothin', I kinda knew she was different. Know what I'm sayin'?"

Alice and Sylvia nodded.

"And then," Rose continued, "when Gregory, Corinne, and the doctor met with me and Zenya in Lancaster a couple of months ago, you shoulda seen them two—Zenya and Gregory. They acted too close, like they knew each other real well."

Alice caught her breath. "I didn't know Zenya had seen Gregory."

"Yeah. They drove down in secret after that Ian fellow contacted me about Gregory having had a seizure. When Zenya found out I was to meet Gregory, she wanted to come. That's why we moved the meetin' place from Coarsegold to Lancaster."

"Gregory must feel terrible," Sylvia said.

"He does." Rose opened her purse. "They sent me beautiful flowers and he enclosed this card sayin' how bad he felt about Zenya. Said he loved me. Called me Grandma." Tears came to her eyes.

Alice put her arm around Rose. "That is sweet. I'm glad everyone could meet."

"Yeah," Rose said, recovering. "So go on now and tell me what you wanted me to know."

Sylvia told about the experiment and Alice talked in simplified terms about how Zenya could have damaged Lawrence Carter and Harley Johnston. Sylvia warned that the media would seize upon this information once knowledge of Zenya's X2 power came out, as it soon would. Sylvia then told of the plan to publish the article, implicitly asking Rose's permission.

Rose hung her head for a few moments. "The reporters have already been askin' me if Zenya is like Gregory. I told them they could come to the service, but no cameras. I guess they'll be botherin' me a lot more. But I won't tell 'em nuttin'. As to that medical paper, if you're askin' if it's okay to print it, I don't mind. But if'n you do, I'd like a favor. Bein' it's as important as you say, put Zenya's name in and say she was a nice girl."

SYLVIA AND ALICE arrived late for the meeting at Sylvia's house. They found Jared, Ian, and Clyde in the living room with drinks in their hands. The first task was catching everyone up on all of the happenings. The second was deciding how to handle the next few months. After dinner and dessert in the dining room, they moved back into the living room for coffee and liqueurs.

"So we're agreed to publishing both articles at the same time—the Zenya experiment and the mitochondrial DNA findings," Sylvia said. "And we'll make fifty copies of the videos of the experiment for distribution."

Everyone nodded.

"And Clyde, do you think you can get both articles in the same *PNAS* issue in about two months?"

"I've already talked to the editor. Once he actually sees what they are, I know he would bump just about anything else."

There were chuckles.

"And everyone agrees that we will tell the media that the information is under embargo until the publication date?" Jared asked.

"Right," Ian said. "Until then, we give them no additional information."

"What do we do after that?" Alice asked.

"Good question," Clyde said. "After the publication everyone will want to know what it all means. How it ties together."

"How should we handle that?" Sylvia asked. "Should we hold a press conference and issue a white paper?"

"That's one option, but there's another that just occured to me," Clyde said. "I'm scheduled for the keynote address at the American Society of Human Genetics meeting in ten weeks. What if I were to use that forum to tell the

Shenko story, as much as we know of it? Of course I'd need your help in preparing for this. We could hand out copies of the talk."

"Great idea," Jared said. "And we agree on including the climate thing, the Z power?"

"Might as well," Sylvia said.

Ian nodded.

"But what about the topic you were scheduled for?" Alice asked. "Haven't the preliminary programs gone out?"

Clyde's face moved mischievously. "The preliminary program has gone out. But I'm happy to leave the title unchanged."

There was a pause as three sets of eyes looked at him expectantly. Clyde looked back but offered nothing.

"I'll bite," Jared said. "What is the title?"

Clyde smiled. "The topic is *Has Human Evolution Stopped?*"

The hoots and laughter were so loud that Carmen rushed in to see if somebody had spilled something.

Sylvia said, "Okay, we have a plan for all of us, but what about Mark, Corinne, and Gregory? What happens to them?"

Jared's eyebrow spasmed. "One concern of mine is how Zenya's death will affect Gregory. By now he must know that his father died from a seizure. These two events might be weighing heavily on him."

"Ian, what have you heard from Mark or Corinne?" Sylvia asked.

"I haven't received a letter since Zenya's death. I'll probably get something in the next day or two."

"Another thing," Alice said, "what happens if the Harrises are found out because of all of the new media exposure?"

"How likely is that?" Ian asked.

"Fairly high if there are all kinds of magazine articles and TV programs with their pictures bandied about. The press will be looking hard, talking to relatives and all that."

Everyone was quiet for some while, pondering the problem.

"I think it will be easier for Corinne and Mark to face the media than for Gregory," Ian said. "Maybe there should be a two-step process. How about—if and when they are found, Mark and Corinne come to L.A. and stay at my place or at your house, Sylvia. They could have press conferences, go on TV news interviews, *Oprah*-type shows, whatever. That would be pretty easy to arrange in this town. Meantime, we keep Gregory away from the media until we think he and the world are ready."

"But how could you keep the media from him?" Alice asked.

"He goes for a two-week sailing trip on the *Tomolo* out of Santa Barbara."

"With you and Jared?" Sylvia said.

"I suggest the crew is Jared, me, Bill Colliver, and Gregory. Colliver will be needed to make Gregory feel comfortable. Those two are very close. The boat would need provisioning in advance. We'd head out to the Channel Islands, maybe cruise down to Santa Barbara Island and Catalina, and when the time is right, end up at Marina del Rey for Gregory's debut with the media. All during that time we can get him prepared."

Jared laughed. "That's brilliant, Ian."

"And hopefully, by then Mark and Corinne will have provided a positive background that allows the public to be receptive to Gregory," Ian said. "The press will have checked on Gregory's school records and talked with his friends and found out just how exemplary this kid is. They'll find his powers have been controlled and are not a problem for society."

"It's good, Ian," Alice said, smiling.

"Then we have a plan?" Jared asked.

"We have a plan," Sylvia said.

Chapter Twenty-Four

THE SUDDEN BREEZE blew ripples on the pond, obscuring the rounded rocks that lay on the bottom like some stone village in a different world. At the pond's muddy edge a small frog rested on a limb, its green body half in and half out of the water, its bubble eyes blinking slowly.

"It shrinks down in the fall, doesn't it," Mark said.

"One year it completely dried up," Colliver said. "But normally it spawns lots of trout, frogs, dragon flies, water skippers, mosquitoes, and god-knows-what every year. It's one of Bret's favorite places, you know."

"I know."

Following Colliver's lead, Mark sat on a granite rock in the meadow.

"Too bad school started. I miss tromping around with him," Colliver said. "So inquisitive, that one."

"Yep."

Colliver threw a pebble into the pond. "So how do you think he's handling the Zenya business?"

"It's affected him a lot. It's not just her death, but a whole set of things—realizing he's not who he thought he was, that I'm not his real father, that his mother and I aren't married, that we came here to hide him from the world, that there are bad people out there like Carter, and so on. He's reading about himself and the Shenkos in magazines and finding out things on the Web. Seems like each day for the past couple of weeks we deal with something new. Last night he connected his seizure with Nick's epilepsy. We heard him crying in his room. It's a wrenching time and the learning curve is steep."

Colliver nodded. "It's tough. A few days ago he asked me why I had taken you guys in. I said only because you were such city types I thought you'd be gone in a month."

Mark chuckled. "Little did you know."

"I told him how he zapped me as a baby and I had no idea what it was. He thought that was funny. But mostly he's not been in much of a laughing mood. Oh, his earliest memory is of us dumping the tub of water on him."

"Why doesn't that surprise me?" Mark laughed, remembering the watershed moment. "At least he's not talking to anyone else about all this. He's keeping the secret."

"He's probably scared of becoming Gregory," Colliver said.

"I think that's right."

After a few moments Mark looked at his watch. "I've got to head back. It's good to get out with you, Bill."

"Nature is curative, especially for pains of the soul. If there's anything I can do to help, just holler. That kid is important to me."

"Just continue being supportive if he wants to talk. See ya."

Leaving Colliver looking at the sunset, Mark trudged home. Gregory was not there but he found Corinne working in the kitchen.

"Hi. Isn't it a bit late for Bret?"

"Sometimes his games run late. He's usually the last to be dropped off by the soccer moms."

Mark moved close to Corinne and massaged her neck as she worked at the sink. "You don't look so good," he said.

"This whole thing is a nightmare. Like waiting for the sword of Damocles to drop."

"What did you think of the plan Ian sent—that when the sword drops, you and I go to L.A. to face the media and Bret goes on the sailboat?"

"I suppose it's fine. I can't think of anything better. I guess that letter from my mother depressed me, how they're getting bombarded by the media. Your family too, no doubt. Probably even Rachel." The name was said with sarcastic inflection.

Mark frowned. "What about Rachel?"

"Mike, when we were back there I could tell that she still had eyes for you. It was pretty obvious."

"I thought you liked her."

"Oh, she's nice. It was wonderful that she arranged for us to hear that astronaut talk at the Smithsonian. Bret was in seventh heaven."

"So?"

"So nothing. I'm sorry. I'm just feeling bitchy. Let's not talk about Rachel. Could you set the table?"

Gregory came in wearing red athletic shorts and jersey, holding his cleated shoes by their shoelaces.

"Hi, Dad, Mom. Sorry I'm late." He gave Corinne a peck on the cheek.

Mark realized that Gregory's voice was now fully in a man's register. It had dropped over the past three years. Mark also saw that the boy's summer growth spurt had made him taller than his mother. He was now twelve, going on . . . whatever.

"Hi, honey, get your sweaty stuff off 'cause we're ready to sit down," Corinne said.

"Dad, am I still supposed to call you *Dad*, since . . . you know, you're not my real father and you never adopted me?"

Corinne wheeled. "Of course you are to call him *Dad*," she said sternly.

"I would like you to, unless you have a problem with it," Mark said.

"No problem. Just wondering. I'll get changed."

As Gregory left the kitchen, Corinne and Mark exchanged a look. "Good Lord," she said.

Over dinner, Mark and Corinne learned that Gregory had scored two goals even though his team lost 4 to 3 in overtime. Corinne talked about author presentations scheduled for the weekend. Mark mentioned seeing a four pointer buck on his walk with Colliver.

"Dad, I read that epilepsy can be cured by fixing a person's genes. Is this true?"

Mark and Corinne's eyes met again. "It's not true yet, even though there's been a lot of progress on gene therapy." Mark looked at Gregory. "The causes of epilepsy are very complex. There may be no specific genes involved or one gene or a number of genes. And even if you could find the particular genes—which could take years and years—the ability to alter them for good effect is still too crude."

Gregory appeared thoughtful. "I also read that you were a gene doctor at MIT before you and Mom came here. When your name was Mark Sandler. Is that true?"

Mark put his fork down. "That is true, Bret."

Corinne grabbed her napkin. "Your dad could have been a Harvard professor but decided to become a children's doctor at SSU. I took you down there for help and that's how he met us. He's sacrificed a lot for us."

"You've been finding out a lot, huh," Mark said. "If it's from the Web, you need to be careful because it can be wrong."

Gregory nodded. "I know."

"Was it a chat room?" Corinne asked.

"Yeah."

"What else did they say?" Mark asked.

"Well, that you were opposed to research on human genes. Are you?"

Mark felt the stab of Gregory's eyes.

"Bret, I worked on the Human Genome Project at MIT, and I left that job because I came to believe that science was moving toward a technological threshold that would change forever what it means to be human. The name for it is germ-line engineering. I felt that neither policymakers nor the general public had much idea what was going on. So I decided to feel better about myself by leaving and making a statement to my colleagues." Mark stopped to see if what he said was registering on Gregory.

Gregory nodded. "Are you *still* opposed to gene research?"

Mark closed his eyes for a moment. "Bret, I still believe we are going down a slippery slope toward techno-eugenics where some day parents will design their children by selecting genes from a catalogue. Companies are already designing genes for animals and plants with digital technology. The explosion of this kind of R & D has continued even faster since I left the Genome Project. But the public is finally beginning to catch on, especially when they read about the poisoning of lady bugs and monarch butterfly caterpillars by pollen from engineered corn plants. Ultimately this is not a problem of science, but of people's philosophy toward all of life and what it means to be human. Does that make any sense?"

"Yeah." Gregory swallowed some rice. "It's sort of like what Uncle Bill says, that we shouldn't be changing all the plants and animals or people because it would be arrogant and screw up a billion years of biological miracles."

Mark smiled. "Yeah, that's right. Well put."

Corinne smiled. "I didn't know you knew the word *arrogant*, Bret."

"Bill told me. He also told me about Wittgenstein. That guy was quite a dude."

Mark and Corinne laughed.

"But Dad," Gregory continued, "if people don't do research on genes, how can epilepsy get fixed?"

Mark nodded imperceptibly. It was the question that had tortured him for years, ever since Alice Masterson had met him at a restaurant in West L.A. It was the question he had hoped Bret would never ask.

"I wish I had a good answer for that, Bret, but I don't. If all scientists were moral and principled, they would only do gene research to advance medicine and cure diseases. They'd draw the line at changing our species. If that were the case, I'd be in favor of more gene research. But many scientists either can't or don't want to see the big picture in relation to what they do. Or, they're paid big money from some company. Some actually make no bones about wanting to change our biology. Some care more about being first in making discoveries than anything else. That being the case, I believe we need to take a stand now, before we enable technology that unethical people can use. I guess personally that means I would rather die of a genetic disease than be a part of making life become not worth living."

A tear rolled down Corinne's cheek. Gregory's lower lip pushed forward as if he were about to cry, then both lips firmed into a frown.

"I know I'm different from everyone 'cause I got the Shenko genes." He looked down. "Can I ask just one more question?"

"Sure, Bret," Mark said.

"Do you think Shenko genes should continue on?"

"Of course we do!" Mark said. "Shenko genes have been around a very long time and they deserve to go on. They have proven their niche in the world. That's part of the reason your mother and I brought you here as a baby. We wanted you to be able to have as ordinary a life as possible."

"We only wanted you to be happy," Corinne said. "Everything we've done has been for that."

Gregory nodded slowly. "I know, Mom." He looked away suddenly, then stood and pushed his plate toward the center of the table. "I want things to go on just as they are. I want to stay Bret. I like it here." Tears rolled down his cheeks and he turned to leave. Corinne jumped up and threw her arms around him, followed by Mark who hugged them both.

"We love you, Bret," Mark said, as he put his cheek against the sobbing boy's head.

NEAHKAHNIE MOUNTAIN at 1600 feet is one of the highest peaks on the Oregon coast-line. On a sunny, late September day Alice and two postdoc friends from the Vollum Institute ate their lunches on the mountain's knife edge of rock that dropped precipitously to the 101 highway and the ocean.

"Alice, how could you possibly give this up to go to Smogville?" her girlfriend said.

Alice shrugged. "What can I do? Craig's kicking me out. Says I have to move on for the sake of my career."

"The physiology department at SSU ist a top place," Horst said in his thick German accent. "Very *gut*."

"Well, let's hope they want me," Alice said.

Alice had the airline tickets in her desk drawer. On Thursday morning she would fly to Sacramento, spend a day seeing friends at UC Davis and at the *Bee*, and on Friday continue on to LAX for her interview with Dr. Ernie Laster and his lab people at SSU. In the afternoon she would give a seminar that would be open to the whole department. That was not something she was looking forward to, but she could lick her wounds later by visiting her father over the weekend.

The day before her departure Alice received a smudged, hand-addressed envelope postmarked from Nevada City, California. She opened it to find a note written in feminine cursive:

> Dear Alice Masterson,
>   I know Gregory Shenko. His real name is Bret Harris. He plays on a soccer team at Grass Valley Union High. He lives on Tyler Foote Road east of North San Juan. I have intimate knowledge that this is him. I don't want this to be public. I hope to talk with you. I don't know if you'll get this. You can write me c/o General Delivery, Main Post Office, Nevada City, CA 95959.
>   Sincerely,
>   Jane Doe Smith
>   Soccer Mom

Alice read the note three times. Each time she mouthed the words, *I have intimate knowledge that this is him.* She looked out the window toward the west hills of Portland. The Douglas firs and hillside houses would not focus. *Oh my god,* she thought.

AFTER ARRIVING AT THE Sacramento airport Alice rented a Ford Escape. She drove east on Freeway 80, turned north on Highway 49, and continued on to Nevada City. In the center of town she pulled into the parking lot of the National Hotel, which her travel book described as the oldest operating hotel in California. Built in 1856, its interior was much the way it was when the Wells Fargo stage pulled in every day.

She took a room on the third floor in the back. Velvet curtains with gold tassels hung alongside the windows. The old wooden bed was large and soft. She changed into jeans, a long sleeve blouse, and sandals. At the small writing desk near the window she wrote out the following note:

> Dear Jane Doe Smith,
>   I received your letter and would like to talk with you. I just checked into the National Hotel and you can call me or leave a note on

*when and where to meet in N. C. You have my assurance of complete
confidentiality.
Sincerely,
Alice Masterson*

In the lobby Alice obtained directions to the main post office and to Grass
Valley Union High. After a brief wait at the post office, she handed the stamped,
addressed envelope to a postal clerk. "Will this be available for pick up right
away?"

"I'll postmark it and put it in the general delivery box right now, ma'am."

"Thanks much."

To stave off mounting hunger she stopped for a fast-food burger, then drove
to the high school, arriving in the late afternoon. Classes had recently let out and
a number of students were talking out front. She approached a boy who looked
like he could be in the tenth grade.

"Hello there," she said cheerfully.

"Hi."

"Do you know a boy named Bret Harris?"

"Yeah."

"Was he in school today?"

"Yeah."

"Do you know where I could find him?"

"Probably on the soccer field."

"How do I get there?"

Following his directions, Alice found the gym and the athletic fields beyond.
Two soccer games were in progress, one with boys and the other with girls. The
boys looked to be fifteen or older. Alice sat on a bench near a youngster with
a cast on his foot and noticed some women nearby, watching and talking. She
wondered if one were *Soccer Mom*. She leaned over to the boy. "Hi, do you know
Bret Harris?"

"Sure."

"Is he out there?"

"Uh huh."

"Which one is he?"

"The forward in the red jersey . . . number nine."

"Thanks."

She found the jersey with a nine. The boy was stocky and muscular with red-
dish brown hair that flew around as he ran. His tanned face had a prominent nose

and deep-set eyes shaded by heavy, dark protruding eyebrows. He handled the ball with assuredness and grace. Where the other boys yelled, he showed a quiet determination. Alice sucked in her breath. He was so large, so grown up. Could that young man possibly be Gregory?

She watched the final quarter, noticing that everyone on the red team tried to feed the ball to number nine for scoring opportunities. The defense converged on him every time he took possession. Late in the game a softly kicked ball was lofted his way. He nudged the ball down with his forehead, stopped it momentarily with his foot, then juked two successive defenders, moving the ball past them as if they were frozen. Suddenly he was in the open, one-on-one with the goalie. Two quick taps, a fake to the right, and an unreal body twist to the left was followed by a powerful left-footed drive. The ball curved into the corner of the net. Alice jumped to her feet and yelled. The fallen goalie pounded his fists on the grass.

As number nine ran back up field, hands high in the air, Alice felt a chill. He was magnificent. But he was not a boy of twelve. He could not be Gregory.

When the game ended with a victory for the red, the young man high fived with his teammates, then walked to the sideline and sat down next to a bulging backpack. People came by and congratulated him. After changing his shoes, he put on the backpack and headed for the parking lot with two other boys. He carried the tied-together soccer shoes in his left hand.

"Bret," Alice called as she stood up and headed for him. He stopped and looked at her.

"Bret, can I talk with you a minute?" He had a querulous expression as she drew up to him.

"You don't know me, Bret, but I just wanted to shake your hand. You're one of the finest soccer players I've seen at your age." She extended her hand.

He smiled with embarrassment but took her hand. "Thanks," he said.

As they shook hands Alice grabbed his wrist with her left hand and sharply dug her fingernails into the inner side while she held his hand tightly with her right hand.

"Owww," he yelled, his face gathering in pain. He tried to push the attacking fingers away with his left hand but the shoes got in the way.

"Oww, stop it!" He tried to jerk free.

With braced feet Alice held tight and dug into his arm with all of her strength. She felt her nails break skin and gouge into flesh. Then it hit. Like someone had slugged her simultaneously on the front and back of the head. She lost consciousness momentarily and staggered. She would have fallen but Gregory's arm around her waist steadied her and she managed to reset her legs and regain balance. Her head was throbbing from the kind of pain that she had never forgotten. Her eyes caught his angry look just before he turned and ran.

Other boys had stopped and were looking at her. She managed to smile at them, then started toward the parking lot. From the Escape she watched the boys pile into several cars. She saw Gregory at a window of a car that pulled by. With his left hand he gave her the finger.

Back at the hotel she checked for messages but there were none. She felt beat. In her room she removed her sandals, jeans, and blouse and stretched out on the bed. She closed her eyes, but her mind raced.

After all these years she had found Gregory! But he was so different from what she expected, it was as if she had not found him. She had found instead a full-sized, athletic specimen carrying ancient hominid genes who passed himself off as an American adolescent. He was a being with such a sophisticated mental attribute that he had taken her consciousness away for one instant and returned it again almost without notice. The quiet, surgical precision of the act was incredible. She tried to imagine the package of neurons, the intricate chemistry, the genes and proteins that had to have evolved to achieve that. It was a wonder. She gasped. Her heartbeat raced and she began to hyperventilate. Stumbling into the bathroom, she turned on the cold water in the shower and stepped in with bra, panties, and hairband. After a few minutes her palpitations eased. She ran a hot bath in the tub and soaked for a long time.

That evening Alice found a family-style restaurant and downed a glass of Chardonnay with dinner. Then she walked the long way back to her hotel. In her hotel room she zoned through a TV movie. Ideas of what to do about Gregory and Soccer Mom dominated her thoughts.

In the morning she picked up the phone and dialed Dr. Ernie Laster at SSU. He wasn't there, but she told his secretary that due to a family emergency she had to cancel. She would call later to rearrange a visit. After breakfast at the same family restaurant, she walked around looking for stores. Spotting a sporting goods shop, she went in and purchased a high-quality soccer ball.

Finding no messages at the hotel, she drove again to the high school. Classes were in session. She waited in the car until just before noon, then walked into the school's office, identified herself as an aunt of Bret Harris, and said she needed to give him a soccer ball at lunchtime. The girl behind the counter gave her directions to a classroom. Alice found it without difficulty and waited in the hall near some lockers.

When the bell sounded, students streamed out, talking and laughing. Gregory, talking with another boy, did not notice Alice in the hubbub. She waited until he moved past her.

"Bret," she called.

He turned and looked at her.

"It's you!" He seemed undecided as to what to do.

"Bret, I have a present for you." She held up the box and took out the shiny, leather ball. He came closer.

"That's for me?"

"Yes. I'm sorry for what I did to you. Is your arm all right?"

He showed her the red scabs on his wrist. "It'll be okay."

He looked at her, frowning. "Why did you do that anyway? Who are you?"

"My name is Alice. And . . . uh, it's a long story. Here take this."

He took the ball and ran his hand over the surface, then looked at her curiously. "Are you a reporter?"

Alice took a deep breath. "Uh, no. I'm a scientist. Look, I know I owe you an explanation, but . . ."

"Bret, are you coming?" a voice called from down the hall.

"Yeah, one minute," he shouted back. "You're a scientist? What kind?"

"A neuroscientist. Bret, if you'll meet me somewhere, I'll explain things."

He looked at her with more interest.

"I can't now. Maybe tomorrow. Would you get me another present?"

She smiled. "Sure. And I promise not to hurt you again."

"I know you won't." The statement was matter-of-fact. "Do you know where I live?"

"On Tyler Foote Road, but I don't know where."

He smiled slightly. "Could you come tomorrow at noon, and meet me behind the big oak tree south of the driveway where you turn in to go to my house?"

"I don't know where that is."

He gave her directions from North San Juan. "You'll see—where a tree root loops out and back in."

"Okay. At noon."

"Bring hiking clothes and food for a picnic. And don't forget the present."

Her mouth dropped.

"Bye," he said.

"Bret, don't tell you parents about me."

He didn't acknowledge the last statement but walked off with his friend, tossing the ball up in the air and catching it.

In the car Alice looked at her shaking hands. Was that a stupid thing to do? If they met, what on earth should she tell him? A hike? Could it be that he knew who she was? Something else bothered her. It was as if she had been the child—an apologetic child—and he was the adult. Maybe she shouldn't show up tomorrow.

On Saturday morning Alice tried to reach Sylvia at work and then at home, but she wasn't available. She left a message on her father's machine letting him know that something had come up and she wouldn't be visiting over the weekend. She would call him later. At the hotel desk there were still no messages from Soccer Mom. Again Alice went shopping and then left directly for North San Juan. As she drove across the bridge high over the south fork of the Yuba River, she found herself nervous but excited. In her new pack, she had sandwiches, potato chips, carrot cake, a container of lemonade, a new Wilson four-finger mitt, and a blanket. She was wearing hiking shorts and light ankle boots and had her hair in a ponytail.

Gregory's directions were exact. She found the looping root and parked in a wide spot off the road. The big arching oak tree, fifty yards from the road, was unmistakable. She sat next to the trunk for about ten minutes before Gregory walked up. He had on baggy pants with a metal cup hooked on his belt and a faded blue T-shirt. A black baseball cap sat reversed on his head.

"Hi," he said, grinning.

"Hi, Bret," she said, getting up.

"I'm glad you have boots on. I forgot to ask if you liked hiking. Some girls don't."

"Sure I do. I've done quite a bit of hiking in Oregon. That's where I live."

"I looked it up. Neuroscientists study brains," he said.

"That's right."

"That must be why you're clever."

She smiled.

"But before that were you a reporter?" he asked.

"Yes."

"Is your last name Masterson?"

"How did you know? From your parents?"

"No, they don't know you're here. I found it out from that website you started and some other places."

"I see. So you know a lot about me."

"I don't know as much about you as you probably know about me."

She laughed

"Anyway, you got the lunch?" he asked.

"Yes. And the present."

"You didn't have to bring a present. I was just kinda kidding."

"I have one anyway. I hope you'll like it."

"Cool. Follow me. I'll show you why no one could find us when I was a baby. We can rap as we go."

As they hiked the narrow trail to the compound, Gregory talked about his parents and his uncle and their way of life over the past ten years. He pointed out birds and animals, berry bushes and special places, such as where a black bear and her cubs had lived in a rock cave. They veered off on another trail and he showed her Medicine Rock. They eventually came to the top of a ridge where, in a small valley below, they saw the convergence of the main creek with a smaller tributary. At the junction was a pond surrounded by a meadow. There were several granite boulders scattered around. Late-blooming wildflowers splashed color in the meadow. Looking up, Gregory pointed to a red-tailed hawk flying in a lazy circle.

"This is my most favorite place," he said.

"It's gorgeous." Alice found her eyes becoming moist, not just from the beauty of the scene, but from the affection for the land that Gregory exuded. She had the feeling of being courted by a suitor showing off his prized possessions.

"We can eat down there, if you want."

"I couldn't imagine a better spot," she said.

They spread the blanket on soft grass among some young pines. They broke out the lunch and talked about Colliver's land and what it had been like for Gregory as a child. After he had downed the sandwich, Gregory looked at Alice with a serious expression.

"I want to know why you wanted to find me," he said.

"I thought you might." She smiled. "It goes back to when you were a baby and I was a young reporter."

Alice talked for some time, giving the history of her contacts with Mark, Corinne, and Gregory as a baby, including experiencing the X power in Fresno. She discussed the family's disappearance, establishing the website, and going to grad school. Gregory asked occasional questions. They had finished the lunch by the time she stopped.

"So that's about it," she said. "You have fascinated me for a long time, Bret."

"I fascinate a lot of people."

She laughed.

"Do you have a husband and kids?" he asked.

"No."

"How come?"

"I never married."

"Why?"

"Well, I never found a man I wanted to marry."

"Why?"

"Boy, you ask a lot of questions."

He laughed. "Well, aren't we trying to get to know each other?"

She laughed with embarrassment. "Right. Okay, why haven't I found a man I wanted to marry? Let's see. I did find one, but he didn't want to marry me."

"Why not?"

"Oh, he had gotten divorced, and men who are just divorced often don't want to marry again right away. Anyway, that's the main reason."

"Did you have sex with him?"

"Bret! What a thing to ask," she scolded.

"Well, people have sex even though they're not married."

"I know, but you don't ask someone a question like that."

"Why not? What's wrong with talking about it?"

She rolled her eyes. "You can talk about it, but only after you know a person really well. We've only met."

"We met ten years ago."

She laughed. "Clever."

"How many times do people have to meet before they know each other well?"

"It depends."

"On what?"

"Oh, on how well they get along . . . how much they like each other . . . whether they have common experiences . . . whether they trust each other . . . lots of things."

"But we're trusting each other, aren't we?"

She looked at him with puzzled amusement. "Yes, I suppose."

"So we can be good friends too?"

She laughed. "You are amazing."

He looked out toward the pond for a minute. "You don't have to talk about your sex life if you don't want to."

"Bret, I didn't have sex with him," she said, exasperated.

"Why not?"

"Look, I don't want to talk about it any more."

He looked at her intently for a few seconds, then began clearing the blanket. After everything was off, he stretched out on his back.

"Lay down," he said. "Get comfortable."

"Why?" she said.

"I want to show you the Y power."

She smiled. "I don't want to experience it. So please don't, thank you."

"It doesn't hurt at all. It feels good. Just relax."

"Bret. Please." As she held up her hand to emphasize the point, a slight wave licked at her insides. Then a second came, noticeably stronger. An unfamiliar thickening feeling in her hips began. Her breasts tingled. Bret was looking at her, smiling slightly.

"Okay, Bret, I feel it," she said. "You can stop."

"Just lay back," he said.

A strong wave went through her. She began breathing heavily. "Okay, Bret, that's all."

The waves died down. He smiled. "Did you like it?"

"Uh, well, it was interesting." She sat up and rubbed her face. "Bret, would you like the present now?"

He sat up. "Oh good, yeah."

She reached into the pack and brought out the glove. He took it quickly, tried it on, and admired it.

"Thanks. It's super. My glove is about worn out. This is great."

She smiled. "You're welcome."

"You're a nice lady," he said.

Alice smiled. "I'm glad you like it."

"I should get you a present."

"Oh no, that's not necessary. Being friends is just enough for me."

She eyed him thoughtfully. "Bret, have you ever used the Y power on anyone besides me?"

"A few times."

"Do your parents know that?"

"No. They don't want me using the powers."

"And for good reason. You should never use the X or Y. It could get you into big trouble."

He looked pensive. "I think I could use the Y if I were in love with someone."

"Well, only if they were in love with you too."

"Yeah. But it would help them fall in love with me."

Alice found herself searching for a reply.

"I mean, like if I did it to you, wouldn't you kind of start to love me?" he asked.

"Bret, I'm more than three times your age."

"But people of all ages can love each other."

She smiled. "I'm talking about romantic love. Love between a man and a woman."

"I'm a man; you're a woman." He grinned.

"Nice try." She laughed.

"What would you have done if I had not stopped?" he asked.

"I would have become angry." Her voice was cautious.

"But you couldn't have because you would have felt . . . you know, like love."

"Oh, yes, I could have."

He laughed. "As smart as you are, you don't get it."

"Get what?"

"It's hard to resist."

"Yeah, I do get that. But I think you should not do it without advance consent."

"Are you mad at me?"

"No."

"Did you like it?"

She smiled but did not answer right away. She loosened her ponytail and ran her fingers through her hair. "To be honest, I did. But I didn't like that you could force it on me."

Gregory smiled.

The sounds of the creek became louder. Gregory was the first to hear Arnie's footsteps. Gregory shook Alice.

"There's a dog coming. Don't be frightened," Gregory said.

She started when she saw the wolf dog.

"He won't hurt. That's Arnie, Bill's dog, which means Bill might be coming."

They stuffed things into her backpack except for the mitt which Gregory hid in the branches of a nearby tree.

"Yo there!" Colliver's voice came from the other side of the main creek. They watched him stone-step across the shallow, rippling rapids and head for them.

"Your name is Alice Grass and I just found you hiking around. Okay?" Gregory said.

"Grass?"

Gregory laughed.

"Afternoon," Colliver said, joining them.

"Hi, Bill, this here is Alice. I found her hiking around. This is my uncle Colliver. He owns all this."

"Hi, there," Colliver said, inspecting her.

"Please to meet you, Mr. Colliver. This is very beautiful land."

Colliver nodded. "Thanks. So where are you from, Alice?"

"Portland." She smiled.

"Portland? Well, I could think of far worse places as cities go."

She nodded.

"She's a scientist, Uncle Bill."

"A scientist? Why does this place attract scientists? So you're just out for a little hike?"

"Yes, I didn't know it was private. I didn't mean to trespass."

Colliver smiled. "I don't mind people enjoying the land as long as they behave themselves."

"Uncle Bill, I have to go do homework. Could you show her our coyote cabin? I was telling her about that."

She frowned at Gregory. "You have to go?"

"It's okay. He'll show you the way back."

"But . . . but . . ." she stammered, looking into his eyes.

"Don't worry. Thanks for everything. I'll see you." Gregory snatched the new glove from the tree.

"Bye," she said softly.

Gregory stopped after taking a few steps. "Uncle Bill, you know that buck that's been around lately?"

"Yeah."

"I got him. Put him down like a baby."

"Huh," Colliver said.

"Gotta go. Bye, Alice. Bye, Uncle Bill." Gregory ran off.

"So long, Bret," Colliver said. When he looked back at Alice he saw her wiping her eyes.

"You okay?"

"How far is it to the cabin?" she asked.

"About a half mile."

"Maybe I could rest a little there. I'm feeling a little weak all of a sudden."

"Here, let me have your backpack. We can go slow."

With Arnie alongside, Alice followed Colliver to his cabin. He made her hot tea and they talked for some time. Then he drove her to her car and made sure she could find her way back to Nevada City in the dark.

At the hotel she asked about messages and the clerk handed her an envelope. She immediately opened it.

> *Dear Alice,*
>
> *I thought a long time whether I should meet you. I decided against it. I just don't think any good would come from you knowing who I am. I'm a happily married woman with three kids and a husband to think of. I doubt you would believe what happened six weeks ago anyway. Nobody would think I acted properly, even though I had no idea what was going*

on until I lost control. I know he somehow caused it. It had to be one of the powers they wrote about. But I don't want to get him in trouble. He's basically a good kid.

I'm not going to soccer games any more because I don't dare get near him. I certainly won't be driving him home again. I'm trying to forget what happened, but it's hard. I hope writing this will help put it past me. In some ways, I don't ever think I'll forget it. I'm sorry you had to come up here for nothing. This is the best I can do. Please don't try to find out who I am or tell anyone.

Ex Soccer Mom

Alice smiled thinly. Soccer Mom sounded likable despite her heart-wrenching experience. She clearly was right about one thing. It would do nobody any good to talk about what happened between her and Gregory.

Chapter Twenty-Five

THE ANNUAL MEETING of the American Society of Human Genetics takes place in mid- to late-October. This year it was held at the Washington State Convention and Trade Center in Seattle.

Sylvia, Alice, Jared, Ian, and Clyde ate dinner at a restaurant near Pike's Street Market. They could see the placid Puget Sound with its ferries plying routes to the west and north. Not far from them the futuristic Space Needle presided smartly over its mountain and water empire.

After finishing up their main courses inside the four-star restaurant, they sipped wine and talked. The conversation turned to Clyde's upcoming presentation.

"I think I have everything down fairly well," Clyde said. "Thanks to all of you for the information you sent. I especially appreciated your suggestion, Alice, that the Y power works by stimulating euphoria-producing neurotransmitters such as serotonin and dopamine. Those dynamics fit with what Zenya told me."

The waiter brought creme brulees and espresso drinks.

"You know," Ian said, "I was surprised at the media firestorm after the *PNAS* article. Front page stories everywhere. I would have thought people were OD'd on this stuff. I'll bet there wasn't much more bold ink for the bombing of Pearl Harbor."

They laughed. "What amazes me," Jared said, "is the ASHG allowing live TV coverage of your talk, Clyde."

"I'm sure they're getting a chunk of money for it," Ian said.

Clyde turned his gaze back from the window. "You know, the one thing that doesn't fit my model is that Gregory has been sexually quiescent. At this point he should be a hormone-driven teenager going after females. He should be trying out that Y power. But he just seems happy with sports and hobbies."

Alice coughed and put her latte down. "He may be more active than we know," she said.

"Possibly," Clyde said. "But you'd think that Mark and Corinne would have gotten wind of it."

Jared shrugged. "The reason is that we successfully socialized him. That is what Mark and Corinne did so effectively. And thank god for that."

"Yes, well, biology usually wins over culture," Clyde muttered.

Ian laughed. "Spoken like a biologist."

As NOON OF THE next day approached, the convention center's large ballrooms were joined into a cavernous hall with theater seating. Even so, there was standing room only when the session started. Media people with video cameras were perched in strategic locations and a television crew had set up on a special platform for the live broadcast. It took several minutes for the president of the ASHG to quiet the crowd.

"We have only an hour to hear the genetic story that has galvanized the world. So I will make a simple introduction in order to get on with what I'm sure you'll agree is a major coup for our Society. It is my honor to introduce Clyde Finlayson—Nobel laureate; member of the National Academy of Sciences; Byron Williams Professor of Biology; and Chair Emeritus, University of Washington. Dr. Finlayson?"

The applause damped quickly as Clyde began speaking.

"You may think you're at a Seahawks-Dolphins game, not a scientific meeting. I think there might be pom-poms and peanuts in the air soon. But that's okay, as long as there are no commercial breaks."

There was laughter.

"I'll spare you further attempts at humor because time is short and the topic does, in my humble view, merit attention from all of the people on this planet, especially scientists. The media coverage could be perhaps more subtle, but their role here today cannot be gainsaid."

Clyde then explained that he would provide "informed speculation" on who the Shenkos were, where they came from, and how their amazing traits might have developed. His comments would be "broad brush" and would not include information previously published or covered by the media. He would speak for thirty minutes and then field questions for the remaining time.

"So let me first address the question that many news headlines have asked: Are the Shenkos a new species? The question as stated is wrong. If the Shenkos are a species separate from us, then they are an old species, not a new one. We are the new guys. But, are the Shenkos a *separate* species? In my view, the answer is *yes* . . . at least more *yes* than *no.*

"I think the genetic Shenko line has been in the process of speciation for at least several hundred thousand years. Like most forming species, they were in geographic isolation for some time, then must have received company—Neanderthal and Cro-Magnon—at which point they developed a strategy of *sympatric speciation*—in other words, keeping separate to significant degree while living in the midst of others. In doing this, they have been able to conserve and pass on their special genes among their group while taking on other genes from surrounding populations.

"But how could they do this without being diluted? How could they possibly keep their genetic line distinct?" Clyde held up a finger. "The answer is, by developing social and mating mechanisms that are unique and utterly astounding! Let me explain."

The huge audience was now hushed. As the TV cameras rolled, the home audience was climbing in numbers surpassing Superbowl ratings.

Clyde carefully described the four traits and the effect each produced, pointing out that only Shenko males had the stun trait X, the seduction trait Y, and probably the Z —the latter being the ability to detect subtle changes in climate, most likely CO_2 levels—and Shenko females had the disorienting trait X2 and possibly the Z.

"The sexual dimorphism of these particular traits carefully evolved over time for the purpose of species survival. Please consider this scenario: About one point eight million years ago Homo erectus became the first hominid to spread into Asia and Europe from Africa. This forebearer to Homo heidelbergensis, to Neanderthal, and to modern man had a large brain, was a scavenger carrying manufactured stone tools, and was perhaps the first user of fire. The Shenkos probably derive from Homo erectus, too. The Z trait itself—and I'm going to refer to these as *traits*, not powers—allowed the sensing of climate change which was important because climate could change quickly in those times—from sudden droughts to rapid ice ages. The existing climate was a key factor in finding food, especially animals to prey upon. These hominids were probably more prey than predators, however. The Shenko line, dating back to possibly three-quarters of a million years ago, must have branched off in Eurasia from Homo erectus as the result of a significant mutation—the initial brain lesion and the X trait it produced. The genes for a prototypical voltage cell lesion must have been in the gene pool for a long time until the particular triggering mutation occurred, resulting in a phenotype. It may have been weak at the beginning, but over time became strengthened. The conditions in the environment that made the lesion immediately useful were the predators—the big cats, wolves, and other large carnivores. The X trait allowed a defense against such ferocious beasts, providing the new hominid more mobility for scavenging. He could range far away from the protective forest. Over time the X strengthened and became a weapon that allowed Shenko hominids to become real hunters, not just scavengers, and to move into geographic isolation in Europe or western Russia during the ice ages."

The audience buzzed with conversation while Clyde drank from a glass of water.

"Now why do I suggest this? I say it because that initial weak X trait, operating like an electric shock, allowed Shenko males to scare predatory animals away, to stun small animals and seize them for food, and to weaken later hominid enemies in close combat. It was a fantastic breakthrough. And over time it developed further, became more precise and powerful, and provided a signficant advance in hunting prowess. It allowed the tribe to trek far distances to where there was better game. It conferred a great defense against hostile tribes. In the basic "meat-for-sex" relationship between males and females, women would be incented to mate and bond with the prolific Shenko hunters, now the better food providers. Some experts think that females, given their greater plasticity in sexual and social attributes, had more to do with hominid evolution than the males. I expect this was especially so with the Shenko line.

"But there was a dark side to this newly evolving hominid. The lesion's downside was that for the males it was accompanied by a life-shortening epilepsy. And the positive and negative aspects of the lesion could not be separated out by subsequent selection processes. So the new hominids continued on with both effects, still able to succeed in environments where other hominids could not."

"He sure knows how to get to the heart of it." Ian whispered.

"An incredible mind," Sylvia said. "I'm glad he's calling them traits."

"Further innovations in sexual attraction and mating patterns were possible and necessary, however, to advance the survival of the lesion. The seduction Y and disorienting X2 traits came along through additional mutations to cement the new species in a creative way. Let's picture an early Shenko tribe in the shadows of the glaciers in the great Ukraine valley. Big herds of mammoths and aurochs, which were wild oxen, were plentiful on the grassy plains. Shenko hunters with their X trait could ambush these beasts and bring them down with precision. It was dangerous, no doubt, but the X was still more effective than wooden spears.

"While the Shenko males, even as boys, could bring home the bacon so to speak, they kept dying young from seizures. Living longer, the women carried the culture, and for this reason the tribes were matriarchal. What was needed was more babies, faster. What better way to have Shenko women of all child-bearing ages produce children rapidly than through the development of the male Y trait—a seduction machine *par excellence*. Women couldn't resist the young males' sexual advances. Maximum sexual enjoyment and maximum offspring."

Clyde shot his arms in the air with a comical expression. The audience roared with laughter.

"What a showman," Jared said, chuckling.

"Maximum message," Sylvia said.

"All the time that the lesion was evolving," Clyde continued, "there was accompanying brain development beyond Homo erectus. Following the herds, coordination of the hunt, increasingly complex tribal organization, and the challenges from sharp coolings and warmings of the environment all contributed to selection pressure for more brain power. Thus the Shenkos' large-sized crania and the evolution of the Z trait. By the way, the human body already has carbon dioxide sensing in the carotid artery system. The carotid body is a small cluster of chemoreceptors and supporting cells located near the fork of the carotid artery. This body detects changes in arterial blood, mainly the pressure of oxygen but also of carbon dioxide. It is not surprising that, during the course of evolutionary development, such a CO_2 sensor migrated into the brain with all the neurons there. The Z trait could even have developed first, before the X. But I digress, maybe we're getting too technical." Clyde then said, "As kids say, 'my bad.'"

The audience laughed.

"So we have the Shenko X, Y, and Z traits that had evolved. Why would the female X2 trait come into being? One reason may have been to prevent mating when it was not healthy for the female to have children, and to prevent sibling matings or son-mother matings. The male X and Y forces had to be counteracted to avoid the genetically deleterious effects of close interbreeding. So from further lesion mutations there develops a sex-linked female X2 trait. What better way for a female to deflate a male ego and penis than to make him sick to his stomach? It might not always have worked, as Zenya told me, but most of the time was probably good enough.

The audience chuckled.

"Now what about the X2 trait exerted *in extremis*—where at maximum strength in close quarters it can cause runaway seizures and even death, as apparently Zenya intimately showed one Lawrence Carter? This feature probably developed to deal with hominid aggressors who might dilute the Shenko genes. We know that from about two hundred thousand years ago Europe was populated by Neanderthals who had also speciated. In addition, there were other ancient hominids around, all descended from Homo erectus along with the Shenkos. There is evidence that

Neanderthals interbred with other hominids, but how much is unknown. All of these early hunter-gatherer groups probably coexisted in states of equilibrium, their growth limited by their ecological niches and food acquisition capabilities.

"Then, about forty thousand years ago, there was a sudden outpouring from Africa of a new, aggressive hominid—our human ancestors—known as Cro-Magnon. These folks had the benefit of a major advance: detailed language, which provided the ability to perform complex coordination and planning. The young of these new humans could learn and perfect tool-making, weapon-building, and group-hunting techniques from Papa, Uncle, and Grandpapa through an oral tradition. This was a great advantage.

"The Neanderthals, the heidelbergenses, and other ancient peoples whose fossils have been found in Europe and Asia were intelligent, but still had a bit more of a guttural larynx, one that probably did not allow as much language as we have. This limited their capacity for generational learning and change. And also, for the Shenkos, there was still the problem of male early death to impede their success. Under the pressure of the new language-speaking Cro-Magnons, about thirty thousand years ago Neanderthals went extinct. The Shenko line, however, in the face of this pressure, came up with a distinct and saving evolutionary strategy. The Shenkos found survival value in interbreeding with the new kid on the block—the Cro-Magnons, i.e., us—but only in a limited and controlled way. The males' Y trait and the females' X2 trait were the key to this."

"Where on earth is he going with this?" Jared asked.

"Listen, it's pretty ingenious," Ian said.

"You know where he's going?"

"Clyde and I worked it out together."

Clyde paused to adjust his notes, then continued. "Shenko males preferred mating with Shenko females and vice versa. With the Y trait there was some mutual brainwave reinforcement for this, such as release of internal opiates that made this attraction extremely powerful. But Shenko males also learned to excite and mate with non-Shenko females. Non-Shenko women could be captured or seduced and brought into the tribe for increased child-bearing. On the other hand, Shenko females evolved a sexual exclusivity for Shenko lesion males in order to increase the frequency of lesion children. The X2 trait in normal dosage allowed them to deter non-lesion males' overtures. But what if the village were attacked by marauding tribes? Shenko women could thwart rapers by using the X2 trait *in extremis*, immobilizing or even killing the assailants. Attempted rape and pillage at a Shenko village brought surprises for the attackers. It was the X2 trait that kept Shenko women from having children contaminated by external genes.

"Are you still with me?" Clyde looked around. "I know this is a lot of information."

The audience murmured as if to say, *Keep going*.

"Okay, so what was the genetic effect of this unusual mating system?" Clyde looked up as if he were searching for hands in the air. "The effects were two.

"One was that it brought some Cro-Magnon genes into the Shenko gene pool, but in a limited way. By mating with women from non-Shenko tribes and bringing them into the village, Shenko men also brought in critical characteristics such as the genes for the physiology that facilitated language. These external genes allowed the Shenkos' continued adaptation for competition and co-existence with the Cro-Magnons. The second and most important effect, however, was retaining lesion individuals within the tribe to continue mating with each other. This system maintained exclusivity of the all important X, X2, Y, and Z traits for the Shenkos. The small proportion of females born in the tribe without the lesion could be traded out or kept for further mating with lesion men. Men born without the lesion would be kept from breeding with lesion females and either stayed in the tribe as second-class citizens or left the tribe.

"Okay. How certain am I of this particular paradigm? Not at all. But some system for genetic exclusion had to have happened. Otherwise the lesion traits would not have survived all this time in one group of people who were interbreeding with others."

Clyde took another drink of water. He looked at his watch and then at Jared, Sylvia, and Ian in the front row. He smiled and winked.

"Let me make one more point before I stop for questions. Why, you might ask, did not the Shenkos with their superb traits take over the world instead of Homo sapiens sapiens, i.e., us? Why are we not all Shenkos? The answer, I suspect, is that it came down to a numbers game. The Shenkos could not proliferate as well as tribes with longer lived males. Moreover, while the Shenkos could hold their own against germs and to some degree, steel, they could not measure up against guns. They could not deal with huge hordes or armies. They probably were forced to hole up in Transcarpathia, high in the mountains. There they could defend themselves against all comers, whether Attila the Hun, the Mongols, or the Russian Tartars, but not so on the plains.

"And make no mistake, the Shenkos would have been deadly fighters. They could drop horses in their tracks as well as men with swords, bows, or pikes. But the Shenkos could not defeat overwhelming numbers of people, especially those with guns, on the flatlands. The Shenko clans were probably thought of as demons, incubi, witches, and such. They were definitely the 'other,' and neighbors and marauders likely left them alone only until such time as their powers no longer held the advantage. From that perspective, it is quite remarkable that they have survived to this day."

Alice said, "Is he still talking about Gregory?"

"Rather impersonal, isn't it," Sylvia said.

Clyde ended his talk and called for questions.

A middle-aged, red-headed woman was first to reach a microphone. "Dr. Finlayson, do you think that the Shenkos interbred with Neanderthals?" she asked.

Clyde repeated the question then frowned. "It is certainly possible biologically. And they were in the same area. If the Shenko Y power worked on Neanderthal females, then it would have happened. I'm told the cranial capacity of Nicholas Shenko was about equal to a typical male Neanderthal and that his son Gregory has heavy supraorbital ridges and a chunky, muscular body. So it's a good bet that they got Neanderthal genes to some extent."

A white-bearded man asked the next question. "If there was Cro-Magnon gene flow into the Shenkos, wouldn't there have been at least some gene flow from the Shenkos out to non-Shenko tribes, especially if non-lesion males left or were forced out of Shenko villages?"

Clyde smiled. "Well, I would think some lesion genes leaked into non-Shenko gene pools. Perhaps some modern humans ended up with lesion powers from time to time. Maybe those famous seducers of women, Don Juan and Rasputin, had the Y power."

Laughter exploded in the audience. "Another?" Clyde asked.

A young man in a dark suit and tie spoke. "If the Shenkos were in the western Ukraine area, I just don't see how they could have survived separately under all the Mongol hordes, Germanic tribes, Russian Cossacks, Bulgars, and others that fought over that land century after century."

Clyde nodded. "It *is* surprising. That portion of the Carpathians, once known as Galitzia, is near the borders of Romania, Hungary, Slovakia, Poland, and Ukraine. It was in the middle of lots of action. Culturally, Sergi Shenko's parents who immigrated here were Carpatho-Rusyns, a Slav mountain people who made their living from livestock, sheepherding, and the like. But there are other ancient peoples who have survived like this. Look at the Basques of southern France, northern Spain, and the Pyrenees mountains. They have a very distinct blood group and a pre-Indo-European language. Some experts consider them direct descendants of the Cro-Magnon tribes who did the cave paintings. Historically, they have been highly intelligent and fierce fighters.

"Remember, too, that most of the wars and sacking of cities in Europe took place in valleys or on the plains. Armies marched through the passes but would have bypassed the high mountains. The Shenkos could have been like gypsies, surviving partly through wits and partly through the formidable X, X2, and Z powers. As a Mongol chief, why would I want to pay the price of trying to get these people out of the mountains? Even if you got some of the Shenko tribe, you probably wouldn't get them all. And you might lose much of your army in the process. Besides, there wasn't much to pillage."

The next several questions were technical, dealing with polygenic inheritance, genetic drift, chromosomal mapping, genes, and alleles. Looking at his watch, Clyde finally said he would take two last questions.

A well-dressed woman intoduced herself as a paleoanthropologist from UC Berkeley.

Finlayson nodded, "I can certainly see why you've come," to which there was a ripple of laughter.

The professor said, "Yes, this is the most astounding development in the world—if it's true. My question: What about the 1.8 million year old skulls found in Dmanisi, Georgia—do these relate to the Shenkos? And second, does the existence of the Shenko line utterly shoot down the Mitochondrial Eve school, that we all come from one genetic line that exited Africa fairly recently?"

Finlayson looked up at the ceiling for a few moments. "To your first question, my understanding of the Dmanisi skulls is that they are an early form of Homo erectus and much too early to directly relate to the Shenkos. As to the Shenkos shooting down the Mitochondrial Eve hypothesis I would have to say, yes and no. Clearly the Shenkos, and to some degree the Neanderthals, succeeded in a strategy of surviving by interbreeding with Cro-Magnons while, in the case of the Shenkos, keeping genetic separation because of the unusual mutations they had. In this sense the existence of Shenkos supports the so-called 'multi-regional' model of human development, i.e., a mixture of all the genes from erectus. But without the special Shenko traits, I don't think this could have happened. Allowing the Shenko separation, I say Mitochondrial Eve seems correct. It's just that nobody could have foreseen evolution producing a Shenko line. We know from Stephen J. Gould and others that mutations can happen frequently, causing very significant evolutionary change in very short time frames. But the geneticists or even the great fossil hunters, the Leakeys, couldn't have predicted the Shenkos. In some ways I guess that the Shenkos were and are living fossils. But they surely didn't appear that different to all their neighbors until interaction occurred. Okay, next."

A distinguished-looking man in a sport coat and silk tie took a mike. "As a doctor and genetic counselor, if a Shenko came to me today, wouldn't I have to look at the lesion as a terrible disease to be avoided? Just as I would advise a couple having a high likelihood of a Tay-Sachs child, wouldn't I need to strongly counsel such persons from having any children?"

Clyde looked down for several moments before responding. "I know where you're coming from. But I think we have to be very careful about applying the medical model here, especially a medical model developed by and for Homo sapiens. I believe we need to have respect—more than that—to have *deference* for a hominid species that has probably survived on this planet for six to eight hundred thousand years." Clyde tapped his finger on the lectern. "Let me read you something." He pulled a paper from a folder. "I think this ethical statement is wise and applies well to this case.

> The American Society of Human Genetics deplores laws, governmental regulations, and any other coercive effort intended to restrict reproductive freedom or to constrain freedom of choice on the basis of known or presumed genetic characteristics of potential parents or the anticipated genetic characteristics, health, or capacities of potential offspring.

"I'll leave it at that. Thank you very much."

The audience jumped up and gave a very long standing ovation.

SUNSHINE, UNUSUAL IN October, continued in Seattle over the next couple of days while the jetstream pointed at northern California. In Nevada City rain fell off and on as weak storm fronts blew across the area. Wet weather always reduced foot traffic at Corrigan's Bookstore, so Corinne decided to box up unsold books for return to the Ingram Book Company, the store's major distributor.

On that Thursday afternoon, as she pulled books off shelves, the bell on the door tinkled. Dottie Winslow, a retired school teacher and avid book reader, stepped inside and shook her dripping umbrella.

"Hi, Dottie," Corinne called out.

"Hi, Susan," Dottie said, coming over.

"Wet out there?" Corinne asked, smiling.

"Just a bit. Susan, I just came from the Bistro and there was a man and a woman reporter from out of town having lunch. They were showing the waitresses pictures of that doctor and the mother of that Shenko boy who's been in the news so much? Said there is a good chance the boy is somewhere around here."

Corinne stood. "Well that's interesting. Why do they think so?"

Dottie looked at Corinne for a few seconds, then said, "Well, they claimed to have traced some airplane to the Grass Valley airport a while back. Friends of the doctor had chartered it from L.A. The reporters think they might have come to visit the Shenko boy."

Corinne laughed. "Well, wouldn't that be something. That'd sure put this community on the map, wouldn't it?"

"Sure would. You know, Beth has worked at the Bistro eighteen years and claims to know most everyone in town. So she looks at the pictures and says she can't recognize anybody. But after they left, Beth says to me the young woman looked like you."

Corinne giggled. "That's a laugh."

"Yeah, I thought so too."

"Did you see the pictures?" Corinne asked.

"No. I was on the other side of the room. Anyway, I'm not looking for books today. Just thought I'd make your day with that story."

"Yeah, it's a good one. Thanks, Dottie. Don't get too wet."

In the back room, after getting off the phone with Mark, Corinne stared through the window at the slanting rain, listening to its drumming on the roof. She had agreed with Mark that they should pack suitcases that evening and keep them in the trunk of the car. At a moment's notice they could get Bret out of school and head out if needed. They had decided to talk with Colliver and have him explain to their bosses that they were called away on an emergency if they suddenly disappeared. Colliver would need to watch the house. Corinne thought about Beth and the pictures. There must be several locals who knew of the incident by now. No, it might not be long.

A bookstore clerk popped her head in the door. "Jeff Weismann is here."

"Can't you wait on him?" Corinne asked.

"He's asking for you."

Corinne walked out and greeted the longtime customer who worked over at the court building on Church Street. Weismann, somewhere in his forties, loved military history.

"Jeff, I'm sorry but I don't think we've got anything new for you to look at."

"That's all right. I actually came to talk to you and wondered if we could go have a cup of coffee."

"Well, okay . . . for a few minutes."

Under his umbrella they crossed the street and entered the deli that advertised espresso with a neon sign. Soon they were sitting at a corner table, leaning over steaming cups.

"Susan, I came to see you on business."

Corinne looked puzzled. "Court business or book business?"

"Juvenile court business. It's about your son, Bret. Does he know a girl named Nina Schuh who lives in North San Juan?"

"Sure. A few years back she used to babysit Bret. We haven't seen her for a while."

"Has Bret seen her recently?"

"Well, I wouldn't know. He hasn't said anything about her. Why?"

Jeff took a gulp of his grande coffee. "Nina is six months pregnant and told her parents that Bret is the father."

Corinne froze for several moments, then slowly shook her head. "No. That can't be. No."

Jeff held up his hand. "Susan, we've been acquainted for quite a few years, right?"

"Right."

"I've met Bret and your husband in the store on occasion. I have a son in school who knows Bret. So I know you are good people, responsible people. I will try to help you as much as I can, but I have to deal with you officially on this."

"I understand."

"I'm going to tell you something and then ask you a question that you need to think very seriously about before you answer. I am an officer of the court. You don't have to respond. You may wish to consult an attorney. But if you choose to answer, you must tell me the truth."

Corinne nodded. Her hands were shaking as she put her cup down.

"Nina's parents told the officer in Juvenile who took the report that Nina claims Bret is the boy in hiding who has the weird powers . . . you know, the one who has been all over the news recently. Gregory Shenko is his name. My question of you is—is this true?"

Corinne tried but couldn't prevent the tears. She covered her eyes for a minute then finally wiped her face with a napkin. Recovering somewhat, she said, "Jeff, what happens if I don't answer that?"

He nodded slightly. "Well, then I think I have to go over to the high school and pick up Bret and have a talk with him. You or your husband can come with me if you want."

"What would be different if I answered the question?"

"If you said, 'No, Bret is not Gregory Shenko,' then I would allow him to go home and stay with you until I investigate this more and decide what to recommend to the judge. Is it correct that he's only twelve?"

"He's twelve."

"Well, Nina's seventeen and that would legally make her the perpetrator and Bret the victim, even though they're both minors."

Corinne nodded, trying to keep her mind tracking. "So what if Bret were this Gregory?"

Weismann looked at her strangely. He shook his head slowly. "Damn," he said softly. "That would change things a lot if what they say about him is true. Then I would be staying at your place tonight and he couldn't leave the house until the detention hearing with Judge Ronke tomorrow morning."

"Why would you stay at our house?"

"So I can keep an eye on him. Otherwise he'd have to go to Juvenile Hall."

"I see. What's a detention hearing?"

"To determine if Bret is a threat to the community and should be confined or not."

"Oh, god."

"I'm thinking you probably should talk to an attorney, Susan. And do it before I see Bret. I can recommend a couple if you like."

Corinne exhaled loudly. "Can we first go find Mike?"

"Sure."

NOBODY GOT MUCH SLEEP in the Harris' house that night. Gregory went to bed in his room. Corinne slipped in later to watch him in the dark from a rocking chair. Mark was in the master bedroom, first talking on the phone to Ian and then Jared, then sitting up much of the night. Jeff Weismann catnapped on the couch.

As she rocked quietly Corinne thought about what her boy had said earlier at the lawyer's office. He had seen Nina a couple of times six months ago. Nina had approached him about going to visit Medicine Rock because she was doing a paper on local Indians. So he had taken her there, but other than looking at the rock and talking, nothing had happened, he claimed. Mr. Kruger, the attorney, had said fine, there was nothing to worry about. Mark had accepted it, also. So why couldn't she just believe it, too? Was it that Nina and Gregory had seen each other twice? Gregory said Nina had needed to look again at the rock because there was something she missed the first time. He couldn't remember what. Or, was it that extra flick of his eyelids that she had seen before when he knew he was in trouble?

The law is in our favor, Kruger had said, even if Bret Harris is Gregory Shenko. But Kruger had not wanted to know if Bret was Gregory—not yet anyway. For the hearing tomorrow it was immaterial.

"Mom?"

"I thought you were asleep."

"I can't sleep."

"Then just stay quiet with your eyes closed."

"How come you came in here?"

"I just wanted to be by you, honey."

"Will they put me in Juvenile Hall?"

"We don't think so."

"I want to stay home."

"I know. We want you at home too. Stop talking now."

"I love you, Mom."

"I love you too, Bret."

THE HEARING TOOK PLACE at 10 a.m. in the old County Court building in Nevada City. The room's judicial bench and furniture had been modernized at some point, but the high windows and ceiling were the originals, lending a formal atmosphere. Except for a man in overalls sitting in the gallery and a bailiff standing in the corner, the room was empty when Mark, Corinne, Gregory, Les Kruger, and Weismann came in. Kruger had his clients sit in the front row near a table close to the judge's bench. Kruger and Weismann sat down at the table and took papers from their briefcases. Soon a side door opened and the judge, a court reporter, and two uniformed police officers came in, one a young raven-haired woman, the other a bald-headed man. Soon William Schuh and his pregnant daughter Nina came in and sat down.

"All rise," the bailiff said. "Family Law Court in the Civil Division of the Nevada County Superior Court, Judge Burke Ronke presiding, is now in session. Everybody please raise your right hands." The bailiff swore everyone in.

Judge Ronke was an obese man in his forties. His black robe flared as he waddled up behind the bench. He looked out from under wiry eyebrows and smiled.

"Hello, everybody. Please be seated." He looked down and read for a couple of minutes, then looked up. "This is a detention hearing in the matter of Nina Schuh and Bret Harris, two minors involved in charges of second degree rape and first degree sexual abuse. We are on the record. Mr. Weismann, would you introduce the case?"

Weismann stood, papers in hand. "Your Honor, we have present the minor, Bret Harris, his parents, Michael and Susan Harris, and their attorney, Les Kruger. Also present are William Schuh, father of minor Nina Schuh, Juvenile Officer Jan Whitedeer, and Chief Rod Lancaster."

"Welcome and thank you for coming," the judge said. "Please continue, Mr. Weismann."

"Nina Schuh, age seventeen, is six months pregnant and states that Bret Harris, age twelve, is the father of her unborn child. She further alleges that she did not initiate or engage consensually in sexual misconduct with Bret Harris, but was the victim of his unwanted advances. Nina Schuh resides at home with her parents and it is Officer Whitedeer's and my recommendation that she remain there due to her condition. We see no evidence that she is out of control or constitutes a threat to the community."

Weismann looked up at the bench. Judge Ronke nodded and turned to Officer Whitedeer.

"Is that your recommendation, Officer Whitedeer?"

"Yes, Your Honor."

"Mr. Schuh," Ronke said, "is Nina under your parental control and will you house and care for her in the foreseeable future and at least during her pregnancy?"

"Yes, Your Honor," the man in casual clothes said, standing up. "And I just want to say that my daughter is a nice girl who has never been in trouble and this problem is all 'cuz of that boy who should be locked up. He ain't natural."

Mark's jaw dropped and he and Corinne glared at Schuh. Gregory shifted in his chair.

"Thank you, Mr. Schuh," Ronke said loudly. "I ask you to please only answer questions that are asked and not to make uncalled-for remarks."

"Yes, sir."

"I have a question, Mr. Schuh," Ronke said. "When did Nina tell you or her mother that she was pregnant?"

"About two weeks ago. We noticed it and asked her."

"Did she say why she waited so long to tell you?"

"She didn't know she was pregnant for a while. And then was afraid and embarrassed."

"Is that when she said Bret Harris was the father?"

"Yes."

"Thank you." Ronke made some notes.

"Mr. Kruger, is there any objection by your clients to Nina Schuh remaining with her parents?"

Kruger, a tall man with brown, curly hair stood up and smiled. "None at all, Your Honor. At this time we do have objection to Nina Schuh's account of the facts, that the sexual act or acts were non-consensual, and that Bret is the father of her unborn child, but we will address those in the Admit/Deny hearing."

Ronke nodded. "Thank you. Mr. Weismann, please continue with the recommendation concerning detention of Bret Harris."

Weismann glanced at the Harrises as he raised himself. "Your Honor, given the ages of these minors, the law provides that Nina Schuh is the offender in this case. Given that, and given Bret Harris's age, ordinarily we would recommend that he be released to his parents, and this is their wish. However, I feel I must bring to this court's attention that Bret Harris is alleged to have a false identity. He might very well be one Gregory Shenko. Gregory Shenko, as I'm sure I don't have to tell anyone, has been reported to have some abnormal powers, including those of seduction of females. This is all hearsay, of course, from media reports, but if there is any truth to the reports, it could have a bearing on this case and on the advisability of releasing him to his parents."

"Your Honor?" Kruger jumped up.

"Mr. Kruger."

"Your Honor, may I suggest to the court that getting into hearsay about who Bret is or is not might be appropriate for a trial when there are rules for evidence, but not here, not today. My client Bret Harris is well known. He has attended schools in Nevada County all of his life and has a verifiable record as an outstanding student, an excellent athlete, and a model citizen. There have been no reports or complaints of any misconduct by Bret from teachers, from law enforcement, from anyone prior to now. Mr. and Mrs. Harris hold responsible positions in our community. This young man, Your Honor, is only twelve years old. In no way does he deserve to be confined."

"Thank you, Mr. Kruger. Mr. Weismann, did you have further comment?" Ronke asked.

"I would ask Chief Lancaster to report to the court what he told me this morning."

All eyes turned to the city's chief of police who slowly raised his large body from a chair.

"Yes, Your Honor. We verified just this morning that the Nevada County DMV fingerprints of Michael Harris match previous Los Angeles DMV prints of one Mark Sandler, M.D., Ph.D., born in Pittsburgh, Pennsylvania, employed by Southern State University. Also, that local DMV prints of Susan Harris match previous Fresno DMV prints for one Corinne Shenko, who previously resided in Fresno. We have searched vital statistics databases and find no record in the U.S. for the marriage of Michael and Susan Harris. We have yet to find any records verifying that Bret Harris has a previous alias as Gregory Shenko, but we expect we are likely to find this by the end of the day."

Ronke stared at the chief for a few seconds. "I see. So you think that this really is the family that has been in hiding all these years. That Bret Harris is actually Gregory Shenko?"

"Yes, sir."

Ronke sat back. "Well now. Amazing." He stared at Mark, Corinne, and Gregory with intense curiosity. "Well, what does this mean, Chief . . . you know, for law enforcement?" he said finally.

"One thing it means is that very soon we will be invaded by the media and the curious from all over the place. My department is making plans for this as we speak. We are arranging for extra help from other jurisdictions. For the next phase of this case I think it means you will need crowd control for this court. It will be a zoo, Your Honor."

Ronke looked astonished. "Really?"

"Really," the chief said.

"What about the boy? Do you think Bret should be placed in detention?"

"I don't consider him a threat to the community. I'm more worried that he won't be able to escape the mobs, friendly and unfriendly. You might want to detain the whole family for their own protection."

The judge looked up as two people came in and sat down.

"We can't do that. Chief, I would like you, Mr. Weismann, and Mr. Kruger to approach the bench."

The four of them spoke in low voices at the back of the bench for quite some time. Finally they all resumed their places. Kruger leaned back and whispered to Mark and Corinne.

The judge spoke loudly. "Mr. Weismann, what is your recommendation concerning Bret Harris?"

"If Bret isn't detained in some way, he and his parents might leave the county and state. I don't think Juvenile Hall is an appropriate place for Bret. I understand he has a medical condition. My recommendation is that Bret be under twenty-four hour electronic ankle monitoring surveillance and that he be required to stay within the city limits of Nevada City under adult supervision at all times . . . that is, when he is not in classes at school. Further, I recommend his parents report in to me each day by telephone between eleven and one."

The judge nodded. "Mr. Kruger, any further comment?"

Kruger stood up. "No objection, Your Honor."

"Good. We will implement that recommendation concerning Bret Harris effective immediately. The Admit/Deny hearing will take place in this room two weeks from today at ten a.m. This hearing is closed."

Chapter Twenty-Six

T HE MEDIA EXPLOSION IGNITED from a story that appeared the day after the detention hearing. The *Union*, a joint Grass Valley and Nevada City newspaper, broke the news. The front page was headlined:

GREGORY SHENKO FOUND IN NEVADA CITY
Exemplary Student Known As "Bret Harris" Faces Statutory
Rape Charge

The article was accompanied by a photograph showing a surprised Mark, Corinne, and Gregory standing on the doorstep of a downtown rental unit. The photo's caption stated:

Dr. Mark Sandler, Corinne Shenko, and Gregory Shenko take
city apartment after having hidden out as the Harris family for
eleven years on North San Juan Ridge.

Within three days of this article nearly every major newspaper and electronic news media organization in the world had shown the picture and run the story about the discovery of the long-sought family. Some of the articles were stand alone pieces while others were written as continuing coverage of the *PNAS* article and Clyde's Finlayson's talk at the ASHG convention. Several newspapers, such as the *New York Daily News*, presented the information sensationally with such headlines as:

NEANDERTHAL BOY FOUND, MAY HAVE FATHERED BABY
and
ANCIENT HOMINID BOY RAPES MODERN GIRL?

The *New York Times* and the *Washington Post* ran in-depth articles giving a complete historical account of the Shenko story, including all of the key persons involved. Radio talk shows were again dominated by discussions of the Shenkos.

Chief of Police Lancaster's "zoo" prediction for Nevada City was an under estimate. Within days of the *Union* article, Nevada City crawled with media trucks and news personnel of every stripe. Curiosity seekers from far and wide converged on the little town, creating traffic jams on all downtown streets. On weekends, bumper-to-bumper vehicles backed up traffic on Highway 49, the main artery to the city. With increasing numbers of police borrowed from other California jurisdictions, Chief Lancaster slowly gained control of the problems, even though traffic checkpoints were required at certain times on Highways 49 and 174 to divert unnecessary vehicles from entering the beleaguered city.

Early on, the Chief stationed guards around the apartment building that housed Gregory and his parents. However, the day after the *Union* article appeared, the landlady refunded Mark's rent money and requested they leave by the end of the day.

"The other tenants can't stand the commotion. Can you blame them?" she said in an explanation that appeared on national TV news.

This misfortune was remedied by a long-term city resident who immediately offered Mark and Corinne a month's free rent in a rental house away from the downtown area. The Chief liked this arrangement because the two-story home had a half-acre lot that could be secured more easily. Unsolicited offers of help, food, cash, and moral support came to the family from unknown people in the city and around the country. This outpouring seemed to mesh with a national poll conducted by *Time* magazine one week later. The question asked of a statisti-cally representative sample was: "How do you view Gregory Shenko? Favorably, Unfavorably, or Don't Know?" Nearly 50 percent said *Favorably*, 25 percent said *Unfavorably*, and the remainder said that they did not know.

Even with this support, Mark, Corinne, and Gregory were overwhelmed by the sudden turn of events. They found they could not leave the house with-out being surrounded by media people taking pictures, thrusting microphones in their faces, and flinging questions. Gregory took the brunt of it. *Gregory, did you have sex with her? Gregory, did you use your sex power to seduce her? C'mon Gregory, give us a sample of your powers now.* After two unsuccessful attempts by the threesome to go to the market, the Chief assigned a squad car and two stout officers to transport them when they needed to leave home. This protection did not eliminate the verbal abuse and Gregory soon holed up in his room and refused to go anywhere or to even look out of the windows.

On the second day after moving into the house, as Mark ran a vacuum cleaner through the downstairs, he began to get angry. He couldn't pinpoint anyone in particular for his wrath, it was just the whole situation. He, Corinne, and Gregory had suffered insults. They had been uprooted twice. He and Corinne were unable to go work and Gregory could not attend school. The rental house was filthy. Despite all of the things that their friends had dropped off, they didn't have enough bedding, food, dishes, and utensils. Most of the stuff they had was still in boxes. Mark clenched his teeth. He felt like smashing somebody in the face. Instead, he slammed the vacuum against the wall. Then he heard Corinne's voice.

"Mark? Mark! Shut that dang thing off."

He turned off the machine and looked around. Corinne, hands on her hips, stared at him.

"Look, Mark, you're not the only one who's got problems around here. Listen once in a while."

"What is it?" he asked sullenly.

"The guard's on the walkie talkie."

"I feel like throwing that thing through the goddamned window."

"Great. That would solve a lot, wouldn't it? Here." She tossed him the transceiver.

He put it up to his face.

"Jack, this is Mark. What's up now?"

"Mark, there is a woman out here who claims she knows you. Shall I let her come to the door?"

"What's her name?"

"Rachel Applebaum."

"Rachel?"

Mark looked at Corinne, dumbfounded.

Corinne rolled her eyes. "Just what we need—a visitor. She's probably dolled up and I look a fright."

"Susan, I had no idea . . ."

"Mark, we can't turn her away. Just tell him to let her in. Maybe she's good at lining shelves."

Rachel came through the door with packages in her arms. She wore, to Corinne's surprise, a denim shirt, Levi's, and tennies and no trace of lipstick or make-up. After greetings and hugs, Rachel smiled painfully.

"I've been so worried. Are you okay? Is Bret?"

"We're hassled, but okay. Bret is hard to talk to right now," Corinne said. "How on earth did you get here so fast?"

"You're the first out-of-towner to find us," Mark said.

"When I saw the news on TV, I threw some stuff in a suitcase and caught the next plane. In San Francisco I stayed overnight, then rented a car and got a roadmap. Here in Nevada City I kept asking people until someone pointed me to this house."

A door opened upstairs. They looked up from the entryway to see Gregory slowly coming down the stairs.

"Hi, Bret," Rachel said, smiling big.

"Hi, Rachel," he said. "What are you doing here?"

"Well, since it's almost your birthday, I found this neat thing at the Smithsonian gift shop that I thought you'd like. So I decided to deliver it in person."

He laughed for the first time in a long while. "That's not why you came," he said.

Rachel picked up a small gift-wrapped box from the floor and handed it to Gregory. "Open it and tell me if it wasn't worth my bringing it out here," she said.

Gregory smiled and quickly pulled off the wrapping paper.

"Count Down," he said, reading the name on the box that contained a CD and a large colorful cardboard diagram of a space shuttle on a launch pad. He read further.

"Yeah, this is cool," he said.

"It goes through one hundred pre-launch steps and explains each one," Rachel said. "It gives the real conversations of all the engineers as well as between Houston and the astronauts."

Gregory smiled. "Yeah, cool," he said. Then he looked at Mark. "But I don't have my computer."

"Well, we're going to get it," Mark said. "We have to go to the house for kitchen stuff and bedding and we need to see Bill because he doesn't know where we are. We'll pick up your computer."

Rachel handed packages to Corinne and Mark. "Your turn."

"Rachel, you shouldn't have," Corinne said.

They opened the presents to find bubble bath soap and a lavender-scented bath gel for Corinne and a small book on Wittgenstein for Mark.

"And Susan, while you're in the bath, you can't feel guilty because I'm going to finish lining your shelves," Rachel said.

"How did you know that is needed?" Corinne said.

"I can see your cupboards open from here, silly."

Corinne hugged her. "Thank you, Rachel."

"Thanks, Rachel," Mark said. "You couldn't have gotten me anything better."

While Mark finished vacuuming and Corinne took a bath, Gregory sat at the kitchen table and talked with Rachel while she lined the cupboards. When Gregory went up to his room to get one of his recently built models to show her, Mark came into the kitchen.

"Why didn't you tell me you were coming?" he asked softly.

"I didn't want you to discourage me. Besides, I can see that you and Susan need some help."

"Yes, but such *chutzpah!*"

She laughed. "Just keep your distance and things will be fine."

Refreshed from her bath and dressed in nicer clothes, Corinne came into the kitchen to find the shelves lined and the counters and table top sparkling. Rachel announced that she wanted to make dinner. She would get groceries at the nearby store. She suggested that Mark and Corinne make the trip to their house while she cooked and kept Gregory company. Gregory was all for it and, to Corinne's and Mark's amazement, he offered to set the table and help with the dishes.

The stirfry, rice, and salad dinner, followed by ice cream, put everyone in better spirits, especially Gregory who was allowed a half of a glass of wine. As they sipped coffee Corinne said she needed to ask something important of Rachel. This immediately stopped the conversation.

"Rachel," she said. "Mike, Bret, and I have talked and we would like you to stay with us instead of at the hotel. If you don't mind the mess, there is a bed in the third bedroom, and I have extra sheets and blankets."

"Please stay here," Gregory said. "I have to be with an adult if Dad and Mom go back to work."

"Well . . ." Rachel said, looking at Mark.

Mark held up his hand. "We do need your help and we can't bear the thought of your having to pay such an exorbitant price for that hotel suite."

"It was the only room left in Nevada County," Rachel said.

"I know, but I've got an idea. Ian, Jared, and Sylvia are arriving tomorrow, and if you're willing, it would be perfect for them," he said.

"Please say you'll stay," Gregory said.

"All right," she said. "Thank you."

HAZE AND SMOG floated over the valley when Ian pulled their rental sedan onto the I-5 freeway from the Sacramento airport. Searching the radio for any reports on Gregory, they soon found KFBK providing extensive coverage on the Shenko case. Jared, Sylvia, and Ian became attentive when a press conference was announced with the Nevada County District Attorney, Morgan Eberhard.

After a recap of the detention hearing and subsequent events by an announcer, the station quickly shifted to live coverage of Eberhard.

"Good afternoon. I am Morgan Eberhard, District Attorney of Nevada County. Because of intense concern expressed by the public and an incredible number of queries from the media about the Gregory Shenko case—from all over the world I might add—I have decided to make myself available today for some questions. I won't make an initial statement other than to say that I will be personally handling the prosecution. I would appreciate you raising your hands to be recognized. No shouting questions, please."

"Mr. Eberhard, will this case be moved to adult court given that Gregory is said to be much more mature than his chronological age and given the nature of his sexual predatory power?"

There was a collective *ahhhh* from the audience.

"Well, I didn't expect the questions to be easy, but you might have started out with a gentler one," Eberhard said to laughter. "But let me see . . . Judge Ronke and Defense Attorney Les Kruger and I have discussed whether the case should stay in Juvenile Court and we have agreed to keep it there for now. If I had been involved prior to the detention hearing, we might well have petitioned to try Gregory as an adult. But I think justice can be done in Juvenile Court."

There was a distant voice.

"Some of you may not have heard that. The question is whether I am comfortable that Gregory is not confined to a security facility. Again, if I had been involved earlier, I would have pressed for the boy's detention in juvenile hall. But, Chief Rod Lancaster is comfortable with the electronic and physical surveillance now in place, so I'm not proposing a change at this point. We'll have to see how the arraignment goes—let me correct that term—how the admit/deny hearing goes. Bail and Juvenile Hall could be revisited."

Jared shook his head. "I don't like the way this guy sounds."

"Sounds like a hard-ass," Ian said.

Sylvia said, "That's all we need."

"Mr. Eberhard, if Gregory's so-called Y power is as coercive as all of the knowledgeable sources indicate, would you consider the use of the Y power during sex as forcible rape?"

"Boy, you folks are tough," Eberhard said. "To answer what I think you're asking, I would have to say that if the Y power was used in a sexual encounter, and the woman did not want to have sex beforehand, then it's an awful lot like the situation of date rape. And date rape in my book is forcible rape. Next?"

"A follow-up, sir," the same questioner said. "Does that mean doing time?"

Eberhard's voiced firmed in a lower register. "If this young man is guilty, absolutely. Forcible rape requires doing time."

"What about the report that she came to see him a second time?" another person asked.

"I can't comment on the particulars. But let me say in general that it would be important in each encounter—the first, second, whatever—to know the woman's state of mind. In other words, what was her intent? It is conceivable to have forced rape on one occasion and not on another. So you could have two encounters with only one legal count of rape."

Jared smacked his hands together. "This guy is bad news. I hope to hell they have a good attorney."

"Mr. Eberhard, have you had any discussions with defense counsel? Are you open to plea bargaining with Gregory's attorney?"

"We are always open to discussion. We've met once so far. But I hafta tell you that I will keep uppermost in my mind what is best for this community and its safety."

"What about the notion that Gregory is a different species and shouldn't be subject to our laws?"

Eberhard laughed. "I've heard such comments. I didn't think they were serious. We're in Nevada County, in the state of California, in the United States of America. The time is now, not the Pleistocene. I am duty-bound by my oath to uphold the laws of these jurisdictions for everyone including Gregory Shenko, also known as Bret Harris. And that is exactly what I intend to do."

"Mr. Eberhard," a woman's voice said, "all of your remarks so far suggest a rather hard-line approach. Given that this case involves two juveniles and that the philosophy of juvenile court is not meting out punishment, but finding the best way to help the families achieve a good solution in the best interests of the children, shouldn't you be less adversarial and have a different attitude?"

"About time someone called him on his law 'n order approach," Sylvia said.

Eberhard cleared his throat. "I don't think you need to tell me about the nature of juvenile court, madam. There are always the competing interests of society and the individual, whether in adult court or juvenile court. I will be mindful of the philosophy of both of these, but my job as prosecutor is to weigh in on society's side. The defense attorney is concerned with the individual defendant. Through this adversarial process will come the best solution. That's our system of justice."

"Do you think this is going to trial?"

"I don't know. It certainly will if the defendant pleads not guilty, or rather denies the offense, to use the juvenile court terminology. If he admits wrongdoing, then there still could be a sizable trial-like disposition hearing to ascertain all of the facts of the situation which, as you know, are quite novel and complicated. But we'll take it one step at a time. We'll know more about the direction this will take in about a week and a half."

"Mr. Eberhard, will there be prenatal DNA studies of the fetus for determining paternity?"

"Uh, I can't comment on that. I think I'll end this now. Thank you."

For the first time, Jared, Sylvia, and Ian realized the seriousness of Gregory's problems. The issue consumed their conversation until they reached the Holbrooke Hotel in Grass Valley, where Mark had said a suite was reserved for them. The Holbrooke, built in 1851, was a Victorian landmark famous for hosting such luminaries as Ulysses S. Grant, Grover Cleveland, Gentleman Jim Corbett, Mark Twain, Bret Harte, and Lotta Crabtree. The old wooden building had the look of history. Immediately upon checking in, Ian called Mark to report their availability for a meeting. Within an hour Mark and Corinne arrived in a Nevada City police car. After heartfelt greetings were exchanged, Mark and Corinne eased into antique chairs in the spacious suite. Two police officers stood guard outside the door. Mark brought everyone up to date on all that had happened since Corinne had been confronted by juvenile court officer Jeff Weismann at the bookstore. Mark found out that they had heard the press conference with District Attorney Eberhard.

"What a bastard," Sylvia said. "Excuse my language."

"It's just our luck that he wants to make political hay," Corinne said.

"How is Bret taking all this?" Jared asked, looking at Corinne.

"He's pretty down. Doesn't like missing school. He's angry about the kinds of things the media yell at him. So he won't leave the house. But his mood improved when Rachel, Mike's friend, came to stay with us. He likes her. But he misses Bill terribly. Bill can't visit because he doesn't want to leave his place with so many people wandering onto his property."

"What does Bret think about the rape charge?" Ian asked.

Mark and Corinne looked at each other.

She continued. "He acts like it's not real. Says the whole thing is stupid. Doesn't want to talk about it."

"Hmm," Ian nodded.

"But doesn't he realize he might be sentenced to a facility. Doesn't he worry about that?" Sylvia asked.

"We know he's been on the internet and listening to the radio," Corinne said. "This afternoon when I went by his room, he was listening to the DA's press conference. So I know he realizes what's going on. What does he think? I don't know. We haven't pressed him because we don't want to worry him too much. We're mostly waiting for the lawyer to tell us what to do."

Jared frowned. "Bret's probably not worried because he knows he did nothing wrong. And I agree he shouldn't be stressed. The last thing needed is to trigger a seizure."

"I think that Bret didn't have relations with Nina," Mark said. "But Corinne's not so sure."

"Who is your attorney?" Ian asked.

"A juvenile court lawyer named Les Kruger," Mark replied.

"What's he think?" Ian asked.

"He's worried. Says the DA's office has taken over prosecution of the case and wants to make it into an adult trial even though it's in juvenile court. Says Eberhard doesn't really want to go with a plea bargain, or if he does, it would be for almost no reduction of a usual sentence. Says the judge is quiet about what he wants and seems dazed by all the notoriety."

"Maybe this is out of Kruger's league," Ian suggested.

"Maybe. Some big-time defense lawyers have contacted us. I like Kruger. I just don't know what's best. We're supposed to meet tomorrow after Kruger has talked more to Eberhard."

"What have the outside attorneys advised?" Jared asked.

"One said Bret should plead *Not Guilty* even if he did it. Suggested the defense is that Bret has genes that he cannot control."

"That's interesting," Sylvia said. "But it would mean everything about the lesion, the traits, and his ancient heritage would get aired in court, wouldn't it? Evolution and science on trial?"

"Yeah. One San Francisco columnist said it could be a modern Scopes trial," Mark said.

"Is there going to be a DNA test?" Ian asked.

"Yes, Nina and her father have agreed to an amniocentesis, and they're planning to do it soon, but it won't be completed before the Admit/Deny hearing," Mark replied.

"What do you think should be done, Susan?" Sylvia asked.

Moisture was noticeable in Corinne's eyes. "Whatever happens, he can't go to a prison. That would kill him. If something could be worked out where he only gets probation, I think that would be okay."

Sylvia nodded.

"One area where we need your advice," Mark said, "is whether we should hold a press conference. The media has been clamoring for Bret, Susan, and I to talk to them. Our lawyer thinks that public opinion may be very important to any verdict or sentencing, and it might help if we met with the media. But if we did, what should we talk about and not talk about?"

"I think it would be a good idea," Sylvia said. "You would show people how normal and nice all of you are."

Ian frowned. "I think you would have to be careful. You shouldn't talk about Bret's traits or what happened with Nina—which is just what the media will want you to talk about. Bret would need to be carefully coached."

As this conversation continued in the dark-paneled suite on the top floor of the Holbrooke, a faded burgundy Camry pulled into Colliver's driveway off Tyler Foote Road. Alice Masterson hit the brakes as she came upon a barricade of sawhorses with flashing yellow lights. A uniformed policeman came out from under an oak and held up his hand, then walked around to the driver's side. He had a clipboard under his arm.

"Where is it you want to go, m'am?"

"I want to go down to Bill Colliver's place."

"Is he expecting you?"

"No, but I'm a friend."

"What is your name?" he asked, looking at a clipboard.

"Alice . . . Grass. It might be under Grass or Masterson."

The man shook his head. "Neither one is on the list. Are you a media person?"

"No. I'm a recent friend who saw him not long ago."

"Well, I'm not to let anyone in unless they're on this list."

"Look, I know Bill. There are two cabins down there near a creek. His wolf dog is named Arnie. Bill has a chipped front tooth. He would be upset if you turned me away."

The officer frowned. "You certainly know the place. I'll let you go in but at your own risk. I'm warning you—if he doesn't know you, you could get shot at. He's in a grumpy mood."

At the bottom of the switchbacks, Alice pulled her car to the side and got out. She saw Colliver's vehicle under the enclosure. There was quiet except for the gurgling of the creek. She walked up to Colliver's cabin and shouted, then knocked on the door. She heard no stirring inside and decided to wait. On tiptoes she pushed herself backward into a hammock hanging in front of the cabin. Stretching out on her back, she looked up at the pine branches and cloud-streaked sky. She closed her eyes and wondered if she could get used to living without the noises of civilization. Just as she was about to doze, she heard footsteps on dry leaves.

"What the Sam Hill do you think you're doing?" The voice was a shout. "If you're another goddamn reporter, I'm going to put a pellet in your ass!"

She tried to step out of the hammock, but fell on the ground. When she got up she saw Colliver a few yards in front of her, pointing a pellet rifle at her feet. Arnie was next to him, fur up and growling.

"Bill, it's me, Alice Masterson. I met you a few months ago . . . you know, with Bret."

Colliver lowered the gun. "Shush, Arnie. Oh yeah—the brain scientist who had been the reporter. Well, hello. Sorry to shout at ya."

"It's okay. The guard up there warned me that you'd been bothered by intruders."

"With all this damn business about Bret, reporters just poke around, take pictures, act like there is no such thing as private property."

"I guess I'm not surprised." She smiled and dusted off her Levi's.

Arnie came up slowly and sniffed. She held out her hand and he moved closer, allowing himself to be petted.

Colliver frowned. "You heard about Bret's problems, I suppose."

"Yeah, that's why I came. To see if I could be of help."

Colliver nodded slowly. "Well, it's gotten fucked up in the court. The DA's a real dick. TV and radio. It's a damn circus. Poor kid."

Alice grimaced and nodded. "Yeah."

Colliver sat down on a log and gestured for Alice to do the same. "Nevada City is all clogged up. Is that why you came over here?" he asked.

"I talked on the phone with Jared, Ian, and Sylvia on my way up. They said there were traffic jams and no accommodations. Said there was no sense for me to go into Grass Valley or Nevada City."

Colliver looked at her, his hazel eyes now softer. "You looking for a place to stay?"

"I have a sleeping bag and could lay it out here on the pine needles if you didn't mind."

Colliver nodded. "Except it might rain. Better for you to stay in the coyote cabin. It'll be musty, but we can air it out. How long are you going to stay?"

"I don't know. I guess until Bret gets through all this. Is that all right?"

Colliver nodded and smiled. "Sure. Maybe we can talk science."

She laughed. "I've heard about your philosophical discussions."

He chuckled. "They're not so bad. Say, I have to get over to see Bret. How about if I got you fixed up and you and Arnie guarded the place tomorrow while I went into town?"

"That would be fine. Could you give Mike a note from me?"

"Sure," Colliver nodded. "I've got stuff you could read. If it doesn't rain, you could lay out here in the hammock with books and the pellet gun."

She laughed.

ON WEDNESDAY the street where the Harrises lived was blocked off for the media conference. A tight police cordon allowed in only media representatives—about two hundred of them. Several domestic and foreign networks set up for live television and radio. Just before ten in the morning, Mark, Corinne, and Gregory stepped up on a platform and formed a small semi-circle around the micro-phones. Mark had on a dark blazer and a maroon-and-navy striped tie. Corinne wore a smartly-styled, knee-length blue dress. She had visited a hairdresser the day before. Gregory, in the middle, had on a forest-green, long sleeve shirt, and charcoal dress pants and held a model airplane in one hand. Seated in the front row of the audience were Jared, Sylvia, Ian, Rachel, Colliver, and Attorney Les Kruger.

Shortly after ten Mark greeted the crowd which hushed quickly. He introduced the three of them by their Harris names, cracking that their other names were already well known. He explained that each of them would say a few words and then answer some questions. He made clear the ground rule of no questions about the charges, the trial, or Gregory's traits. At this a groan went up from the crowd.

Mark held up his hands to quiet the crowd. "Many people have asked why Susan and I gave up our other lives to come up here and hide. I would like to say that our only reason was to provide a regular life for Bret. We felt the only way he could grow up normally was to be away from public scrutiny. So that is why we took on different names and told nobody who we really were. Bret did not know he was Gregory Shenko until fairly recently. Although we lived in a remote place, we didn't really hide. Bret went to school, I went into the health adminis-tration field, and Susan took jobs at the library and at Corrigan's Bookstore here in Nevada City. We've had friends and a nice social life. We kept in touch with our families and some colleagues from before. If we have broken any laws or hurt anyone by changing our identity, we are sorry. We will try to make things right once we get the court situation with Bret straightened out. With that, I'll be pleased to answer a few questions."

An elderly woman with a pencil in her hair asked the first question. "Dr. Sandler, how could you give up such a wonderful career in science? That was a huge sacrifice and a great waste, wasn't it?"

Mark smiled. "On one level, it was a sacrifice. But my life up here has been rewarding in many ways. I don't subscribe to the concept of *highest and best use* in real estate and I don't think the concept applies in life either."

"Then would you do it all over again?" a man asked.

"Would I do it all over again?" Mark repeated, more to himself than the audience. "I don't know. I guess there are some things I'd do differently. I'll think about it and let you know." There was mild laughter. Mark answered a few more questions and then asked Corinne to talk.

She stepped forward, remembering to keep her feet together, and to point her toes at a forty-five degree angle. "Hi, I'm Susan, Bret's mother. I think one misunderstanding out there is that we raised Bret in secret. This is not correct. As a baby, we took him to other people's houses for get-togethers. He entered pre-school at age two and second grade at age four because he was surprisingly mature. He's been in public schools ever since. He's had good friends and done things most kids do. He's an excellent soccer player. This past year we took him to the Smithsonian which he loved. So I just wanted to correct the notion that Bret was a secluded child. I'll be happy to answer questions." She stepped back and smiled.

"Mrs. Harris, are you saying that Bret is just a normal boy?" a young woman asked.

She again moved forward to the microphones. "He clearly is different in certain things because of the lesion, and he's matured faster than most kids. But for the most part, he's just like any boy. Once it came out who he was, all of his friends and teachers were shocked. They had no idea."

Another woman reporter got the nod. "Susan, I understand you lived for several years under primitive conditions—no electricity, no hot water, only a woodstove for cooking, hand-washing clothes . . . how on earth did you do it?"

The audience laughed. Corinne put one hand on her chin. "Well, it was hard at first. And don't tell Bill Colliver, but I took clothes to a laundromat sometimes."

Gregory started laughing, looking at Colliver.

"But you know," she continued, "it was romantic. It was like we had gone back in time and had to make do. Then, after a while, I got used to it. I even got used to not taking baths very often, especially in the winter. When Bill smelled, Mike smelled, Bret smelled, and I smelled. So it was like nobody smelled. It didn't matter."

The audience laughed along with Gregory and Mark.

"So, in lots of things like that, Bill was right. In modern society we worry too much about the wrong things."

A man with a camera around his neck was next.

"There has been all this talk about Bill Colliver being a recluse, hating technology, living a life of the Middle Ages. What makes him tick? What is he like to be around?"

"First, he's not a recluse," she said. "He has many friends. He was at times frustrating, you know, putting his philosophy out there and forcing you to deal with it. But his bark is worse than his bite. Most of the time he was caring, generous, and fun. We could not have done it without him. He found out who Bret was and accepted him completely. He and Bret got along like peas in a pod." She looked at Colliver. "Thank you, Bill."

After a few more questions, Mark cut it off and said Bret would say a few words. The crowd quieted completely.

Gregory stepped forward and pulled on one ear. "Well, as you know, I'm Bret—the guy that all this ruckus is about. My favorite things are hiking and hunting, soccer and baseball, and model building. I have thirty-seven models I built and this here's one of them. I like school and do pretty well, I guess . . . get all A's. I don't know what else I can tell you. So do you have any questions?"

Surprisingly, there was no sound for a few seconds, then hands shot up everywhere.

Mark selected a questioner from the back.

"Bret, you mentioned hunting. What animals do you hunt? Do you use a rifle? Where do you go and who with? How successful have you been?"

Gregory smiled. "I hunt only on Bill's property, sometimes with him, mostly by myself. I try to find any kind of animal—bear, cougar, deer, coyote, raccoon, skunk, porcupine, marmot, squirrel, birds, whatever. I don't shoot them, though. I just watch them and try to get close. I pretend that I can stun them mentally."

"With your power?"

"Well . . ." Gregory looked at Mark.

"Let's go on to another question," Mark said.

A young woman in a red dress was selected.

"Bret, do you feel that you're different from everyone? That the Shenkos are a different species?"

Bret smiled. "Yeah, I'm a Neanderthal who's come from the past to get even. No, I'm just kidding."

The audience laughed and hooted. Mark winced and Corinne shook her head.

"I think my Mom's right. Mostly I'm like everyone else. And the differences I have are just kind of special for me and other Shenkos. I don't think about it a lot. It's just part of me . . . who I am."

Mark held up his hand. "I think we'll stop now."

More would-be questioners raised their hands and shouted.

"All right. We'll take one last one," Mark said, pointing to a man close to the front.

"Bret, what does the word *rape* mean to you?"

"Well . . ." Bret started.

"Hold it," Mark shouted angrily. "That's off limits. I would suggest to you, sir, that you read some Wittgenstein. Wittgenstein made clear that what a word means is not some object everyone agrees on but rather a psychological feeling. A word means something different to each person because it produces different feelings. Forms of life and ways of living were critical in communication for Wittgenstein. So don't think rape can be just defined. Wittgenstein said, 'If God had looked into our minds, he would not have been able to see there whom,' or in this case what, 'we were speaking of'.'" Mark glared at the questioner in the dire calm following his outburst.

"Well, Dr. Sandler, I meant no offense . . ." the man said.

Gregory stepped up to the microphones. "Everybody, don't take my dad too seriously, even though Wittgenstein was quite a dude, and you might want to read him. One last thing I wanted to say is—this airplane is an extra, so would anyone like to have it?"

The audience laughed and a large number of hands shot up.

Gregory grinned. "There's too many. Well, I'll just send it out there."

He sailed the small plane out over the group. People bunched and jumped, trying to snag the aerodynamic model that passed over everyone and landed in the street. The video and picture of Gregory, arm throwing the plane in the air, was the one that appeared on most TV news shows and in newspapers and magazines around the world after the media conference. Headlines varied, but perhaps that of the *Seattle Times* was typical:

DAD LOSES IT, GREGORY AND MOM DELIGHT

After the event Mark, Corinne, Rachel, Jared, Sylvia, Ian, and Colliver met together in the rental house. A giant pizza was delivered along with a birthday cake labeled "Happy Birthday Bret" and they rehashed the media conference before the party started.

"Listen, Mark," Sylvia said, "the media will probably poke fun at you, but the event overall was a great success. You guys came across as very human—a nice American family. And Bret had star quality."

Ian said, "I agree. But I predict that the Wittgenstein message will begin to seep out once they begin to understand it."

Ian's comment turned out to be sagacious. Corinne discovered later in the day that at Corrigan's, all Wittgenstein books and every philosophy book mentioning the philosopher had been sold. This trend was noticed at bookstores and libraries across the country.

TWO DAYS PRIOR to the hearing Mark and Corinne traveled via patrol car to the office of their attorney, Les Kruger. The purpose was to learn of his negotiations with District Attorney Morgan Eberhard. They also were eager to hear about Kruger's private meeting with Gregory earlier in the day. Kruger greeted them warmly and guided them to a small conference room. They pulled up club chairs around a walnut table covered with smokey glass.

"So has Eberhard budged any?" Mark asked.

"He's budged a lot. I think your meeting with the media really paid off. He must be getting immense pressure to go easy on Bret. But he refuses to do probation only. He says if Bret will admit to one count of rape, he will accept Bret serving one year in a minimum security residential facility. That's much less than the three years in a maximum security facility he originally proposed. As a part of the deal, he agrees that if the DNA test shows Bret is not the father, the sentence can be negotiated down to probation only. I consider this a good offer."

Kruger looked at Corinne. "So what to you think, Susan?"

"Can we wait for the DNA results before deciding?" she asked.

Kruger laughed. "That's the stickler. Eberhard wants to force Bret into admitting or denying before the DNA results come back. If he allows Bret to wait and the results come back negative, then Bret could deny having had sex and be off without even probation. Eberhard believes Nina's version of the story. He says she's a nice girl, does not run around, does not have any boyfriends."

Mark tossed his head. "How about this? What if Bret denied at the hearing in order to wait for the DNA results? Could we then change his plea if the DNA were positive?"

"Yes, but then Eberhard would want Bret to do a lot more time. Bret would no longer appear as a nice young kid. He would have lied. Public support would swing."

"What if Bret denies and we go for a trial?" Mark asked.

Kruger scratched his forehead. "If you do that, you will need a top-notch trial lawyer. I'm not that person. The case would probably get moved to adult court and you'd have a different judge. The trial would be end up being a national media event lasting months. Good lawyers and lengthy trials cost a lot of money."

"Do you think that is what Eberhard wants?" Mark asked.

"Big, notorious trials are every prosecutor's dream."

"Money may not be a problem," Mark said. "One prominent lawyer told me he would take the case pro bono."

Kruger shook his head. "Well, that's really something."

Corinne straightened up. "How did it go with Bret this morning?"

Kruger nodded. "I explained all this to him, and he seemed to understand it. I said he needed to level with me as much as possible if he wants me to help him. But you know, he just clams up. Doesn't want to talk about what happened with Nina. I kept asking why. When I suggested he was afraid of something, he said, 'It's not 'cause I'm afraid, it's because it's such bullshit.' I asked if he meant by that what Nina said. He said, 'No, I mean the DA, the court, the laws, this whole bullshit society.'"

"He said that?" Corinne asked.

"Yes."

Mark said, "Well, when you told him of your conversation with Eberhard, did he say how he wanted to plead?"

"No."

ARNIE LOPED UP to meet Mark's car coming down the last switchback into Colliver's compound. The wolf dog smiled but did not prance as he accompanied the vehicle to the side of the lean-to. Arnie is getting old, Mark thought. Or, maybe he just finds nothing to be excited about these days. Probably misses Bret. Mark got out and rubbed Arnie lovingly, then walked around to Colliver who was hanging clothes on a line near the cabin.

"How's it going, Bill?"

"I need to get these wet things out to dry while the sun's high. Figured I'd better have something clean for picking up Rose Shenko tonight and for the hearing tomorrow."

"Probably a good idea. We appreciate your putting up Rose and bringing her in tomorrow."

"No problem. She's going to sleep in the coyote cabin with Alice."

"That's nice."

"And speaking of Alice, you'd better get down to see her. She's been nervous that you haven't come. I gather she has something important to tell you."

"I've been meaning to see her. Things have been crazy."

"I know."

As he headed for the smaller cabin Mark felt nostalgic. The smells of woodsmoke and the sounds of squirrel chatterings all triggered heavily laden memories. He knocked on the door and it was quickly opened. Alice wore Levi's and a bulky sweater and her hair was tied back. She extended her hand and smiled, showing the white, even teeth he remembered.

"Hi, Mark. It's good to see you."

"Hello, Alice. Been a long time since the SSU days."

She laughed. "That's for sure. Come on in."

A fire crackled in the woodstove. They sat in chairs a few feet from the flames and sipped apple spice tea. They reminisced briefly and then discussed Gregory's legal status and the pending hearing. Alice reported that she had been listening to the news about Gregory every evening up at Mark's house and then relaying the information to Colliver.

"Are you coming to the hearing tomorrow?" he asked.

"No, I'm going to stay here to keep an eye on things so Bill can attend. Bill will feel better if I'm watching his place."

"It will be a bedlam outside, but hopefully not too bad in the courtroom."

She nodded, her gold-streaked eyes momentarily unfocused.

"Your note said you had something important to tell me," Mark said. "I wasn't sure if Susan was supposed to come. She wanted to stay with Bret anyway."

"I was hoping she wouldn't come. Telling this kind of thing to a mother— especially Corinne—would be hard. But I felt it was something you needed to know before the trial if you weren't aware of it."

Mark frowned. "So, what is it?"

Alice picked up Soccer Mom's two letters and handed them to him. "Read the one in the stamped envelope first."

As Mark read slowly through both letters his body sagged. At the end of the second one, he dropped the letters to the floor and hung his head.

"I'm sorry, Mark," she said softly. "I see that this is something you didn't know."

"Mmmh," he said, slowly bringing his head up to look at the fire. "It's funny," he said, "Susan would have been readier for this than I."

Alice nodded. "Can I get you more tea?"

"Thanks, but I think I'd better get back."

Mark slowly pulled his jacket on. "So now it all makes sense," he said softly.

Chapter Twenty-Seven

HEAVY DEW STUCK to leaves and lampposts on the morning of the hearing. A low cloud clung stubbornly to the trees, resisting the sun. A swath of Church Street was given over to barricades, police cars, trucks with dish antennas, and minions of the law enforcement and reportorial professions. Most noticeable were eight policemen on horses that stood calmly despite the noisy generators and shouting workmen.

None of the equipment was going inside the building as Judge Ronke had ruled out video and audio recording in the courtroom. He had granted privileged access to thirty domestic and foreign news organizations whose reporters could only sit in the back and take notes and draw sketches. Cell phone cameras were prohibited. The rest of the media remained out front, awaiting the arrival of Nina and Gregory and their families and attorneys. A small podium with microphones sat next to the sidewalk, evincing optimism that either or both sides would make statements after the hearing.

During the past week there had been profuse media speculation about whether Gregory would admit or deny sexual relations and the use of his Y power on Nina. Most commentators thought that plea bargaining would occur, with Gregory admitting fault in exchange for probation. At the same time, the media salivated for a trial—a meaty contest of Neanderthal boy meets modern maiden, mutant throwback versus the civilized state.

The arrival of Colliver and Rose on foot was initially overlooked by the milling crowd. Then someone recognized them and called out their names. Media people quickly closed around them. Colliver refused to answer questions and strode forward, pushing an escorting police officer ahead and pulling Rose behind him.

She waved and tried to converse. "I came to be with my grandson . . . Excuse me . . . No, I don't know what they decided to plead . . . Now don't push . . . I cain't hear if you all talk at once . . . Well, I just met Mr. Colliver yesterday and he is a nice fella . . . Excuse me . . . Sure I miss Zenya—that's stupid . . . Well, if that girl's baby ends up my great grandbaby, of course I'd love it . . . Please let me get by . . ." Once into the courtroom they were seated in a section up front reserved for relatives and friends of Bret Harris.

Jared, Sylvia, and Ian arrived in a taxi. The vehicle was quickly surrounded by police who kept the swarm at arm's length. In wedge formation the small group, led by three officers, forged into the building. None of the Angelenos tried to understand, much less respond, to the mishmash of questions shouted at them.

As the doors closed behind those three, three squad cars with flashing red-and-yellow lights pulled up. In the backseat of the middle car were Mark, Corinne, and Rachel. Gregory sat up front on the passenger's side. Officers from the front and back cars joined others in forming a tight circle around the center car and helped the occupants get out. The shouting began.

"Bret, how are you going to plead? Did you use your Y power on Nina? Throw us another airplane." Gregory smiled but kept his eyes forward and followed the officer in front of him. "Are you going to marry Nina? Susan, can you tell us what the Y feels like? Is there a deal with the DA? Go for the trial, kid."

Attorney Les Kruger met his clients in the lobby and escorted them into the courtroom where no open public seats remained. A collective murmur surged through the crowd as all eyes followed Gregory, Mark, and Corinne to a table in front. Gregory sat down between Kruger and Corinne while Rachel took a seat next to Rose in the gallery.

"Did you decide how you're going to plead?" Kruger whispered to Gregory.

"Almost," Gregory whispered back.

Kruger gritted his teeth. "You have about five minutes to make up your mind and I'd sure like to know."

Gregory nodded, then whispered to Kruger. "I plead 'not guilty' because I could not be the father of Nina's baby. Even though we had sex, I withheld my sperm. I've never told anyone this, but I can prevent myself from ejaculating. It's just another Shenko thing, I guess."

Kruger's mouth dropped. "You're not serious!" he whispered loudly.

"I am serious. And the paternity test will show it," Gregory whispered back.

"Do your parents know this?"

"No."

The courtroom doors opened again and the Schuhs came down the center aisle. Nina, showing moderately in a full dress, walked between her parents. District

Attorney Eberhard led them to the plaintiff's table as low voices emanated from the audience.

When the Schuhs stepped through the gate of the low railing separating the tables from general seating, Gregory stood. He and Nina exchanged a long look. Gentle, upward curves came to the corners of her mouth. Gregory, hand at his side, gave a subtle wave with his fingers, and she returned it in kind. Mr. Schuh stepped between them and guided her to a chair on the other side of Eberhard.

"Bret Harris, please sit down," the bailiff said loudly.

Gregory sat down and looked slowly around. He saw Chief Lancaster and Officer Whitedeer sitting where they had before. The chief held a small transceiver on his knee. Two police officers with pistols and nightsticks on their belts stood against the wall near the chief. There were two officers with similar gear standing just inside the court's main door. The court reporter squeezed her fingers nervously at a small table near the judge's bench. Gregory faced ahead again, a slight smile on his face.

The side door opened and Judge Ronke entered.

"All rise," the bailiff said."Family Law Court in the Civil Division of the Nevada County Superior Court, Judge Burke Ronke presiding, is now in session."

Everyone in the packed room stood up and watched the judge move pachyderm-like to the high-backed swivel chair behind the bench. Once settled, he looked around the room, dwelling on Gregory for a few seconds.

"Welcome, please be seated everyone." After the audience had quieted, he said, "Let me cover some ground rules. This is a court of law. There is to be no video or audio recording while we are in session. No use of cell phones and no ringing. Turn them off. No talking. I expect complete decorum and dignity during this proceeding. Is that understood?" He looked around imperiously. The court room quieted noticeably.

"All right. This is an 'Admit/Deny' hearing only. We are on the record."

The judge looked at Gregory. "Bret Harris, you have been brought here to juvenile court to face two charges brought against you by the Nevada County, California. The first charge is that you as a minor had sexual relations with another minor, Nina Schuh, and as a result are the father of her unborn child. The second charge is that your sexual encounter was forced upon Nina. Do you admit to or deny these charges?"

Les Kruger stood up. "Your Honor, I am Les Kruger, attorney representing Bret Harris.My client denies that he is the father of Ms. Schuh's unborn child. He denies that any relations between the two minors were forced."

Murmuring loudly filled the room.

Judge Ronke said in a raised voice. "Quiet, quiet." He brought down his gavel and the room quieted some.

Then he said, "Thank you, Mr. Kruger. But I want to ask something directly of your client. Bret, please stand. Son, please tell me . . . did you have relations with Nina?"

Bret stood. "Yes, Your Honor. But I am not the father of her child."

"But if you had relations, how do you know you are not the father?"

"Because no seed of mine went into her," Bret said quietly.

Kruger stood up. "We understand that a paternity test will be done, Your Honor, and Bret will fully cooperate. I am advising my client to answer no additional questions, pending the result of that test being available to the court. I presume no trial would occur without that major piece of evidence."

Attorney General Eberhard jumped up. "Your Honor, this is highly irregular. The defendant's answers do not make sense. Surely you will allow us some questions."

Judge Ronke said. "I must remind you Mr. Eberhard that this is a juvenile court where the interests of the children and their families are central. So I agree that there should be no more questioning until the paternity evidence is available."

Ronke looked at Gregory. "Son, you will continue to wear the ankle bracelet and be under surveillance until the paternity evidence is available and I issue further orders in this case. Understood?"

Gregory stood. "Yessir, Your Honor. Could I make one request?"

"What is it?" Ronke asked.

"That when they take me out, they allow me to say something to the media."

Ronke jerked his head in surprise. "Humpf . . . well . . . just a short comment, I guess would be okay. Bailiff and officers, please allow Bret to say a few words at the microphone outside. This concludes this court session . . . we are off the record."

The bailiff stood and shouted, asking the public to file out in an orderly fashion. The hubbub was loud. Reporters ran to get outside first. Amid the noise, Kruger leaned toward Mark and Corinne, talking at length. Gregory noticed Mark shaking his head.

Eberhard pushed back the crowd and got out before others from behind the balustrade. Once outside, he walked the narrow pathway through the crowd cleared by the police. He heard shouts from reporters.

"DA Eberhard, what do you think now?"

"Make a statement."

"Will you move it to adult court?"

Eberhard shook his head, waived in protest, said nothing, and headed out to a waiting county car and driver.

Word had passed from reporters in the courtroom that Gregory planned to talk briefly to the media. The huge crowd pressed around the platform, flowing into the street. The network video camera operators rechecked their camera settings and views. Someone rechecked the sound level of the speakers, saying *testing, testing*, at the microphone.

After all people had exited the courtroom, police escorted Gregory, Mark, and Corinne out the front door. A large cheer erupted from the crowd. Gregory waved an arm, then pointed to the platform with the microphone. A policeman escorted him to the platform.

"Can you hear me?" he asked, in front of the microphone. The crowd indicated they could and quieted down.

"I will not answer questions. But I have two things I wanted to say," Gregory said, as the sound from the speakers was heard far and wide. "The first is that my friend Nina is a very nice young lady. I want to thank her and her parents for going ahead with the paternity testing. They are good people. And uh . . . the second thing I wanted to say is that when all this court stuff is cleared up, I will be pleased to accept the challenge from Pepe Hernandez to a boxing match as soon as it can be arranged. And I say to Pepe: *Be careful what you wish for, amigo.* So that's it. Thanks to everyone. Bye."

There were several yelled questions, but Gregory quickly stepped away with the officer and joined Corinne and Mark. All three were threaded through the boisterous crowd by a number of officers who got them into a police car with a driver. He drove the family back to their temporary quarters.

While enroute, Mark asked Gregory, "Bret, who is that Pepe Hernandez you mentioned? What's with the boxing match?"

Gregory replied, "He's the World Lightweight Boxing Champion. He's been dissing me and my powers on some national sports websites. Said the X power is bunk and that he'd like to get me in the boxing ring."

"Bret, why on earth would you want to do that?" Corinne said, flabbergasted. "It's crazy. Especially announcing that right after a serious court proceeding? What's gotten into you?"

Mark shook his head. "I can't believe what you said, Bret."

Gregory smiled. "I could take Pepe easily. And it would be a way to make some money, right? Since I'm no longer hidden, I might as well get out there and do something interesting. Besides, that Pepe has a big mouth."

~

THE NEXT DAY many TV media and newspapers were critical of Gregory. Editorials often had headings similar to: "Has He No Contrition?" or "Where's the Remorse?" The arguments went that he was in serious penal jeopardy, yet acted as if it was nothing, and talked of a future boxing match. Other media were a little more sympathetic, pointing out that young Gregory was acting just like an adolescent.

Two days after the hearing, Pepe Hernandez, on a major news network, furthered the plot by saying he welcomed a fight with the "Neanderthal Kid" and would teach him what "throw back" really meant. Suddenly the match was what people and the media were talking about. Most people, especially males, wanted to see the *Boxing Match of the Ages*.

In the late morning, two days after the Admit/Deny hearing, Mark, Corinne, Ian, Colliver, Sylvia, Jared, and Alice sat on chairs around a table in the backyard of the house where Gregory was sequestered. Rachel stayed indoors to keep Gregory engaged in games so that he wouldn't listen to the outdoor conversation. Colliver had hired a couple of more guards to watch his property so that Alice could come.

"So, Ian, what do you make of Bret's saying he can withhold ejaculation?" Mark asked.

"It's amazing if true. We can call it the W trait, for 'withhold.' So now Gregory has W, X, Y, and Z. And Shenko women have the X2 and perhaps more. Absolutely incredible. As to the rationale for the W, I think it fits with Finlayson's ideas on Shenko gene seclusion. W further allowed Shenko males to have children only with whom they wanted, not just any female. With this capability, the lesion didn't spread easily beyond the Shenko species. In other words, it served the genetic sequestering function in males as the X2 did in females, which sympatric speciation required."

"That's why Bret is so dang confident that the child isn't his," Colliver said.

"Apparently," Jared said.

Sylvia put down her cup of coffee. "But I sure wish Bret had not been so confident and had not talked about Pepe Hernandez and accepting a boxing match. That sure didn't help him with the media and average folks."

"True," Corinne nodded. "Maybe we shouldn't have allowed him to talk to the media after the hearing. But we had no idea he would say that."

Alice raised a finger. "My journalism courses always held that stories can change rapidly, going from one feature to another. It appears that the boxing match is becoming dominant and the court case is past news. Quite a few people are lining up to root for Gregory over the cocky Pepe."

"Yeah, but if Ronke and Eberhard are ticked as a result, that may be bad," Mark said. "They might find some way to get Gregory even if the paternity test is negative for him."

"Maybe Gregory needs to apologize in public?" Sylvia asked.

"I think he should just stay mum at this point," Ian said. "Don't say anything more about anything until the judge says something to him."

They talked on for quite a while, but the consensus was for Gregory to say nothing further in any public way.

TWO WEEKS LATER a meeting was quickly called by Judge Ronke with Attorney General Morgan Eberhard and Gregory's attorney, Les Kruger. They gathered in the judge's office.

"Thanks for coming on short notice," Ronke said. "I learned the results of the paternity test from the Head of Genetics at county hospital. Nina's father had approved my being told as soon as results were available. So I want to share this and my decision on further adjudication of the Bret Harris case." He looked at both Eberhard and Kruger firmly.

"Well, okay. Don't keep us in suspense," Eberhard said.

"All right then," Ronke said. "The DNA results on the fetus show that Bret Harris is not the father of the child. It is not clear who is, but Nina, who was confronted on this by her father, admitted that there could have been another young man—a cousin who lives down in Auburn."

"Wow. So Bret was right," Kruger said.

"Yeah, but this is only the matter of paternity," Eberhard said. "There's still the issue of rape."

Ronke cleared his throat. "Well, the problem is whether the act was between consenting minors or not. Nina is much older than Bret and so is more legally liable. The investigation indicated she had gone to visit Bret on the Colliver property. There was no reporting of force by her at the time. So I don't see how force can be charged against him."

Eberhard leaned forward. "Well, there is all this evidence of that so-called Y power. You just can't have someone with that capability going around seducing women."

"The Y power, if it exists, is highly improbable hearsay," Kruger retorted. "I doubt if any jury would believe it."

Ronke held up his hand to cut the discussion. "What I've decided is that the case against Bret should be dropped. I don't see anything worthwhile coming out if it were pursued. And I would strongly advise, Morgan, that you *not* move it to adult court."

Eberhard glared at Ronke. "Well, that will be my decision and I'll let you know. And anyway, everyone is clamoring for the boxing match—not even caring about justice. Hell!"

"Just so you know," Ronke said, "I will make a public statement that the paternity test shows Bret is not the father and that the case in juvenile court is being closed."

Eberhard nodded.

"Thank you," Kruger said. "I'll relay the information to my client and his parents. If this will be reopened in adult court, Morgan, please give me the courtesy of an advance head's up."

Eberhard nodded. "Sure."

After a few days Eberhard called Kruger and said, "I'm giving you the advance heads up that the Bret Harris case will *not*, repeat *not*, be opened in adult court. After thinking about it, I'm letting the matter drop. That kid is clearly winning the PR war."

Chapter Twenty-Eight

DECEMBER CAME AND the weather turned wintry. For five days wind-driven rain drenched Colliver's canyon. Colliver and the Harrises were happy because it reduced the number of media people and "lookie-loos" coming around to try and see Gregory. After getting word of Judge Ronke's decision, the Harrises had moved back into their old coyote cabin to be as far away from the main road as possible. A party was held at Colliver's cabin to celebrate the decision and to say farewell to Rachel, Jared, Ian, Sylvia, and Alice who were returning to their normal lives. It was also decided to go back to using the old names of Mark, Cory, and Gregory

Mark thought about Jared's advice—that the boxing match be canceled. Jared was worried that the excitement and physical activity might cause a seizure. Colliver, on the other hand, had thought the stress would not be any greater than Gregory's soccer matches. As far as the actual bout with Hernandez, Colliver said Gregory would easily keep his opponent at bay and ultimately put Hernandez down just as he did large animals. Gregory, of course, lobbied strongly to move forward with the match. Ian, Sylvia, Alice, and Corinne stayed neutral. The next day, Mark gave his okay to making plans for the match.

Two days later Gregory picked up the mail from the Colliver mailbox and shouted, "Whoopee!" He ran to Colliver's cabin. "We got it. We got it. Express mail."

Colliver stepped outside. "Got what?"

"The letter from that ESPN exec guy you know, Jed Adams."

Colliver opened the letter and started reading silently. Suddenly he gave a thumb's-up sign. "He'll do it. But he wants to come meet us first. He's probably left already."

"Yay . . . yay . . . yay . . ." Gregory hollered.

Corinne came up. "So who is this guy and how do you know him, Bill?"

Colliver chuckled. "He was a neighbor kid when I was growing up. He became a big success in the sporting world. I haven't talked to him in fifteen years or so. That is why I sent the letter to his mother's address. She must have called him. I figured Jed would recommend someone who could handle all the negotiations and management from our side, but his letter says he will take a leave of absence from ESPN and handle everything himself."

"First you know Ian, then this guy . . . for a bumpkin you're pretty amazing, Bill."

Colliver laughed. "So he'll probably show up here soon . . . let Mark know that we're going to have to start deciding things. I hope he doesn't show up wearing a suit."

Jedidiah Adams was stopped by a guard, but after giving his name, drove on and pulled up to Colliver's cabin in a new green Jeep. He honked the horn and stepped out, looking around. He was wearing a red flannel shirt, hunting vest, Levi's, and boots. Colliver waved as he came out the door. He sent Arnie down to get Gregory and his parents, then hugged, shook hands, and greeted his old childhood friend.

"Geez Jed, what's with the Jeep and hunting get-up?"

Jed laughed. "Well, I heard that this place is rugged, according to the media reports. I thought I might have to wrestle a bear just to get in here. But it was just a guard."

Colliver laughed. "Same old Jed, I see. Great to see you, buddy."

They shook hands again and Colliver clapped him on the shoulder.

Gregory and Arnie came running up. Soon after Mark and Corinne could be seen walking fast in their direction.

"Are you Gregory, the Neanderthal Kid?" Jed asked. "I'm Jed."

"Yeah, I guess," Gregory said, embarrassed. "Nice to meet you." They shook hands and Gregory felt a hard handshake and so squeezed hard back. Jed rubbed his hand as if it were damaged and all three laughed.

By then Mark and Corinne had arrived and were introduced.

"I'm incredibly impressed with this amazing, amazing story about all of you," Jed said, shaking his head. "You too, Bill."

"Well, I made some hot tea," Corinne said. "Why don't we go down to the creek near our place and get acquainted."

"Sounds great, but first I need to sample the goods." He opened the tailgate of the Jeep and brought out four boxing gloves. He put on one pair and tossed the other at Gregory. "Put 'em on, Gregory. Then let's see what ya got. I can't take this job unless I'm backing a winner."

Colliver and Gregory laughed while Mark and Corinne frowned. Jeb ran at Gregory and threw a right punch which Gregory dodged easily. Jeb turned around.

"C'mon, give me some of that X stuff," Jed said.

Gregory looked at Jed, then zinged him with a slight amount of X. Jed suddenly staggered dizzily, almost falling down. "What the hell?" he said, trying to regain his composure. "Feels like an electric shock."

Gregory asked, "Do you want me to put you down?"

"Yeah, I dare you!" Jed lunged at Gregory again.

Gregory gave a moderate blast. Jed's knees buckled and he fell heavily to the ground.

"That's enough, Gregory," Mark said in a firm voice. "Turn it off."

Jed shook his head repeatedly, then slowly sat up, still on the ground. After a minute he was able to stand. He stared at Gregory, slowly shaking his head. "So it's true. Absolutely unbelievable."

Colliver said, "Now that you've had the *come to Jesus* moment, Jed, let's all get some tea."

Gregory handed his gloves to Jed.

"All right," Jed said, still slowly moving his head around. "This match is gonna be big . . . huge," he said, as if talking to himself. "Might be the biggest audience ever. It'll get lots of non-boxing fans. It'll be tremendous. Wow."

They sat in wooden chairs around a small table next to the brook. Corinne poured hot tea from a teapot and passed around a basket of crackers. Colliver and Jed talked about their childhood friendship. Everyone made small talk for a while.

"Okay," Jed said. "We need to start talking about the match and the arrangements. But before I give any of my thoughts, I need to hear—especially from you, Bret—what you want, what ideas you have."

Gregory nodded slowly. "Well, here's what I want: I want there to be the largest TV and radio audience around the world as there can be. I'm not interested so much in maximum money, but in a wide audience. Second, one week after the match, I want time on all the same networks and stations to talk to all the world's people for about an hour. It would be part of the overall deal. You know—if you cover the match, you have to cover my talk. I have things to say to people of the world . . . who I am, the traits I have, what it's like for the Shenko line, stuff like that. There could be questions by a panel or something for the last thirty minutes, but most of the time would be for me. 'Cause after the match, people will know I'm for real, then they'll want to know what makes me tick. Only I can do that."

The four adults stared at Gregory. In the sudden silence, finch and blue jay sounds could be heard above the burbling of the water. Mark looked in the distance and thought he saw a doe come to the stream for a drink. He thought, *What is going on here? Who is this grown-up boy who had just acted like an adult? My god, Gregory has matured. How did that happen?*

Jed said, "Well, all right. I think those things can be arranged." He looked at Mark, Corinne, and Colliver who all exhibited body language that said . . . *Okay with me, if that's what he wants.*

Jed continued, "That means we should not give exclusive rights to any networks—just make it available for all comers. And given that, we should price on the basis of audience share determined *post facto* by rating firms, taking into account final advertising rates. We'll get up-front fees of course. I'll need some staff for all this, but I can arrange it."

Gregory said, "Can it be held somewhere nearby, like in Reno?"

"No," said Jed. "We have to do it in Madison Square Garden, New York, if the boxing commission will allow it as an unofficial event, which I think they will. That city has the best electronic connections to the world. Tell me, have you been contacted by any of Pepe's people about arrangements?"

Colliver grunted. "Yeah, there are some letters that have come in. I've got them all in a pile for you, unopened."

"When would the match be?" Gregory asked.

"I'd like to try for early spring," Jed said. "But we'll just have to see what the availability is at the Garden and with Pepe, and make sure there is enough time for all the arrangements and marketing. I'm going to be damn busy. But some of my old staff I think will come in on it."

"What kind of contract do we need with you, Jed?" Colliver said.

"I'll put together a simple contract and term sheet for your review in the next few days. Getting liability insurance will be the hard thing. Sound okay?"

Colliver said, "That would be good. We'll have to trust you for the most part. But if you do anything wrong, Arnie and I will be coming for you." Colliver looked at Arnie, then pointed at Jed. "Arnie, give Jed a growl."

The wolf dog suddenly bristled with a low growl focused on Jed.

Everyone laughed and soon Arnie was wagging his big tail.

"I get the message," Jed said. "You won't have anything to worry about. I'm more interested in making this happen than in money. But there is going to be a lot of money coming in and perhaps you need to think about what you want to do with it, how to avoid heavy taxes. Maybe you want to form a non-profit foundation or two. You should get yourselves an accountant and a tax attorney. And a lot more guards for this place. The media will be crawling around every square foot. Also, Bret, I'm going to refer you to a media strategist I know. When Pepe calls you a 'fraud' or a 'phony,' you'll need to know what to say."

SHORTLY AFTER NEW YEAR'S DAY, a joint announcement by Jedidiah Adams, representing Gregory Shenko, and Jorge Cruz, manager for Pepe Hernandez, took place in San Francisco. Taking turns, they announced that a boxing match between Pepe and Gregory Shenko would occur the evening of April 1st in Madison Square Garden. Tickets would go on sale in February. The match would be open for all TV and radio networks around the world to broadcast, once prior contractual arrangements had been made with Adams. Jed gave a website, email, and phone number for his new organization, "Match of the Ages." The press conference ended with Cruz saying that Pepe was looking forward to this and would go easy on Gregory, not putting him out until the fifth round so that fans could get their money's worth. Adams responded that the Neanderthal Kid would put Pepe down easier than he "X'd out" a buck deer. The media began hyping the match from that moment on. Public interest skyrocketed worldwide.

The media specialist, Dwight Branson, had asked Gregory to keep a low pro-file with the media, but to stay reachable by phone every other day. This led Colliver to reconnect the unlisted phone in the front house previously occupied by Mark, Corinne, and Gregory. Pepe made comments to the media about once a week, mostly saying the alleged powers were a hoax, but Branson had Gregory respond in kind only about once every two weeks. Colliver had to increase the number of guards. The quantity of media and other people trying to catch sight of Gregory was "astonishing" as Colliver put it. There were even a few people who hiked in from the far perimeters of Colliver Canyon property to avoid the guards.

On the days when Gregory was not on phone duty, he often went hiking, mostly with Colliver, but sometimes alone. Colliver always brought Arnie and his pellet gun on the hikes, keeping a sharp eye out for uninvited people on his land. In one instance he shot a fellow carrying a camera who challenged him as owner of the property. The shot, at a low number of pumps, stung the man in the thigh and provided quick motivation for him to run away.

One day in late February, Gregory was hiking alone near his favorite meadow. The sun was out and birds and squirrels were moving around. Thinking he was alone, Gregory zapped a brown squirrel running up the trunk of a tree. The squirrel fell to the ground, then recovered and ran off. Only then did Gregory notice movement behind a granite rock. A young man rose up, put his smart phone in his pocket, and started running away. Gregory considered zapping the fellow, but thought better of it. Jed had forbid him to use his X trait between December and April 1.

Three days later a short video of the squirrel dropping off the tree trunk with a recognizable Gregory in the foreground appeared on a highly popular public video website. It could be accessed by searching 'Gregory Shenko' or 'Squirrel zapping'. The number of hits on the video climbed into the millions daily and the site stopped operation for a while, trying to upgrade software and equipment to cope with the volume. The video was also rebroadcast on news outlets in every country. This hugely ramped up interest in the 'Match of the Ages' and led to some of the best Madison Square Garden tickets—long sold out—being resold for tens of thousands of dollars each.

Soon after the video came out, Pepe held a press conference. "That video is crap," he said. "The squirrel just lost its footing. It quickly ran away after hitting the ground. It wasn't dazed. Anyone can see that. This 'X' power is a hoax . . . 'cause nobody could possibly have such a thing. And I'm going to prove it on the first of April. The only fools will be Gregory and anyone who drinks the Kool-Aid that his side puts out."

After careful coaching by Branson, Gregory made a rare trip to Nevada City where he gave a short press conference in Pioneer Park. Advance notice had been given to the police department and to a selected few media outlets who had maintained skeleton crews in Nevada City ever since Gregory's juvenile court appearance. A small crowd quickly assembled around a makeshift platform. Gregory used a bullhorn provided by the media people.

"Good afternoon," Gregory said. "I just wanted to give a short response to my boxing opponent, Pepe Hernandez, who keeps saying my X trait is a hoax. I'm here to say that my special trait is not a hoax. That squirrel video is proof that I can disorient animals at close range. Pepe is not a small animal, but he will learn first hand that he is susceptible. While Pepe is not a squirrel, he does seem to be acting pretty squirrely, don't you think?" There was a ripple of laughter from the crowd.

"I'm sorry I can't take questions, but I encourage everyone to watch the match and then watch my interview. That interview will occur one week later on the same stations. Thank you again." Gregory then left with Colliver and Mark who had brought him.

His videotaped response to Pepe was broadcast worldwide on many media outlets. The betting odds in Las Vegas changed after the squirrel episode and Gregory's media conference. Prior to the squirrel zapping the odds favored Pepe over Gregory 80:20. Afterward, the odds changed to nearly even, Pepe retaining a slight advantage.

One week before the match, Jed visited Colliver Canyon. He held a meeting in Colliver's cabin with Gregory, Colliver, Mark, and Corinne.

"Okay," Jed said. "I just want to go over everything before it's time to leave so we are all on the same page. We have a private plane leaving Sacramento Airport the day before the fight and a private van will pick up all of you and your luggage at six a.m., so please be ready. Jared and Sylvia will join us at the airport as you requested, Mark. They were able to get an early flight from LAX. And of course, I'll join you at the airport. Bill, I'm pleased you will be the coach in Gregory's corner. There will be front row seats at the Garden near Gregory's corner for the rest of us."

"Yeah, but do Gregory and I have to wear those stupid clothes you sent with 'Neanderthal Kid' on them?" Bill asked. "What's wrong with just a gray sweatshirt?"

"It's marketing, Bill. We want to hype the crowd and the TV audience. Right?" Colliver shook his head. "Whatever."

"I've also arranged a large private suite with four bedrooms and other rooms with some fold-downs so we all have a place to stay. The rental is located in midtown not far from the Garden. We'll have a large van, a driver, and bodyguards, and I've coordinated with the NYPD. Security needs to be tight because of all the weirdos that can come out of the woodwork. Is everyone still planning to stay the full week after the match to watch Gregory's talk?"

Everyone nodded. "Jared and Sylvia are too," Mark said.

"Good. I've reserved a small auditorium at the United Nations building for Gregory's interview. It will accommodate all the expected media. They also have separate rooms for a lot of language interpreters who will be broadcasting in various languages. So when you talk, you'll need to speak slowly and enunciate well, Gregory."

Gregory nodded.

"What's the revenue situation now?" Mark asked.

"It's just unbelievable," Jed said. "So the world population is seven billion and probably two to three billion of that are babies and young kids who wouldn't be interested in the match. That leaves about a four billion potential. Our people are projecting a TV and radio audience of one- to two-billion people. *More than one billion people* all around the world. Can you believe that? This will be the largest audience of any media event—ever. It is estimated that about five hundred million watched the first moon landing in 1969, which for that time was incredible, given fewer TVs and fewer people. But this will top the moon landing. And as for the money, we are now estimating eight hundred million to come in from all sources, and that after expenses, Pepe and Gregory would split around seven hundred million."

"Oh my god," Corinne exclaimed.

"Damn," said Mark.

"Wow," said Gregory.

Colliver just closed his eyes and shook his head.

"What size audience do you project for my interview?" Gregory finally asked.

"We don't have a good handle on numbers for that," Jed replied. "It could be much less or much more. We'll just have to see."

CHAPTER TWENTY-NINE

ON APRIL 1, Manhattan was experiencing clear weather and bedlam. The latter was due to the match that evening at Madison Square Garden. Bumper-to-bumper traffic, especially taxis, jammed the avenues. City foot traffic walked more quickly, and New York's "finest" were out in full force. Sports bars with huge TV screens had accepted pricey reservations for their seats. The *New York Times* had run a separate section—an unusually detailed six-page article, including pictures, on the history of Gregory Shenko, Mark Sandler, Corinne Shenko, Bill Colliver, Jared Weymouth, and Shenko family members. It seemed that everyone in the city that day was reading up on Gregory.

The night before, Gregory, Mark, Corinne, Colliver, Jared, Sylvia, and Jed had arrived by private jet and large van. Everyone had enjoyed watching Gregory first discover the city from the airplane window at dusk. Other than the trip to Washington, D.C., he had never been in a skyscraper city before. Nevada City was a small forested dot in comparison to New York. Jed had requested that the Gulfstream 200 pilots get as close to Manhattan as permitted before landing at JFK airport. As they approached the island Jed identified key landmarks to Gregory, including the Statue of Liberty, the Freedom Tower at Ground Zero, the Brooklyn Bridge, Wall Street, the Empire State Building, Central Park, and Madison Square Garden.

"In one of my classes we saw the planes hit the World Trade Center towers," Gregory said, staring intently. "Oh yeah, Central Park . . . are there any wild animals there?"

"Not like you're used to," Colliver said. "Squirrels and birds mostly."

Gregory nodded. "That's the trouble with cities . . . no forests, no animals." He looked back at Madison Square Garden. "I didn't know it was round like that. They should call it Madison Round Garden. I didn't know it would be so big."

"It will be full tomorrow night for you and Pepe," Jed said, smiling. "Pretty amazing, huh?"

Gregory nodded, then seemed to smile at some internal thought. "Yep."

THE GARDEN'S 20,000 seats filled up earlier than usual. The number of paid seating would have been higher if large amounts of specialty space had not been assigned to domestic and foreign media personnel and their equipment. The high-power overhead lights lit up the boxing ring's white floor and red containment "ropes." The hubbub of the crowd suddenly broke into an almost deafening roar when Pepe and his two coaches walked in, the coaches assuming their positions in one corner of the ring. Pepe moved to the center of the ring, raised an arm and glove, and turned slowly around, gesturing to the loud, supportive crowd.

The audience reaction to the entry of Gregory and Bill Colliver was polite but noticeably less in volume. Some people chuckled at the bright yellow "Neanderthal Kid" on the shiny purple background of Gregory's warm-up jacket. Gregory strode to the center of the ring and jabbed his right boxing glove in the air, looking over at Pepe whom he'd met earlier in the Garden's warmup gym. The crowd slowly responded with cheering.

A popular sports announcer named Kelly interjected at that point in his on-air TV commentary: "So, does this Gregory kid really have Neanderthal genes? That's what they want you to believe. He does look the part, I have to say. Look at those huge jutting eyebrows, protruding face, the size of his chest. But the real question is: does this Gregory really have some sort of strange powers as the people interviewed in the *New York Times* article claim? I guess, like Pepe, I'm not sure I believe that squirrel video that appeared on the Web. But that's just my opinion. We are sure going to find out very soon. We will find out if this will be a boxing match or a magic show . . . or a hoax."

A Garden official in a dark suit and red tie came to the center of the ring and welcomed the crowd to the "Match of the Ages." When he said that "the combined TV and radio broadcasts around the world may make this the most watched and listened to sporting event ever," the crowd cheered. Then he successively introduced World Lightweight Boxing Champion Pepe Hernandez and special challenger, Gregory Shenko, as the cheering continued. When the referee was introduced, Colliver leaned close to Gregory's ear.

"Now remember, Gregory, he may charge out of his corner and throw a quick haymaker, so be ready."

"I'll be ready," Gregory said, smiling.

The referee brought the two combatants together in the middle of the ring to touch gloves and told them things that couldn't be discerned above the roar of the crowd. After they went back to their corners, the bell rang, starting the first round.

As Colliver predicted, Pepe charged out quickly toward Gregory. Gregory backed up and stepped to the side, then gave some X to Pepe, just as the latter started to swing. The effect was immediately noticeable. Pepe's left and right punches went wobbly and Gregory easily ducked away. Pepe stood strangely for a minute, not moving, shaking his head. The crowd had noticed, voicing a collective, "Ohhh Ohhhhhh." Gregory, standing to the side, waited for the next charge.

"Get him, Pepe," someone in the crowd yelled.

Kelly, the popular announcer, said in low tones, "Well, that might have been a zapping of Pepe by Gregory, because Pepe's charge appeared interrupted and his punches were uncontrolled, kind of rubbery. Very weird, I have to say."

Pepe danced some and moved more slowly toward Gregory. "Don't let him get too close," Colliver shouted.

Gregory danced to the right and then left, allowing Pepe to get closer. At about six feet apart, Pepe again charged, swinging his left. Gregory gave some low level X but Pepe's left still landed strongly to the delight of the crowd. Gregory reeled back, shaking his head. Then Pepe charged again, seeing an opening. But the straight right Pepe intended missed wildly due to the strong X blast Gregory delivered. Pepe faltered, then slipped down on his knees, shaking his head.

The crowd loudly booed. Gregory looked around at the audience and saw some people giving him a *thumb's down* gesture. The puzzlement on Gregory's face was noticeable.

Kelly's commentary at that point reflected the feelings of many in the audience. "Clearly, that was another of those X power shots, done after poor Pepe had landed a good left that Gregory couldn't deal with. I think this crowd is booing because they want to see a boxing match, not repeated epileptic zapping—or whatever it is. So far, Gregory has not thrown a single punch. Pepe is now up again, the ref having checked him. He says he's okay. Oh . . . now there's a sign to Pepe coming from Pepe's coach. Looks like it's two fingers, whatever that means."

Pepe danced and shadow boxed some, but didn't charge Gregory, who stayed relatively in the same position close to ring center. After about a minute of this, without Pepe or Gregory trying to engage, the crowed started booing.

Kelly's commentary to his large TV audience resumed: "So maybe that two-finger signal by Pepe's coach was for Pepe just to hang back. Maybe the

Hernandez team is hoping Gregory will move against Pepe. But Gregory has yet to show any boxing talent—all we see is an occasional zapping to stop Pepe's charges. The crowd is booing and justly so, I think."

As the clock drew down toward the end of the first round, Pepe suddenly charged again with a flurry of punches. Gregory covered his head with his arms and gloves and kept dancing backward. Pepe threw a hard left at Gregory's middle, causing Gregory to double over.

"Kill him, Pepe," shouted someone at ringside. The crowd noise rose, cheering the action.

But Pepe could not land the obvious uppercut right he intended because the bell sounded, ending the first round. The referee quickly jumped between the two fighters and pushed them toward their corners. After the cheering died, a low chorus of boos could be heard.

"Well, we finally had some action," Kelly said, "even though it was all on Pepe's side. At least there was no more of the weird zapping. This crowd is clearly not happy after Round One."

Gregory sat on the stool in his corner.

"Bret, why didn't you zap Pepe once and for all when he charged?" Colliver said.

Gregory winced. "I thought of that, but the crowd wants us to box. They don't want to see the X power."

"Yeah, but the X is what you advertised," Colliver said angrily. "You can't beat Pepe at the game of boxing. So, just get it over with this next round. You're not here to please the crowd."

Gregory stood and leaned over to Jed. "Jed, please write down on a small paper the mailing address of our organization, *Match of the Ages* and give it to me. Thanks."

"Bret, what the hell is that about?" Colliver asked. "Look, this next round you have to stop playing games and just zap Pepe for the ten count. I'm serious, Bret."

Gregory said, "I hear you."

Jed stood up and passed a paper to Gregory who took it and put it in a pocket of his trunks. He also smiled and waved at Mark, Corinne, Jared, and Sylvia sitting next to Jed and looking concerned.

A loud buzzer gave warning that the next round was soon to start.

"Look at me, Bret," Colliver said. "You are here not to box, but to put Pepe down with the X. That's exactly what we said we'd do. And the time is now . . . this round. Understand?" Colliver's eyes had burrowed into Gregory's.

Gregory nodded. "Yep."

"Okay," Colliver said. "You're doing well, by the way."

Gregory laughed as the bell rang, starting Round Two.

Pepe came out slowly, dancing in boxer style. Gregory moved toward Pepe slowly, step by step. At a distance of about six feet from each other, they both paused, circling counter clockwise.

Again there were shouts that could be heard. "Knock him on his butt, Pepe." "Forget the zapping, Gregory . . . we want boxing."

Pepe began inching closer to Gregory, who put his gloves in proper position and began boxer dancing. Neither showed signs of backing away. As they got closer, suddenly Gregory threw a hard left at Pepe who had not expected it. The strong punch landed on Pepe's cheek bone. Both Pepe and the crowd felt it. A cheer went up. Realizing there had been no zapping, Pepe stepped back into position, saying to Gregory, "C'mon, c'mon, is that all ya got?"

Gregory stepped up and threw another left. But Pepe, expecting it, pulled his head back and the punch missed, leaving Gregory open and off balance. Pepe moved in and threw a hard right punch that landed heavily on Gregory's left jaw. Gregory's knees folded and he fell to the canvas. Cheers and groans came from the audience. The referee quickly moved Pepe to a safe corner, came back, and started counting as Gregory sat confused on the canvas for several counts.

"Get up, get up!" Colliver was shouting from the Kid's corner.

Gregory staggered up at the count of 'Seven.' The referee grabbed Gregory's gloves, looked closely into his eyes, and then whistled the match to continue.

Pepe, seeing an opportunity, moved quickly toward Gregory. There was more cheering and moaning from the crowd.

As Pepe closed in to throw more heavy punches, Gregory opened his mouth and let a powerful X blast go. It was accompanied by a short scream. The level and length of the blast was the same as Gregory had used on deer and other big animals on Colliver's land. Pepe's eyes rolled up white and he dropped to the canvas like a rag doll. Gregory moved quickly to a neutral corner and the referee stepped near Pepe and began counting. The crowd yelled for Pepe to get up, but the champ lay there, out for the full count. The referee motioned the medical crew into the ring, and with smelling salts, they were able to slowly coax Pepe to his knees, then up on his feet. The referee came to Gregory and held up his right arm, the gesture of the winner.

Most of the crowd stood and booed, long and loud.

Kelly's commentary at that point went as follows: "Well, there it is. Amazing. The Neanderthal Kid has won. And he did it with the use of his X power in Round Two. Only twice did he throw punches, and when that happened, it looked like we were going to get a boxing match. But after Pepe knocked Gregory down for a seven count, it was clear that Gregory was not going to be able to stay with

Pepe, who then moved in for the kill. So Gregory gave out a helluva blast and poor Pepe had no chance. You still hear the booing because the crowd is pretty ticked off. We only went about one and a half rounds. They wanted boxing. Oh, wait. Oh, wait. Now Gregory is motioning for the microphone to be dropped down . . . he wants to say something. But will the crowd let him? He's got the mike, so let's try and listen."

Gregory had pulled the small paper from his pocket. He motioned for the audience to quiet down, but the audience wasn't cooperating. Gregory began talking, and the crowd quieted.

"I want to thank Pepe for being game. He put up a good fight." Gregory waved at Pepe who sat in his corner. Pepe waved back.

Now the crowd became more silent.

"I want to thank all of you for coming, even though you definitely did not get your money's worth."

The crowd, surprised, gave approval to that, and some waved their ticket stubs.

Gregory continued. "Because you did not get your money's worth, I am going to refund your ticket costs." Suddenly the crowd was very silent. "So for those who feel gypped, save your ticket stubs and please send them to me, Gregory Shenko, at 'Match of the Ages'" at the following address." Gregory slowly read out the address and repeated it. "And remember, you can always find that address at 'MatchoftheAges.com'. Be sure to include your name and return address. I'm very sorry this fight was not what you expected. Thank you."

Suddenly the crowd began cheering. Gregory waved, let one of the officials take the microphone, moved to his corner, and then slipped out between the ropes with Colliver to join the security personnel who surrounded them.

Kelly's commentary had a querulous tone. "Can you believe that? Knowing that the crowd was unhappy, the Neanderthal Kid just promised to pay back everyone who sends in his or her ticket stub. Incredible! How much money does that involve? Let's say the average ticket price is two hundred dollars, some a lot more and some less of course . . . that would be twenty thousand seats times say two hundred dollars—what is that, somebody—oh yes, it could come to four million dollars. That's serious money. Now we know they had a huge purse to share, what with all the media and advertising, but even so the match time frame was so short, it's hard to believe that there weren't clauses to limit monetary payments.

"Folks, let me sum up. It's clear we did not see a boxing match. But we did see something absolutely unique. We witnessed a person with the ability to mentally disable another person—not just disable—but to knock him out for a ten count. And to do that without touching the other person. So, I don't know about you, but I guess this show was . . . I can't think of a word . . . *dumbfounding*, I guess. Was it worth the money just to see that? Wasn't that better than anything Hollywood does? How often would you ever see that? Despite my criticism of the boxing, let's face it . . . we've all just seen something incredible in this world, something unknown in human experience. This Gregory must be who he claims to be . . . a strange and different species. So what now? What now? I have no idea. I'm paid to talk to you and here I am—a babbling baboon."

DUE TO THE SLOW-MOVING crowds, it took nearly an hour for the special group—Gregory, Mark, Corinne, Colliver, Jared, Sylvia, and Jed plus bodyguards—to get into the condominium with all security in place. A few from the audience on their way home shouted when they recognized who the group was.

"Hey Gregory, I'm going to send in my ticket stubs. I'll need six hundred dollars back"

Gregory didn't reply to any of the remarks, except for the next one.

"Gregory, are you going to get a license for that weapon?"

Gregory shouted back, "I'd like you to listen to my talk in a week. That will be part of it."

The condominium suite, recently remodeled, was on the fifth floor of a brownstone-like building. Looking out the west windows during the day, one could see narrow views of the Hudson River with ferries and ships moving about. That evening, after obtaining coffee or tea and munching on cake and cookies in the kitchen, everyone gravitated to the living room for serious talk.

Colliver cleared his throat. "So I have to ask: What did everyone think of the match?"

Corinne said, "I was very nervous when you tried to box him, Bret—I mean Gregory."

"When you went down, my heart jumped into my throat," Sylvia said.

"Yeah, the whole thing made me very nervous for you," Jared said.

Colliver nodded. "That's for sure."

"But they wanted a boxing match—they didn't want to see my X," Gregory exclaimed.

"That may have just been the Garden audience," Mark said softly. "It'll be interesting to see what the general TV audience thought."

"Why don't we turn on the TV and see some media reaction?" Jed asked.

A popular cable news show was brought up on the forty-inch flat screen. A panel of two men and a woman, publicly known and experienced journalists, were being called upon for their opinions on the match. The program was just starting. The moderator—a popular cable news anchor, Natalie Simms—said,

"I've just learned that Pepe told the press that the X power is for real and that Gregory and his powers are for real. So Roger, please tell us: What does this all mean? What has transpired at this so-called Match of the Ages?"

The camera narrowed on a gray-haired man of about sixty. "That's the question of the ages," he said, chuckling. "I understand that the Garden audience may have been looking for a boxing match and for Pepe to easily win it. But that outcome would have been insignificant compared to what we've just seen. A new species of hominid, with incredible traits, just appeared before our eyes. Some of the traits, including the X that we saw, seem to defy biophysics. Yet there it was, unquestionably proven before our eyes. This turn of events is totally *mind blowing* if you'll pardon that word. And I think it's going to take a while for this reality to soak into people. I think that Gregory Shenko's talk in a week will have an even larger audience than the worldwide record-breaker we just saw. People are going to want to know what the hell is going on here and who this kid is."

Natalie nodded seriously. "And how about you, Stephanie, what do you think?"

The camera focused in on an attractive brunette in her mid-forties. "Well, I have to admit that I had not followed the Shenko stuff until recently when I read the *New York Times* piece—three times over. I agree with Roger that this is 'mind blowing.' One doesn't want to believe it, but there it was happening right on TV. But what really gets me, and I think it will be the case for most women, is that Shenko men, in addition to the X power, have a Y power that supposedly excites women uncontrollably to want sex. Say what? The curiosity about this will flood every woman on the planet. And apparently Shenko women have powers too. They have an X2 power that can make men in close proximity sick to their stomachs. So if you don't like some guy putting moves on you, you can make him throw up. All I can say is—these Shenkos must have come from a different planet. Seriously."

Natalie laughed, then looked over at Gordon, the third panelist. "So Gordon, how do you think the public is going to react to Gregory?"

The camera honed in on a person in his late forties or early fifties wearing thick glasses. "Well, I don't think the public will be at all pleased with learning about these Shenkos. Most people have the notion that Homo sapiens sapiens, which is us, are the endpoint of evolution. Some believe the religious teachings that we are made in God's image, and that the Creator made us different from all the animals. In other words, most people think: We're it. We're the top of the heap. We are better than all the lower animals and have the right to rule over them. Some other people call this 'speciesism'. But now, with the Shenkos, everyone is forced to realize that we may not be 'it.' These Shenkos have some amazing traits and they are quite athletic and intelligent. So a lot of people are likely to be angry, resentful, and negative toward this new 'Other' who's suddenly appeared on Earth. Speciesism may take on a whole new meaning."

"That's an extremely good point," Natalie said. "Anything else?"

Roger jumped in. "Ever since the Shenkos were first written about, I've been doing some reading in paleontology. Probably the leading advocate for the idea that evolution occurs in a directional and goal-driven way was a French Jesuit priest and paleontologist named Teilhard de Chardin. He thought that we Homo sapiens were predictable and inevitable as the endpoint of evolution—that if the process were set back to the beginning and run again, it would end up the same. He was quite influential and not always appreciated by his Catholic hierarchy. But now here are the Shenkos and they are evidence that this whole Chardinian view is totally wrong. It's too bad that he's no longer living, because his commentary now might be very interesting."

Gordon continued, "According to some scientists, the Shenkos may be more of an older species, closer to Homo erectus than to us. And the famous paleontologist, Richard Leakey, has written that he believes the key qualities of humanness—i.e., consciousness, compassion, morality, language—arose to some extent in such earlier Homo species well before Homo sapiens. So all of this is going to be debated now, because of what happened tonight and probably because of what happens when Gregory Shenko talks to the world in a week. Society is in for the 'Debate of the Ages,' I think. And I strongly suspect they will not be happy about facing up to this."

"Wow," Natalie said. "I guess we'll all have to stay tuned. Thank you everyone."

After the television was turned off, Colliver turned to Gregory. "Bret, uh . . . Gregory, did you understand all of that?"

"Not all, but quite a bit," Gregory replied. "But can we now talk about what's going to happen this week?" Gregory looked around at everyone, his heavy brow furrowed.

"Sure," said Jed, who looked at the others.

"Fine with me," Mark said.

Corinne nodded and Colliver shrugged.

"So tell us what you want," Jed said. "By the way, we put the *New York Times* article up on the website. People can access that along with the speech given by Clyde Finlayson at the American Society of Human Genetics meeting. The number of hits on the website is soaring, but we were prepared for this."

Gregory looked down at his feet. "Yeah, but I don't understand that Dr. Finlayson speech. I need some help with all this 'paleo-tology' or whatever it is. What I'd like is to have Ian come to New York so I can talk to him about this."

Corinne perked up. "Well, then let's ask if he would come."

"Doesn't he have classes to teach?" Colliver asked.

"I think he would find this far more important than teaching classes," Mark said.

"Sure," Jed said. "We have the budget to fly him out here immediately. And as far as career importance is concerned, I'd think he'd come in a flash."

"It's still early out there, so let's call him," Corinne said.

"I'll do it," Mark said, pulling his phone out of a pocket. Mark stepped into the kitchenette and spoke in low tones for a while. When he returned, there was a broad smile on his face.

"He will catch the earliest morning flight to New York. He's delighted to come. And he'll let us know his arrival time. Said he would bring a sleeping bag and air mattress."

"Great," Gregory said. "Thanks . . . Dad."

"What else?" Jed asked.

Gregory thought for moment, turned red, then said. "I need to discuss the Y thing with some ladies. Sylvia, you will be great. But do you think Rachel and Alice would come too?"

Mark showed surprise. "Rachel? I know she would come up here at the drop of a hat. And Alice? I'm sure she would come too. But why them? What do they know about the Y?"

Gregory said, "I like them. Both are smart and easy to talk to."

Corinne laughed. "At least Rachel doesn't have to line any shelves this time."

Sylvia smiled. "I think Alice would be very pleased to be here, given what's going on."

Mark chuckled. "Let me call them." Again he went into the kitchenette and spoke quietly. Returning, he announced, "Both will on morning planes. Jed, can you get a place for them to stay?"

"You bet," Jed said. "I'll get someplace close by, maybe in this building."

Gregory smiled. "That's terrific. With Ian, Jared, Sylvia, and those two helping me, I know I can be ready for the broadcast."

Jed smiled. "Very good. And is there anything else, Mr. Shenko?"

Everyone laughed.

"Uh, yeah." Gregory was thoughtful. "I want everyone who hears my broadcast to be able to text message the answer—yes or no—to a question I'll ask on the air. The text message will need to be sent in during the last half hour of the broadcast. And then all the answers that come in will need to be tallied up at some point."

"I don't know if we can arrange that," Jed said. "It could be too technically complicated."

"Well, it's very important to me," Gregory said. "I'd appreciate your making it work."

Jed gulped. "Okay. We'll look into it and do our best. Do you know what question you want to ask?"

"Not yet. I want to talk to Ian and everyone. But it will be really, really important to me." Gregory's chin jutted out as he stared at Jed.

"Well . . . okay. We'll do our best," Jed replied in deference. "I'm going to call our technical guru first thing in the morning."

All the adults looked at Gregory with awe—the teenager going on CEO.

Gregory suddenly slapped his head. "Ohhh . . . There *is* one more thing. The panel for the second half of the hour. I need a panel." He looked around at everyone.

Colliver cleared his throat. "What about those three panelists that were on the cable show tonight? They're pretty sharp. And they would have credibility."

"But we don't know them," Gregory responded.

"Well, perhaps all the more reason to get them. They will have journalistic integrity and high credibility with the public," Colliver said.

"Do you think they would agree with only one week's notice?" Gregory asked.

Jed chuckled. "I think I could line them up. This would be the biggest audience they would ever have. And we could get that Natalie Simms to open the program and introduce you, then chair the panel. Let me work on it tomorrow."

Jed looked again at Gregory. "And now, Mr. Shenko, sir, is there anything else we can do?"

"I'd like to turn in for the night."

Laughter filled the room.

Chapter Thirty

GREGORY PEERED OUT his window at the boats and ships maneuvering on the Hudson River. The water glinted in the morning sunshine. It would be a warm day, he realized . . . a great day for going to Central Park with Colliver. The question was: How this could be done, given the notoriety of the Neanderthal Kid and all those people down there?

A milling crowd, including many paparazzi and some media people, was on the street in front of the condo building. They faced an increased number of policemen that morning because Jed had passed word that Gregory might like to venture out. But the lieutenant coordinating security for the NYPD advised Jed's security chief that it might be much better if Gregory wore a disguise and slipped out a back way, to be whisked away by an NYPD special taxi and accompanied by a plainclothes officer. This plan was accepted and Gregory and Colliver put on hooded sweatshirts and sunglasses provided by the NYPD.

"Now don't be late," Corinne said. "You'll need to shower before dinner. Ian, Alice, and Rachel will be here—we're having dinner brought in."

"I'll see that we get back no later than five," Colliver said.

The plan of a surreptitious building exit followed by incognito walking in Central Park went well. Gregory and Colliver spent several hours in the huge park, including lunching at a corner food stand. They wished the plainclothes policeman, also in hooded sweatshirt, didn't have to follow them, even at a distance. But they quickly put him out of their minds as they avidly looked for wildlife.

"There are *so* many different plants and trees," Gregory remarked.

"I read somewhere that there are fifteen hundred different species of plants," Colliver said.

"You'd think that deer would love a place like this," Gregory said.

Colliver shook his head. "If it weren't for all the idiot people harassing them, maybe a small deer herd could survive on all this vegetation. Normally, though, deer need a much larger area to roam."

"Do you think we can find some wild animals, Uncle Bill?"

"If we look hard enough—but we have to get off the people paths."

WHEN THE NYPD taxi dropped off Gregory and Colliver near the back of the condo building, it did not go unnoticed by a few people now watching the rear doors. Colliver told the plainclothes officer that Gregory might like to go out again the next day in the afternoon. The officer said that a new plan might have to be worked out for maintaining their anonymity, but he would work on it. Then he thanked both Gregory and Colliver for showing him so many unusual animals in Central Park—he had no idea the animals were there.

Ian, Alice, and Rachel had already arrived at the condo. When Gregory and Colliver came in, the greetings were warm and loud. Rachel asked how the walk through Central Park went. Ian shook Gregory's hand strongly and Alice gave him a hug.

"We saw some wild animals," Gregory exclaimed. "We saw an opossum hanging from a high tree limb. We saw racoons, turtles, squirrels, fish—a huge amount of birds."

"That's wonderful," Rachel said.

"Yeah, the variety of vegetation and trees was surprising," Colliver said. "But there are no big animals like we see at home."

Ian laughed. "I guess you weren't counting homo sapiens as big animals."

"Precisely, Ian. If we were, we'd have seen thousands."

"You guys need to shower," Corinne said.

"Yes, Mother," Colliver said, bringing chuckles from the others.

During dinner, Ian, Alice, and Rachel updated the group on their activities while everyone consumed the pepperoni-mushroom-goat cheese pizza and Caesar salad with gusto. After tiramisu and coffee were served, Gregory finally broached the topic the group awaited.

"Ian, Alice, and Rachel—did you see the match on TV?"

"Yes," Rachel replied. "And the suspense almost killed me." She laughed.

"Certainly did," Ian said. "And I was ticked off that the Garden crowd favored Pepe."

Alice said she didn't watch some parts because she was so worried.

Gregory grinned. "Yeah, it didn't quite go as we expected."

"But it turned out all right," Corinne said. "Especially when you offered to rebate the cost of the tickets."

Colliver nodded. "Yeah, in hindsight that was brilliant, Gregory."

Gregory smiled appreciatively. "Now I want to say something to everyone. I very much appreciate all that you have done for me. Many of you have sacrificed your careers. Some of you have not agreed with others about me. Dr. Weymouth, Sylvia, Alice, Ian, Rachel—*thank you* so much for being concerned and helping me all these years. And Mom, Dad, and you, Uncle Bill, I owe you so much, I can't even say . . ." Gregory suddenly broke down into tears. Mark ran over and held him.

"It's okay, it's okay," Mark said soothingly. "We all thank you, Son, for those kind remarks. Everyone, I'm sure, appreciates it."

Everyone in the room then expressed in different words their appreciation for Gregory's maturity and difficult journey. After this there was a period of silence.

Jed finally said, "But now the big event is Gregory's talk. And judging from what my staff and the media are saying, this will be far bigger than the match. Gregory knew all along that the one would set the stage for the other."

Gregory smiled and nodded. "Is the text messaging going to work?" he asked.

"Yes, but we're needing separate numbers for quite a few of the countries. Local announcers will break in to give these numbers out. It's the best we can do."

"But the results can all be totaled up?" Gregory asked.

"Yes. We should have it all within a few hours."

"Okay, good. Thanks, Jed. You, too, have been just super." Gregory seemed thoughtful as he poked at the tiramisu, making tiny piles as if intended for mice.

"So how do you want Ian, Sylvia, Alice, and me to work with you?" Rachel asked.

"Well . . . how about if Ian and I talk every morning from 8:30 to 10:30 and you ladies meet with me from 10:30 to 12:30? We can meet in my bedroom—move some chairs in. That way, we'll be free in the afternoon."

Rachel, Silvia, Alice, and Ian looked at each other.

"That works," Ian said. "Okay with you ladies?"

They nodded.

"Yes, that's good," Rachel said. "It gives me time to see my aunt who lives uptown."

Gregory nodded slowly. "Okay, let's start tomorrow. But I have one more question and it's for everyone here."

The adults waited expectantly, looking at Gregory.

"How do you think I should act while I'm talking?"

Nobody responded. "What do you mean?" Mark finally said.

"Well, you know, should I act like I really know a lot of science and stuff?"

Alice smiled and raised a finger. "I think you should act like who you are—a boy telling what it's been like for him growing up, discovering all your traits, discovering who the Shenkos are . . . in other words, just be yourself."

Colliver said, "Yeah, just be yourself and talk normally, Gregory."

Jed nodded. "You're already so much ahead of your age group. Maybe you should start with 'Hello, everyone. Thank you for tuning in. My name is Gregory Shenko and I'm fourteen years old. I want to tell you my story' . . . something like that."

"I agree," Corinne said. "It might work better if you don't use much scientific language. You'll connect better."

Mark nodded. "I think so too. Probably more than nine out of ten people listening won't be scientifically literate."

Gregory looked at Ian and Jared.

"I agree," Ian said. "We can talk about the science here, but when you go on the air, it will be better if you put things in your own words, at your level of understanding."

Jared nodded. "I agree with that. Most people don't understand science, so keep it simple."

Gregory smiled and looked at everyone. "Okay. I appreciate that. Thank you."

FOR THE REMAINING DAYS before his media event, Gregory held the meetings as planned and then made sightseeing trips in the afternoon, either with Colliver or with Mark and Corinne, the plain clothesofficer always following. The NYPD found the best way to deal with the crowds was to load Gregory and companions into a police van in the guarded underground garage entrance and then switch them to the undercover taxi in an NYPD-guarded parking garage several blocks away. While in the van, clothes, make-up, hats and sunglasses were provided to maintain their anonymity. In this way Gregory was able to visit the Statue of Liberty, Empire State Building, South Street Sea Park, Times Square, and Coney Island without being recognized.

Meanwhile, Jed lined up the cable news panel and made sure that all arrangements with the U.N. and television and radio broadcast services were ready. Jed personally purchased a new set of "nice casual" clothes for Gregory.

Chapter Thirty-One

Natalie Simms cleared her throat. "Good day or good evening, whatever time it is for you. Welcome to a special broadcast featuring Gregory Shenko, also known as the Neanderthal Kid. My name is Natalie Simms of CNB News and I will briefly introduce Gregory Shenko, and then, in the second half of this broadcast, I will coordinate a panel of three journalists who will ask Gregory questions. But first let me announce that Gregory, near the end of his talk—that would be in about a half hour—will ask you, the audience, a question. And he wants every one of you, using your cell phone, to text yes or no in answer to the question. This should be done during the second half of the program or within fifteen minutes after the entire program ends. We are now going to pause for thirty seconds for your broadcaster to give you the number where you are to text your answer. Be sure to write it down. It will be given again later. So we will be right back in thirty seconds."

"Welcome back. I am Natalie Simms and it is now my pleasure to introduce the amazing young man who has captured the world's attention. I give you Gregory Shenko. Gregory?"

Television cameras moved to Gregory—wearing his new clothes—sitting in a comfortable chair, looking at the camera, and smiling.

"Hello to everyone. Thank you for tuning in to hear me. My name is Gregory Shenko and I am fourteen years old. But I'm way different from you. Way, way different. Because of that, I want to tell you my story. I will talk about what I've learned about myself and my special traits and why some people call me The Neanderthal Kid."

A different camera came on briefly showing Gregory's side profile. The forward jutting eyebrow ridges, the forward projection of his face, and the slightly bulging 'Neanderthal bun' on the back of Gregory's head were easily seen.

"When I was just a baby living in Fresno, California, my dad, Nicholas Shenko, died suddenly of an epileptic seizure. My mom, Corinne, had taken me to a Fresno doctor who worried that some eye-rolling I had, along with my father's problem, meant I should be seen by a specialist at Southern State University in Los Angeles, a Dr. Jared Weymouth. Of course, being a baby, I didn't know what the heck was going on." Gregory laughed. "But this is what I'm told happened."

"So anyway, down at the university, even though I did just fine with the usual baby tests, they found on an EEG that I had five times the normal voltage I should have had coming off the back of my head." Gregory cupped his hand over the occipital area. "Back here."

"Also, I should say that one of the young doctors we saw there was Mark Sandler, an up-and-coming genetics researcher from MIT who was changing his career to pediatrics. I was one of his first patients. I'll say more about this later, but he and my mother eventually decided to hide me in northern California. He became my father . . . kinda, and my mom's husband . . . sorta."

Gregory smiled knowingly. The camera technicians snickered, holding back laughter.

"But I didn't have anything to do with the hiding decision, 'cause I was a nine-month-old baby at the time we went north. You could say I was just along for the ride."

Gregory couldn't help noticing the camera operators smiling and he grinned.

"Anyway, continuing on, I was brought down to the university a second and third time for more testing. And this time my X power and Y power traits were discovered. Dr. Sandler held an ice cube against my bare foot and I got angry, I guess, and let go with my X trait. In those baby days I couldn't focus it, or adjust the level like I did with Pepe Hernandez. I just screamed and let it go, hitting everyone in the room. And the way the Y trait was discovered is that this nice lady psychologist was playing some board game with me, and I guess I was having fun, got into the game, and the Y just quietly came out. It affected both the nice lady and my mother who was holding me on her lap. Both of them became sexually excited. But being a baby, I had no idea what was going on."

Gregory held his hands up and raised his large shoulders in a shrug. Again the camera technicians, two men and a woman—all young—tried to hold back laughter.

"Well, after that there was some infighting by SSU professors over me and a reporter found out about my X trait and wrote a newspaper article. Some

L.A. militant religious guys who read it came up to Fresno and threatened my mom about me, scaring her. Then the university president got involved and Dr. Weymouth, the head doctor, was in trouble for keeping my traits secret. Apparently it was a *real* mess, all coming to a head. Other professors wanted me to be studied—you know, become like a laboratory rat with needles in my head. So a professor named Ian Trevor, a close friend of Dr. Weymouth's, suggested privately to my dad and mom that they take me up to hide out on some remote land on San Juan Ridge in northern California. Ian knew a guy who owned a lot of acreage up there and this guy—Bill Colliver—took us all in, letting us have a small unused cabin that had no electricity. At the time he didn't know who we were and we didn't tell him.

"So why would Uncle Bill do that? I call him Uncle because he became like a favorite uncle to me. He took us in because he's kind of a good-guy hermit. He's into the environment and philosophy—stuff like that—and he likes living a rustic life. The word 'rustic' means he has rust on him—no, just kidding."

This time the camera operators' laughter could be heard on the air and one gave a thumbs up sign. Gregory laughed in response.

"So we lived with kerosene lamps, we heated the place with a woodstove, and got ice for a cooler or put things in a nearby creek to keep them cool. Mom would wash clothes in the creek. Now and then we'd take hot showers at Bill's place. It was a simple life, like living in the eighteen hundreds, I'm told. I really liked it. Bill had all this acreage with deer, bear, and other animals.

"My parents' big problem was trying to prevent me from using my X and Y traits as a baby and young kid. Before arriving at Bill's, we had changed our names to the Harrises—Mom was Susan, Dad was Mike, and I was Bret—and we kept to ourselves at first, not venturing out anywhere. When I'd get upset or angry I'd let go with the X, not knowing how to control it. And I guess one of those times was when Uncle Bill was nearby, and he got zapped. He eventually connected the dots, realizing we were the baby, mother, and doctor who had been in all the news. He was amazed, but thankfully, he still wanted to help us and kept our secret."

Gregory took a drink of water and breathed deeply a few times. Then he held up the glass.

"One of the ways my parents learned to control my traits was to throw water on me if I started doing the X or Y. And it mostly worked. A half a cup of water in my face got my attention and I'd stop. I do remember when I was a toddler—it's one of my earliest memories—I was having a tantrum in front of Uncle Bill's cabin, screaming and doing the X as strongly as I could. Uncle Bill and Dad filled up this big wash tub in the creek, and when I finally stopped the X they came and dumped the whole tub on me. I thought I'd drowned."

Gregory shook his head. "But it did the job. After that I stopped doing my powers for fear of getting doused. I learned I could control them."

Gregory laughed suddenly, thinking of the far-off incident. Then he looked at the camera and his face became serious.

"So you're probably wondering how my strange powers can work. Well, the scientists don't really know. My real dad, Nicholas, had them, and probably his dad, going way, way back for tens of thousands of generations. And Shenko women had powers too, which I'll explain later. The autopsy on my dad, Nicholas, showed a gigantic, never-before-seen conglomeration of huge neurons packed together in his head. The whole thing was the size and shape of a short-handled hammer in his brain. I must have the same thing right up here."

Gregory tapped his head.

"And this had to have come about from many mutations over hundreds of thousands of years when early hominids occupied Europe and Asia. It also means that the Shenkos are a different and older species than Homo sapiens, meaning all of you. The Shenko line is probably some offshoot species that evolved in Eurasia from a combination of Homo erectus, Homo heidelbergensis, and the Neanderthals." Gregory quickly studied a paper in his hand. "That was from a hundred and twenty to eight hundred thousand years ago, a period called the Middle Pleistocene. This was well before modern humans came out of Africa about forty thousand years ago in what is now called the Holocene period. I'm not really this smart about science. I've had some help, you know.

"The X trait had to have developed to allow those ancient Shenko hunters to knock down antelope, reindeer, and other big animals for food and also to protect against dangers, such as lions, saber-tooth tigers, and the huge woolly rhinoceros with a four-foot horn. It was also a defense against other hominids. Anyway, that is what professors have told me. What do I know?"

Again, Gregory held up his hands and shrugged, chuckling. The camera technicians laughed again.

"But, you know, a lot of strange traits have evolved in animals." He held up one arm. "Do you know there is an electric eel about the size of my arm that can shock its prey, or defend itself against predators with its shocks? And it can do this at will?"

Gregory again studied his paper. "This eel's voltage can measure up to six hundred volts at one full amp of DC, direct current. Now if that were RF, or radio frequency energy, it would amount to five hundred watts of power, similar to a ham radio station that can broadcast and be received halfway around the world. So I have to ask: If an eel can develop such a thing, why is it so surprising that ancient hominids like my ancestors developed something similar? The X power evolved over millennia, tailored to the Shenko way of life during the various ice ages. Anyway, that is kind of how I think about it. The proof of the pudding is that it works. I have been able to put down a big buck deer at twenty feet."

Gregory drank more water, then put on another serious expression.

"Now what about the Y power—the sexual trait that Shenko males have? The explanation of this gets a little more complicated but it is quite understandable. And why did Shenko women develop the X2 trait—the ability to make people in very close proximity sick to their stomachs? For those of you who, uh . . . uh . . . you know, appreciate science, I recommend you look at a speech on the Match-of-the-Ages website by this Nobel professor, Dr. Clyde Finlayson. He says all this much better than me. It is kinda complicated."

"But let me try a little more. See, the power neuron chunk in the male Shenko brain went down into the primitive parts of the brain where, you know, anger, sex, and base kind of appetites are. And it makes sense that sexual waves could come out of that area the same way as the anger waves. But what was the purpose for that Y trait coming about? The professors say it was because all Shenko men died young from seizures, just like my real dad, Nicholas, did. So in order for the Shenkos to keep their own species going with their exclusive traits, the women needed to have lots of babies. And men with the Y power would excite the women to, you know, make love a lot."

Gregory shrugged. The camera technicians' laughter could not be concealed and Gregory laughed.

"I'm sorry, I don't mean to laugh, but these camera people out here are laughing. So anyway, why would Shenko women develop the X2 power, in other words, the ability to make men sick? Well, that too makes sense. The vomit power—which is what I call it—allowed Shenko women to defend against rape from marauders which is a significant capability for keeping Shenko genes only within the Shenkos. Also, if they didn't want to make love with their mate, they could zap him, canceling the effect of his Y power. Some people say it's, you know, like women saying, 'Not tonight, sorry, got a headache.'"

This time, in addition to the technicians, laughter was heard from Natalie Simms and the three panelists sitting just out of camera range. Gregory smiled, looked at her, then looked at his watch.

"But there is one more trait that maybe you've not heard much about—the Z trait. As I was growing up, my parents will tell you that as soon as I could read and learn stuff, I became obsessed about global warming, reading everything I could. In school I wrote book reports on it. I'm the leading fourteen-year-old expert. Seriously."

Again, laughter from the camera technicians.

"I think there was a reason for my obsession. And that is because from an early age I have been able to sense that our climate has been warming. It's given me a signal a little bit like ringing in the ears, but slowly changing in pitch. I think all of the Shenkos have an ability to sense the amount of a greenhouse gas, CO_2, in the air. But why would this trait evolve? Because in those early hunter-gatherer years the climate changed a lot, swinging back and forth between cold glacial periods and warm interglacial periods. Sometimes it could change quickly in a matter of weeks or months, going from year-round freezing to drought. The Shenkos needed this climate change signal for knowing in advance when to move to areas that their game would be moving to. The four-legged game moved a lot faster than the two-legged Shenkos, so the latter needed this advance warning. And it evolved in their brains from mutations that were selected, like all changes to animals and humans."

Gregory smiled. "And one other thing—I've talked a lot about the Shenkos. But most of Shenko development and progress came from mating with and bringing in genes from Homo sapiens, in other words, interbreeding with people like you over the millennia. I wouldn't be what I am today without all those many people like your ancestors who contributed to the Shenko's intelligence, language development, and other talents."

Gregory looked at his watch. "I need to wrap things up. Let me say that my childhood was wonderful. Uncle Bill and I would go around on his huge acreage of land looking at wildlife. I loved that. I was considered smart and excelled in preschool and elementary school. I did well in sports and especially liked soccer. I don't remember ever using my X power in all those years, except on animals. Oh, and I did it once when I thought these motorcycle guys were going to pound me. So for people who think the X is dangerous, I'd say it's not any more danger-ous than having a gun that you shouldn't use anywhere but for hunting or target practice.

"I did use my Y power a few times which I regret. A couple of the times were just kinda trying it out. In most of those few cases, I thought my partner actually wanted to experience it. But I offer no excuse; I shouldn't have done it."

Gregory looked at his sheet of paper. "Well, I think that's about what I wanted to say. Many people have helped me in my life, particularly Drs. Jared Weymouth, Ian Trevor, Sylvia Auerbach, Alice Masterson, and Rachel Applebaum. But I could not have survived as I did without the love and help of three key people:

Corinne, my mom; Mark, my second dad; and Uncle Bill, my mentor. I thank each of you from the bottom of my heart.

"Now I have a question for all of you in the audience. This is the question I want you to answer by sending a text message. The announcer will come on and tell you again the number for texting in your area after I give you the question. You can text this in the next half hour of the program, or, if you want to wait until I've answered all the panel questions, you can text in the first fifteen minutes after the program ends. Your answer will be very important to me, so I hope you make sure to do this.

"So the question is this: Do you think the Shenko line should continue on as a separate species, being part of society?

"I repeat the question: "Do you think the Shenko line should continue on as a separate species, being part of society?

"Please give it some thought and text your answer. Thank you very much. We'll take a brief break for the stations to give the text numbers for your area. And then we are going to have a panel of reporters ask me questions, led by Natalie Simms."

During the break, a table and four chairs were brought out and the panel assembled and sat down. Natalie adjusted the microphone attached to the front of her dress.

"Welcome back," she said. "Thank you, Gregory. That was an amazing story. I'm Natalie Simms of CNB, and coordinator of a distinguished panel of reporters who will now ask Gregory questions based on his presentation. Let me introduce, from left to right, Roger Peterson of CBR News, Stephanie Strickland of CNB News, and Gordon Masters of NNC and columnist for many newspapers. Welcome, panelists."

The panelists all responded verbally or nodded.

Natalie continued. "Let me lead off, Roger, by requesting that you ask the first question."

"Sure," Roger said, looking down at his notes. "Gregory, isn't the Shenko X power a lot more dangerous to society than a gun because it is so surreptitious and powerful? And isn't the Y power a real danger to women because they can be seduced against their will?"

Gregory cleared his throat. "Well, one thing I didn't mention is this: If a Shenko child was raised by a true Shenko family . . . with parents having the X and X2 powers, that child would quickly learn to not use his powers because he would be zapped or made sick by the parents immediately, in that way teaching the child not to use the powers. My mom and dad found out they could douse me with water and eventually this worked. A Shenko child should learn not to use the powers for the same reason any child learns what behavior is unacceptable. And this self-discipline carries on into adulthood. A child learns never to point a gun, and the Shenko child should learn the equivalent. Of course, there is a difference from being shot with a gun and getting zapped with the X power. You can recover easily from the latter, but not the former. As to the Y power, in my case, I should probably have been instructed more about never using it. As I said, I have regrets about the couple of times that I used it."

Natalie said, "We appreciate your honesty, Gregory. Now let's go to you, Stephanie."

Stephanie looked directly at Gregory. "Gregory, you said Shenko males die young from seizures. Apparently, your father, Nicholas, died while you were a baby. Do you worry that you will die soon from this epilepsy that affects Shenko males?"

Gregory rubbed his face and looked upward. "Boy, these are hard questions."

"Don't answer it if it's too personal," Stephanie said.

Gregory nodded. "No, I'll answer. And the answer is *yes*, it does worry me. My grandmother told me that some males live longer than others, into their late twenties even, so I'm hoping I'll be one of those. And with all the advances of medicine, who knows what cure might happen. But, yeah, I don't want to die."

Natalie, caught by emotion, suddenly teared and pulled out a handkerchief from her purse. Stephanie then asked to borrow it.

"Well . . ." Natalie said, recovering. "I didn't realize how personal this panel would be. But moving on—now it's your turn, Gordon."

Gordon nodded. "Is everyone ready?" he asked, looking at Gregory and the others.

Gregory said, "Yeah, go ahead."

"All right. Gregory, a number of current religions say that modern man and woman, meaning Homo sapiens sapiens, were made in the image of God. And such believers probably think that the Shenkos, and specifically you, were not created by God and, therefore, don't deserve treatment any different from an expendable animal. What would you say to such a religious person?"

"Wow," Gregory muttered, slowly shaking his head. "Hmmm. Well, it's clear that that religious guy—Lawrence Carter and his OCS group who threatened my mother and killed my aunt Zenya—thought that way. It appeared to my parents that I was in real danger from him, and that's one of the reasons I was put in hiding. What right did Carter have to say I wasn't made in God's image and what happened to Thou Shalt Not Kill? And who's to say that Adam and Eve were not really Shenkos? Maybe Adam and Eve were aided by the Y power. Look, I'm not knocking religion because sometimes I have religious feelings, especially when

I'm out in nature. Uncle Bill once said the wilderness was his church. I feel that way too."

Gregory rubbed his forehead. "I guess I would say to thoughtful religious people that Homo erectus, an early ancestor to Homo sapiens, had tools and used fire. And their brain size was almost as big as Homo sapiens'. Neanderthals had even larger brain capacity than Homo sapiens and many experts think they had some language and hunting capabilities that for a while were much better than Cro-Magnon's, your modern ancestors. Recent studies have shown that modern people have some Neanderthal genes, about one to four percent. So it's clear that interbreeding between species occurred to some extent. Given this, how can anyone say exactly what 'made in God's image' really is? Didn't God make all the earth and the animals? Anyway, I guess that's all I want to say on that. Don't you folks have some easy questions?"

Natalie and all members of the panel laughed. "Now I'm going to ask a question," Natalie said, "but I'm not sure it's an easy one. Gregory, I recently read about your juvenile court trial that took place in Nevada City. I don't know how to say this delicately, but do you have the ability to withhold your sperm from ejaculation?"

Stephanie sucked in her breath. "And *my* question was personal?"

Gregory laughed. "Actually, it is an easy question. The answer is yes. And if you wanted to have a letter for it, maybe W for withhold. I had thought all men could do that, but maybe only Shenkos can. So, that's just the way I'm made, I guess."

Natalie's jaw dropped. "*Amazing*. Built-in male birth control. Well, let's take a brief break." Natalie gave out Gregory's question for the audience again and asked people to text a yes or no per the instructions of the stations that came on with the numbers.

"WELCOME BACK to the panel questioning of Gregory Shenko. I'm Natalie Simms. Let's go back to you, Roger."

"Thank you. Gregory, this is simple, but I'm just curious. Do you consider yourself more athletic and smarter than other kids your age?"

Gregory smiled. "My coach said I was a terrific athlete and one of the best soccer players he'd seen. It may have been partly that I've matured faster than my classmates. But I will leave that question and answer to others. Smarter? I don't think so. I pretty much got A's in my classes, but I didn't have television or smart phones or electronic games or computers until later, so studying became my entertainment. Most of my classmates were distracted by their electronics and didn't study enough. So I don't think I was, you know, natively smarter. Is that enough on that?"

"Okay," Natalie said. "Let's go over to Stephanie now."

"Gregory, given that the Shenko men died young, do you think that the Shenko peoples were matriarchal in their tribal days?"

Gregory nodded. "I've talked with Ian Trevor, who's a cultural anthropologist, about this. And *yes* it would completely make sense. Nobody has any evidence, of course, but I would guess that the older women made the important decisions for the tribe. I don't know, but my guess is that they had the climate-detecting Z trait and decided when the tribe would move to a better climate or to find game. They may have even decided who the men or boys would mate with. If there was a shortage of males, there may have been a kind of polygamy—though marriage itself was unlikely. The older women undoubtedly helped with child-rearing, as grandmothers do today. So yes, I think the Shenko women must have run the tribes.

"Oh, one other thing. Ian thinks it's even possible that the women could have accelerated the selection and development of the Shenko traits by making sure males and females with the best traits mated and had lots of kids. That's speculative, but possible."

"Hmm, interesting," Natalie said. "Okay, I think we have time for one more question and answer. So Gordon, that leaves you with the last one."

Gordon glanced at some papers. "Yes . . . Gregory, I'd like to follow up on the climate subject, since you're the smartest fourteen year old on climate."

Gregory, the panel, and the camera technicians all laughed.

"My question is . . . what do you think is happening to climate on the planet now? And do you think all the world's countries should be doing more about global warming?"

Gregory leaned forward. "Actually, that *is* a good question. People need to realize that our planet has cycled through ice ages and warm periods for many hundreds of thousands of years. And the difference in *average* temperature from one to the other is comparatively small—experts say today's average temperature is only 9 degrees Fahrenheit warmer than the last ice age. Let's see, oh . . . people should also know that the cycling of ice ages and warm periods results from many things such as Earth's orbit, the sun's brightness, volcanic activity spewing out CO_2, changes in ocean currents, and 'forcings' such as arctic ice melting allowing more heat absorption by the ocean—lots of different stuff. We've been lucky to be in a long warm period over the past twelve thousand years—what some people call the 'long summer'—that's allowed agriculture, cities, and modern civilization to develop. But given the ice coring evidence from the past nine hundred thousand years, that all could change and rather quickly because it has before.

"See . . . now we're emitting greenhouse gases so strongly it's causing a superfast warming in what had been a very slow cooling phase. Many experts think we're basically screwing with nature, and we don't appreciate that 'nature bats last.' Some scientists think we could trigger a sudden ice age. Others think we're going to bring on droughts in many places and cause the loss of the Greenland and Antarctic ice packs resulting in major flooding of coastal cities on all continents. And more and more, we're seeing really weird and dangerous weather.

"This whole thing is *personal* to me because I'm a Shenko and my CO2 sensor signal has been getting worse every year. It's like *quick . . . we got to move somewhere!* But where on the planet can we go? The problem is everywhere. Animal and plant life is greatly affected by climate change and also by the huge, growing human population. Our out-and-out destruction of wild animals and habitat is causing the sixth major extinction event in Earth's entire history. That is just *unforgivable!* The more I learn about all this, the more unhappy I get. The Shenkos were able to survive and evolve because there was lots of food—you know, animals and vegetation— and our tribes were adaptable, flexible, and migratory. I think all the people on the planet now are in for *real* problems soon if we don't change our ways."

Gregory took a breath, then a drink of water. "Anyway, that's more or less it."

"I'm really impressed," Gordon said. "Yes, I agree that you are the smartest fourteen year old on climate issues."

Gregory smiled and then said. "Well, I hope I didn't overdo it."

Then he looked directly at the camera. "Okay, that ends this thing. I would like to thank all of you who were willing to listen to me, to hear my story. I'm a strange bird for sure, but I hope you realize that I had no choice about it. I am who I am. And I bear no enmity to anyone. So, please remember to text your answer to my question. It's very important. Good bye to all of you. I wish you well." Gregory stood, waved at the camera, and smiled.

CHAPTER THIRTY-TWO

THE EARLY SUMMER DAY was warm. The sound of beach-goers, volleyball, and children at play could be heard, along with the muffled waves beyond Ian Trevor's beach house, by all who had, one by one, gathered in the previous hour: Gregory, Mark, Corinne, Colliver, Jed, Jared, Rachel, Sylvia, Alice, and Ian. They sat around a large folding table that Ian had brought into his den. Corinne sat next to Ian and Mark sat next to Rachel.

"Did any of you get recognized?" Gregory asked.

"No, it looks like our disguises worked," Mark said.

"I don't want to be a cleaning lady again," Corinne said.

"I'll trade you the barefoot beach dude clothes," Jed said to laughter and chuckles.

"I guess only I was fine in my hospital scrubs," Jared said, smiling.

"Yeah, I'm getting tired of hoodies and huge sunglasses, but thanks for coming," Gregory said. "This second official meeting of the Good Times Ahead Charitable Foundation is now opened. And let the record show that all board members and officers are present."

Rachel, duly-appointed secretary of the new foundation, nodded as she wrote notes on a small computer.

"And thank you for surviving that marathon first meeting," Gregory said. "At least we covered the key issues. As always, I want to thank you, Jed, for all the staff work your people did and continue to do. By the way, are we still getting inundated with email and letters?"

Jed nodded. "Sure are," he said. "It's down to about a thousand a day now. More than half are women who want to meet you. Many send pictures. We answer them all."

"Any more religious stuff?"

"Some. Of those a few are threatening, but most just take issue with the notion that Adam and Eve were Shenkos. You know—if that were true, the Old Testament would have said so, and the apple and snake wouldn't have been there, etc."

"I sure wish I hadn't said that." Gregory shook his head.

"The positive letters far outweigh the bad ones," Jeff said. "And I pass along some of the great ones to you."

"True and I appreciate it. But let's get on with the agenda."

"So we have the sperm bank set up now," Gregory said, "and I'm continuing to provide the key ingredient. And the idea to put the clinic into a semi truck and bring in couples at rest stops was just great. That super-dedicated doctor and nurse you found, Dad, are terrific. Thanks."

"Yeah, they're committed to the cause but will be highly professional," Mark said.

"So we'll be taking applicant couples from Canada and the Ukraine at first?"Colliver asked.

Gregory nodded. "And both husband and wife have to sign on, have a good income, and they have to have some rural or forest area nearby where the kid can go."

Corinne shook her head. "I still can't believe that only those two countries scored beyond the seventy percent 'yes' on the text messaging answers. And that the U.S. was below fifty percent. Unbelievable. Anyone know why that would be?"

"I think Canada has always been fairly tolerant toward immigrants and its indigenous peoples," Jared replied.

Ian shrugged. "Ukraine is somewhat a mystery, but the Shenko name is Ukrainian and maybe there was some experience with the Shenko peoples there so that the locals weren't scared of them as apparently was the rest of the world. As for the U.S., there is a lot of anti-illegal immigrant feeling here and there are a lot of fundamental religious groups."

"We'll of course pay the travel expenses for Ukrainians, Canadians, and any-body else to come over here for the sperm treatments," Jeb said.

"Well, we can still make exceptions for some U.S. couples, especially for those from states that scored high and where the couple has rural or forest land available," Gregory said. "Places like Washington, Oregon, Colorado, and northern California would be good. So all of this is written in the plan that Jed set down, which is in a folder in front of you," Gregory said. "Why don't we look it over one more time, and then approve a motion to make it official Foundation policy."

Corinne looked at her son affectionately. "So Gregory, are you happy now that there will be lots of little Shenkos appearing in the world in the next few years?"

Gregory smiled broadly and looked around at everyone. "Definitely. And I ask that you all keep tabs on them and bring them together in a Shenko reunion sometime down the road, even if I'm not around."

Everyone nodded without smiling.

ABOUT THE AUTHOR

A FOURTH-GENERATION Californian, Richard Sessions grew up and attended college in the San Joaquin Valley. After a stint as an intelligence officer in the U.S. Navy, he moved to Los Angeles and received a Master's degree from USC before taking a position at UCLA in pediatric research administration involving "high risk" infants. He held other senior administrative positions working closely with medical scientists and engineers while obtaining a second Master's degree from UCLA. After 19 years he was recruited by a neuroscience institute at Oregon Health & Science University in Portland, Oregon. Eleven years later, he co-founded a couple of start-up biotechnology companies. All of these scientific and academic experiences provided grist for *Gregory's Anomaly*, which Sessions calls his academic medical thriller.

Richard Sessions' first novel, *Island Woman*, was published in 1997. This historical fiction novel takes place in the early 1700's off the west coasts of the Americas. Abbie Spence, a recent graduate of Reed College, is put back in time against her will and encounters Chumash Indians, Spanish warships, hacienda landowners, and much more during the time when Spain controlled the New World. The author was inspired to write this book based on his sailing experiences to the Channel Islands off the coast of Santa Barbara. To learn more about this unusual novel, go to the author's website, www.richardsessions.com

www.ingramcontent.com/pod-product-compliance
Lightning Source LLC
Chambersburg PA
CBHW031143050726
47495CB00018B/501